THIN, Rich, Pretty

THIN,
Rich,
Pretty

Beth Harbison

ST. MARTIN'S PRESS

New York

THIN, RICH, PRETTY. Copyright © 2010 by Beth Harbison. All rights reserved. Printed in the United States of America. For information, address St. Martin's Press, 175 Fifth Avenue, New York, N.Y. 10010.

www.stmartins.com

Book design by Kathryn Parise

LIBRARY OF CONGRESS CATALOGING-IN-PUBLICATION DATA

Harbison, Elizabeth M.
Thin, rich, pretty / Beth Harbison. — 1st ed.
p. cm.
ISBN 978-0-312-38198-1
1. Female friendship—Fiction.   2. Self-realization in women—Fiction.
3. Chick lit.   I. Title.
PS3558.A564T47 2010
813'.54—dc22
2009047043

First Edition: July 2010

10   9   8   7   6   5   4   3   2   1

In memory of a generation gone but not forgotten:
Judge Craig Starbuck Atkins, Margaret Denty Atkins, John Anthony
McShulskis, Helen Dargis McShulskis, Capt. Emory C. Smith,
Dorthlyn Smith, Barr V. Washburn, Bernice Washburn, and
Col. James A. Stewart.

Also to Gregg Lyon; he knows why.

Acknowledgments

The thing about book acknowledgments is that it's a really cool way to thank people for things that they've done whether it was for the book or not.

So for things to do with the book, I want to thank Jennifer Enderlin, Meg Ruley, and Annelise Robey, as always, and for help with this book in particular; and I want to thank Marsha Nuccio, Mary Blayney, Annie Jones, Elaine Fox, John Harbison, and Mimi Elias for the support they've given to my work and to me in the writing of my books.

And for various things from long ago that have nothing to do with work, I'd like to thank Cinda O'Brien, Lucinda Oliver Denton, Peter G. Nash, Diane Nash, Tammy Nash, Kim Nash Amori, Dana Carmel, and Amy Bowes.

THIN, Rich, Pretty

1

Camp Catoctin, Pennsylvania
Twenty Years Ago

I don't want to do this," Holly Kazanov said half to herself as she stood on the lakeside next to the rickety wooden rowboat that Counselor Brittany was holding for her.

"Just *go*," Brittany snapped. She was the worst camp counselor ever. Even though she was supposedly seventeen, she acted like she was twelve.

The boat was made of splintering whitewashed wood and had the name *Fat Oxen* stenciled on it in chipped blue paint. There was an old house in town called Fat Oxen, too; someone had said it meant "wealthy" because to the Pennsylvania Dutch, having a fat ox meant you could feed it well.

To Holly, and to everyone around her at the moment, it just meant "fat."

In fact, just today, Sylvia had referred to Holly's hair and eyes as *cow brown* when they'd passed a cow pasture while they were out on a trail ride. Ironically, Holly had just been thinking how pretty a color the cows were, and what a cool picture it would be of them spotting the green hill like chocolate chips in a cookie.

She didn't think so now.

Now she just thought she was far too cowlike.

I am too fat, she thought frantically as the water slapped the side of the boat. *I have terrible balance. The boat will tip over and everyone will see! I'll die in front of everyone and they'll remember me forever as the Big Fat Idiot who drowned falling out of the* Fat Oxen *boat.*

Out loud she asked, "Are you *sure* it's safe?"

The best she could hope for was that Brittany would roll her blue-lined eyes and impatiently tell her to forget it and go back to the cabin.

She wasn't so lucky, though.

"Sure," Brittany said, tossing a glance—at least her fiftieth in the past fifteen minutes—toward Danny Parish, a counselor who was a year older than she was, had brown curly hair and blue eyes, and looked like Kirk Cameron. He had no idea all the girl counselors were panting after him with flying hormones. "It's fine. Just *get in it already!*"

But Holly could see the water seeping in through waterlogged wood. It smelled like metal and rotting fish. Should it really be wet *inside* the boat? They'd only *just* put it in the water! And the fact that Brittany didn't even *look* at it made Holly even more nervous.

"I don't want to!" Holly cried, drawing the attention of several campers nearby. "Can someone come with me?"

Obviously Brittany was more interested in Danny Parish than she was in anything Holly did, including, like, *not drowning,* so Holly was on her own with this. "These are for one person, stupid," she said to

Holly, anger animating her body language, hands on the edge of the boat, her knuckles white . . . and her eyes . . . well, her eyes were still darting toward Danny. "Just get in the fucking boat." Holly hated that she said *fucking* when no one was around to hear her. "Everyone else is doing it. You don't get to cop out just because you're scared."

"I'm *not* scared." Holly put one foot into the boat. It rocked madly beneath her Dr. Scholl's sandal, and she drew back, immediately hitting her ankle hard on the edge. "I'm *right*. It's leaky."

"It is *not* leaky." Brittany averted her eyes, and again they landed on Danny Parish for a lingering moment before returning to Holly. "God, you are being *such* a crybaby."

Brittany was lanky, with bad skin and the thinnest brown hair that Holly had ever seen. She looked more like a camper than like a counselor. She'd been chasing after Danny like a dog in heat ever since camp began, and he hadn't noticed her for so much as a second. Even in her vulnerable state, Holly knew not to worry too much over what Brittany said about her.

"Do they inspect these boats for safety?" Holly asked, sounding, to her own ears, just like her overcautious father.

"Oh. My. God." Brittany sloshed through the shallow water and gave Holly a push on the back so she toppled into the boat. "Danny *just* had Lexi and Sylvia bring this out of the boathouse, which is where they *repair* anything that even *might* be wrong with it. Get in it!" She gave the boat a surprisingly strong shove, sending it rapidly into the deeper water.

"But—" Holly stopped. Anything she might say about safety checks or repair tickets would only be answered by another snipe about it having come out of the repair area of the boathouse.

Holly had very little faith in that.

For one thing, rumor had it that the boathouse was where the counselors had sex after everyone was supposed to be asleep. It was easy to imagine the counselors forgetting something as trivial as boat safety in the throes of passion.

And for another thing, Mr. Frank, the camp director, seemed to put way too much faith in the teenage counselors. He trusted them more than Holly did—that was for sure.

"Just row out into the lake with everyone else before it's time to come back already, would you?" Brittany didn't wait for an answer. With enough eye rolling to make a lesser person nauseated, she stomped off to the shed, where Holly had noticed Danny going just a second earlier.

"But I can't swim!" Holly yelled after her, taking her one terrible secret—the thing she hadn't wanted to admit in front of anyone—out of her pocket and throwing it into the atmosphere with the hopes that the counselor would stick around to make sure she was safe.

But Brittany pretended not to hear.

Holly knew Brittany was pretending because she saw the counselor's shoulders flinch when she yelled.

So Holly looked at the lake, where everyone else was paddling around like ducks in a carnival game. It was probably another ten yards to them and, thanks to the current, maybe twelve yards back to shore.

But was there *anyone* out there in the lake who would help her if she needed help?

There were a few people Holly didn't recognize, so *maybe* they would help, but the other five girls consisted of Lexi Henderson—Queen Bitch of the camp—and her posse of suck-ups, including Sylvia Farelle, Tami Ryland, and Kira Whatsername, who pretended she didn't mind that her mom sent Figurines diet bars in care packages from home.

Holly wished Nicola were here. Nicola was her new friend, also in cabin 7, and was way nicer than Lexi and her stupid friends. But she had arts and crafts this morning, and Brittany hadn't allowed Holly to go to the director and try to switch to that because she was already in two other art classes. She wanted to be an artist, not an athlete, so why did Brittany care how many art classes she had?

She didn't. She was just mean.

Holly's best hope was to row calmly back to shore and just wait there until this particular exercise was over. Why not? It wasn't like the counselors were going to notice at this point. They were too busy flirting in the boathouse.

"Okay," Holly said to herself. "You can do this. Just paddle back to shore, and stupid Brittany won't even notice."

"Look! It's the *Fat Ox!*" Lexi Henderson was so mean. Leave it to her—in a boat called *Billy Idol*—to point out the embarrassing name on Holly's boat.

"Shut up, Lexi!" Holly shouted, clutching her oars hard despite the sharp splinters of wood that pushed against her skin. A cloud of gnats hovered around her face, and she was afraid to take a breath to say more, in case one of them flew into her mouth.

"Or else what?" Sylvia taunted, her eyes lit with pure spite. "You'll come get her? Trample her with your big fat ox hooves?"

It was a stupid joke, it made no sense, but still the brownnosers who surrounded Lexi giggled.

And still Holly felt her face grow hot.

"You know," Sylvia continued, gliding effortlessly in circles on the lake while Holly scrambled to row toward shore, "this isn't a fat camp. I mean, look at the rest of us. You're in the wrong place."

"Yeah," Lexi agreed, and her agreement was all the more painful because of how pretty she was.

Holly had been waiting for someone to pull out that little gem of truth. It was camp, but it wasn't *fat camp*, and someone who looked like her would fit in only at a fat camp.

Fat girls at skinny camp sank canoes and died humiliated.

"What's the matter, fatso?" someone asked. There was no way to know for sure who it was because Holly was too busy trying, vainly, to make her oars work, but she just knew it was Lexi.

It was like one of those nightmares where you're running but not moving. Holly paddled fiercely, but the boat barely moved. She tried to keep her expression calm so Lexi and her friends wouldn't have the satisfaction of knowing how freaked out she was, but the more she rowed, the less she seemed to move.

Then she noticed the water bubbling up into the bottom, like blood oozing from a deep wound. She glanced toward the shore, but it seemed miles away and there were no counselors there. They were probably in the boathouse. How long did sex take? If her boat was going down, would they finish before she went under?

"Um," she said, her voice thin, as if too much volume would make things worse. "My boat has a leak." No one responded, so she cleared her throat and tried again. "My boat has a leak!"

Of course it was Lexi who heard and answered, "You better put on your life vest!"

Right, like Holly had one with her. She hadn't wanted to go through the humiliation of trying—and failing—to find one that fit around her chest, so she'd skipped that part.

She dropped her oars and cupped her hands to bail the water out of the boat, but the effort was too small and the leak too big. "Help!" she called toward shore. "Help!"

The water came in faster now, and the boat was being dragged down quickly. Panic hummed through her, but her movements felt useless. She was vaguely aware of voices calling out, though she couldn't tell whose they were or if they were laughing at her or trying to help.

"Put on your life vest, stupid!" someone shouted.

"I don't"—panic took over—"have one!"

It was impossible to say how long it took—a few minutes or maybe even just a few seconds—but the boat dragged downward and pulled away from her. For a moment, as she and the wood parted ways, she thought she might float, but almost immediately she went down, water bubbling up around her mouth and nose as she paddled crazily, her limbs moving every which way without propelling her anywhere but down. "Help!" she cried again, but that one staccato syllable was interrupted by water filling her mouth, thick and dirty, tasting like mud.

With a new burst of energy, her arms sprang up and pinwheeled while her legs ran on ground that wasn't there.

She went under again.

And this time, despite her spastic efforts to save herself, she only went down faster. She opened her mouth to scream—an instinct she couldn't help, and the lake rushed into her, pushing her farther down.

Then she felt an arm hook under hers and lift her through the water at warp speed.

Was it Jesus?

Her nana had always said Jesus would save her even if she didn't believe, and she'd always been glad of that, since she pretty much didn't believe and found it hard to believe just in case of emergency. But now, as her body shot upward like a rocket into the air, her only thought was that Nana had been right and she'd never doubt again.

She gasped at the air like an old woman grabbing her chips at a slot machine, taking it in and reaching for more, more, more. She coughed and water came through her mouth and her nose. She didn't care. When she drew breath in, it was air that came, not water. She wasn't drowning anymore.

She wasn't drowning.

"Are you okay?" a male voice asked.

Jesus?

She couldn't focus on Him.

What she *did* see, out of the corner of her eye, was Lexi Henderson staring at her, wide-eyed.

So she was either alive or . . . not in heaven.

"Jesus," another voice said.

So it *was*—

"She's just being dramatic," the voice went on. "She wants attention because—"

"Shut your mouth, Brittany." And then he came into focus: Danny Parish, her savior.

Well, her rescuer, anyway.

"Call nine-one-one," he said to someone over his shoulder.

"I'm okay," Holly said, weak and with a lot of coughing.

"Deep breath," Danny said to her, staring into her eyes with an intensity that, under other circumstances, would have made her heart skip a few beats.

As it was, though, her heart was just trying to catch up.

She took a deep breath and felt water percolate in her lungs. The next thing she knew, she was throwing up all over his Dockers.

"Ew!" was the consensus of the girls around her.

She'd never live this down.

But, impossibly, Danny said, "Good. Feel better?"

And, improbably, she did. She nodded feebly. "Lot of water," she said, like that would explain things and somehow help her save face.

"That's what happens when a moron sends you out in a boat with a hole and no life vest." He tossed a pointed glance at Brittany, who first looked shamed and then shot a hostile gaze at Holly.

Like this was more embarrassing for Brittany than for Holly.

"Can you sit up?" Danny secured his arm behind Holly's shoulders and eased her upward. "Feel okay?"

She looked into his vivid blue eyes—the same color as the sky behind him—and fell just a little bit in love. "Yes." She nodded.

"Cool." He smiled. It was a bright white surfer smile.

"So she's gonna live?" Lexi asked, peering down at Holly as if, for some reason, she needed to see it for herself.

"What's your name?" Danny asked Holly.

"Holly Kazanov."

"Holly's fine," he announced, "so back off." Then, to Holly, he added, "Why don't you go back to your cabin and lie down for a while? This probably really sucked for you."

She nodded. It had sucked, all right.

"Thanks," she managed, and sat up. She felt magically strong and capable. As long as they didn't put her back in a boat. "I think that would be good." She hauled herself up, aware of her bulk and of the fact that plenty of people here would probably blame that for the boat going down.

But at the moment, she didn't care.

She was alive.

And she'd met her soul mate: Danny Parish.

". . . he *saved your life?*" Nicola Kestle grabbed Holly's care package from home—a cardboard box containing 3 Musketeers bars, a Marathon Bar, Ho Hos, Wacky Packages, gum, and a *Teen Beat* magazine. She put her hand over the top to block Holly's view and get her attention. "Danny Parish *saved your life?*"

They were sitting on the top bunk, enjoying a few minutes as the only two in the cabin since everyone else had gone to the campfire sing after dinner. The only light came from a small battery-operated lantern hanging from the post of the bed, and it cast their shadows, large and dramatic, on the wall next to the open window.

Holly kept thinking it would be a cool painting, and she wished they'd let the campers work with oils in art instead of primary-color tempera paint. There was no way to capture the colors of the cabin at night with blue, green, red, orange, and purple tempera.

"Yes." Holly nodded, proud. Her shadow echoed the motion big against the wall, like a shout. "So doesn't that mean I, like, owe him my life?"

"Well"—Nicola frowned, and the light emphasized her nose, which she was very self-conscious of—"in *some* cultures. Though I have to say I've never really understood that. I mean, it could be a drag to save someone's life and then have them hanging on you forever, offering to be your slave, getting in the way of everything all the time."

The door opened and Lexi walked in, took one look at the two of them, and rolled her eyes. "What are you guys *doing?*"

"Just talking." Nicola pushed her coppery hair back, the way she always did when she got self-conscious.

"About what?"

"None of your beeswax!" Holly snapped, sounding braver than she felt.

For a split second, Lexi looked shocked. Obviously she didn't think Holly had it in her to confront the Great and Powerful Lexi Henderson.

Good. Maybe she'd think twice before tormenting Holly again.

"Just shut up and go back to pigging out," Lexi said, going to her drawer and getting something that she put into her front pocket. "It's what you're best at." She tossed her head—and her light golden hair bounced like she was on a shampoo commercial—then she flounced out the door, letting it bang behind her.

"Whatever." Holly opened a Marathon Bar and wished it were frozen, so she could whack it against the wall and break it into a hundred pieces, as the packaging suggested. Instead it was just like a chewy 3 Musketeers. "So back to Danny—I wouldn't mind following him around forever."

Nicola snorted, and both she and her shadow threw up their hands. "Then you better get in line behind Emily Delaney."

"Who?"

Nicola peeled the thin chocolate off her Ho Ho. "You know, the blond counselor who just came in a couple days ago? The one who wears really, really short shorts?"

"There's no new counselor!"

"Uh-huh. She was at crafts today. She had the coolest shell necklace I've ever seen." She popped the Ho Ho chocolate into her mouth.

Holly, on the other hand, was beginning to lose her appetite. "And she's pretty?"

Nicola nodded and started to unroll her now-bare Ho Ho. "She looks *exactly* like Stacy on *T.J. Hooker.*"

Now Holly felt genuinely sick. "*Heather Locklear?*"

"Yup."

Holly grabbed Nicola's wrist, making her drop what was left of the Ho Ho. "Are you serious?" Her shadow looked fat and formless on the wall, a stark contrast to Nicola's wiry, thin one.

"Hey!" Nicola objected. "Now you need to give me another one!"

"Fine. But does Emily *really* look like that? Is she really that pretty?"

"Yeah, why? I'd think you'd be glad someone has come along to rub Brittany's stupid face in it."

There *was* that.

The problem was that Holly felt *exactly* the way she hoped Brittany would feel: hideously ugly, incapable of ever being able to compare in any way to a girl who looked like Heather Locklear. Suddenly the romantic fantasies of Danny that had carried her along like a gentle wind all day felt like embarrassing words tattooed on her forehead.

Outside the open window, the crickets and frogs seemed to amplify their echoey songs.

"I'm glad," Holly said weakly, then looked at the Marathon Bar in her hand.

It wasn't helping anything. It, along with the Ho Hos and the Juicy Fruit gum and every other favorite thing her mom had packed for her were all serving to keep her from the one thing she really wanted: Danny Parish.

"You know," she said as casually as she could, "I don't think I want this after all." She dropped the chocolate over the side of the bed into the wide tin bucket they used as a trash can.

"Are you *crazy?*" Nicola looked over the side, clutching the bed rail with both hands like she might jump for it. "*I* would have taken it. It's better than corned beef, which you totally know they're going to serve again tomorrow night."

"Then I won't eat anything," Holly resolved right then and there. People always told her she had "such a pretty face," sometimes even adding, "if you could only drop a few pounds."

She hated the part of herself that kept on eating anyway. She hated how she felt when people looked at her with pity and scorn, and she hated, even more, how she felt when she ate a Twinkie or something after that. It was stupid of her, and she knew it. She had to change.

Now she would. She was determined.

She'd drop a few pounds, even if it killed her, and see if maybe—just *maybe*—she could be pretty enough to win over a guy like Danny Parish.

The Present

N o wine for me, please," Holly Kazanov said, handing her menu to the waitress. "Seltzer with lemon or lime would be fine."

Randy Peterson, her boyfriend of four months, nodded approvingly, ordered his steak with mushroom sauce, Cakebread cabernet sauvignon, and handed his menu over. He watched the waitress—a slender redhead dressed in the usual tuxedo getup that made girls with her shape look like boys—walk away before he turned back to Holly and said, "That was a good choice."

Holly glanced after the waitress. "What was a good choice?" The pants? Holly didn't think so. They were too tight, making her proportions seem even bigger, like a woman in a Fernando Botero painting.

Holly was feeling like a big, fat Botero subject herself at the moment.

"Your diet. I didn't want to say anything myself, of course, but I'm glad you've made the healthy choice."

She looked sharply at him. "I'm sorry?"

He frowned, his sandy eyebrows changing his expression from pleasure to concern. "You ordered the chicken and skipped the wine. I assumed that meant you were dieting. Doesn't it?"

"*Should* it?" Suddenly it felt like her gut expanded by six inches. The Lycra in the waistband of her pants seized and pulled inward. She'd been feeling okay about herself just minutes earlier, but this was all it took to rock that confidence.

Had he been noticing—*observing*—everything she ate?

"Sweetheart." He reached his hand out and put it on top of hers. His fingers were long and tapered, as opposed to the overstuffed sausages that extended from her hands. "I only care about what's best for you."

"So you think I'm fat." Were her rings actually getting *tighter*?

"No, no, you're . . . What's the word? For that painter who did portraits of chubby women?"

Holly felt ill. "Rubenesque?"

He snapped and pointed a finger gun at her. "That's it! You know your art."

She should. She was a co-owner of the Macomb Gallery on Macomb Street in Northwest D.C. It was the only thing that appealed to her after getting her masters in art history.

As it turned out, all that experience had narrowed itself, in this conversation, to the information that Randy thought she was, at best, "chubby." People meant a lot of things when they said *Rubenesque*, and if they knew anything about Peter Paul Rubens's art, they didn't necessarily mean *big fat whale*, but Randy had said right up front what he meant.

That painter who did portraits of chubby women meant "like you—you're chubby."

It didn't exactly indicate that he viewed her as sexy.

"I'm not sure that's all that flattering," she said with a short humorless laugh. She didn't want to snap at him. She just wanted him not to call her fat.

"I want you to be healthy." He gave her hand a squeeze. "I want you to be with me for a long, long time."

Time froze.

Was he talking engagement?

Marriage?

If so, how could he even find a ring to fit her ridiculous fingers?

She'd thought several times over the past four months that maybe this relationship had what it took to go all the way. She'd *hoped* Randy felt the same way, but she hadn't brought it up.

How could she? She still couldn't believe her luck, that a good-looking guy like Randy was interested in her. It would be pushing her luck to hope for more.

Yet she couldn't help it.

"Wow," she breathed, both excited and humiliated. It was a strange combination of feelings. She wanted to fall into his arms and run away all at the same time.

Running would be a very poor choice, though. Particularly in light of this conversation, he did not need to watch her chugging away, breathless and wheezy.

"Do you"—he looked into her eyes and gave her hand a squeeze—"feel the same way?"

"Yes. Absolutely. I could definitely—" Whoa! She was overstating her case. "I'd like to see where things go."

He gave a half smile. The laugh lines around his left eye deepened, reminding her of George Clooney. "Is that all? Do you just want to wait and see? Or do you want to make it happen?"

"I want to make it happen!" God, she sounded like a game show contestant. *I want to go for it, Pat Sajak! Big money! Big money!*

But Randy looked at her as if she were his dream woman. "I think you're on the right path. Ah." He leaned back as the waitress brought their food. "Perfect timing."

The waitress set his Cholesterol Special in front of him, and the grilled chicken that had inadvertently put Holly on the road to marriage in front of her.

What if she'd ordered the steak? Or the pasta? What if she'd ordered the pasta and asked for extra cheese, as she usually did? Or salad, with extra blue cheese on the side? What if she'd made just one slightly different move that had said to Randy that she didn't care enough about her health and living a long life by his side?

Would this conversation even have come up?

Had fate just been testing her?

If so . . . had she passed? She had, right?

She ate only half the chicken breast and avoided the rice altogether. Randy didn't say anything, but a couple of times she caught him looking at her with what looked like pride.

She was doing this for him, and he *appreciated* it. That was so refreshing!

In fact, for the rest of the meal, the more he glanced at her, the smaller her bites got. It was the most satisfying meal she could ever remember having.

"You have got me so hot." Randy took off his shirt, did a quick fold, and set it on the cedar chest at the end of his bed. "You have no idea. . . ." He ran his hands along Holly's shoulders and down her back, expertly snapping her bra open.

Holly flushed with pride and warmed with passion. "I'm not even doing anything yet."

"You don't have to. It's just *you*. And this whole night." He sucked in his breath as he unzipped his pants.

Holly sort of thought she should be doing that, but the last time she had, the zipper got caught on his underwear and, long story short, the mood died.

"You're just amazing," he finished.

"So are you." She moved in and kissed him.

He responded hungrily, pressing his hands on her shoulders and kissing her deeply before pulling back just long enough to take his pants off and drape them over the wooden valet next to the bed.

Holly pulled off her cotton dress and let it drop in a pile at her feet.

He glanced at it, then at her, and kissed her again, guiding her onto the bed. He paused for only a moment to turn off the lights, then gave her his full attention.

It was the most exciting sex they'd ever had.

Afterwards, while he was in the bathroom, she lay in bed trying to figure out exactly what was going on tonight.

She wanted to call someone. She wanted to call her friend Kim or, no, she wanted to call Nicola. Nicola had been living in L.A. for years now; she'd grown very wise in the ways of men and relationships and everything. Nicola was a huge success, so she would undoubtedly know what to make of this almost ordinary day in suburbia.

Holly glanced at the clock. It was nine fifteen. Randy had been in the bathroom for about three minutes so far. Usually he took about six. But she couldn't be sure. Hell, she didn't even know what he was doing in there, but whatever it was, he jumped up and did it every single time after they had sex.

Sometimes he took longer, but once in a while he came out sooner. She didn't want to be on the phone if tonight was one of those quicker nights, so she just lay back on the pillows and looked at the changing shadows on the ceiling, wondering where the night would lead from here.

"Sorry," he said, coming out of the bathroom wrapped in a bathrobe. "Just needed to clean up."

So that's what it was. Holly gave a laugh. "Just couldn't wait to get me off you, huh?"

He took off the robe, hung it on his bedpost, and got back under the sheets with her. But he was wearing his briefs now, and she felt overdressed. "Cleanliness is next to godliness, isn't that how the saying goes?" He kissed the tip of her nose.

"That's how it goes." She wasn't sure she wanted God as part of a threesome, but she was even less sure of how to say that without sounding like a humorless heathen.

"One of the things I love about you is how understanding you are." He drew her closer.

One of the things he *loved* about her? They'd never exchanged *I love yous* before, and in all the tense excitement of the night, somehow she'd forgotten that little detail.

Now that he'd said it—well, *sort of* said it—she felt a little more confidence in pursuing clarification.

Holly lay in the crook of his arm, trailing her fingers across his smooth bare chest and trying to screw up the courage to be up front. "So when you said you wanted me to be with you for a long time . . ." It was the perfect time to look meaningfully into his eyes, but she couldn't. What if he shot her down? She didn't need him having a close-up of her burning humiliation. "Just how long were you think-ing?" There. That was good. Not too needy. Kind of flirty. Definitely open to interpretation.

He took her hand in his. "Look at me."

She did.

He smiled that smile she loved. The brown of his eyes seemed to darken to liquid ink. "Are you asking me if I could marry you?"

She gave a small gasp. Yes, she probably *had* been asking that, in a way. But it wasn't like she was going to ask it flat out like that.

And now that he'd asked her if that's what she was asking . . . would her answer constitute a proposal?

At the end of the night, would the story be that *she'd* proposed to *him*?

She swallowed. That was *not* the way she wanted this to go. "Well . . . I think I'm just wondering what *you* have in mind." She shrugged, which was awkward, given her position. "I hadn't really taken it much further than that."

"Hmmm." He looked at the ceiling, clicking his tongue against his teeth thoughtfully before asking her, "Do you think you could marry me?"

Her breath caught in her chest. So much so, that for a moment she felt panicked. Was *this* a proposal? It didn't feel exactly like one, but then again, no one had ever proposed to her before. How would she know what it felt like?

Maybe it had been a proposal all along and she kept throwing a wrench in the works.

"I don't know." Better to play it coy, she decided. "You'd have to ask."

"What if I am?"

"Are you?"

He rolled over onto his side and she slid onto the mattress, facing him. "How about this: we call this a pre-engagement."

"A *pre*-engagement." Somehow this wasn't adding up to the magical moment she'd always imagined. "What does that mean?"

He touched her cheek. "Contingent upon you getting healthy."

She drew back. "I *am* healthy. Jeez, Randy, you're making it sound like I have to give up my cigarette and meth habits."

"Sugar can be just as addictive."

"I don't eat that much sugar!"

"Shhh." He shook his head gently. Like he was patiently dealing with an idiot child. "You said it yourself tonight, you are on a diet, and making healthier choices so you can stick around for the long haul." He reached down and caressed her left ring finger with his thumb and index finger.

"Y-yes." She *had* somehow ended up saying that, hadn't she?

"So I want your long haul to be with me. And I want to help you get there."

"So what are you saying?" she asked. "Exactly?" There had been enough nebulous intimation tonight.

"You lose some weight." He frowned and poked out his lower lip for a second. "Say—I don't know—thirty pounds?"

"Thirty?" She was only five-four. If she lost thirty pounds, she'd look like a child! "Is that how fat you think I am?"

There was a moment's hesitation—or at least she *thought* there was—before he said, "Okay, let's say twenty. When you lose twenty pounds, we will get engaged. Officially."

"I—" She what? This was both thrilling and horrifying. It was a night for contrasts. She didn't want her first engagement to be tainted by body-image issues, but then again . . . Wait, why was she thinking *first engagement* at all?

This would be her *only* engagement.

And what he was saying was actually perfectly reasonable. He wanted her to be healthy so she'd live a long time, so they could grow old together. It was a beautiful thought, really. A very loving sentiment.

So what was she doing being such an exacting pill about it?

"I agree," she said, nodding more vehemently as the idea took hold. A lot of women lost weight to fit into their wedding gowns. It was a perfectly healthy, *normal* thing to want to do.

"You'll do it?" he asked, looking almost as giddy as she felt.

"I will," she said firmly, then laughed and put her arms around him, rolling him on top of her. "I will."

"Congratulate me! I'm pre-engaged!" Holly looked at Lacey Schmidt over a crate of paintings they'd just acquired from an estate sale. She always hoped she'd find a Rembrandt or a Monet in estate sales, but the best she'd done so far was come across a forty-five-thousand-dollar Mark Strauss cow painting. Forty-five thousand bucks was nothing to sneeze at, but it wasn't forty-five million, either.

Lacey raised a pierced eyebrow. "Pre-engaged."

"Yes!"

"What the hell is pre-engaged?"

Another person might have been discouraged by Lacey's less-than-enthusiastic response, but Holly knew this was how Lacey was. Always. She was a short, round fireball with pink hair, multiple piercings, and although she herself was an artist, she had a "thing" against the pretentiousness of most of the artists they dealt with.

And Lacey was always ready to be skeptical. As a matter of fact, pessimistic was her default setting.

"It means," Holly said, "that we are *going* to be engaged."

Lacey stopped and looked at her, her pink spiky hair standing straight up like exclamation points. "When?"

"I don't know." She didn't want to reveal the whole weight-loss thing. Other people might not understand. "Soon."

"That's the stupidest thing I've ever heard." Lacey returned to pulling nails out of the wooden crate, but never one to let something rest if it didn't sit well with her, she stopped again. "I mean, that's like being a pre-lottery-winner."

"No, it's not. You never know if you're going to win the lottery. *Afterwards* you might look back and remember when you *were* a pre-lottery-winner, but you can't say you are in advance."

"And that's different how? Are you *sure* you're going to be engaged?"

"Yes." Wasn't she? "Absolutely."

"Then why aren't you calling it engaged?"

Together they lifted a canvas out of the box and began to unwrap the packaging.

"Because *engaged* implies a date that's already been picked out."

"Does not. I know people who have been engaged for years."

Holly raised her eyebrows.

"I know," Lacey said, returning to the unwrapping. "That's a whole different argument. We're talking about you right now. So the date isn't the thing, and don't bring up the ring, either. I notice you don't have one."

"Yet."

"Yeah." Lacey snorted. "Not till you're engaged."

Even though this was just the sort of thing Holly had expected from Lacey, she was starting to feel a little deflated. "I practically am! You don't understand, Randy and I had a whole conversation about this. We made an agreement."

"To be pre-engaged."

"Exactly."

"So you *know* it's going to happen."

Twenty pounds. She'd done it before; she could do it again. "Yes."

"Then by the same token, I'm pre-dead."

Holly leveled a gaze on Lacey. "Correct."

Lacey thought about it for a moment, then shrugged. "Okay. Then please accept my pre-congratulations."

"Thank you." Holly smiled. "Now, was that so hard?"

"Pretty hard, yes." Lacey was so deadpan that Holly didn't know for sure if she was kidding or not.

But, then, that's the way it usually was with Lacey. Holly opted to believe she was kidding.

The best move at this point seemed to be to change the subject so that Lacey didn't manage to dampen the mood further. "This is nice," she said, gently brushing dust off an oil still life. "People love still life."

"It's just that I don't like that jerk snowing you into thinking *pre-engaged* is a good thing," Lacey said abruptly.

Holly was taken aback. "I'm sorry? *That jerk?*"

"Sorry." This time Lacey sounded like she meant it. "It sounds like a blow-off to me, and I don't want you to be disappointed. There. I said it. And you can hate me for it if you want, but at least I got it out."

Holly smiled. This was the warmest she could remember Lacey ever being. "Would it make you feel better if you knew *I* was the one who wanted to put off the engagement?" It wasn't *entirely* true . . . but mostly. It was too soon to get married, which had to mean it was too soon to get engaged, plus the whole "getting healthy" thing was for her, not for him, so, when she thought about it, she was as 100 percent behind this idea as Randy was. Which made it true.

"Yeah . . . were you?"

"Yes." Holly took a box cutter and carefully slit the packaging on another canvas. Better that than her wrists. She didn't want to look at Lacey, even though she believed what she was saying. "Yes, I was. Now, let's get back to work. Time is money, and all that."

Holly's parents and her brother had reactions similar to Lacey's. Her mom had tried to be encouraging, asking if she might consider getting married on their boat down in Tampa, but there was doubt about the whole thing in her voice.

Her father had been so confused as to what *pre-engaged* meant that she felt stupid for having mentioned it at all.

And her brother Sam flat out told her she was stupid, although he'd tempered it with, "Hey, seriously, if you're happy, that's all that matters. I'll support you no matter what."

So that little moment was nice, if pitiful.

But almost immediately after changing her Facebook status from *Holly Kazanov is tired of her iPod breaking* to *Holly Kazanov is pre-engaged*, the phone rang.

"Oh my God, you're pre-engaged?" It was Nicola. The most supportive person Holly had ever known in her life.

"Yes!" Holly shrieked. She moved from her office chair to her bed to settle in for a long gossipy chat with her oldest friend. "I am!"

"Tell me everything. Who is he? What's he like? What does he look like? And what's the difference between pre-engaged and engaged?"

Holly's heart sank a little. She'd hoped Nicola would understand it all right off the bat. Then again, she had to admit that a pre-engagement wasn't all that standard. She knew Nicola would understand once she explained it a little. "Well, it's like we've set a date to become engaged."

"Why? Does he have to save up money for a ring?"

"No." Damn! That would have been a perfect explanation for Holly to give Lacey. She wasn't going to lie to Nicola, though. Maybe it was all the time they'd known each other, maybe it was the distance between them, but Nicola was one person Holly always felt like she could tell the truth to. "Can I tell you the truth?"

"You better."

"I actually want to lose weight before we're *officially* engaged."

"Hm." There was a long moment that felt like electricity crossing the phone wire—or air, at least in Holly's case, since she was on a cordless phone—between them. "He asked you to marry him, and you said not until you drop a few pounds?"

"Sort of." Holly's shoulders sank. "Not exactly. It was a little more roundabout. . . ."

She explained it all to Nicola. The dinner, the accidental "diet," Randy's reaction, and the subsequent conversations. Relaying it this way reinforced Holly's feeling that it was all fate—one fortuitous thing after another.

Nicola, on the other hand, was hesitant. "Why does he want you to lose weight before he'll commit to you?"

"It's not like that. That's just how this happened to come up. He didn't lay down the conditions in a 'do it and we will, fail and we won't' way."

There was silence on the other end of the line. Then, "You've done that before, you know."

"What?"

"Changed yourself for a guy."

"When?" Holly straightened her back. She had *not* done that. "Name me one time."

"Andy Tervis had that whole Rollerblading thing he wanted you to do with him, even though you told him you weren't athletic and you had a bad feeling about trying it."

"That was a matter of *doing things together*," Holly contended. "It wasn't like he *made* me do it." And frankly, it had been eight years now and her tailbone *still* hurt.

"Fine. What about when Seth Goldstein wanted you to convert to Judaism just to date him?"

"Gold*berg*, and he didn't insist."

"Would he have dated you if you hadn't at least looked into it?"

Maybe not. "It was interesting to learn about another religion," Holly dodged. "I don't regret that."

Nicola sighed. "Hol, even back at camp, you starved yourself into the infirmary because you wanted that counselor Danny to notice you."

"Danny Parish." Holly couldn't help but smile. "Lord, he was *so good-looking*. Wasn't he?"

"He was."

"I wonder what ever happened to him."

"He married some chubby girl and had a bunch of happy, healthy babies."

Holly gasped. "How do you know that?"

"I don't, but that's what the smart guys do."

"Randy is a smart guy," Holly said. "That's why I want to hold on to him. But believe me, Nic, there is nothing wrong with me dropping a few pounds before getting engaged. If *I* hadn't brought it up, we never would have had the conversation at all." That much she believed. "I *promise* you, he didn't sit me down and give me an ultimatum."

"Phew! You had me nervous for a minute, there."

"Oh, no, he's not that guy."

"So you're doing this for you, not for him?"

"Yes, *absolutely*." She said it just a little too loud, maybe. But Nicola didn't notice.

"Then congratulations on your pre-engagement!"

"Thanks! Now, tell me about you. What's life like out in Hollywood these days?"

"Busy. I have a huge audition tomorrow for a movie with Steve Carell. It could be my big break."

"Haven't you already *had* your big break?" Holly asked with a smile.

There was a pause. "I mean that it would be a great opportunity." Nicola's voice was suddenly tight, and Holly realized that she must have accidentally insulted her best friend by insinuating that it was too late for big successes.

"I didn't mean anything by that—"

"I know." Nicola sighed. "It's just always stressful to go to another audition. The preparing, the waiting in a room full of people prettier than me, the waiting . . . I wish I'd wanted to be an accountant."

Holly gave a laugh. "That's a hot business these days."

"Too bad I can barely count." Nicola laughed, and the conversation moved on to the other small details of their lives.

Over the past twenty years of their friendship, there had sometimes been long periods during which they didn't talk, but they were available for each other. And whenever they took the time for a long gab session, it was like no time had passed at all.

Holly always found this comforting. It was like having her own private Dear Abby on the other side of the country, someone she could call in the middle of a cold, dark night who would answer, cheerfully, in the warm light of the other coast.

Until now, Holly had never held anything back from Nicola. She'd always been completely up front, no matter what was happening. But maybe that was because usually whatever was happening was totally, and clearly, beyond her control. If a storm flooded her basement, or a job was forced to cut back her hours, or if she failed a test because her stupid professor based it on material he hadn't taught yet (she would contend to her dying day that that one wasn't her fault), she could report on any of it and it didn't reflect badly on her.

But if her boyfriend put what might appear to Nicola like aesthetic conditions on the survival of their relationship, she didn't feel she could be totally up front about it. Not that Randy had done that, exactly. She half believed it when she told Lacey and Nicola that she was fully on board with this plan.

Privately, she wondered. *Was* this really okay with her? Or had she wanted a husband—and kids, and a house, and yard with azaleas blooming in the spring—so badly that she was, at thirty-three, willing to make sacrifices to make it happen?

Even slightly degrading sacrifices?

She sat with that for a moment.

Then she dismissed it.

Because what she'd said to Nicola was true: Randy hadn't sat her down and given her an ultimatum. She'd agreed. She'd participated wholly in the conversation, and she'd decided to make a change in herself.

And it was a change she'd wrestled with all her life. She was too quick to be complacent with her shape. Every time she stopped thinking about dieting, she slipped up and found herself with a cookie in her hand.

She had to stop that. She *wanted* to stop that.

That put her in control of the situation.

Didn't it?

Camp Catoctin, Pennsylvania
Twenty Years Ago

I wish I had some makeup," Nicola whispered to Holly.

They were, as usual, on Nicola's top bunk, looking down at Lexi, Tami, and Sylvia, who were giggling and putting on powders and eye shadows and all sorts of cool things that came in sleek plastic containers with fun names written in crazy fonts.

"We're not allowed to use it here," Holly said, sounding kind of glad that she didn't have to try. "We'd get in trouble."

Nicola rolled her eyes. "Like Brittany's going to notice anything besides Danny Parish."

"She hasn't seemed to notice Emily Delaney attached at his hip." Holly sighed and leaned back. "By the way, I'm not going tonight. I can't."

"*What?*" There was a dance tonight with the boys from Echo

Lake, and Nicola had changed her clothes three times so far, trying to look just right in hopes that Steve Grudberg would be there again this year. "You *have* to go. I *can't* go by myself!"

"My stomach hurts."

"If it does, it's because you haven't eaten all week." That was another thing Brittany—the world's worst camp counselor—hadn't noticed: Holly was on some sort of starvation diet. Nicola was actually getting a little worried about Holly until finally Holly broke down and had three Ho Hos this afternoon.

"That's not true—I eat!"

"No kidding!" Sylvia chirped from below, and she, Lexi, and Tami giggled and got back to their makeup and gossip.

Nicola noticed Holly's face turn a deep, hot red.

"Okay, whatever," she said quickly to try to erase Holly's embarrassment. "The thing is, I've been really looking forward to this because of, you know"—she lowered her voice—"*Steve Grudberg*. And I'll look stupid standing there all by myself, hoping for him to notice me."

"Then ask him to dance."

"Right."

"I'm serious." Holly dropped her fake-stomachache voice. "If he says no, it's not like you'll ever see him again if you don't want to."

Nicola shook her head. "If I ask him and he says no, he will probably end up moving in next door to me."

Holly laughed—making it now totally obvious that she wasn't really sick and that she didn't want to go because she was self-conscious—and said, "Look, you want to be an actress, right?"

"Yeah . . . but what does that have to do with anything?"

"So tonight just *act* like the most confident person in the world. *Pretend* you're already Steve's girlfriend and that he's dying to see you. When you get there, pretend he's *thrilled* to see you."

Like you're pretending you're sick? Nicola thought but didn't say. She felt let down that Holly wasn't going to be there for her, but she knew her well enough to know that once she decided something—like that she wasn't going to the dance tonight—there was no changing her mind. "That's stupid."

"It is not. I heard that's Diane Keaton's secret. She pretends she's already in the situation so when she acts it out on-screen, it's like it's already real."

Nicola really admired Diane Keaton. She'd watched the old movie *Annie Hall* multiple times, even though Woody Allen was creepy. "Okay, I'll try it," she agreed, only half convincing herself.

"Good."

A few minutes passed with only the sound of the other girls' prattling and the buzz of a fly trying to get out through the ripped screen in the window.

"So," Nicola tried again, "are you sure you don't want to go?"

Holly made a clearly self-conscious effort to wince. "No. I really don't feel good."

The dumb fly continued to bump into the screen.

Holly must have thought Nicola was as stupid as that fly if she thought she'd believe this story.

If it were Nicola, she would have gone to help her friend, even if she didn't want to.

She was hurt that Holly wasn't willing to do the same for her.

"Then you should probably go to the infirmary," Nicola challenged, knowing it was obnoxious yet hoping it might change Holly's mind. "Maybe it's something serious."

Holly shrugged. "It's probably something I ate."

"But you've barely eaten *anything.*" Nicola saw the chance to drive home her point *and* hone her acting skills. She arranged her features into an expression of serious concern. "If you'd had breakfast or lunch, then, yeah, maybe I'd think it was just something you ate, but . . ." She shrugged and let her implication drop like a tennis ball into Holly's court. "If you're too sick to go to the dance . . ."

Holly's brow twitched downward. "Fine. I'll go."

"To the dance?"

"No way!" It was a heated response for one so "weakened" by illness. "To the infirmary."

Disappointment tickled at Nicola's hopes, but not surprise. "I'll walk you there."

"No, it's okay. I'll go by myself. You need to get ready." Holly pushed off the bed and made the awkward trip down the ladder, and for the first time, Nicola wondered if maybe she really *was* sick, because ordinarily she never would have given Lexi, Sylvia, and Tami such a golden opportunity to mock her.

"Look out!" Sylvia cried, crossing her arms in front of her face. "If she falls, it's all over for us."

The other girls laughed—of course—and Lexi added, "Maybe you shouldn't be hoarding all that candy, Holly. If you shared every once in a while, you might not be so big."

"I *do* share." Holly, red-faced, tugged at the wedgie her shorts had given her on the way down. "Just not with bitches like you!"

Nicola gasped inwardly.

Holly had called them *bitches*!

Right to their faces!

It was shocking. Kind of cool, of course, but *shocking*.

If Brittany had heard her say it, she would have sent Holly straight to Mr. Frank's office.

In fact, Nicola often thought Brittany would take *any* opportunity to get rid of Holly and Nicola because she thought they were fat and ugly and it embarrassed her to have them in her cabin. Truth was, Nicola suspected Brittany thought Danny Parish wouldn't look at her because her campers weren't pretty enough.

Brittany was probably like that because of her own insecurities, but that didn't make Nicola feel sorry for her one bit. Nicola had plenty of her own insecurities—with this nose, how could she not?—but it didn't make her act like a jerk to other people and try to hurt their feelings in order to boost herself up.

Even a thirteen-year-old like Nicola could see what a stupid plan that was.

But a seventeen-year-old like Brittany would probably never see it. She hadn't been in with the popular group when she was a kid, probably, and now she had the chance to be in with Lexi and company, so even though they were only thirteen, it was better than nothing.

The screen door squealed on its hinges and banged thinly against the doorframe, like a screaming guitar lick to Holly's heavy, percussive steps across the front porch and down the wood steps into the thick, buggy night.

Apparently Nicola was the only one who cared that she was gone.

". . . so look what I got from my Stepmother Dearest," Lexi was saying to the other two as she unzipped the pocket of her suitcase. Her cheeks were a pretty Maybelline pink with a light sheen of gold powder under her eyes.

She looked almost angelic.

She pulled a gleaming ring with the biggest diamond Nicola had ever seen in her life. It was like a golf ball.

Even Sylvia and Tami gasped.

"She *gave* it to you?" Tami asked in disbelief, blinking muted mauve eyelids and echoing Nicola's thoughts and perhaps a smidgen of her skepticism.

Nicola noticed then that she had the ring on a gold chain. Lexi slid the ring, chain and all, onto her finger and said, "Of course not. I *took* it. She'll kill me if she finds out." She held her hand up to the light. "But, of course, she'll never find out. She'll just think it was one of the maids or something."

What if a maid gets blamed and fired? Nicola wanted to know. But she wasn't about to have that argument with these three. She knew where they would stand on the matter, and it wasn't the same place she stood. So she pushed her concerns about it aside and tried to keep up with the conversation without anyone noticing.

The ring was amazing. The diamond was just huge. It was probably worth a million dollars. Nicola's father owned an insurance company, and she'd heard him talk many times about the value of the jewelry people were insuring.

"It's supposed to be mine someday, anyway," Lexi said, absently fingering the chain. "It was my mother's."

The light in the cabin wasn't great, but from where Nicola sat on the top bunk, she thought Lexi's expression tightened for a moment.

"Then you should totally keep it," Sylvia said, crossing her arms in front of her. "It's yours anyway."

"To-tally," Tami rang in agreement.

Lexi looked uneasy. She glanced up, and Nicola looked away quickly, hoping she wasn't going to get yelled at. She felt like she'd been eavesdropping on bank robbers and would be in huge trouble if she were caught.

But instead, Lexi said, "Hey. Nicky."

Nicola didn't correct her, even though no one called her that. "Hm?"

"Are you going to the dance?"

"I don't know." She didn't sound half as casual as she was trying to. "Yes."

"We're doing makeup if you want."

Nicola couldn't believe what she was hearing. "If I want what?" she asked, trying to sound neutral instead of both hopeful and skeptical.

"If you want to put some on," Lexi said. "*Duh.*"

"Oh." Nicola propped herself up on her elbows. "Really? *Your* makeup?"

Lexi made another *duh* face and said, "Um, unless you brought some?"

"No, I didn't," Nicola said eagerly.

Too eagerly.

The girls exchanged a look that said it was *obvious* Nicola hadn't brought makeup.

"Cool." Lexi turned and flounced back to the spot on the floor where they'd laid out all the little compacts, containers, pencils, and so forth and sat down, patting the floor next to her. "You sit here, and we'll do your makeup for you."

"We'll what?" Sylvia snarked.

Lexi flashed her a silencing look. "It's always better if you have someone else do it. We can see better in here."

Nicola thought to herself that maybe Lexi wasn't so bad after all. Maybe she and Holly had given her a bad rap unfairly.

"Okay, so put your hair back in this." Lexi held out a ponytail band and waited while Nicola put her hair into a quick braid. Ever since she'd seen *Little House on the Prairie* she'd preferred braids to ponytails, and she'd gotten quick at doing them.

Lexi shook a bottle of base and poured it onto a little triangular sponge. She dabbed it on Nicola's cheek, then moved back and narrowed her eyes.

"It's the *perfect* color for you," she pronounced.

Nicola felt her face flush with pleasure and hoped it didn't ruin the perfect match.

"So." Lexi swabbed the sponge across Nicola's nose without making even one snide comment. "What's the deal with you and Fatso?"

The right response would have been something along the lines of *Who is Fatso?* but Nicola knew exactly who Lexi was talking about, and everyone in the room knew it.

"What do you mean? There's no *deal.*"

"Um, you guys seem totally, like, close—and I just don't get *why.*" Lexi screwed the lid back on the bottle and picked up a square black compact, opened it, held it up to Nicola's cheek, nodded, and took out a fluffy blush brush. "I mean, you're so cool and she's so, you know."

"Fat and stupid and boring," Tami offered.

Lexi shrugged, but it was a gesture of agreement.

"Well . . ." Nicola knew she should defend her friend. Worse, she knew that, if the shoe were on the other foot, Holly would defend *her.* But something about the way Lexi was brushing the blush across her cheeks, the hypnotizing feel of the feathery bristles gliding across her skin, lulled her onto the easier path of betraying her friend. "We're just . . ."

For a long time after, she hated herself for what she said next.

". . . bunkmates. It's not like we knew each other before we came here or anything."

Lexi smiled.

It was distinctly triumphant. Subtle but triumphant.

That was something else Nicola would remember for a long time to come. "That's what I thought. It's the only thing that makes sense."

Guilt rose like bile in Nicola's throat. "But I like her," she hastened to add, wishing she'd defended Holly—wishing, at the very least, she'd said *nothing.*

But she couldn't take back her words. It was like trying to put toothpaste back in the tube.

"Hm?" Lexi paused, her brush halfway across Nicola's right eyelid, forcing a wink Nicola did not mean to give.

"I don't really understand what you have against her," Nicola said, trying to walk the fence.

Lexi shot a look over Nicola's head and said, "You don't? Seriously?"

Nicola scrambled for an answer. She was on the verge of joining the popular girls for the first—and maybe *only*—time in her life. It was like someone was holding a golden ticket out to her and she was shoving her hands into her pockets and asking for a better deal.

It was insane.

"I—" The pause between that one word and all the words that *should* have followed seemed endless. "Can you just tell me?" she asked, like she was *on Lexi's side* and just wanted to help her. "What's your problem with her?"

"She's selfish, she's mean"—Lexi resumed her work on Nicola's eye shadow, but her touch was a little heavier now—"and she totally doesn't belong here. Camp Catoctin is for *serious athletes.*"

"Oh." Nicola had never heard that. She glanced down at her lap, at her ordinary thighs and nonmuscular arms. "Really?"

"Mm-hm." Lexi nodded authoritatively. "You know, girls like us."

"But . . . we don't really do a lot of sports here." All they did was some boating and swimming. But it was every day. "I mean, she's here for the art. She's a really good artist."

Lexi stopped. "Are you defending stupid Holly? After what she said about you?"

Nicola's face went hot again. "What did she say about me?"

She braced herself for some terrible truth she hadn't seen coming. It wouldn't be the first time she'd trusted someone she shouldn't have.

When would she *learn*?

"What did she say?" she asked again, hoping her voice didn't betray the nervous pounding of her heart or the way her stomach had lurched into her chest.

Lexi pressed her lips together. "Nothing."

It was bad, then.

Had Holly told everyone something Nicola had confided in secret? Like her dreams about John Stamos? Or the time she got her period during math class and *everyone* had seen?

"Tell me!"

Lexi hesitated, biting down on her lip, then shook her head. "I don't want to hurt your feelings."

For a long minute, Nicola was torn.

Had Holly bad-mouthed her?

Or did she believe it only because she'd been so ready to do the same herself, in the interest of being one of the popular girls?

"She just said . . . she said you have a big nose and that there was no way you were ever going to be an actress with 'a honker like that.'" Lexi splayed her arms. "I didn't agree, I'm just saying . . ."

Hot tears immediately sprang to Nicola's eyes. This was way worse than the John Stamos or period stories. If there was one thing—and there was—that made her more self-conscious than anything else, it was her nose. It ruined her entire face. It ruined her whole look.

It was the one thing that she worried might keep her from being a famous actress, and she'd told Holly that!

They'd *talked* about it. Holly had said it made her *interesting*, that famous painters would love to put her image on canvas for all time. Holly had told her she was *lucky* to have such a "cool look"—and that Nicola would get famous that much faster because she was beautiful without looking like every other girl in Hollywood.

She'd wanted to believe her. And Holly had said it all with such earnestness. Had she *really* been so two-faced?

How could Holly be so convincing talking to her, then turn around and say something so hateful to Lexi? *She* wasn't the actress; *Nicola* was.

"I don't believe she said that," Nicola said.

Lexi's eyes widened and her hand drew back. "I'm sorry?"

There was a moment where Nicola could have backed down—she could have said that what she meant was she just couldn't believe what a bitch Holly was.

But Holly was one of the nicest people she'd ever met, and she just couldn't imagine giving that up and spending the rest of her time at camp—another week and a half—avoiding Holly and feeling weird every night when it was time to sleep on the same bunk.

Her instincts told her who the liar was.

And it wasn't Holly.

"I don't believe you," Nicola said again, with more force. "Holly wouldn't have said that."

Lexi's eyes darted from Tami to Sylvia, and her voice wasn't nearly so confident when she said, "Well, I *guess* I might have misunderstood what she said."

"Finish her makeup," Sylvia said, reaching her hand in front of Lexi.

Suddenly Sylvia was the boss?

"You need to blend here"—she rubbed Nicola's cheek, under her left eye, hard, her nail scratching—"and here." She did the same on the other side. "We're going to be late now, thanks to this stupid conversation."

Lexi looked like she was stifling tears.

Tami, on the other hand, sort of looked like she was laughing.

That was how they were, Nicola concluded. They weren't even nice to each other. Only to the meanest one.

"Come on." Tami grabbed her hand and pulled her to her feet.

"Wait, I want to look in the mirror," Nicola said, reaching for the small hand mirror on the floor.

"You want to miss the dance?" Tami asked, tightening her grip on Nicola's wrist.

"N-no . . ."

"Then come *on*," Lexi said.

They all ran out the door and through the gravel pathways to the dock, where a group of girls was gathering in the dark. The frogs were loud here, and the dank smell of the lake was strong, particularly in the dark, but Nicola kept her spirits up, reassuring herself that Lexi—who looked *fabulous*—had done her makeup, so she must look good.

At least she knew she was wearing her best, most flattering tank top.

They waited there in the dark, slapping back mosquitoes and rubbing their arms against the increasing chill of the summer night, until finally the covered, utilitarian boat pulled up to take the girls from Camp Catoctin to Echo Lake.

It felt like a long ride in a big cold metal boat that smelled of old fish and seaweed, but Nicola couldn't help the trill of excitement that ran through her in anticipation of the night ahead.

Steve Grudberg would almost certainly be there. He'd been there the past two years.

And Nicola had just had her makeup done by Lexi Henderson herself!

They glided across the lake, and Nicola looked out at the dark silhouette of evergreens on the shore, the sky only slightly lighter above and sprinkled with stars. She knew this should be the sort of memory she held on to forever—she'd heard this kind of thing in the old songs her grandparents played at Thanksgiving and Christmas—but all she could think about was Steve Grudberg, and would he notice her?

It became a mantra for her as they crossed the lake.

Steve Grudberg.

Steve Grudberg.

Please be there, Steve Grudberg.

By the time they finally arrived at the dock on the opposite side of the lake, Nicola was feeling a bit wilted from the heat and dizzy from concentrating on Steve Grudberg.

When the boat pilot gave her a second look on her way past him onto the dock, she barely noticed.

When girls around her *on* the dock giggled, she didn't really notice at all. Or at least, she didn't think it had anything to do with her.

They went to the large wooden meeting hall. It smelled of woodsy smoke from the fireplace, and the entire place was lit by low-watt lightbulbs in wall sconces that looked like old-fashioned lanterns.

To Nicola, it was like something from a fairy tale. The woodsman's cottage, the place where the prince would come to find Sleeping Beauty or Snow White, and his kiss would bring her to life.

It was on the heels of that thought that someone in the crowd stepped aside in front of her, and there he was.

Steve Grudberg.

She would have known him anywhere—that wavy black hair,

those cool blue John Stamos–like eyes with the enviably long dark eyelashes, that jaw with the muscle that twitched when he chewed. He was taller this year, by maybe like four inches, but it only made him look better. His thin frame was wiry and strong. She just knew he was probably the fastest runner at his camp.

She'd thought about him for a year. Fantasized about his hand touching her face, him bending down to kiss her. She knew just what it would feel like. Her whole body tingled just thinking about it.

Thoughts of Steve Grudberg had carried her through some of the loneliest nights of junior high. When she wasn't picked for teams in PE, when her voice cracked during a solo in music, every time she had been ostracized, laughed at, or otherwise demoralized, she had gone home to the safety of her room and her thoughts of Steve.

Her pretend boyfriend.

Now here he was, right in front of her.

She had to do something. If she let this opportunity pass, she might never see him again. It was almost a miracle that he was here this year!

If she talked to him, even for a few minutes, it would be a lot more than she had last year. And, who knows, maybe he'd really like her. Maybe the fact that she liked *him* so much was actually a *sign*.

Maybe he'd ask her if she wanted to go out to the dock and make out.

Her pulse quickened. Suddenly her mouth was dry.

She *had* to do this.

She straightened her back, took a short breath, and started toward him. Her only hesitation came when she thought she heard someone say her name, but it wasn't directed at her. With Holly faking sick in the infirmary, there was no one here who had anything to say to her.

So she sped up, refusing to allow that moment of faltering to stop her from doing the one thing she knew she had to try.

It seemed to take hours to get to him. Her knees threatened to buckle with every step. Still, in the first instance of self-confidence Nicola had ever forced upon herself, she headed strongly toward her mission.

The crowd seemed to part as she walked toward him. People stood back and talked in hushed tones—or was that her imagination? She was almost sure she heard her name once or twice.

This was her destiny.

Finally she was before him. He was talking to Perry Sullivan, but they stopped when she got close, and both of them looked at her with (she was almost sure) interest.

"Hi, Steve," she said, a little breathless.

He frowned. "Uh-huh?"

Wait. That wasn't the answer she was hoping for. It wasn't even close.

Uh-huh?

What could she say to that?

She took a quick breath and tried. "So . . . are you having a good time? You know, at camp. Or here. Camp or here, whatever. Is it fun?"

He and Perry exchanged a look, and Perry put his hands up and backed off.

Which was . . . good. Right? Maybe Steve had been telling him he liked this girl and maybe, just *maybe*, that girl was Nicola. Like, maybe she was picking up on his feelings all along.

She gave Perry a smile and told herself his bark of laughter was a childish reaction to Steve's affection for her.

But Steve wasn't really being affectionate.

In fact, he was looking at her like she'd just dropped a dead kitten at his feet.

"What's your problem?" he asked.

"My . . . problem?" Heat rushed into her cheeks. Something was very wrong.

"Yeah, what's with the"—he gestured at her with disgust—"makeup or whatever that's supposed to be?"

Her hand flew to her cheek. She hadn't looked at herself before leaving the cabin. Maybe it looked too heavy in this light.

She swallowed hard and tried to improvise some sort of response that would make her seem less clownish than she apparently looked.

What would Diane Keaton do?

"It's just . . ." *What? What?* "I was . . . we were . . . doing . . . a play? Because . . . I'm an actress? So . . . ?" She just wanted to drop dead, right here, right now. Or disappear into thin air. That would be better—then her stupid body wouldn't be lying here, proving that this had really happened.

"So what? What would you act in? *Frankenstein* or something?" He shook his head and walked away, clearly revolted by her, shamed by the attention she had pinned to him and him alone.

The crowd that had seemed to part in the romantic wake of her journey toward him now gathered around her, looking at her, pointing, laughing.

The sound got louder.

Finally, somehow, Nicola's legs got enough strength to move her, slowly at first, then more quickly, toward the bathroom. By the time she got there, her breath was coming out in soft, pitiful whimpers.

Yet as bad as she felt, as humiliated and embarrassed, it was nothing compared with the utter mortification she felt when she saw her face in the mirror.

She wasn't prettily made up like Lexi, Tami, and Sylvia. There was no soft mauve shadow in her eyelids or shimmery gold dust highlighting her Maybelline pink cheeks.

No, her eyelids were dusted with an ugly, stark white. Her forehead was streaked with blue. Her cheeks were a vivid red, worse even than the flush that grew even hotter by the second. The gold powder that looked so pretty in a light dusting under Lexi's eyes was painted onto her nose, creating a gleaming bold beacon on the one feature she prayed every day that people wouldn't notice.

In case there was any doubt about that, though—the idea of people noticing—there were two wide black eye pencil arrows on each of her cheeks, pointing at her nose.

What she'd thought was Sylvia's nail scratching her in her haste to make her makeup pretty was, in fact, Sylvia deftly drawing on her, etching humiliation into her skin.

Nicola turned on the tap and a pathetic, cold dribble of water spat out toward the drain. She cupped her hands beneath it until finally she had enough to work the dry, brown-cracked bar of Ivory next to the sink into a measly lather. She rubbed it on her face, her eyes, her forehead, fervently hoping that she would—*please, please, please*—be left alone long enough just to get this mess off her face and try to leave, if not with dignity, then *at least* with some anonymity.

It wasn't easy. The water ran out before she was finished, so she took a handful of the hard beige paper towels and rubbed them on her skin until Sylvia's artwork was gone. Never mind that she'd left a tender red burn behind; it was better than actual *arrows*.

When she'd done the best she could, she unlocked the door and paused. She couldn't go out there again. Everyone had watched her run in here. They were probably still standing there, waiting for her to emerge so they could all continue their big laugh.

Well, screw them.

She turned away from the door and went to the window. It was small, and painted shut, but she wasn't going to let that stop her. With the choice between parading her degraded self in front of everyone at the dance or leaving through the window, she'd break the glass with her bare hands if she had to.

Fortunately, she didn't have to. With determination, she was able to open the window about ten inches. Enough to wedge herself through and land in the sharp holly bush below.

It didn't matter.

She had to get back to the cabin.

She wanted to go home.

She ran through the marshy ground toward the lake, hoping someone was there, operating the boat. It had taken only about five minutes to cross the lake, so they could easily run her back to Camp Catoctin and return well in time to bring the other campers back.

After running what seemed like forever, Nicola saw the dock within view. But the big boat that had chugged them across the water was nowhere to be seen.

It must have been back at the Camp Catoctin dock. Or—who knows?—maybe these canal-like offshoots wound to other places, too. Nicola was just going to have to sit here and wait until it came back to pick everyone up.

Which meant she'd have to sit here and wait for everyone else to come down to the dock, where they'd probably have nothing better to talk about than the reappearance of the stupid girl who had come to the dance with writing on her face and gold dust on her big nose, and who had tried to escape out the bathroom window.

Maybe drowning in the dark water would be better.

Not that she'd *really* consider that, but looking out across the glassy black expanse, she did notice a little boat at the end of the dock. With hope thumping in her heart and a quick glance behind her to make sure she wasn't being watched, she went to the boat. It was a splintery old wooden rowboat, affixed with a rusty outboard motor.

But it smelled like gas, which meant it had been used recently. She couldn't tell if there was water in it—but if there was, it wasn't much, because the thing was still on top of the water and not at the bottom of the lake.

By an incredible stroke of luck—and, given the night she'd had, *any* luck felt incredible—Nicola knew how to start an outboard motor and steer a boat through murky waters.

She hadn't spent summers at her grandfather's bay house in Shady Side for nothing. Granted, she'd never had to navigate a strange craft through the night with no one watching her, but she was willing to take that chance.

She climbed into the boat, feeling relief at the sound of the water slopping up against the side.

The sound was *so* much better, right now, than Journey singing "Don't Stop Believing."

She unlooped the tether from the end of the dock, pulled the starter cord, and the motor coughed and sputtered out. She pulled again. And again. And finally it putted to life and she steered it with shaking hands out into the open water.

This is crazy. This is really stupid. In twenty years, I won't even remember these people—they are not worth dying for in the middle of the night in the middle of some mucky lake. . . .

It was easy to imagine the worst-case scenario on the lake, but it was even easier to imagine the even-worse-case-scenario of going back to the dance—possibly drenched with dank water and with reeds and fish in her hair—to admit defeat.

So she steered the boat onward, her heart leaping with every choke of the engine, heading straight into blackness. Several times she thought about going back, but she didn't know if she'd already passed the halfway point and figured that, if she had, it was wiser to keep going.

So with only a modicum of faith and possibly even less gas, she chugged forward, trying to quell the eerie retellings of urban legends that played in her head—the bloody hook hanging off a car door handle in the woods; the slimy creature raising a glistening hand from the swamp—and concentrating on the fact that, if she kept going straight, she'd *have* to hit land eventually.

But time wore on, and she saw nothing before her. Had she gone in circles? Woven around in such a way that she was always out of sight of land?

She was about to lose heart, but she heard the distinct sound of an engine starting, and the boat that had taken them over to Echo Lake sprang to life in a hail of little lights.

Camp Catoctin's dock was directly ahead.

The larger boat drew back and passed her, unknowing, creating a wake that caused her own boat to buck wildly. But it didn't matter because her destination was close enough to swim to if she absolutely had to.

Within minutes, she was on land. She'd let the little boat go, knowing that anyone who missed it would find it easily in the lake tomorrow, and hopefully would believe it had accidentally gotten loose.

When she got to cabin 7, she peeked in the window first to make sure Brittany wasn't sitting up, waiting for her campers to return or, worse, waiting for Nicola to return so she could question her about the missing boat.

But Brittany wasn't there. No one was except Holly, so Nicola went in, deliberately letting the screen door slam shut behind her.

"Well, thanks a lot," she said, peeling off her wet clothes.

"What?" Holly looked up from her sketchpad.

"Turn around. I'm undressing," Nicola barked. Then, when Holly did so, she continued, "I've just had the most humiliating night of my life, and you could have stopped it, but, no, you had to pretend to be sick."

Holly set her sketching and charcoal aside. "What happened?"

"Like you care!"

"I *do*!" Holly insisted. "I'm sorry I wasn't there for you, but . . . I just couldn't go. But I'm here for you now. Tell me what happened."

So Nicola told her, including every terrible detail, saving nothing for private embarrassment, until finally she was just crying in Holly's warm arms.

"I'm sorry." Holly fretted. "I just didn't want Lexi making fun of me anymore."

"You were right." Nicola hadn't seen it clearly until just now. She'd tried to befriend Lexi and her stupid friends so she'd be cool. It was a stupid, stupid mistake. "It's not your fault at all."

"But I'm still sorry!"

"Me, too!"

They had only about twenty minutes before everyone got back, but it was long enough for them to lie in the dark on their bunk beds, plotting revenge against Lexi Henderson to the soundtrack of crickets and bullfrogs.

Lexi was *finally* going to get what was coming to her.

She was going to pay—big time—for what she'd done to Holly and Nicola.

The Present

Y ou want me to be honest with you, right?"

Nicola always hated that question and its implication that what followed was bound to hurt.

But what could she say? No? Of course she needed the truth. Especially when her agent had information that could get her out of the "homely girl makes good" roles and into some serious, Oscar-contending parts.

Because, of course, you have to be beautiful for that. And, more often than not, uglied down for the role.

Nicole Kidman in *The Hours*.

Charlize Theron in *Monster*.

It was ironic.

"Yes," she said, mentally bracing herself. She'd just auditioned for a movie that promised to be one of the biggest of the year. It would be the biggest break of her career. If there was anything she could do to make it happen, she had to do it. No matter how hard. "Of course I want you to be honest with me."

"You're not going to like it." Mike Varnet was a good agent with a clumsy bedside manner. He'd risen to the top with Nicola when she starred as the homely girl who got the hot guy in the sleeper hit *Duet*, but he had somehow managed to stay up while her career had drifted back downward. She'd had only one more starring role, in a movie that failed miserably at the box office *and* on the shelves, and then a series of increasingly diminished parts; from the bitter lesbian sister of the hot guy in a frat house comedy to the quirky neighbor on a TV pilot that went nowhere.

"Tell me." Her voice was tight. Every muscle in her body was tight.

"Well . . ." He sighed. She could picture him leaning back in his chair and fiddling with a pen, the way he had since he'd stopped smoking. "The general consensus is that you're just not pretty enough. You're too scrawny and your nose is too big. You just don't fit the ideal for a lead actress. Unless they remake *Popeye* and need an Olive Oyl. Rob Leiman said that, by the way, not me."

Nicola sat down.

It was finally out in the open. *Finally*, after all her years of insecurity, all her years of therapy and self-help books, all her years of telling herself that she was okay with who she was and that she was far more critical of her own looks than anyone else would be, someone had *finally* come out and said what she'd suspected since third grade.

We've all been talking and we all think you're ugly.

In fact, you're too ugly to be near us, so just go away.

This was not a surprise. Or it shouldn't have been.

When *Duet* had come out and become the sleeper hit of the summer, everyone raved about Nicola's "unusual beauty," "exotic looks," and a million other euphemisms for "she's not Meg Ryan," and Nicola had made a conscious effort to believe the press. She'd tried hard to feel good about being "a new kind of pretty." But even then, she'd known the truth, and even then, she'd been bracing herself for an ambush just like this.

The failed follow-up, the subsequent minor roles, had all felt more familiar to her. Auditioning for the lead and ending up as the sidekick felt a lot like her all-girls high school, when she always got the *male* lead because, Miss Bradshaw said, she was more talented than whatever fluffy blonde got the lead, and that it required more talent to take on the male role.

"You there?" Mike sounded impatient. He probably had more successful, more attractive clients to call.

Nicola struggled to find her voice. "I'm here. I just . . . I don't know what to do. I don't even know what this means." It wasn't just the Carell project she was upset about now. She had to worry about everything else suddenly, too. "Am I just not going to get work? Ever? Anywhere? Should I just resolve myself to performing as Anne Boleyn in a traveling Renaissance festival?"

"That would be three years' worth of work at least."

"*What?* Are you joking?"

He didn't answer fast enough.

"Mike, are you seriously telling me that I should give up on the film industry entirely and move to community theater? *Really?*" Her voice rose. She couldn't stop it. Hysteria bubbled in her chest.

Could it really all be just *over?*

Just like that?

"Cool it, Nic. I'm just telling you the feedback I'm getting. It's a tough business. You know that."

Of course she knew it. She'd always known it. Well enough to invest the disproportionately high paycheck she'd gotten for her second major movie and parlay it into an ostrich-sized nest egg.

That didn't mean she wanted to retire now.

And it damn sure didn't mean she wanted to *fail.*

"What should I do, Mike?" She hated how desperate she sounded. And how desperate she felt. But now was the one time in her life that did not call for acting. It called for honesty. "I'll do anything to get my foot back in the door."

"Are you asking me who you should blow?"

"No!" *Was* there someone? "I'm asking if there is anything within my power that I can do. Maybe more acting classes, or a new method—"

"You're a great actress. No one's got a problem with that. This business is about looks as much as that, maybe more. You know that. Get yourself a nose job and eat a cheeseburger, and we can talk about bigger roles. Short of that, you're looking at more of the same."

"As I said before, the bruising and swelling will still be somewhat dramatic at first." The doctor's voice was soothing and his touch light and nimble as he removed the bandages from Nicola's nose. "If I could keep my patients from looking in the mirror at all for the first couple of weeks, I would, but everyone wants to see."

"Including me," Nicola confessed. "I haven't told anyone about this, and my friends and family are starting to wonder why I don't want to go out."

This was the very beginning of what she was thinking of, to herself, as the New Nicola Project.

It was the only project she was 100 percent sure she'd be part of these days.

Dr. Bernstein chuckled mildly and gave the last of the adhesive a quick yank. "This will be quite the surprise for them." He sat back and looked at her. "Excellent. *Excellent.* This is some of my best work. It was quite a challenge, you know."

That could have been insulting, but Nicola realized he was talking solely about the level of difficulty of his task. The truth was the truth.

"So it's going to look exactly the way it did in the three-D model you did beforehand?"

He shook his head and clicked his tongue against his teeth. "Even better."

Her heart leapt. *Even better!* He was looking at her right now, apparently looking as if she'd been hit by a truck, and he believed that the results would be even better than the ideal he'd done on the computer beforehand.

A surge of energy flowed through her.

She couldn't wait to go on an audition.

"You must be very careful, Nicola. You will be surprised how many times in the course of a normal day you might touch your nose. It's of the utmost importance"—he looked into her eyes—"I cannot stress it too much, that you are careful. Don't overexert yourself. Don't participate in any contact sports."

"No problem." She was already planning to lie around reading scripts and sipping milk shakes to try to add some curves to her coltish figure.

"Then you're ready to go. I'll see you back here in two weeks to check the progress. But first"—he reached into a drawer and took out the sort of hand mirror a hair stylist might use—"I want you to take a look and let me address any questions you might have before you leave."

She took the mirror and turned it to face her.

Despite all the warnings, she must have been expecting to see an improved version of herself rather than the black, blue, and yellow impressionist flower that bloomed in the center of her face. With the white bandages on, even the black eyes had been obscured, but now she could see all the bruises in all their glory.

And her nose looked like Marcia Brady's had, right after she got hit in the face by a football.

"Questions?" Dr. Bernstein prodded. He obviously expected her to ask when she would stop looking so scary, but he probably didn't want to bring it up first, on the off chance that she *wasn't* thinking that.

She forced herself to look away from the mirror and at the doctor. She *had* to ask. "Are you *sure* this is normal?"

He laughed outright, breaking the tension somewhat. "Nine times out of ten, that is the first question, and I do understand why, but yes, Nicola, this is absolutely normal. It wouldn't be possible to perform such an operation without bruising and fairly substantial swelling. It's ironic that you look worse before you look better, but that's just the process."

"Yes, but . . ." Logic told her he was right. In fact, all the Googling she did on rhinoplasty before having the procedure had told her to expect this. However, looking at the mess that was her face, she couldn't help but wonder if this was more extreme than what most people got. After all, she'd never heard phrases like *frightening children* used in connection with a nose job.

Then again, her case might have been more extreme than most people's to begin with. She was realistic about that. It wasn't that her nose was so *big* really, but it had a bump in it that made it harsh, and it was crooked enough to look like maybe she'd been in a fight when she was younger. So Dr. Bernstein had been dealing with a lot.

"Even the swelling"—she pointed to the bridge of her nose—"here? And this much? It's normal?"

"One hundred percent." He smiled, and she took a moment to wonder who his dentist was.

Surely a plastic surgeon who cared that much about his *own* looks cared as much about his reputation with other people's looks.

"I've been doing this for over two decades now," he said, "and I can see already how good this is going to look."

Nicola looked back in the mirror. It was hard to imagine, but she had to believe it. "So—"

The speaker on the wall buzzed, and the receptionist's voice came through. "Dr. Bernstein? Tammy Morgan is on line one, and she says it's urgent that she speak with you."

Dr. Bernstein's face reddened. "I've told her not to reveal my clients' names," he muttered to Nicola. Tammy Morgan was the latest Disney-teen-queen-cum-hot-starlet, and there had been a lot of speculation in the tabloids lately about whether or not she'd had some work done. "Please don't repeat that."

"Sure." Nicola waved him off. She was glad to hear he had such high-profile clients. It only strengthened her conviction that she'd made the right choice in doctors.

"All right, then." He stepped back and assessed his work with obvious pleasure. "If you don't have any further questions, think you're ready to go home and begin healing?"

"I'm ready!"

"Remember, a liquid diet for the first couple of days and *no alcohol whatsoever.*"

She nodded. "Does that thin the blood too much or something?"

"No, it makes people clumsy," he said with a completely straight face. "We can't afford to have you tripping and falling into a Dumpster and ruining your nose."

That was pretty specific. Tripping and falling into a Dumpster. She wondered who had done that.

"I promise you I won't," she said, getting up to leave. She was eager to go home and take her time examining her new face but also apprehensive about leaving the only person who could really reassure her that everything was going normally.

Staying wasn't an option, though.

She gathered her things, gave a brave smile—which tugged on her nose a little and hurt—and said, "See you in two weeks!"

One thing Nicola was not excited about was telling Holly what she'd done.

Holly had never been judgmental about anything Nicola had done; it wasn't that. But ever since they were children, and right up to—and beyond—Nicola getting the role in *Duet*, Holly had been a cheerleader for Nicola.

Exactly the way Nicola was.

When she'd had trouble at camp with girls who made fun of her, Holly was right there to boost her spirits and tell her that they were just jealous of what a nice and happy person Nicola was.

When Terese Ordman asked Billy Ryder to the prom right when it was obvious that he was about to ask Nicola, Holly comforted her by pointing out that Terese had seen what Nicola was unable to—that Billy had the hots for her and the cheerleader couldn't stand being shown up by the studious girl.

And when Nicola had endured one painful rejection after another after moving to L.A., it was Holly who had staunchly supported her, *assuring* her that someday someone would see her unique beauty and she would make a fortune.

Well, Holly had been right about that. But what she hadn't realized—actually what Nicola hadn't realized at the time, either—was how fleeting that success and appreciation would be. Before she knew it, Nicola was right back at the bottom of the heap, and now, instead of being just "homely," she was now "homely" and "getting long in the tooth."

It was a terrible combination.

So she'd sincerely felt she had little option but to fix the thing casting directors were saying was "wrong" with her. She needed to do it for her work, for her livelihood.

She honestly felt like she'd had no choice.

But.

There was undeniably a certain shame in it because she knew that, in a big way, she'd given in. She didn't change her look because she was passionate about looking *this* way. Nor was she particularly passionate about looking different from the way she had before.

She'd given in to society's view of what a woman's appearance should be, and she'd tried to become it. In order to get money, she'd changed herself. Wasn't that almost prostitution?

Would Holly see it that way?

Probably not. Holly wasn't like that. But Nicola knew that Holly would be disappointed in her for giving up something so integral to her *self* as her very appearance.

And, worse, she knew that a small part of her was disappointed in herself for the same reason.

Nicola sat cross-legged on the floor in front of the full-length mirror, examining her image.

It had been two weeks since she got the bandages off, and the worst of the bruising was gone and the swelling was down quite a bit. With the careful application of some concealer and a topcoat of powder foundation, no one would be able to tell anything was amiss at all.

Dr. Bernstein had been right: Her nose was coming along just perfectly. It was surprisingly exciting. She was already just a little bit of swelling away from the look she'd been going for. It was an incredible feeling to change this way. Yes, it was also disconcerting to have a new face every time she looked in the mirror, but if it led to her getting work, it would be worth it.

That she wanted to keep working was a given. It fulfilled her in a way that nothing else did, nothing else could.

But the truth was, she wanted to know what it was like to be perceived as *pretty* for once in her life. She'd been called ugly plenty of times, particularly as an adolescent, she'd been called average, and she'd been called unique, but just plain pretty? Never.

All her life, she'd wondered what it felt like for beautiful people to walk around like that, being admired, being noticed, being envied.

Now maybe she'd get a small taste of what it was like.

She could hardly wait until the last of the swelling went down.

A week later, she wished the swelling would *stop* going down.

She didn't know if she'd overiced or if the homeopathic arnica root gel was so effective it had diminished actual flesh, but Nicola's nose had turned to a straight, sharp little blade.

On another face, it would have been great. In fact, on Michelle Pfeiffer's face, it *was* great. But to Nicola's eye, it looked . . . fake.

Well, maybe not *fake,* but it didn't look like *her* anymore. At all. When she looked in the mirror, someone else was looking back at

her. At first, it had been a kick. But slowly it had gotten . . . disconcerting.

Disturbing.

It turned out the rest of her face was pretty symmetrical. Her blue
eyes were even and well set, if not striking. Her brows were straight.
Her mouth was Goldilocks medium: not too big, not too small, with
even teeth and a nice-enough smile. Her chin was just a chin—not
jutting, but lacking the charm of, say, a gentle cleft.

All her uniqueness had been in the shape of her nose.

It's probably your imagination, Holly wrote to her in an e-mail after
Nicola had finally told her about the surgery. *I had a mole removed
from my cheek once, and the difference seemed huge to me, but of course,
no one else even noticed.*

Nicola tried to agree, but privately she worried that she might
have made an enormous mistake.

There was a benefit for ovarian cancer at Iota on Friday night, and
Nicola had decided that was as good a time as any to reveal her new
self to the world.

On Friday afternoon, Nicola had a professional makeup artist
come to her house to do her makeup for the evening. Also, she'd purchased a flowing Stella McCartney gown—in stark contrast to her
usual tailored style—to complete her new look.

She was ready by four o'clock, which gave her a couple of hours to
stop and visit with her grandmother, which was test number one in
the New Nicola Project.

Nicola's grandmother lived in a beautiful Dutch Colonial house
on a tiny curve of road just on the outskirts of Beverly Hills. Her
second husband had been Barney Klotz, a Hollywood bigwig—well,

medium wig—back in the forties and fifties. The house had been in his family since it was built in the twenties. Cary Grant and Randolph Scott had rented the pool house for a few months when they were just starting out in the business.

Nicola's grandmother—everyone called her Vivi, including Nicola—met Barney when Nicola's grandfather had died in the late sixties. The story was that he stopped her on the street in New York and told her she was the most beautiful woman he'd ever seen and that she could marry him right then and there or hold out while he pursued her.

"But make no mistake," he'd said, according to Vivi. "You will be my wife."

So, to the horror of everyone in the family, Vivi married him two days later.

And somehow, the one, single impulsive act—the only one anyone in the Kestle family had ever made, it seemed—had worked out. The marriage lasted until he died in 1988, and since then, Vivi had been living on her own, going to parties and events almost every day of the week and hanging out with cronies who knew virtually every golden age star by their real names.

Nicola loved going to Vivi's. When she'd first moved to L.A., she herself lived in the pool house, and she would have been happy to stay there forever, except that it would have proved her parents' point that acting was a "pipe dream" and that she needed to go back to school to get a "practical degree" in order to get a "real job."

So she'd moved to a tiny apartment in West L.A. and allowed Vivi to secretly give her grocery store gift cards until *Duet* provided her big break.

Still, going to Vivi's always felt like going home, and never had Nicola needed to feel that more than she did now. Normally she would have let herself in, but she wanted to see Vivi's face, to gauge her honest reaction, as soon as she saw Nicola.

Nicola could hear Vivi's voice as she approached the door, apparently on the phone. ". . . must run, darling, my Nicola has come to see me. Ta!"

The door swung open, and Vivi stood there in a whooshing blue satin muumuu that matched her ice blue eyes. Her silver hair was cropped short and made her tanned skin seem even darker. Her small bow lips, always smiling, formed an O.

A long moment passed before she said, "Yes?"

This was not the reaction Nicola had expected. "So . . . ," she prompted, taking a step forward, "what do you think?"

Vivi stepped back and closed the door a fraction. "I'm sorry?"

"Of my nose! Come on, Vivi, what do you think? Is it that bad?"

"I don't—" Realization dawned in Vivi's clear eyes, followed by a moment of warmth that was quickly obscured by—clearly—embarrassment.

She hadn't even recognized Nicola.

"Come *in*," Vivi effused. "Darling, come in, let me look at you."

But she *had* been looking at Nicola—and she hadn't even known who she was seeing.

Nicola had spent days telling herself that she was being oversensitive to the change, that other people might not notice it at all, or might—ideally—just think she looked wonderful but be unsure as to what was different.

All she had changed was her nose.

How was it that that seemed to have changed her entire face?

Nicola followed her grandmother out to the lanai, where she had set tea and those Pepperidge Farm butter cookies she kept on hand for every imaginable occasion.

When Vivi turned back to look at her, her expression was still clearly troubled, though she was trying to mask that. "Well. How do you feel?"

Nicola sat down heavily. "Like a pod person." The truth came spilling out. No more trying to jolly herself along or pretend everything was hunky-dory. "I feel like I'm playing dress up."

Vivi frowned. "Darling, you look beautiful."

"Thanks." Her voice was limp. So were her spirits. "I look different."

"That's . . . true."

"Too different."

Vivi pursed her lips for a moment, then shrugged and said, "Too different for what?"

Too different to keep living my own life, Nicola thought with a touch of hysteria. She felt like she was standing on the edge of a really big, irretrievable emotion. It was all she could do just to maintain her composure, to keep calm.

"Too different . . ." She couldn't finish. Instead, she cried.

"Oh, darling, darling." Vivi's arms were around her almost immediately, the drape of her sleeve like a shawl across Nicola's uncharacteristically bare arm. "You *do* look beautiful. You *do*. Anyone would say it. Someone who saw you walking down the street would say, *Look at that beautiful girl.* But it's not familiar to you yet."

"That's for sure." Nicola sniffled. "How can it ever be? It's not me! And I'll never be *me* again!"

Vivi drew back and held Nicola's arms hard within her narrow clutch. "Listen to me, Nicola Dean Kestle." She looked hard into Nicola's eyes, and her mouth was a thin line as she spoke. "Don't you *ever* say that again. No one in our family is foolish enough to think who we are has anything to do with what we look like. If you truly believe that *you* is contingent on how you look, then you are not the girl I believed you were."

"But—"

"But nothing!" Vivi could be fierce when she had an idea. "If someone were disfigured in an accident and said to you that they were no longer who they thought they were, would you listen to that nonsense?"

Nicola's other grandmother, Grandma Parker, would have been knocking wood and *God forbidding* at this point.

"No," Nicola admitted. "I'd be saying the same thing you are."

Vivi released her grip. "There you go. And you didn't even have the misfortune of disfigurement. You look like a soap opera star."

And that hit the nail on the head: a soap star. The kind of face that would fit into the Barbie-and-Ken world of soaps.

Nicola no longer had a face that felt expressive, that communicated something about her before she even spoke. She was going to have to work that much harder to get half as far. And she knew that was the truth, even though she knew Vivi was right, at least in part, about the fact that this wasn't due to a tragedy.

Tragic stupidity, maybe.

Tragic vanity.

But not random tragedy.

At least she had that on her side.

There was no way she could go to the benefit at Iota tonight. She wasn't ready to get the world's reaction all at once. She had to start with Mike.

Then she'd go from there.

Camp Catoctin, Pennsylvania
Twenty Years Ago

Talk about stupid.

Lexi had tried to stop dumb Nicola from actually marching into the dance with that ridiculous makeup on—it was only supposed to be a little joke!—but Nicola totally *totally* ignored her. She even sped up to get away from her.

What else was Lexi supposed to do? Chase her down?

Um, no.

She would admit that it wasn't supernice of her to put ugly makeup on Nicola, but it wasn't like she'd drawn the arrows. That was Sylvia.

That kind of thing was always Sylvia.

And if Lexi had tried any harder to help Nicola, she would never have heard the end of it.

Anyway, Nicola and Holly probably deserved everything they got.

Like when Holly almost drowned the other day—Lexi had *told* her to put on her life vest. Duh! How many times was Lexi supposed to try to help these jerks? She was sick of it. They were so nasty to everyone else, always whispering together, laughing, eating all that great candy Holly's mom sent and never *ever* sharing *any* of it. Holly got a care package like every other day, filled with the best stuff in the world.

But did she ever offer even a single Dubble Bubble to anyone else?

No. She knew perfectly well that the Camp Catoctin food was total crap. Lexi would have given *anything* for a Twinkie or a Ho Ho. Even just a *bite* of one. But Holly kept it all to herself and Nicola, knowing everyone else wanted some, too.

In fact, she probably shared it with Nicola only to make the point that she *wasn't* sharing it with Lexi. Every time Holly even glanced Lexi's way, she made it clear she hated her. It was so bad that, even though Lexi loved art and wanted to be a painter or a sculptor someday, she made sure she didn't have any art classes with Holly.

And, of course, Holly was taking, like, *all* of them.

So on top of everything else, she was screwing up Lexi's future as a famous painter.

Lexi could have taken the classes anyway, of course, but the idea of sitting through forty minutes of icy glares three times a day sucked. There was no way she was going to do that. It was enough just dealing with Sylvia and her mood swings and temper.

So she wasn't making friends, so what? It wasn't like she'd be back again next year. A lot of people went to camp, nearly died of loneliness, and forgot about it later, probably.

Lexi wished she didn't care.

If her mother hadn't died last year, she would have been sending care packages, too. Lexi knew it. There would be Marathon Bars,

Zotz, Candy Dots, 3 Musketeers, Ho Hos—all of Lexi's favorites. And there would be little notes, too, like the riddles she used to handwrite on her ANNA HENDERSON notepaper from the kitchen.

Q: *What's smaller than an ant's mouth?*
A: *What the ant eats.*
Q: *What shoes should you wear when your basement is flooded?*
A: *Pumps.*
Q: *Why did Lexi's mother die on Lexi's twelfth birthday?*
A: ———

Lexi felt tears rise, hot and embarrassing and unwelcome, and she blinked hard. It was so unfair that her mother was gone. Just *gone*. Almost like she'd never existed, like she was a figment of Lexi's imagination.

Then her father married that wicked witch Michelle the very next Christmas, which made it even *more* like her mother hadn't existed. The man who was married to her for fifteen years didn't even miss her—he just got a replacement! Lexi's grandparents were gone, and her mother had had no siblings, so it was up to Lexi to remember her mother all by herself.

So she couldn't find a replacement like he had. She could barely even look at her father, for fear that it would erase the one place Anna Henderson still did exist—in Lexi's memory—and then she'd be forgotten completely.

Lexi wouldn't let her mother be forgotten. She couldn't make anyone else remember, but she could hold on to that herself.

That's how she did most things anyway—by herself. The truth was, she had no one in the world she could really turn to for . . . well, anything. Not comfort, not advice, not a shoulder to cry on.

Not even a stupid Ho Ho, much less a friend to tear the chocolate outsides off with.

Lexi reached into her front pocket and felt the chain and ring she'd put there. She liked to have them with her, especially here at camp, where she felt so homesick. She couldn't wear it on swimming days because she wasn't sure if the water was bad for it, but during arts and crafts day and horseback riding, she could keep it with her.

At night, she looped it over her bedpost, and the ring hung like a dream catcher, keeping her safe from nightmares.

"Hey!" Brittany called behind her.

She was next to the stable, a few yards from the classroom building, where she had hoped no one would see her, but she'd know Brittany's shriek anywhere.

Lexi turned around. "What?"

"Aren't you supposed to be at art or something?"

"I came out to find a rock for a project." Lexi lied easily these days. Sometimes she herself was amazed at how quickly things came to her.

"Oh. Whatever." Brittany waved it off and left, undoubtedly in hot pursuit of the other counselors.

Lexi took a deep, wavering breath.

She wished like crazy she was home, in her room. She'd be alone, but it was better than being with these people.

She hated it here.

She hated everyone here. Especially her "friends," Sylvia and Tami.

She'd left arts and crafts class because Sylvia had been talking—in a really loud whisper—about how dumb-looking Tami's mom had been in her big Jackie O. glasses on the day everyone got dropped off.

Lexi had noticed Tami's mom, not because of the glasses but because of how hard she hugged Tami when it was time to leave. Like she didn't want to let go.

The driver Lexi's dad had hired—she couldn't pronounce his name, though she read it over and over again on the license he had on the glass divider in his Town Car—let Lexi out at the wrong building, and she'd had to walk like half a mile to get to the check-in.

Obviously she hadn't had any tearful good-byes.

And it made her really sad that Sylvia was so spoiled that she could just make fun of someone for having a mom who loved her. Lexi would have said something, but if she did, Sylvia would turn the same wrath on her that she did on *all* the people she thought were weaker than she was. Like Nicola. And Holly.

It was Sylvia's idea to get the boat for Holly. She thought it was hilarious that it said *Fat Oxen*. They didn't actually *know* it had a leak, and Lexi couldn't believe it when Holly didn't put on her life vest, even once the boat started sinking.

But, honestly, that's what she got for eating all that candy her mom sent by herself.

And Nicola had ignored Lexi when she tried to stop her on the way into the dance, so what had happened was *her* fault.

Lexi didn't need to feel sorry for either of them.

Her hand started to hurt, and she realized she had made a fist around the chain in her pocket. Hard. Her knuckles hurt. Her palm was scratched by the ring.

Worse, she didn't feel like anything of her mother had come through to her. That was the real reason she'd brought the thing—because her mother had worn it all the time. Lexi couldn't remember a time when she didn't have it on.

It *had* to have absorbed some essence of her mom.

Hadn't it?

A tear dropped onto the laces of Lexi's blue Keds.

"What's wrong with *you?*"

Sylvia!

Lexi closed her eyes and rubbed them. "I got a gnat in my eye," she said with a sniff. "It's killing me."

"Lemme see." Sylvia yanked Lexi's hands down and put her hand under her chin to look. "I don't see anything." She narrowed her eyes. Her breath smelled like Skittles.

"My eyes watered so much, I think he might have floated out." Lexi gave a fake laugh, but it was more like an old dog barking. "I hate those things."

"Me, too. Fucking things." Sylvia had been experimenting with cuss words lately. "So, you know Gabriella Sanchez?"

"Sort of."

"She farted in music today. It was so fucking funny."

"Oh, my God, are you serious?" Lexi was so glad it hadn't been her. "Did anyone notice?"

"Um, *obviously*." Sylvia rolled her eyes. She was wearing eye pencil on her inside eyelid, which made it look really creepy. "What kind of person *does* something like that?"

A couple of days ago, Gabriella Sanchez had split her last piece of gum in half to share with Lexi. Lexi thought she was really nice.

"Fool," she said to Sylvia, choosing the safer route of agreement over the potentially fatal route of arguing. If she didn't, Sylvia would get mad and start saying the same kinds of things about her, and then she would be friendless *and* a laughingstock.

She honestly didn't think she could take that.

"How dumb," she said instead.

"I know." Sylvia nodded, apparently satisfied that Lexi was complying with the Rules of Sylvia. "So . . . what are you doing out here anyway? Didn't you want to make a pot holder for Mommy?"

Lexi looked at her sharply.

"Oh, sorry. Forgot." She said it so breezily that she might have been talking about whether or not Lexi had a cat. "Well, you could make it for your stepmommy. It's almost the same."

It occurred to Lexi only now that the fact that everyone was making their pot holders for their moms probably had a lot to do with why she suddenly felt like she had to get out of there when Sylvia started ragging on Tami.

Now Lexi did start to cry. "Like I'd do anything for that bitch," she said, the word *bitch* tingling illicitly down her spine. It was better to call Sylvia's attention to that than to her tears. "She could burn her hands right down to the bone before I'd give her a pot holder."

Sylvia snorted with laughter and thumped Lexi on the back. "You are *so funny*. You just crack me up." She thumped her again, and it kind of hurt. "So what should we do until lunch? I do *not* want to go back into the classroom. Tami's all mad at me and crying because I dared to insult her mommy."

"How does she know?" Lexi hadn't told her. She wouldn't do that.

"She got dizzy from the heat during riding, so they sent her to arts and crafts instead. It was, like, right after you left, so when she came over and sat down, I thought she was you and I added that Tami's mom also had the ugliest shoes on that I've ever seen. They looked like those special shoes people wear when they have clubfoot, you know? I was totally right, but she got all upset."

"Did you apologize?"

Sylvia laughed immediately, like it was a joke. "Um, no. Duh."

"Oh. Yeah."

"Hey." A light came into Sylvia's eyes. "Want to go down to the boathouse? Maybe we can see someone doing a blow job."

"Cool." It was the last thing in the world Lexi wanted to do. "Probably Emily, right? I heard she and Danny are doing it down there all the time." She hadn't heard any such thing, but it was a pretty logical guess. And, more to the point, it was the kind of risqué thing to say that made everyone think Lexi was cool.

And she would much rather they thought she was cool than know she was a wimpy little kid, crying over her mommy.

Two nights later, Lexi left the meeting hall early because she had cramps.

Fortunately, there wasn't anyone around to convince of her ailment, because, in truth, she was self-conscious about "women problems" and tended to ride them out in agony under normal circumstances. But as usual, her counselor, Brittany, was nowhere to be found, so she took the opportunity to sneak out the back of the all-camp meeting and creep through the darkness to cabin 7.

Unfortunately, Nicola and Holly had beaten her to it.

Of course.

They always did. They *always* seemed to be wherever Lexi wanted to be alone.

Fuckers.

She felt sort of guilty for having that last thought—influenced, undoubtedly, by Sylvia—but she felt good about it, too. Because these two girls—with their secret conversations and pig-out sessions and letters from home—weren't what you'd call nice.

They thought they were so great, they didn't *want* anyone else around them because that would ruin their little club.

Well, tonight Lexi didn't care. She wanted to be alone, and no matter where she went, someone was there and she'd thought coming all the way back to the cabin from a *mandatory* assembly would mean that she would *finally* and *definitely* be alone to cry or whatever, but no, here were these two.

Again.

"Um, what are you doing here?" Lexi asked, knowing she sounded meaner than she felt, and only hoping that might chase them away so she could finally breathe. "Aren't you supposed to be at the assembly with *everyone* else?"

Nicola made a nervous move to get off the bed, but Holly stayed put, biting down on her lower lip. "Aren't *you?*" she challenged.

But there was just enough of a waver in her voice to let Lexi know she didn't have the confidence of her convictions.

"*I* was excused," Lexi lied. "But *you* weren't. And"—she tried a bold move—"they were wondering where you were after roll call."

"They took roll?" Nicola asked in full panic.

Lexi nodded. "And Brittany's coming to look for you."

"Oh, crap!" Nicola scrambled down from the bed, followed more slowly by Holly.

"Yeah, you'd better hurry." Lexi egged them on, knowing full well that no one was coming to look for them. No one had even noticed they weren't there to begin with.

Holly's pudgy heel stuck on the blanket and pulled it through the ladder of the bunk bed. Something clattered to the wood floor.

"You dropped something." Lexi had just enough time to pick up the small round dough ornament—the kind she could remember making for the Christmas tree when she was younger—before Holly thumped to the floor and snatched it from her.

"You can't have that!" she cried.

"Who said I *wanted* it?" Lexi grabbed the item back, heedless of how that contradicted what she'd just said. It was a rope of dough, swirled into a circle with tiny perfect individually painted alphabet noodles, spelling out WORLD'S BEST DAD! (The exclamation point was made from a carefully broken *l*.) I LOVE YOU, (the comma was a broken piece of an *O*) HOLLY XOXOXO.

And for reasons Lexi wouldn't fully understand for a long, long time to come, it infuriated her.

"*Give that to me!*" Holly cried.

Like Lexi wanted it! "What, *this?*" She held it up, taunting Holly. She knew it was wrong, but she was so mad at the way Holly and Nicola thought this whole cabin was theirs alone, and the way they freaked out on Lexi every time she came anywhere near them. Like she wanted to steal their candy or their stupid dough ornaments or whatever. "You can have it. I don't want the stupid thing."

She didn't want the stupid thing with its stupid message for Holly's stupid dad.

So she hurled it at Holly.

And Holly, who probably wouldn't have been able to catch so much as a firefly if it landed on her arm, put her hands out in a pitiful attempt to grab the thing, only to accidentally bat it away.

It hit the wall and smashed to the floor in a pile of dough shards and little painted noodle letters.

Holly looked at it in horror, then looked at Lexi. "You did that on purpose!" Tears filled her eyes. "You are such a jerk!"

"Oh, please." She hadn't, of course. But she wasn't sorry to see it, either. So Holly had a mom who sent care packages and the "world's best dad"—what right did she have to whine about anything? She should be glad for all the stuff she had, not yelling at Lexi. "Get a life."

"I *hate* you!" Holly shrieked. She glared at Lexi while Nicola moved forward to inspect the broken ornament.

"Oh, no!" Lexi mocked, putting a hand to her chest. Her heart was thumping hard; she could feel it. "What a *huge* surprise."

Nicola glanced back at Lexi but said nothing.

"Why don't you just get out of here? Go back to Tami and Sylvia and ruin your own lives instead of everyone else's!"

Lexi wanted nothing more than to leave the cabin, to leave the entire camp. Sometimes at night she fantasized about sneaking out to the highway and hitchhiking all the way to California to start a new life.

But Lexi wasn't so much of a dreamer that she didn't know what a failure it would be. She'd seen *Dawn: Portrait of a Teenage Runaway* on TV, and she didn't want to end up in a life of prostitution and drugs.

"I'm not going anywhere." Lexi plopped herself down onto her bed, willing herself to stay there and look obstinate, rather than running away and revealing a weakness to these two.

"God!" Holly then whispered something to Nicola, and they spoke in hushed voices. If Lexi had really wanted to hear what they were saying, she probably could have, but the fact was she *didn't* want to. She didn't need to know what terrible things they were saying about her.

So she took the chain out of her pocket and hung it on the thumbtack she'd pressed into the bedpost.

The whispering on top of the bunk increased.

She didn't brush her teeth or change her clothes because she didn't want to give those two the chance to talk about her out loud.

Instead she climbed in between the sheets, turned off the small bedside light, and lay in the semidarkness, staring at the ring as if its years on her mother's finger might give her magical powers (or at least protect her from evil) until tears burned her eyes and she closed them.

She was *not* going to let Holly and Nicola force her out of the cabin and back into that boring assembly.

She was *not* going to let Michelle force her out of her home and into a life of drugs and prostitution.

She was going to stand her ground and lie here until one of them left first, even if that took all night and into the morning.

So she kept her eyes fastened on the ring, watching the facets sparkle in the changing light. The chain seemed to have a soft glow, a faint line in the dark. Her mother had looked at the same thing, probably hundreds of times—were her thoughts and memories caught in there somehow? If Lexi tried hard enough and long enough, would she feel her mother with her?

She tried. And tried.

Finally she fell asleep.

The Present

Lexi sat straight in the hard leather chair opposite her father's personal attorney, Larry Larson. The tissue she'd brought with her, *in case she cried,* was already damp, wadded, and torn, and she held it in her clenched fist because there was no trash can nearby.

"You sounded like this meeting was urgent," she said to Larry. She had just sat down and wondered how urgent it could be. Her father was already gone; he'd died almost three weeks ago from pancreatic cancer. Since that terrible moment when Lexi watched him close his eyes for the final time and take one last labored breath, it didn't feel like anything else really mattered. She was numb.

She was alone.

What could possibly be urgent *now?*

Larry was in no hurry to let her know. "Can I get you anything?

Coffee? Coke? Maybe a beer?" His hand hovered over the intercom button, and Lexi got the feeling that his secretary, Ellen, was ready to come running in with any or all of the above.

"No. Thanks." Something wasn't right. "Why am I here?"

"Michelle has employed me to handle the affairs of the estate," Larry said, leaning back and taking a deep breath, like the weight of the world were on his shoulders.

"You mean *Dad* hired you," Lexi corrected. It was bad enough that she'd have to deal with that witch for the rest of her life; she wasn't going to let anyone act as if the great Alexander Henderson and Michelle were *interchangeable.*

"Alexis, your father and I had a good working relationship for many years. I remember when you were born." He reached for a cigar on his desk and chomped on the end. He never lit them anymore. "It was the happiest I ever saw him, and that includes the day he married your mother."

Lexi felt tears burn in her eyes and darted her gaze around to see if Larry had tissues anywhere. All she saw was a carved mahogany box across the room that might have been a tissue holder but was more likely a cigar case. So she looked skyward, hoping the tears would somehow sink back in before she had to produce the little wad of hell she was holding in her hand. "Thanks, Larry. I appreciate that."

"That said, my legal obligation to your father ended with the execution of his will."

Lexi nodded and swallowed hard. "When will that be done?"

He moved forward, and his seat groaned under his weight. "But for a couple of small details, it's done now, Alexis. The will was relatively straightforward."

"Oh." She was confused. There would be terms she'd need to understand. Transfers. Power of attorney. All kinds of financial stuff she didn't want to think about but would have to learn to handle. Though she'd never had to do anything financial herself, she did know that the estate involved millions of dollars and she was going to have to, if nothing else, find a good financial adviser.

Her first thought was to ask her dad.

Her second thought, the follow-up thought she knew she was going to be surprised by over and over for a long time, was that she couldn't. She could never ask him anything again.

"What do I need to know?" she asked, her entire body tense.

"He left everything to Michelle, Alexis."

She nodded, not absorbing the words. "I knew she'd get something, obviously."

"You're not following me." Larry's face colored, and he cleared his throat. "He left his entire estate to Michelle. Do you understand what that means?"

"I . . . guess not." It *sounded* like he was saying that her father had left her nothing, that *everything* was going to Michelle, but there was no way that was possible.

She and her father weren't *chummy*, but he was all she'd had, and she knew he loved her in his way. There was no possibility that he would leave her destitute!

She smiled halfheartedly. Fear was bubbling up deep inside her. "I guess you'll have to talk to me like you'd talk to a first grader."

"Your father's will didn't earmark anything for you, per se. No money, no property, no investments. He left his entire estate to Michelle, meaning literally all his worldly possessions, with the written request that she divide it between herself and you as she sees fit."

"Oh . . ."

"Meaning it was entirely discretionary. She's not legally obligated to do a thing for you." His words fell like heavy stones in an avalanche.

"Since she and your father never had any children, I imagine he had in mind that this would be a bonding experience for you and Michelle."

Lexi snorted.

"Interestingly, that is much the same reaction Michelle had."

Lexi wasn't so stupid she didn't understand *that*. "How dare she! My God, she's helped herself to my father's money, my mother's things, *my* things, for years! She's siphoned off money, sold jewelry—Dad knew that! Why would he leave her everything?" It was unimaginable. He wasn't a cuckolded old fool. Or at least she'd never thought he was.

"He trusted her," Larry said, "with everything."

"Including my life. You're saying that my father left me nothing, *assuming* that Michelle would somehow"—she searched for the words—"*do right* or something?"

Larry nodded.

The conclusion was horrifying. "And that her response to that was . . ." Lexi shrugged and made the same dismissive snort she had a moment ago. "As in I'm out of luck?"

Larry continued to nod. "For lack of a better way of putting it, yes. I think you've hit the nail on the head."

"She's known me since I was twelve. She's tried to get me out of the way since I was twelve, but she's known me since I was a child. Are you seriously telling me she didn't have it in her to show even a morsel of generosity to her husband's daughter?"

"Well . . ." Larry drew the one syllable out. "She *has* given you until the end of June to vacate the house."

Lexi's stomach dropped. "That's hardly any time." Her eyes fell on the desk calendar in front of Larry. "A little more than a month. To move my whole life."

"She'll be out of the country during that time," Larry offered, like a gift. He was reaching the end of his bad-news-delivery speech and would undoubtedly have a more pleasant appointment following this.

"She's in the Caribbean." Lexi had caught Michelle on the phone with her travel agent planning a trip to Saint John's *two hours* after her dad had died.

"Correct. And she did ask that you don't take anything from the house without her permission."

Lexi gave a dry laugh. "How's she going to stop me?"

Larry looked down for a moment and cleared his throat again.

Lexi knew exactly what that meant. "You're going to chaperone me there."

Now Larry did not meet her eyes. "If you can just tell Ellen when exactly you'll be moving, I'll meet you at the house."

"Well, that's really nice of you, Larry." Lexi felt sick.

The betrayal was enormous. Not only because of what Larry was doing to her but also because of what he was doing to her father. They both knew damn well that Alexander Henderson had written his will with the intent—seriously misguided though it was—that his daughter be taken care of.

It had been almost twenty years since he'd married Michelle, but right up to the end, he hoped as he'd hoped from the beginning: that Michelle would take the place of Lexi's mother, Anna. Both in his heart and in Lexi's.

Lexi didn't believe for a minute that he'd loved Michelle the way he'd loved her mother. Maybe that was the problem: Maybe for all these years, Michelle had felt like a second-class citizen.

But she'd never been *treated* like one. At least not to her face.

Still, that didn't give her the right to take Lexi's entire birthright away from her! Michelle was spiting her faithful, good-hearted husband every bit as much as she was spiting Lexi.

She didn't have that right!

Lexi didn't realize she'd said it aloud until Larry answered her.

"Yes," he said. "Unfortunately, she does have that right. And—" He paused again. Lexi was starting to realize his clients paid a lot of money for those endless pauses. "—that is, unfortunately, that. Meanwhile, I suggest you start looking for a new place immediately, in order to give yourself plenty of time. Also, you'll probably want to find work."

That's that. How simple. "Is she able to drain my bank account?"

Larry shook his head. "That's the good news. Whatever assets you have in accounts in your name are yours to keep. Likewise, debts and credit in your own name are also your own, though I believe your father had you as a rider on most of his accounts."

"That's right." She'd never had to pay a credit card bill in her life. She whipped those babies out at the store and never had to think about them again.

"Alexis." He looked at her meaningfully. "I suggest you invest, if you have enough, and begin to bring in a new income as soon as possible. I can't stress that enough. You need to be cautious and to save."

"But get someone else to advise me." Lexi looked at him, and it was all she could do not to roll her eyes. "Because you're working for the enemy now."

"Alexis—"

"Maybe you should call me Ms. Henderson now that we're no longer what you'd call friends. At least, I *assume* we're no longer friends. I *assume* you wouldn't treat someone like this—take money to cut them off from everything they've known—and then call them your *friend.*" Her anger built with every word. "I realize that maybe, just *maybe,* you couldn't stop my father from writing the will the way he did. But you know damn well it was never his intention that"—she didn't even try to find a gentler word—"that *bitch* cut me off."

"I don't believe that was his intention."

"Then why are you helping her do it? Why are you protecting her new interests instead of having some loyalty, Larry? What about ethics? Do you feel good about this?" She waited a moment, and when he didn't respond, she demanded, "Well? *Do* you?"

He steepled his hands in front of his face, looking thoughtful, and for a moment she thought she might have gotten through to him. But then he said, "Unless you have any further questions, I think we can call an end to this meeting, and I'll see you when you're ready to move out of the house."

Unless she had any other questions. How about, *What kind of person would do this to her husband's child?*

Why did her father write a will that depended upon Michelle to do the right thing by Lexi when she had never once in her life demonstrated any desire to do so?

Why did Larry let her father write such a crazy will?

Why did Larry then abandon Lexi, whom he'd known, as he'd just said, since she was born, in order to support Michelle in cutting her off this way?

And, the most painful question of all, what kind of man married a woman who would do this to his only offspring? Particularly after he'd been so happily married to her mother? So in love with her mother.

Why did Lexi's father do this to her?

"I don't have any questions," she said, standing up and leveling an icy gaze on him, "except one: How do you sleep?"

Lexi Henderson had never had to make her own way in the world. Not by any stretch of the imagination.

But that didn't mean she'd never suffered any hard knocks, or that she wasn't prepared to stand up to the task, whatever it entailed.

The one thing she decided with absolute certainty as she took the gilded elevator down twenty-nine floors from Larry Larson's office was that she wasn't going to beg.

Her inheritance, her birthright, the funding she'd gotten very comfortable enjoying these past thirty-three years, was gone. It was almost unbelievable, yet it was undeniably true. She had no illusions about that, and no plans to file for a costly and unlikely appeal. Her father had made a choice—a choice she thought straddled the line between stupid and cruel—and she had no power over it now.

She didn't have power over her anger or sense of betrayal, either.

She was stopped in the lobby by Benny . . . Something. She couldn't remember his last name, but she'd met him several times at her father's business functions. He probably worked for Larry's firm.

"Ms. Henderson!" He looked delighted to see her.

He must not have worked for the law firm. They were never delighted to see anyone who couldn't pay them exorbitant retainer fees. Even Larry's good-bye had held the implication of *good riddance*.

"Benny!" she trilled back, as if she knew exactly who he was. "How are you?"

"Well, thanks. I did hear about your father—I'm so sorry."

Suddenly, without warning, she felt like she might cry again, only this time it wasn't the same sense of grief and aloneness that hurt. "Thanks. I was just up talking to Larry about the terms of the will." She watched him carefully to see if he registered any sort of knowledge.

But he just frowned and said, "Larry Larson?"

"Yes."

"I'd heard he was representing Mrs. Henderson now, but I didn't realize . . ." He cleared his throat and changed the subject. "So what are you doing now, Ms. Henderson?"

She could have given an airy answer about moving on, hiding her predicament. It's what her father would have wanted. He was the king of the stiff upper lip. She'd often thought that was why he got involved with Michelle so soon after Lexi's mother had died—so no one would suspect he was grieving.

Don't let on, her father's voice said in her head. *Protect the dignity of the family name.*

Screw that.

"Looking for work, actually."

"Oh?" He looked like he was hiding surprise. Badly.

And for some reason, that one small polite-but-false gesture set her on edge. This was just one more example of someone not shooting straight with her. She was sick of it.

She was angry that her father had done it. And that Larry had done the same thing, albeit with a completely different aim. He'd given her the cold, hard facts, with no warning, and expected her to take the hand he'd just dealt her and work with it.

Well, she would—she *had* to—but it still alarmed her that so many people she'd trusted effectively ambushed her with this.

And she was pissed.

"Things are hard," she said, adding the one final word that would probably have her father spinning in his grave, "financially."

"Yes. Yes, indeed." Benny suddenly looked sympathetic. "The economy is in a very rough way, and, without good advice, one might lose it all."

"I pretty much just did."

Benny looked shocked.

"Well, not my father's whole estate, of course," she hastened to add. "It just—" She wanted to say it. She wanted to tell the world what a stupid son of a bitch her father was. But she couldn't. "—feels like it."

"I understand completely."

"There are so many things to consider now that my father is gone."

Benny nodded. "Perhaps even more than you know. I'd be very glad to help you in any way I can. As you know, I'm a financial adviser—"

She nodded, although she hadn't known.

"—and I would be happy to discuss your financial plans with you at any time."

"Thanks." He wouldn't say that if he knew how little he'd be dealing with.

"So you know where we are, third floor, same as always." His eyes darted around. He was clearly looking for some reason to excuse himself from what had undoubtedly begun to feel like a prolonged conversation.

"Sure." But she didn't know where his office was.

She didn't know anything.

She didn't know what to do.

Apart from cling, conversationally, to Benny Whatshisname, who was standing in front of her, looking like he'd just stepped in gum and couldn't get it off his shoe, desperate to get away from this conversation with her—but she wasn't going to let him off so easy.

"And if you know of any suitable jobs, let me know."

"Where did you go to school? Sarah Lawrence?"

"The Maryland Institute."

He frowned. "I don't know it."

"It's an art school. Fully accredited, of course," she added, though that wouldn't hold water with a guy like this. "You can get regular degrees there. Bachelor's, master's." She trailed off, unsure if it was possible to get a doctorate there.

"I see. Well, I'll keep it in mind. I'm not looking to hire anyone myself right now." He gave a short laugh. "Apart from someone to paint my house, that is, but if I hear—"

"I can paint your house!" Granted, she hadn't finished at the Maryland Institute, but not because she wasn't talented. She could paint! She just wasn't into all the academics that came with a design degree.

Benny's face colored. "Ms. Henderson, I really don't think that's a good idea."

"Actually, Mr. . . . Benny, that's one thing I really love to do. I paint." She smiled and shrugged. "Call me crazy, but I find it relaxing. So you'd really be doing *me* a favor. And I bet I can underbid any other painters you've talked to."

Benny's posture stopped being one of escape. "Really?"

"Sure! I'd really love to."

He looked dubious. "You've done this before?"

This was one of those moments where she could barrel on with a new blunt honesty thing, or she could take the age-old path of deception to get a job.

She was angry and shocked and desperate, but she wasn't stupid.

"I certainly have. I might even have done your neighbors' houses. Where do you live?" She took a stab. "McLean?"

"Potomac."

Better still! "Do you know the Chapmans on Belmart? I painted their house for them."

He looked impressed. "They just had it renovated."

She nodded, though she hadn't seen the Chapmans since fifth grade, when she used to go horseback riding with their son. She thought she'd heard they'd gotten a divorce. Maybe this was a new Mrs. Chapman. Not that it mattered. "I did it after the renovation."

Benny looked genuinely shocked. "I don't know what to say, Ms. Henderson, I feel funny about this—"

"Please call me Lexi."

He gave a chuckle. "Okay, Lexi." He took a card out of his pocket and a pen, and scribbled on the back. "Here's my address. What would you say to coming by Saturday morning so you can let me know what you think it will cost?"

She glanced at the card. Benjamin Hutchinson. Had she *ever* known his last name? It didn't ring a bell at all. The address was 134 Alloway Drive. He did live near the Chapmans. Hopefully that wouldn't come back to bite her in the butt. "I'll be there. Does nine A.M. work for you?" Nine A.M. sounded really early to her, which she hoped meant it was a really good time for the normal working people.

"It's a little late," he said, frowning. "Could you make it at seven thirty?"

"In the morning?"

He paused. "Yes." The silence afterwards added *obviously*.

"You've got it. I'll see you then."

He smiled and gave a shake of his head. "Are you absolutely sure about this? I can't quite see you painting."

"You will soon!"

"Excellent. See you Saturday."

"At seven thirty," she said, then added, "A.M."

It was with great optimism that Lexi went to the art supply store and stocked up on everything she'd need in order to paint Benny's house. Canvases, oil medium, every color paint including double alabaster, since that always went first. She also picked up a sketchbook and a nice selection of charcoal and pencils, so she could sketch it out first.

And a fabulous leather case for the pencils. It was as soft as butter but also very practical, as it would hold a large assortment of pencils but could be folded over to quite a compact size.

She also picked up a portfolio—also leather, because when she pictured herself taking it out in fifty years to show her work to her grandchildren, she knew it would look amazing, as opposed to the paper ones that would be in tatters if they still existed at all.

Her mood, which had been so lightened by shopping, was ruined when she got home. Or *to the house*, she supposed she should begin thinking of it. No longer was the big brick edifice her home; it was a building in which her enemy lived. A building in which she was so unwelcome, it felt as if there were a gravitational *push* coming from it. No longer was this wide sweep of green lawn a place of happy memories, birthday sack races, improvised obstacle courses for her ponies, and so on. Instead it was a sad, ghostly shadow of a place she had once known and once loved.

And a place where she had been loved.

A long time ago.

Now it was a place where she looked over her shoulder, hoping no one was watching her and tapping a stilettoed foot on the gleaming marble floor in impatience for her to leave.

Lexi put the Go-Go's *Beauty and the Beat* album on her ancient turntable as a musical score to her packing. She chose that because she remembered the Christmas that "Santa" had given it to her.

It was funny, but after two decades, she still knew all the words.

And she could hear her mother's voice singing along. Or maybe she just imagined her mother was singing along. Maybe it was just Belinda Carlisle.

The automatic arm on her record player lifted and replayed side two about ten times over before "This Town" accompanied her taping up the last box of clothes. She'd packed a couple of suitcases of things for the summer but figured she'd have a new place before she needed to see the fall and winter stuff again.

She booted up her laptop and went to Craigslist to look for a place to live. Though she knew it was unlikely she could reasonably afford to rent a house in the area, she still checked that out first, only to find they were far, *far* more expensive than she could have anticipated.

She switched over to apartments and condos and was surprised how much even those were. Once upon a time, she would have thought condo living was for people a lot poorer than she was.

One ad caught her eye, and she jotted it down:

Available for Rent: Potomac—Beautiful new brownstone with rooftop terrace, 2 BR/1.5 BA, gourmet kitchen. Must see. $3800. 2 month deposit.

The location was right. She could make do with two bedrooms. One could be a home studio that she could convert into a spare bedroom if anyone came to visit. One and a half baths was modest, but it was enough. The rooftop terrace sounded fantastic, and the gourmet kitchen just made sense, since she was going to have to do a lot of her own cooking now instead of going out.

She called the Realtor, but no one answered, so she left a message asking how soon the place would be ready and if she could see it.

She hated waiting. At least, the *old* Lexi did. *New* Lexi was going to have to be more mature. She may have been spoiled, but she wasn't so dumb that she didn't realize it.

With the "business" out of the way, she decided to call her friend

Maribeth and go out for the night to try to shake off the stresses of real life. Tomorrow she would take a look at her bank account, and hopefully at that condo.

Then she would continue packing.

The next day she'd go to Benny's and hopefully begin her life as an artist.

It really wasn't so bad, striking out on her own. Truthfully, she probably should have done it a long time ago. It felt good to contemplate a future in which she would have her *own* place. Not that she didn't have all the freedom and independence she wanted here, but she had a feeling it was going to be all the sweeter, even in a smaller place, knowing that she was taking care of herself.

Maybe Michelle had done her a favor after all.

Forty-seven thousand, one hundred twenty dollars and thirteen cents.

That was everything Lexi had.

It kind of sounded like a lot. She didn't usually buy things that cost a thousand bucks, and here she had forty-seven thousand of them.

But, though Lexi was inexperienced with handling her own finances, she was not a fool. With the help of a calculator, she realized that her monthly purchases probably added up to about fifteen thousand dollars. And that was without paying for rent or food.

So obviously she was going to have to change her habits and be a lot more careful.

Good thing she was already on the trail of a job.

But first she had to find a place to live. And it had to be a place that cost a lot less than the one she'd already made an appointment to see: the Potomac condo with the rooftop terrace and what she had originally regarded as a modest one and a half baths.

It was Friday afternoon, so there were a lot more listings in the classifieds than there had been a few days ago. Unfortunately, nothing was "free" or "in exchange for a pleasant face," of course, so she had to rework her budget.

Somewhere she'd heard it was wise to have six months' worth of bill payments ready in the bank, so with that in mind, she figured she could rent for as much as two thousand a month, just with what she had in the bank now, and that would give her *twenty* months' worth of payments. And, of course, the money she made from her art would pay for incidentals.

With that in mind, she noted ten apartments and condos to see over the weekend and packed up her supplies for her first job "interview" on Saturday morning.

When she arrived at Benny Hutchinson's house at 7:25 on Saturday morning—itself a miracle for which no one would likely give her kudos—she was armed with just the sketchbook and the new pencils she'd purchased. After all, she wanted to look professional. She was here to give him an estimate for the commission, and she didn't want to look like some fool who thought she could just sketch it out on notebook paper with a Bic pen.

She also brought her new portfolio stocked with her old art, mostly projects from school, but a few paintings and drawings she'd done back before school. No one would know they were fifteen years old.

And there was no reason to worry that she wouldn't be able to tap back into that vein.

She'd done some research, including calling one of her favorite professors from school, and learned that five thousand dollars would be a reasonable amount to ask. Given the new, lower rents she'd been looking at, that would cover more than two months' worth right there, so it seemed perfect.

Really, she wondered why it had never occurred to her to pursue her art before. She loved painting and drawing in school; it was the mandatory English, math, and language requirements that had made it miserable for her. But for some reason, she let it all fall by the wayside when she'd left school.

She even threw out all her supplies, which *then* she hadn't given a second thought to, but which *now* seemed like a terrible waste.

That was all water under the bridge now.

She put her car in Park and pulled up the parking brake. *Breathe,* she told herself, remembering the calming yoga breathing from a class she'd taken once. *You can do this.*

And with a final deep breath, she got out of the car and made her way to the front door, ringing the bell one minute early.

"Alexis!" Benny looked exactly the same as he had when she'd seen him at the office. He even smelled of the same cologne. It was as if the weekend was no different from weekdays for him.

"I'm here," she said stupidly, splaying her arms, as if it were as surprising to him that she'd made it there at that hour as it would have been to anyone who actually knew her.

"Okay, then. Come on in." He stepped back and made a sweeping motion with his left arm to usher her in. "I'll show you what we need to have done."

That *what we need to have done* gave Lexi her first clue that there had been a misunderstanding.

Wasn't she supposed to paint the house? As in a *picture* of the house? Why would she need to come in to see what needed doing? No one wanted a painting of their dining room, unless they wanted their dining room walls painted—

"We were thinking of a colonial blue," Benny said, stopping in the foyer. "And then that could lead into a pale, pale butter yellow for the dining room." He led her, actually, to the dining room, then looked at her expectantly for her response.

Her first reaction, always, was to fake it. To pretend she had known all along what this meeting was about. To contend that she'd brought her sketchbook because she always liked to sketch out a room for her own reference before painting the walls. But to do that now would be to commit herself to painting walls. For a sum of money she couldn't even begin to determine.

Plus, it would be stupid.

Before she could say anything, comprehension registered on Benny's face. "Oh, no. Alexis, we've had a misunderstanding about what I'm hiring for, haven't we?" He looked at her sketchbook, and it was as if a light went on. "Did you think I wanted to commission a painting *of* the house?"

God, she wanted to lie. To say that *of course* she understood what she was here for. The impulse to grab on to whatever small shred of dignity she could was almost overwhelming, but there was no point. If she were to try to act that part now, she'd fool no one.

She nodded, mute.

"I am so sorry." He shook his head. "I should have realized—honestly, Alexis, this is all my fault. I thought it was odd that you were in the housepainting business, but I just didn't connect the dots."

"It's fine." She tried to smile. It was then that she saw, on the wall behind him, a series of four gorgeous paintings of the house in all seasons. She gestured at them. "So it was a good idea, but just one you already had." She gave an unconvincing laugh.

He looked halfway back, then returned an uneasy gaze to Lexi. "Yes . . . we had those done some time back. . . ."

Lexi nodded. The air was thick with discomfort. "They're nice. Well. I guess I'd better be going now." She started for the front door. "If you know anyone, or should hear of anyone, who needs their house painted—" She stopped. "I mean, a painting done *of* their house—" Then, unexpectedly, she started crying.

Benny asked, "Alexis, are you all right?"

"No," she squeaked. The truth came spilling out of her without filter. "My father's wife was given control of the entire estate, with the understanding that she would divide it with me appropriately, and she's decided to keep the whole thing."

Benny actually took a step back. "Oh."

"And now I'm suddenly out in the real world without any tools to make it. I have no job, no skills, no degree. Nothing to fall back on at all. I've got some savings, but not enough to carry me for very long. Certainly not enough to survive while I try to get a degree or something. I'm just so lost." She looked at him. "How am I going to survive?"

"Hm." He looked thoughtful. "I would have to know more details of your financial situation."

She didn't know if he was actually *asking* for them, but she gave them to him anyway: "I have forty-seven thousand dollars, and soon I will have no place to live."

"That's got to be hard, getting pushed out of your home like that. With so little notice."

His response was gratifying. At least one other person seemed to think it was unreasonable.

She nodded.

"Clearly you need a job."

She scoffed and looked at her sketchbook. "Clearly."

She cursed her father. Not for the fact that she needed to work—she was well aware that most people did—but that she needed to find out this way. Under these circumstances.

Circumstances that seemed to get worse by the moment.

"A *regular* job. With a salary and benefits. Do you know where you stand as far as health insurance goes?"

She shook her head. "All I have is the money in my bank account."

"And that's it? Larry Larson confirmed that for you?"

Yes, Larry Larson had done her that one tiny favor. He'd clarified the extent of her destitution. "That's *it*."

"Perhaps a temporary agency would be a place for you to start."

"A temporary agency?"

"A company that places office personnel on a temporary basis. You might work for a week or two for each assignment."

"Wouldn't I need a bunch of computer skills for that?"

"You know how to do *some* things, right? I assume you have e-mail and have used some social networking sites like Facebook."

"Yes."

"Then you could possibly work as a receptionist." He hesitated and added, almost to himself, "Though these days, often receptionists need to do more than answer the phones and greet clients."

"I don't know what ninety percent of the programs on my computer do." She thought for a moment. "Actually, I'm not even sure my computer is mine."

Benny looked like he didn't know what to say.

And what *could* he say? He was way out of her league now. He wasn't used to dealing with little people who had no money.

She honestly didn't blame him.

"I'm sorry," she said. "I really should be going. I've wasted more than enough of your time today."

Benny looked at her for a long moment before saying, "If you'd like me to, I can at least help you start to make a plan."

"But you already have plans for today, don't you?"

"I'll cancel."

"Oh, I don't want to put you out—"

He raised a hand to stop her. "Your father did me a good turn once. If I could help you, even a little bit, I'd like to. I don't know why he constructed his will the way he did, but I cannot believe he intended for you to be out on the street."

Two hours later, after a phone call from Benny to Larry Larson at home, Benny and Lexi had a full picture of what her assets were. There was the money she knew about in her bank account, plus everything that had belonged to her maternal grandmother, which amounted to a moldering mink coat that Lexi wouldn't wear under the best of circumstances and several paintings that were so badly in need of cleaning that they looked like photos taken at night without a flash.

"It's not much," Lexi concluded.

"Actually, Alexis, it's a lot more than many people have—"

Not people he normally worked with, she was sure.

"—but, then again, most people don't find themselves homeless and completely cut off financially at your age, so I can see where this feels dire to you."

At your age. Depressing, but there was no arguing it. "How long do you think it will last?"

Benny leaned back in his chair. "Best-case scenario, say you were able to find an eight-hundred-dollar rent, and we'll assume half the utilities on a two-bedroom apartment—"

"Why half?"

"Because you'd be sharing with a roommate, who would pay the other half."

"Whoa! Where did this roommate come from? I don't want a roommate!"

"I don't see what choice you have." Benny looked sympathetic. The lines softened around his eyes. "I know it's not your ideal, but we have to be realistic, and that means that someone your age—"

There it was again.

"—starting out in the workplace with no marketable skills is unlikely to make enough to afford a one-bedroom condo in this town."

"But I've got all this money." She pointed to the column on his paper that included her bank balance. "Can't I supplement the rent with that?"

"Until what? Until it's gone? Then what? Then you have no savings whatsoever. *Then* where would you be?"

"I guess you're right," she agreed halfheartedly. She knew he was right. She just didn't want him to be right.

"Alexis." His voice was surprisingly forceful. "Think about this: What if you were in this same position you're in right now, with no home and no job, but you had no money?"

"I don't know—"

"*Think about it.* Be realistic. You would have no place to go. At least not for the long term." He sighed and shook his head. "Alexis, you seem to have no idea how lucky it is that your bank account escaped the settlement of this will. If you didn't have that money, you could literally be living on the street."

"But I have credit cards!"

"How would you pay them with no money?"

She didn't know. "I could get cash advances . . . ?"

"You could never catch up. Soon—and we're talking months—they'd cut off your credit, and you might even end up with a judgment against you."

She tried to smile. "If I went to jail, that would solve the whole problem of housing and board."

"I don't think you want that."

"No," she agreed. "I don't."

"So thank your lucky stars you have this money. Invest it. Don't touch it, apart from a few thousand to start you off. Get a job—any job you can, Alexis—and look for a place to live that's eight hundred dollars a month or less. That's my best advice to you."

The reality of what he was saying started scraping the surface of her nerves and slowly chipped deeper and deeper. "So you're really serious? I need to have a roommate?"

He nodded. "At least one. Given your budget, you might have to live in a group house."

It was a horrible prospect. She'd had a couple of friends in college who shared a rambling Victorian place on Pratt Street. Every room smelled funny, the floors were warped, and the bathrooms and kitchen were too filthy to act as either bathrooms or a kitchen.

"I see."

"Look in today's listings under 'housing to share,'" Benny went on, a little more gently. "The less you pay, the more you can save and the more likely it is that your nest egg can grow into something that can give you a comfortable retirement."

"When?" she asked hopefully.

"In about thirty-five years."

She looked him in the eye. "This is really the truth, right?"

He looked right back at her and gave a single nod. "It's the truth. It's not the perception of an elitist financial manager. It's the facts, according to a guy who had to share a house with six other people through graduate school and for two years afterwards." When he said that, she really felt the fear tremble through her. He knew exactly what he was talking about. It was the straight truth, and he wasn't sugarcoating it.

"Eight hundred a month," she echoed.

"Or less, if at all possible." He gave her a kind smile, but it was clear he was finished with his pro bono advice session. "Be very careful with your money, Alexis. Spend as little as possible; save as much as you can. Believe me."

As if that weren't stressful enough, when Lexi returned home, she found a contractor's truck in the driveway and the front door standing wide open.

It probably would have been wiser for her to stay in the car and call the police, or at least enlist a brawny male friend, but she was so inflamed that someone was in her house that she marched up to the door and threw it open.

It struck something solid on the other side.

Something that cussed.

She peered around to see a guy with wavy brown hair and one squinty blue eye. The other was covered by his hand. There was a measuring tape on the floor.

"Do you always enter a house that way?" he asked, removing his hand to reveal a matching blue eye and a slightly reddened forehead.

"I do when there are strangers here who shouldn't be," she snapped, reaching into her purse for her phone. She closed her hand over the metal and took it out like a gun. "Who the hell are you?"

"Mrs. Henderson?"

"Funny, you don't look like her."

He touched the tender spot over his eye and winced. "Okay, you're *not* Mrs. Henderson. Who are you?"

"That's what I asked you, and if you don't give me a damn good answer right now, I'm calling the police."

He laughed and shook his head. "Bad call there, Blondie. A criminal would have that phone out of your hand in no time flat. You could use a little basic self-defense education. But to ease your mind, I'm Greg McKenzie. I own the contracting company you hired to renovate in here. That is, assuming you're the daughter Mrs. Henderson warned me I might run into."

"*Step*daughter."

"Actually she made that distinction, too. And she said you'd have attitude."

Lexi's jaw dropped. "She said I'd have *attitude*?"

"I believe her exact words were, 'Ignore her when she takes an attitude with you.'"

Lexi fumed. "Do you have a work order? Something to prove you were really hired?"

"I have the key." He indicated the open door, then pulled a piece of paper out of his pocket and handed it to her. "And this."

Lexi looked. It was a printout of an e-mail from Michelle's private account, instructing Greg@McKenzieRenovations on all the things she wanted done to the house, including widening the front entrance—which must have been why he was standing there with a measuring tape when Lexi came in—and knocking out walls to turn Lexi's room and the one next to it into one large master bedroom with views of the street, the fields next door, and the pool house out back.

There were also instructions to work as early or late as they needed to, to ensure that the work would be well under way, if not finished, by the time she returned.

No need to validate further.

This was *exactly* the kind of thing Michelle would do.

Lexi looked around at the foyer. She'd come through this threshold almost every day of her life, pushing open the solid oak door and crossing the wide expanse of Mediterranean tile to the wide stairway that led to her room—the one place that had been her safe haven for twenty years.

Now it was going to be Michelle's.

And God knew where Lexi would be.

Obviously Michelle didn't give a damn.

"Get out," Lexi said suddenly.

"Sorry?" Greg had just picked up his measuring tape and looked at her with surprise.

"You heard me. Leave. I still live here, and as far as I'm concerned, you're trespassing. Until I'm gone, you're going to have to *get out*."

"What, you mean for like fifteen minutes or so?"

"Try days. You can come back next month."

He shook his head. "Sorry, Blondie, but I've got a crew starting here tomorrow. Unless Mrs. Henderson tells me to call it off, we'll be here at six A.M." He shrugged. "Meanwhile, I'm going to finish what I'm doing, so if you'll excuse me . . ." He shut the door and opened the tape. Then he gave her a quick, sympathetic look and said, "Sorry."

Lexi had never wanted to hit someone so badly in her life, but she knew this wasn't his fault. She also knew he had the right to do his job because he'd been hired by the actual owner of the house, as distasteful as the idea was to her.

Wordlessly, she walked away from him, up the nineteen steps to the second level. She paused in the hallway, noting—for the first time, really—how Michelle had slowly replaced Lexi's mother's colonial-style furniture and mirrors with tacky, gilded crap that looked like it belonged in Zsa Zsa Gabor's house instead of here.

Michelle had taken over like a virus. Like black mold. There was no way to eradicate either one of them, and even if she could, Lexi would still not have a place to live.

This was a serious situation for her. Much as she wanted to turn away and pretend everything would be all right, she had to face the fact that she needed to get out of there, no matter how entitled she felt to it as her home, or else she would lose the few things she did have.

Including her dignity, if she ended up having to sleep in the streets.

Camp Catoctin, Pennsylvania
Twenty Years Ago

S he's asleep," Holly said to Nicola from the bottom bunk.

It was after midnight, and Lexi, Tami, Sylvia, and Brittany were all sound asleep.

"Now's our chance to make our move."

"What move?" Nicola asked.

"You *know.*"

Lately, she'd gotten the feeling Nicola was more sympathetic toward Lexi for some reason, so she was cautious in referencing her at all. But she wanted some sort of satisfaction in the matter of *Holly and Nicola v. Lexi*, so she couldn't just let it go.

"It's our chance to get back at her," Holly whispered.

"Who?" Nicola asked groggily.

"*You know who,*" Holly rasped, then, when Nicola looked down over the side of the bed, gestured directly toward Lexi.

"*Oohhhh!*"

"We *have to* get back at her," Holly said.

"How?" Nicola sounded doubtful, which made Holly *feel* doubtful.

"I don't know, but there's got to be *something.*" Her eyes kept falling on the diamond ring hanging from Lexi's bedpost like a gargoyle. Did she dare take it?

Actually, come to think of it, did she dare *not* take it? Lexi had been horrible to both her and Nicola for weeks—it would totally serve her right to lose the one thing that seemed to matter to her.

Even though it was too big to be real and was obviously a big, fake Barbie "diamond," made of cheap glass and hung on an ordinary gold chain, like you'd find at the mall.

It was the *gesture* that mattered at this point, though. Not the actual *value.* Stupid Lexi treated that thing like it was a good-luck charm, clutching it at night or gazing at it when she put it on the post. One day, Holly had even noticed Lexi just sitting there, winding the chain around her fingers and sighing. It was weird.

"Let's hide that stupid ring of hers," Holly suggested. Saying the words out loud made the idea even more exciting.

Nicola gasped. "It's worth a fortune!"

"*Maybe.* If it were *real.* But there's no way it is!"

"I don't know. . . . That could be, like, major theft."

"Come on, your dad sells insurance on this stuff." Holly's whisper was getting so loud, Nicola couldn't believe it wasn't waking anyone up. "Do *you* think it's real?"

Nicola looked down and angled her head so she could see the ring.

"Look how huge it is," Holly prompted. "Like no one would notice she'd taken a *real* diamond that size."

Nicola didn't know a lot about insurance values, but she had heard her dad talk about the importance of keeping a supervaluable piece under lock and key, like in a bank safe-deposit box.

"You're probably right," she agreed. Strange that Lexi would be so attached to it.

"I am. Let's get it." Holly threw back her covers and tiptoed over to where Lexi slept.

Nicola kept a nervous eye on the door. "Hurry."

Holly stepped away from Lexi's bed to whisper, "The chain is hooked around the post, so I can't loop it over."

"Unfasten the chain!"

"Good idea." Holly went back and worked for a moment, moving her pudgy fingers on the cheap chain until, after a minute or two, she held up the ring.

Nicola gave her the thumbs-up and beckoned her outside into the muggy night, surprised at her own boldness in this exercise, which she knew was wrong.

The night was still, the air so thick, it felt like they were standing under water. The only sound was from crickets, frogs, and the cicadas in the woods.

It was as if they were the only two people on earth.

It was exhilarating.

Then . . . overwhelming.

"What now?" Nicola asked.

"I don't know."

"Well, we can't just stand here with it!"

"I know! Let me think." There was a pause; then Holly added, "You think, too. Where can we hide it?"

"Are you sure this is a good idea?"

"After everything she's done to us? After all the names she's called you? After what she did to you at the dance? This is the perfect way to get back at her. Let *her* feel upset and insecure for a few hours."

"And then give it back to her?" After Holly's reminder of how awful Lexi had been, suddenly Nicola felt disinclined to do anything nice for her.

Holly shrugged. "We can put it back where we found it, like, tomorrow night or the next. Like it was never gone."

Nicola sucked in her breath. "Oooh, I like that! Like it was never missing! She'll think she's going crazy! And so will everyone else."

"Exactly. But what do we do with it in the meantime?"

"Last year, Carrie Freedman lost three dollars, and they got everyone from her cabin to stay there and empty their pockets and suitcases and everything else until they found the money."

"And did they? Find the money, I mean."

Nicola nodded. "It was sopping wet, in the toilet."

"Yuck."

"I know!"

"That won't work in this case."

"It didn't work in that case, either."

"So what should we do? We need the perfect hiding place. Someplace we can find again easily but where no one else would ever think to look."

"And it can't be our sock drawers."

"No, obviously not."

Nicola frowned. "I have an idea. . . ."

Holly leapt on it. "What?"

"I'm not *sure* it will work—"

"What is it?" Holly kept her voice low, but she was beginning to fear that someone would hear them and come out and find them with the ring. "Close by?"

Nicola nodded. "On the bridle trail. There's a robin feeder—really high up in the air."

"You mean like a birdhouse? With little compartments in it?"

"Yes. It's in a clearing that used to have a house—it's kind of creepy because you can see some of the stones from the house still. Someone lived there, and now it's just . . . like it wasn't ever there. Except for the birdhouse still is."

This was great. Perfect. "Let's go. Do you know where it is?"

"Totally. Every time we go out riding, we take the same stupid trail. I could find it in my sleep."

"Good thing, since we're not on horses. Show me the way."

They walked through the small field beside the cabins and into the dark woods. The good thing about Camp Catoctin was that it was pretty small overall. It was fairly easy to find your way around, even in the dark.

The bad thing was that it was hard to feel far enough away from other people because of the small campus. There was no such thing as "alone" at Camp Catoctin.

"I wonder if we should have taken something better than this," Holly said after a few minutes. "Since it's fake, I mean."

"Nah. It doesn't matter that it's fake. She's all wrapped up in the idea that everyone *thinks* it's real." Nicola snorted. "She must think we're pretty stupid to believe her."

"Well, *some* of us *are*. Tami, Sylvia . . . they probably believe it's the Hope Diamond."

Nicola paused for a moment, then confessed, "I sort of thought it was, too."

"We *all* did," Holly reassured her. "At *first*. But come off it—why would she hang something that was supposedly that valuable up by her bed every night? If it were real, she'd keep it under lock and key. She wouldn't leave it hanging out there."

Nicola thought, then nodded. "We look pretty stupid for believing her."

Holly shrugged. "Either that or she believes it herself and we're the *only* smart ones."

Nicola considered that for a moment before shaking her head. "I don't think so," she said. "One thing about Lexi: She isn't that good a liar. She's a lot of things, but she's not that good a liar. I think she really took it from her stepmother."

"Boy, I bet her stepmother hates her."

Now Nicola shrugged. "She sure seems to hate her stepmother."

They made their way through the thick darkness, startled by every noise and giggling after every startle. It was exciting and exhilarating and terrifying all at the same time. But as time wore on, the excitement and exhilaration began to fade. As the blackness of the night seemed to close behind them like a zipper, Holly was left with only the terror.

"Are you sure you know where you're going?"

"Pretty sure." Nicola's voice was thin.

Holly stopped. "*Pretty* sure?"

"Well, it goes a lot faster on horses."

Holly looked around fretfully. "And you're usually riding in daylight. What are we going to do if we can't find our way out? What if we walk and walk and walk and it keeps being more of this and we never get anywhere and we just die here in the dark woods?"

"Stop it! We're not going to die, and if worse came to worst, the sun would come up and they'd come find us."

"Yeah, because *Brittany* would tell them we were missing? She *hates* us!"

"It's not up to her anyway—" Nicola stopped. "I think that's it ahead."

"Where?" Holly couldn't even tell where *ahead* was.

"I think that's the clearing." Nicola took her arm and started moving forward at an alarmingly brisk pace. "See?"

"No!"

"Jeez, Holly, calm down. Do you see that light patch ahead? Look up. You can see where the trees thin and you can see the sky."

Holly looked. "I *think* so."

"That's it! The robin house is really high in one of the trees."

They tripped through the thicket, finally bursting, breathless, into the clearing.

"The robin house is right over there." She pointed over to two o'clock and picked through the clearing. "Don't go over there, by the way." She pointed behind Holly. "Louis Corel puked there earlier."

"Great." Holly looked up the length of the trees. She couldn't see exactly where the robin house was, but the trees seemed to go up forever before she finally saw sky. "By the way, who's going to climb up to hide the ring?"

"I will!" Nicola didn't hesitate.

"But what if you get hurt?" Holly tried to picture herself making her way back through the woods to get help. "I'm not sure this is a good idea." She *was* sure it was a bad idea. A really, really bad idea.

Lexi Henderson wasn't worth all of this. She was just a nasty, rotten girl who got everything she ever wanted. This wasn't going to mean much to her. She could probably just have her father buy her a new ring, real or not real.

It certainly wasn't worth Nicola and Holly risking their lives.

"As a matter of fact," Holly went on, "this has probably gone far enough. Let's go back to the cabin and just forget about it. It's too dangerous for you to climb that high up."

"Almost there," Nicola said, and her voice sounded far away.

Holly looked up. She couldn't exactly see Nicola, but she could see a shadow moving in the shadow of the trees.

And it was *way* up there.

"Oh my God." Holly gasped. "You're going to get killed!"

"I am not!"

"Come down! Come down now!"

"I'm almost there!"

"I don't care—you're going to get killed if you keep climbing up there."

"I'm fine."

Holly's heart was positively pounding in her chest. So much that she thought she might drop dead of a heart attack. And Nicola would probably fall out of the tree and land right on top of her. And when they finally found them—*if* they finally found them—they'd wonder what on earth had happened.

"We can't die for Lexi."

This brought either a scoff or a laugh from Nicola. At this distance, Holly couldn't tell for sure which it was. "We're not going to, Holly. Geez, get a grip." There was the sound of crackling branches and falling leaves. "I can't quite reach."

Now Holly was *sure* Nicola would fall to her death. "Then stop trying! Seriously!"

"We came all this way." More crackling. "Hang on, I'm . . . almost . . . there."

Holly worked to keep the hysteria out of her voice. "Nicola. Come. Down. Now. I mean it."

"Got it!"

Holly let out a long breath that she hadn't quite realized she'd been holding.

She watched intently in the dark as the shadow of Nicola moved slowly but surely down the tree, branches breaking under her movements. "Slow down!"

"I'm fine."

Holly couldn't help but admire her, even while she wanted to go over and strangle Nicola for scaring her so much. She wished she were so brave. She also wished she were as thin so she could do things like climb a tree or swing effortlessly onto the top bunk, or ride horses without fear of getting taunts for "torturing" the animals with her weight. There were a lot of things she envied about Nicola, but her mobility and the confidence she had in her body doing what she needed it to do were right up there.

Holly heard the sound of Nicola jumping to the ground, then heard her footsteps coming toward her accompanied by her dark silhouette.

"I can't believe we did it!"

"You deserve the credit. I can't believe you were brave enough to climb up there in the dark."

"It's not a big deal."

But it was. "So what did you do? Did you hang it from the birdhouse?"

They started walking across the inky terrain, picking their way carefully over the path, accompanied by the songs of crickets and frogs and the occasional owl hoot.

"Nope, I just tossed it through one of the little holes." Nicola sounded tremendously pleased with herself. "The ring went in, but the chain's probably still hanging out. I can just pull it back out."

Holly tripped over a ropey root in the ground and felt Nicola's hand shoot out to steady her.

"Next time, let's bring a flashlight," Holly said with a nervous laugh.

"Good idea."

They continued on through the dark. This time Nicola led with a lot more confidence, and it seemed to take far less time to get where they were going.

When they were within sight of the half moon of cabins at the edge of the lake, Holly stopped Nicola.

"Whatever happens, we can't ever admit what we just did."

Nicola gave a somber nod, which Holly could barely see by the light of the waning moon. "Agreed."

"Even if they torture you. Even if they tell you I confessed, you *cannot* believe them, because it will be a lie. Okay?"

"Okay. You, too. No matter what they say, it won't be true. Only believe what you hear from me."

"Pinkie swear." Holly held out her pinkie.

Nicola linked hers with Holly's, and they looked at each other and nodded before letting go.

"I wonder what she'll do when she wakes up," Nicola said excitedly.

Holly pictured Lexi waking up, realizing her loss, and wailing miserably before realizing that it was all due to her own horrible actions. Maybe she'd have a big turnaround then. Apologize to everyone she'd wronged. Try to make it right.

". . . don't you think?" Nicola asked.

"Sorry, what?" Her pleasant imaginings disappeared.

"She's going to have a cow."

"Oh." Holly nodded, and they began to walk toward cabin 7. "Yeah. She'll totally have a cow."

And hopefully it would all give her something to think about other than ways to torment Holly and Nicola.

9

The Present

"Have you ever modeled?"

The question took Holly by surprise. She looked behind her, completely certain that Guy Chacon, an artist whose work sold extraordinarily well in the gallery, was talking to someone else.

In fact, she was ready to think worse of him for using such a tired cliché of a come-on, but when she looked around, there was no one there.

He laughed. "I'm talking to *you*, Holly."

She raised a hand to her chest. "Me?"

He nodded. "Is that so hard to believe?"

"Honestly, yes." She narrowed her eyes. Surely this man she'd liked so much over the years wasn't trying to make a fool of her. "Why would you ask me that?"

"Because I'd like to paint you."

"Huh."

"I'd actually like to do a figure study in a series. It's hard to find a woman with curves these days who's willing to pose."

Holly looked at him. "I find that very hard to believe."

He raised his hands in surrender. "You got me. It's hard to find a curvy woman with a lovely face who is willing to pose. And that's the truth. You are perfectly proportioned, and you have a beautifully feminine figure." He shrugged. "And I think you know me well enough to know that this is not me making a pass at you."

Actually, she knew *herself* well enough to know that *that* sort of thing didn't happen to her.

"By *curvy* do you mean 'fat'?" She pictured herself, recognizable, in a series of grotesquely exaggerated paintings.

"No." He looked genuinely surprised. "I mean 'feminine.'"

"Not exactly by today's standards."

He sighed. "By *my* standards. A voluptuous figure is a lot more interesting than the skeletal ones so many models have. I've done those. Admittedly, jutting bones and deep hollows *are* an interesting challenge for an artist, and can be beautiful"—he said this with a completely straight face—"but there is a cry for more traditional figures these days. Surely you've noticed."

"What do you mean? In art?"

"On the runway, on television, in magazines, and yes, of course, in art." He smiled. "But I'm not looking to talk you into this. If you're not comfortable with it, you're not comfortable with it."

She scrutinized him very quickly. Was he serious? He looked serious. Could she really do it? Probably not. But how flattering! Guy Chacon was an up-and-comer. Almost there. A real talent. It was an honor that he'd asked. But there was no way she could do it. Take off her clothes for a man she barely knew? It was hard enough to take off her clothes for a guy she *did* know, as Randy could attest.

Then again, Randy wanted her to lose weight, and Guy wanted her just the way she was.

For artistic purposes, that was. Not for sex. Which made the whole comparison irrelevant and actually kind of stupid—

". . . Holly?"

She returned her attention to Guy. "I'm sorry. You know, I am so flattered that you'd ask. If you're serious." She raised a questioning brow, even though he'd just said he was.

Patiently, he nodded and said, "I am. My offer stands. But I can see you aren't ready to accept."

"I'm not. I'm not sure I ever will be." She felt her face flush. "But thank you."

Guy gave a nod and stepped back, surveying another painting on the wall. "How does Heller sell?" he asked. The look on his face made it clear he didn't think Heller should sell very well.

Truthfully, Holly didn't, either. She wasn't going to complain, but one of Erik Heller's paintings—a canvas painted entirely with acrylic white and signed with a toothpick so the signature was visible only at certain angles—had merited a bidding war that took the price up to 400 percent of her initial asking price.

But she was smart enough not to alienate Guy with that news. "We choose only artists who sell," she said lightly. "But you know you're one of our best sellers."

He didn't acknowledge what she'd said, but drew his mouth into a tight line, looking at Heller's *Blue Sky at Night*.

It was a ridiculous painting: a silly mixed-media experiment with an acrylic, oil, and fingerpaint on barn wood, with primitive dispro-portioned cows stamped all over a background of blue sky and white blobs that were apparently supposed to look like clouds, but that looked more like spilled paint. A child could have done it. In fact, a child *might* have done it. In Holly's estimation, Erik Heller was *exactly* the kind of guy to let his four-year-old paint on a canvas, sign it, and then, literally, laugh all the way to the bank.

But Holly was in business, so for her to stand on some moral ground and say that was wrong would have been to cheat herself out of some pretty handsome commissions, so she said nothing.

Eventually, Guy turned away from the painting and said, "There's much to be said for integrity."

"I agree one hundred percent," she said honestly, then went behind the register and opened the safe where they kept commission checks. "And I'm not going to say anything more than that." She winked and handed him the envelope with his name on it.

He took it and smiled at her. "You are much more beautiful than you know, Holly. I hope you'll change your mind and let me paint you."

She felt her cheeks grow hot and cursed the gene that made her blush so damn easily. "I appreciate the thought, Guy. Truly." But there was no way she could ever *ever* have the kind of figure that she could show to another person. Even with her dieting, there were too many horrible imperfections. One or two could be charming. Or ignorable.

But she was full of them.

"But there's no way," she finished.

He tilted his head. "You know where to find me."

She nodded, then looked over his shoulder as the bell above the door jingled and a couple of middle-aged women walked in.

"Good-bye, Holly," he said, then gave a gallant bow to the women before passing them.

"Was he an artist?" one of them asked eagerly as soon as he'd left.

Leave it to Guy to give her the perfect in for a pitch. "As a matter of fact, he is. If you look at this wall right over here, you'll see his latest collection. . . ."

"I'm not sure, but I think there's less to love here." Randy pinched Holly's hip four weeks into what felt, every minute of every single day, like starving.

It hurt. "Ouch!" She stepped away from him, and from the stove. Because of course, this kind of conversation had to take place in the kitchen while she was trying to prepare a romantic—and low-fat—dinner for him. For them both. "It doesn't pull off, you know." She rubbed the spot. "At least it's not supposed to."

"It feels like you've lost a few ounces already."

A few ounces? That was like throwing a couple of deck chairs off the *Queen Mary.* "I think it's at least a couple of pounds," she corrected tartly. She'd been afraid to get on the scale and confirm, but her pants were quite a bit looser. One pair—once known as her "fat pants" but now merely her "gray pants"—even needed a belt.

In almost a month, Holly was pretty sure she'd lost something in the neighborhood of ten or twelve pounds. She'd thought the change was dramatic. Certainly the dieting had been.

And every day she'd waited for Randy to say something complimentary about it, and every day, instead, there would be some small barb about whether or not she really wanted to eat that tiny nibble of cheese (which was Cabot's half-fat cheddar) or if using stimulants (coffee) was the healthiest way to go about losing weight.

Granted, these small things were said amid a lot of bigger, more important and less critical things. Daily talk, about politics, the people at the office, the people who came into the gallery, TV shows, and so on—they had normal, *good* interaction apart from the occasional weird and controlling moments he'd had about her eating habits.

Which was why it was hard for her just to write him off.

When they weren't talking about her weight, she really loved being with him.

So why was it that when they *did* have these little tangles, every nice thing he said and did went out the window and all she could think about was the criticism?

"Really," he said, arching one eyebrow. "A few pounds?"

"Yes."

"Well, that's good, then!" He sniffed the chipotle-lime-honey glaze she had cooking in a pot on the stove. "Needs more orange."

"There's no orange in there."

He gave a laugh. "Maybe that's the problem."

"Is there really a problem with not adding orange to a *lime* glaze that doesn't call for it?" she snapped. But she heard herself and realized immediately that her anger was disproportionate to his offense. "Sorry. I'm a little cranky."

Because you've barely eaten for weeks, she could hear Nicola admonish in her head.

Or maybe that voice she always attributed to Nicola was, in fact, her own conscience.

"Don't worry about it," he said, and kissed her cheek. "And, seriously, that's really good if you've dropped a couple of pounds." She noticed the *if,* but maybe she was being oversensitive. "I'm proud of you."

She knew he meant that last part kindly. Supportively. But something about *I'm proud of you* sounded so condescending, it made her want to scream.

She needed a snack.

"Thanks," she said. Her voice was stiff; she could hear it herself.

Apparently he could, too. "Now, come on." He put an arm around what he undoubtedly thought of as her considerable waist and pulled her closer. "I know this is a sensitive subject for women. That's why I'm not really sure what to say. But believe me, I am impressed with the effort you're putting forth. I know it can't be easy."

"It's not." She swallowed. No point in acknowledging the coffee-all-day method *might* be a little easier than eating sensibly and exercising. "But this is my fault. I've got a bit of low-blood-sugar personality withdrawal." She picked up a piece of celery from the crudité platter and dipped it in the light caramelized French onion dip she'd made. Hopefully the light sour cream had a little bit of protein in it. "I'll be fine."

The dip was good.

At least she'd gotten that right.

Randy watched her do this, and she was worried he was about to say something about how she shouldn't be eating creamy dips or something when he actually said, "I think this is my fault."

"What is?"

"This"—he waved a hand in front of her—"weight issue. You're freaking out about it and maybe trying too hard to diet. I think I made you feel like you had to do this for me—and, Holly, that is *not* the case." He moved toward her and pulled her into his arms. "I love you exactly how you are."

She couldn't believe her ears. For weeks, she'd been attributing every hunger pang, every snappish response to a customer, every fist on the car horn in traffic, to *Damn Randy* and his whole *Dieting for Matrimony* idea, when it turned out she was doing it all to herself.

She should have realized that, though, because she'd barely spoken to Randy this week. The fact that he was in her head, wagging his finger at her, required considerable imagination, in retrospect.

"I love you, too." She sank against him. "I'm sorry for being such a bitch."

"It's okay." He stroked her hair. It should have been soothing, but he may as well have been tugging on it.

There was a long moment of silence. She felt like crying, but now that the crisis was over, that would have been stupid.

Finally, Randy drew back. "So what are you making to eat, here?"

Holly wiped her eyes. "Broiled chipotle lime shrimp on brown rice with oven-toasted almond green beans."

Randy's jaw dropped. "Have you been watching the Food Network again?"

She nodded. "It's my porn."

He chuckled. "Lucky for me."

"So, are you hungry?"

"I could eat. Is there wine?"

Wine. She missed wine. But the empty calories were inexcusable. "In the fridge."

"Do you mind?" He gestured toward the door.

"Not at all." She stirred the glaze as it thickened on the stove. "Can you hand me the lime juice?"

"Sure." He took the bottle out and handed it to her.

She was tempted to ask for the butter, too. That would have taken the glaze to a new, silky, luscious level.

But she wasn't supposed to go there right now.

"Thanks." She squirted some lime juice into the pan, hoping that it would satisfy Randy's request for orange. Surely he'd just meant citrus.

For the next twenty minutes, Holly deveined, stirred, broiled, cooled, stirred some more, then did a final quick sauté, all the while feeling Randy's eyes on her.

"I love watching you cook," he said.

A thrill ran down her back. "Anytime."

"If this tastes half as good as you look making it, I'm going to be in heaven tonight."

She smiled. She loved this. Cooking was one of her greatest pleasures, in addition to being one of her greatest liabilities, so the fact that Randy was hot for her food *and* for her thrilled her to the bone.

She stopped stirring the glaze and turned the heat on the burner down to low. "How hungry are you?" she asked, skimming her fingertips down the side of Randy's chiseled cheekbones. "Or maybe I should ask, what are you hungry for?"

He eyed the stove behind her. "Is that okay?"

She glanced over her shoulder to make sure it—or she—wasn't on fire. But no, the liquid was simmering very slowly. She easily had a half hour or forty-five minutes before it had reduced at this rate. "It's fine. How about *you?*"

She wasn't great at flirting.

Never had been.

"I'm good." He bent down and kissed her.

This was going to be her *fiancé.*

Her *husband.*

This was the man she was going to spend the rest of her life with. Happily.

Why was she worried about flirting adequately with him?

Holly closed her eyes and imagined the life they'd have together. A home. Maybe children someday. Maybe a dog or a cat. She didn't like cats, but Randy did, and she was willing to make that sacrifice for him.

They were going to grow old together, and just knowing she'd never have to date again thrilled her. What luck, she thought. Finally, *finally* the hunt for a soul mate was over. And here he was, right in front of her, holding her.

She moved her hands around his hips to the front of his pants and started to undo his belt.

He drew back. "That smells so good." He gestured unnecessarily at the pot.

It *did* smell good, but . . . she'd been about to unbuckle his pants.

She frowned. "So you want to . . . eat . . . first?" She felt so awkward. She never made the first move with a man, because the fear of being rejected was huge, but this time—this *one* time—she thought she could because *this* man wanted to marry her.

But he was rejecting her.

Actually, sort of pushing her away.

"Yes. I'm starved."

She couldn't help but look down at the front of his pants, half-hoping there would be evidence there that the body was willing even if the gut was hungry.

But nope. Zip. Nothing.

"Randy," she started, then paused for a moment before going on. "Did I just do something to turn you off?"

"What are you talking about?"

"Well, we were just . . ." She gestured limply. "I thought maybe we'd move to the bedroom."

He gave a laugh. "A guy's got to have some energy, right? I'm sorry, Holly, but the shrimp just smells so good."

She gave the pot a stir. "If you're ready to eat, I can heat things up." She was conscious of the double entendre, but immediately embarrassed by the fact that she was the only one in the room who would have seen it as a double entendre.

"Bring it on!"

"Take a seat, and we'll eat."

"Excellent." With enthusiasm that could have been construed as flattering or insulting, depending how one looked at it, he hurried to the table and sat himself down at one end, watching expectantly for her to go finish the dinner preparations.

That part was easy. She turned the gas to High under the glaze and gave it a stir before arranging the shrimp on a broiler pan. When the glaze had thickened, she painted it onto the shrimp with a pastry brush and put it in the oven. As the timer ticked down the first two minutes of the shrimp's cooking time and she stirred the rapidly evaporating glaze mixture that may or may not have needed orange juice, Holly contemplated her situation.

Maybe a character on TV would have been more interested in boning his girlfriend at a moment like this than in eating the shrimp, but wasn't domesticity what she really wanted? Wasn't it, in fact, her ultimate goal in getting married and settling down?

Holly had never wanted to travel the world and be where things were *happening*. She liked a quiet home life graced with simple pleasures.

Randy and she were a picture of that right now.

Actually, it was kind of flattering that the smell of it was making him so hungry, he wasn't interested in Other Things. It wasn't fair to expect him always to be ready to go like a teenager. He'd had a long day at work, he was hungry, he should eat, not be forced to perform.

She pulled the shrimp out of the oven and carefully removed them to a platter with tongs, just as she'd seen Paula Deen do on the Food Network. It looked perfect.

And Holly felt proud.

She took out two plates and handed one to Randy. "Eat up."

"After you." He gestured toward the platter.

She hesitated, then spooned a little bit of rice onto her plate and topped it with a couple of shrimp. She would have loved to pour the sauce over the whole thing, but that would have been ridiculously caloric, so she stepped back and made room for Randy.

"Is that all you're going to have?" he asked, eyeing the platter rather than her plate.

"It's plenty."

"So you don't mind if I take the rest?"

It was unfair that men could do that—take a dozen shrimp, a softball-sized portion of rice, and top the whole thing with half a cup of buttery sauce—without gaining weight, but it wasn't Randy's fault. Sure, he was a *little* doughy around the waist, but nothing like Holly— that was for sure.

They sat down at the table, and Randy raised his glass of wine to Holly's water glass. "To my future bride. You're looking better all the time. I'm proud of you."

"Thanks," she said. But she clinked her glass against his just a little too hard.

Randy didn't notice.

Mike was half an hour late meeting Nicola for lunch at a new restaurant downtown called the Pier.

So this was how it was now. He couldn't even bother to show up. She'd jumped through hoops to try to revive her career; he wasn't even going to see the new her and give her a chance to make a new start.

He'd already written her off as a has-been. She'd waited too long to make the change, and she'd lost the only real conduit she had to the industry. She might as well get a job application for Barnes & Noble.

"This comes compliments of the gentleman over there," the waiter said, pointing to a guy two tables away. He was probably mid-thirties, pretty nondescript, sitting with another guy of the same description. They had to be tourists, unused to the beauty around here, because there were far, far more attractive girls than Nicola to send drinks to. Unless maybe he recognized her from *Duet*.

He gave a little wave when Nicola looked his way.

She gave a half wave back, then saw that what the waiter had brought was a bottle of Cristal.

And one glass, so he obviously wasn't thinking he could come over and join her.

"That's very nice, but it's not necessary," she said. Obviously it wasn't *necessary*. Kind—or patronizing—gestures from strangers were never *necessary*. "But thank him for me, please."

It was the second time this week something like this had happened.

"The bottle's open," her waiter said in confidential tones. "You might as well."

And it was tempting. It had been easy to refuse the tequila shot someone sent to her at Cacique, but she hadn't had really good champagne for a couple of years now, and as great as it was for celebrating a big occasion, she thought it was even better as a pick-me-up when times were hard.

Sitting here, all alone and conspicuous, in a little place no one had ever heard of felt like a great time for a pick-me-up.

"No, really—" She stopped. How stupid to refuse. The guy had sent it, already paid for it. All she had to do was pretend this happened all the time, give a gracious wave, and drink the champagne.

God knew it would make her feel better.

And she certainly wanted to feel better.

"I'll take it," she said.

The waiter chuckled. "Good call. He's sending it because you're hot, but you can drink it just because you're thirsty."

She laughed out loud at that. No one had ever called her *hot* before. Three months ago, she might have sat in this very seat with her hair on fire and Mr. Cristal wouldn't have noticed her. So why not drink his champagne now?

The waiter poured it into her glass. Apparently they did away with the formality of pouring a small amount for her approval first when the wine was sent from another patron.

She took a sip. The bubbles tickled down her tongue, improving her mood instantly. "That's good." She smiled. "Turns out it's just what I needed." She raised her glass to her anonymous benefactor.

He raised an Amstel Light in return.

She looked away before there was a question in his eyes or a gesture that would require an answer.

Luckily, her phone rang, and grateful for the chance to do anything besides sit alone at her table looking like a loser with an expensive bottle of champagne, she flipped it open without first looking to see who it was. "Hello?" Maybe it was a telemarketer. Normally that would piss her off, but today a nice long conversation about her taste in radio stations would suit her just fine.

"Where the hell are you? I don't have time for this bullshit!" It was Mike.

She matched his anger and upped him indignation. "I'm at the Pier—where the hell are *you?*"

"What pier? San Francisco?"

"That's a wharf. I'm at the restaurant, and you were supposed to be here"—she looked at her watch—"forty minutes ago. But this is a nice defense. Good offense and all."

"I'm at the Pier, and you're not here."

"Yes, I am. Where are *you?*"

"Out front. Where are *you?*"

"Inside." Dumbass. "You weren't here when I got here, so I took a table. You know, the way we *always* do it."

"I *looked* inside." His pause also implied *dumbass*. "And you weren't there, so I decided to wait *outside.*"

She frowned and looked around. "Well, I'm here."

"Where?"

"Along the wall. Like three feet from the fountain." She saw him, then, by the hostess's stand, squinting and looking with blind eyes around the room. "Right *here*." She waved a hand.

What was with him? Was he suddenly blind?

"Wait . . . where?"

She waved again, looking directly into his eyes. *"Right. Here."* She gestured for him to come over.

His jaw went slack. "I . . . see someone waving . . . but . . . it's not you. What the hell is going on? Am I being *Punk'd?*"

She sighed. "Mike, you're not nearly famous enough to be *Punk'd*. Now get the hell over here and stop this bullshit."

But he didn't move.

That's when she realized that she looked different to him. He hadn't seen her since the nose job.

The nose job that was supposed to make her look like herself, only better, but that had, in fact, rendered her unrecognizable to her own grandmother and, now, to her agent, with whom she'd been working for ten years.

She flipped her phone shut and got up to walk over to him, moving with the kind of caution the Incredible Hulk had to use when he was big and green instead of nice old Bill Bixby.

"Mike," she said when she got close enough. "It's me."

His brow furrowed into a collection of lines. *"Nicola?"*

She was embarrassed now. She felt like she'd gotten a Halloween mask stuck to her face and she couldn't get it off. She couldn't remove the visage, prove who she was. All she could do was talk, in an increasingly pleading manner, to a friend she'd known for a decade who was now looking at her like she was a stranger.

"Yes," she said, her voice more confident than she was. "God almighty, Mike, I only had a nose job. It's not like I was disfigured in an accident."

"But you look completely different!"

"No." Her voice grew thin. "I don't." But it sounded more like a question than an answer. *Did* she?

"It's great." He smiled. Finally. "You look wonderful, but, wow, what a difference." He scrutinized her as unashamedly as one might look over a cow at a small-town agricultural fair. "You must have had more than your nose done."

She shook her head. "Nope."

"A little lip injection?"

She scoffed. "No."

"Eye lift?"

"Mike, I'm serious—I didn't have anything else done." She shook her head. "But, for what it's worth, you're not alone. My grandmother didn't recognize me, either." She took him by the arm. "Come on, let's go sit down. We're getting a lot of looks."

They went back to the table and sat down.

"Champagne," Mike commented with an approving nod. "Good call."

"It wasn't my call. It was that guy over there." She smiled at the guy again and he smiled back. "He sent it to my table."

"One glass, I notice."

"Go figure. I guess he's not psychic."

Mike was still looking at her: up, down, side to side. She couldn't even take it personally; it was so obvious he was trying to connect the dots and make her into someone he recognized. "So you had your nose done."

"Yup."

He blew into his cheeks, then out in one long stream, like a balloon losing air. "I gotta say, you look hot."

"Thanks." To the point. "Can you get me work now?"

His gaze shifted instantly from detached appraisal to scrutiny. "As Nicola Kestle?"

She was taken aback by that. "What are you talking about? Of course as Nicola Kestle!" But her words, so obvious and so rightly forceful, hung uncertainly in the air. "Why in the world would you ask that?"

"Because you're not Nicola Kestle anymore."

"Yes, I am." She was incredulous. "I don't even know how to argue with that. Just tell me you can get me some good jobs."

"I can try," he said, steepling and unsteepling his hands in front of him. "But . . ." He met her eyes. "You don't really look like the Nicola Kestle people expect anymore."

This was stupid. "But I *am!*"

People from several tables around looked in her direction.

"I *am,*" she said again, more quietly but with equal force. "How could I get work as anyone else?"

Mike laughed. "I'm not suggesting you go out and try to get work as Angelina Jolie—"

"I didn't say that!"

"—only that *you* are not the Nicola Kestle that *I* made famous."

She was no longer *the product* that *he* had supposedly made famous. Though, frankly, she kind of felt like he'd just gone along for the ride once she lucked into the *Duet* role.

Then he'd gotten off when the bus slowed down.

"Then who am I?" She caught his gaze and held it. "Seriously, Mike, who am I if I'm not me?"

He winced and twined his fingers some more, but he didn't shy away. "That's hard to answer, Nic. Because your stock-in-trade was your whole ethnic-looking girl-next-door cuteness. Now you look like a new person. A beautiful woman," he hastened to add. "But not the cute, ethnic girl next door. The kid from *Duet*. So how do I sell you?"

"The same way you always have: as an actress."

He laughed outright at that. "Honey, that just ain't possible in this day and age. You've got to have a *thing*, and ideally it's a thing everyone identifies with you. Don't get me wrong—you look pretty gorgeous. But as far as the industry goes, you're starting over at zero."

This was incomprehensible. "What are you talking about? I realize I'm not Jennifer Aniston these days, but I've got a name. People know who I am!"

He raised his glass. "Not anymore." He drank.

"But . . ." This wasn't how she'd planned things at all. "I had only a minor rhinoplasty."

He snorted. "It made a major change."

"You said I needed that change!"

He shrugged. "You're right. I did say that. I was only reporting what I'd been hearing. But, sweetheart, you look like a different person. It's one thing to have a small nip or tuck to make you look like *you* only better." He drank again. "You're unrecognizable."

How could she argue with that? Even her own grandmother didn't recognize her.

"So you're saying I'm a complete unknown all over again. Aren't you up to that challenge?"

He flattened his hand and tipped it side to side. "A complete unknown of a certain age. That's what makes it difficult."

She groaned. "So now I'm old and anonymous."

This had been a mistake. This had been a *colossal* mistake. On some level, she'd known it as soon as the swelling began to go down and the magnitude of what she'd done became clear. She'd wanted so badly to be pretty—and now she was—that she hadn't thought about all the other implications. The possibility that she would no longer stand out, the possibility that she wouldn't be any "type" at all anymore.

And on top of that, the more she walked around being generically pretty, the less she felt like she had any identity herself.

"Well, you do look terrific for your age," Mike said, evidently thinking he was being encouraging.

Frustration choked the words out of her. What could she do? What could she say? She was devastated, but she knew it would be days, maybe *weeks,* before the tears came.

She'd gone through a surprising amount of physical hell, followed by an ongoing dose of emotional hell, because Mike—and, more important, *all the casting directors in the United States*—had indicated that she didn't have a hireable look.

So she'd changed it.

According to their specifications.

Now she was no one.

"Get me some auditions," she said quietly but firmly. "I did what you told me to do—now take up your end of this."

"I didn't tell you to become Actress Number Three or Girl at Bowling Alley. I said to just alter your snooter a little bit."

She didn't want to hear any more of this. "It's not up to you, Mike. It's up to people way, *way* more powerful than you. Get me the auditions. Let me take it from there."

"But—"

"I mean it. You've got nothing to lose and everything to gain. Get me"—she took a breath—"the auditions. Get them. I won't let you down." *Or myself,* she added silently.

Especially myself.

"It's not just anyone who can feel sorry for themselves because they're attractive," Holly said to Nicola on the phone a few days later. "If this were anyone but you, I'd have no patience for it at all."

"Come on, Hol, don't miss the point: Whatever is attractive about me now isn't any different from what anyone else with an extra ten grand could have." Nicola meant it. She was very aware that the work she'd had done altered her into someone else, and she could no more take credit for her looks now than she could take credit for the workmanship that went into her Marc Jacobs boots.

It was all someone else's work. She was just reaping the benefits; that was all.

"But why are you letting this make you feel *bad?*" Holly sounded impatient. "That is so stupid!"

It *wasn't* stupid.

It was just sad in a way that no one could fully understand unless they'd been there.

"He didn't send it to *me.* He sent it to the woman sitting in the restaurant. If she'd had my real face, he wouldn't have given her a second look."

"You *were* the woman sitting in the restaurant! That's who you are now."

"Not really." She had to make her point. "That's the point. I *look like* her, but I'm *not* her. And I feel bad that all it takes is a nice face to get free champagne and good tables at restaurants and, hell, to be allowed to cut into traffic. What that says to women—like me—who aren't born with classically beautiful features is that they're not worthy." Tears burned in Nicola's eyes, and she was glad Holly couldn't see her right now. "Even while I accepted that guy's champagne, I felt bad for the woman I really am, a woman he might not have braked for in traffic, much less sent a two-hundred-dollar bottle of champagne to."

"All right, I know this isn't just about the champagne. And I get what you're saying about how this isn't fair in the greater scheme of things. Looks count. That sucks. *Believe* me—I know that sucks."

"Holly, you're not—"

"Don't give me a pep talk. I'm in the middle of a point. And that point is that you need to own how you look. It really *isn't* who you are. If some guy in a restaurant thinks it is, and you get a nice little buzz because of it, then be glad you're the kind of person who is smart enough to enjoy that kind of thing even though you know his intentions are kind of sucky and you wouldn't want to date him."

Nicola laughed. "I did drink it."

"*All* of it?"

"Every drop."

"Lush."

"I know."

"But good for you. I wish you'd enjoyed it more instead of sitting there feeling bad about poor old you with the big nose."

Nicola sighed. It was exactly what she was doing. And she couldn't stop. "I found out this morning that I didn't get a role on a new sitcom because I'm too *pretty*."

"What?"

"Mike, my agent, called this morning to tell me that this sitcom I'd gone out for—after they'd *specifically* asked for me—turned me down because they think I'm too pretty. They said they were looking for someone, quote, 'more ordinary,' because the character, quote, 'married late' and, quote, 'was now trying to get pregnant.' In other words, someone so ugly, no one would marry her until it was too late to get pregnant."

"But you wanted the role?"

"Absolutely. It had some great stuff in it about trying to get pregnant. There's a lot of funny stuff out there about that. I think it might be good in the right hands."

"Then I'm sorry you didn't get it."

Nicola closed her eyes and took a deep breath. "It's not just that. I also lost a role on a new teen drama as a mom."

"A *mom?* To a *teenager?*" Holly scoffed. "Well, *duh*, obviously you weren't old enough for that."

"Yeah? Kelly Rowan was thirty-seven when she was playing a mom to twenty-four-year-old Adam Brody on *The* O.C. You go from ingénue to mom in ten years in this business."

"So why didn't they want you for *that* role, then?"

Nicola smiled. "They said I was too young."

"Too young, too pretty, too old, too ugly"—Holly made an exasperated noise—"I don't know how you can take being in that business. I really don't."

"It's not very different from real life, if you think about it. Maybe a little more concentrated, a little harsher, but we women get judged and either accepted or rejected every moment that we're out in the real world."

"Then you should be *happy* that the judgment is now in your favor!"

"I'm pissed off that it exists at all! I'm pissed that people—men, in particular—think they are free to treat women however they want, according to their perception of them."

"You've been in L.A. for too long," Holly said. "You've lost track of the real world. It's not nearly as bad as you think."

Nicola disagreed. "There was this time"—she hated this memory—"when I was nineteen and I was driving in Arlington. To my mother's, actually. I remember it distinctly because I had just been dumped by Todd Kampros and I felt like total shit. Anyway, I went to a four-way stop and arrived like a split second before this guy in a pickup truck. We both stopped, then I started to go because, like I said, I'd gotten there first, and he started to go at the same time. I guess I didn't notice right away, so he slammed on his brakes, and when I looked at him, he threw his hands in the air and yelled, 'You're so ugly!'"

Her chest ached just thinking about it. That *so* had tipped it over the edge. *So* ugly. Not *merely* ugly. Not *unattractive*. *So* ugly was about as bad as it got. It had been the absolute worst thing he could have said at the worst time for her to hear it, and even though the guy was not worth the breath she'd wasted relating the story, she'd thought about him so many times in the past thirteen years that he could have had a memorial brain cell in her head.

"Just 'you're so ugly,' like it was a completely reasonable judgment and like he was the guy to deliver it."

"That's awful." Holly's voice broke. "Obviously the guy was just a jerk with a tiny dick."

This was what she loved about Holly. The woman was a fierce defender of Nicola but could always make her laugh in the process.

"I know. That's why it's so ridiculous that I've let him occupy my memory at all, because *obviously* there's a *lot* wrong with a guy who would act that way toward a stranger at an intersection. Even though I was totally clear on who the asshole was at the time, it still hurt.

That crap about not feeling hurt by someone unless you respect them is bullshit."

"You're right."

"I am?"

"Well, yeah. I wish you weren't, but you're right. But you're actually kind of making my point. It would be ideal if you weren't given special treatment now just because you look good, but if you're going to accept the shit for being supposedly ugly—and you *did* accept the shit, *and* you've carried it for *years*—why the hell shouldn't you accept the perks for being attractive?"

Interesting. "You may have a point."

"I *do* have a point. Neither of those things should affect the *real* you."

And that was true, too. She didn't take the flattery to heart. Why was she so ready to take the insults to heart? Diving into that part of her psyche was more work than she had time for right now.

"Aw, you're just saying that because I'm gorgeous," she joked.

"Obviously. You don't think I'd be wasting all this wisdom on some ugly old cow, do you?"

"Of course not." Nicola smiled. Holly did have a way of making her feel better. "So tell me, oh wise one, what's going on in *your* life? Is all this good advice the product of a happy pre-engagement?" Or was it the by-product of contemplating marrying a man who wanted his girlfriend to lose weight before he'd let her call herself his fiancée?

"I've been so busy, I haven't even been able to *think* about the engagement."

"Really?" That was interesting, but Nicola knew she had to tread carefully. "Gallery business is good, huh?"

"Weirdly good. Usually we don't get this kind of business unless it's Christmas or the Cherry Blossom Festival, but we have exclusive licensing on an artist who was just on *Oprah,* so the place has been hopping."

"Oh my God, are you talking about the woman who uses her own hair as a paintbrush?"

"Rapunzel herself."

"Way to go!" Nicola's call waiting beeped. She glanced at it and saw it was Mike. She'd asked him to call her this afternoon with three potential auditions for her or she was going to fire him. At this point, there was no telling which it would be. "I've got to run," she said. "Let me call you back later, okay?"

"Whenever you've got time," Holly said. "Bye!"

"Bye." Nicola switched over. "Mike."

"Man, I *hate* caller ID."

"Makes you wonder about all those girls who 'aren't home' when you call, doesn't it?"

"Funny. So listen, I've lined up some auditions. You give me an ultimatum, you do them on my time, so I'll be e-mailing the details to you. But something interesting came up. Ed Macziulkas called my office and left word that he wanted to audition you for a *Nicola Kestle role*—how do you like that?"

"Are you kidding? He *said* that?" It crossed her mind, briefly, that she didn't look exactly the way she used to, but that would be true even if she hadn't gotten her nose fixed. She was older now. Hopefully he'd think she looked better.

"Those were his words exactly. Seems that's what the screenwriter had in mind when he wrote the part. Anyway, you're up for that."

Her heart was pounding. This was the best news she had gotten in *years.* "My odds of getting that seem pretty good."

"Hell, baby, you never know. But, yeah, I'd say if he's got a *Nicola*

Kestle role, you'd seem to have an edge there. So check your e-mail, and we'll talk later in the week."

"Okay." She couldn't hide the excitement in her voice. She didn't even want to try. For the first time in she really didn't know how long, she felt optimistic. "And, Mike."

"Yeah?"

"Thank you."

11

The weeks passed quickly for Lexi. Too quickly.

First, she'd muddled through the shock. The initial shock, anyway. She had a feeling she was going to feel shocked for a long time to come, because that's how a person feels when her childhood home, and every feeling of safety she's ever had, is ripped out from under her like a tablecloth in a clumsy magic trick.

Then she'd been pissed. Seriously pissed. For one solid week, despite an initial vow to move on and forget the idea of contesting the will, she had contacted lawyer after lawyer, eventually trying even the ambulance chasers who advertised on weekday-morning TV, trying to find one who would work on spec for a percentage of the settlement Lexi was *certain* Michelle would owe her.

But everyone's answer was the same: Unless there was fraud, she couldn't take legal issue with her late father's decision over what to do with his money.

It was only then, when it was getting down to the wire, to where she would have to get the hell out of the house and start her own life, that she realized she was really going to *have* to get a job *right away*. And the truth was, she did it then only because every Realtor and apartment manager she spoke with told her she needed a verifiable income.

"Why don't you just tell them *I'm* your boss?" her friend Maribeth asked. "They can call me, and I can say, yes, she's my personal assistant, I pay her X, and there you go."

Lexi looked at Maribeth. They were sitting at café tables, having coffee outside Nordstrom. Five weeks ago, having Maribeth pretend to be her boss might have struck Lexi as the solution, too.

Now it just sounded pitifully out of touch.

"Because you're *not* paying me X."

"So?" Maribeth pulled a face. "God, Lex, since when are you so high and mighty about lying?"

"I'm not worried about the *lying*. I'm worried about the *paying* after I've gotten into a place I lied to get into."

"Don't they take credit cards?" Maribeth pursed her lips. She'd just gotten Clinique's Angel Red lipstick after reading that Nicole Kidman wore it in *Moulin Rouge,* and it looked great on her, particularly since she'd just cut her hair into a flapper-style bob and colored it a glossy deep black. "And don't tell me that's a dumb question. Even my doctor takes credit cards these days. They have that Visa/MasterCard sign right on the check-in desk."

Lexi had, in fact, been ready to make a Marie Antoinette "let them eat cake" joke, but Maribeth would have thought she was calling her stupid. "You don't understand—you need to *pay* credit cards every month. You can't just use them and use them and never pay." Even though this hadn't been an issue in her life until recently, Lexi learned it fast and well, and she resented the hell out of the fact that she'd had to.

"I know that." Maribeth rolled her eyes. "But you don't have to pay the whole thing. Jesus, Lex, you don't have to give me so much shit for trying to help you."

"It doesn't help to tell me to lie about having a job then charge my rent on a credit card." Lexi sipped her latte. It was cold. And fattening. And way more expensive than it should have been. In old movies, people paid a dime for a cup of coffee. This explosion of ash-flavored cream had been almost five bucks.

"Then what do you want me to do? Lend you money?"

Lexi felt like she'd been slapped. "No! Why would you even *say* that?"

"Because all you've done for weeks now is complain about how broke you are and how supposedly expensive every little thing is and how you can't go out and do the things we've always gone out and done." Maribeth ran a manicured finger across the lid of her cup, then flicked the foam off her finger and looked evenly at Lexi. "Frankly, it's hard for us not to conclude that you're asking for money."

"*Us?* Who is *us?*"

Maribeth shrugged, as only someone who had no sensitivity to anyone but herself could at a moment like this. "Well . . . everyone. When we went out the other night and you made us all divide up the check by what we had instead of dividing it evenly? You might as well have asked us to cover you."

Lexi's face felt hot, remembering how foolishly *good* she'd felt that night, surrounding herself with people she thought were her friends. But it had been a hard week. She'd had a salad and a glass of white wine. Why should she have kicked in an even amount for people who'd ordered the prime rib and three bottles of Montepulciano?

Particularly since everyone knew what had just happened to her. There was no keeping a secret in that crowd. Whispering and maybe pity were to be expected. A hundred and twenty bucks for a salad and an eight-dollar glass of chardonnay? It wasn't fair.

And Lexi was sure that if misfortune had fallen on *any* of them, she would have been a *lot* more sensitive to it.

"I can't believe you're saying this to me," Lexi said.

"Frankly, I can't believe I have to. But I suppose it was coming. We all thought *someone* might have to talk to you about it."

There it was again—a bold statement that the people Lexi had thought were her friends were not. They were catty, bitchy monsters who were dropping her like she was the weakest in a pack of jackals.

Maybe she didn't slow them down, but she cramped their style.

It was so *awkward* to associate with someone of more modest means.

Lexi gathered her purse and the bags of clothes she'd foolishly bought at Nordstrom. She was only trying to look normal, she realized now, putting on a show for Maribeth when she was the last person in the world who deserved the time or effort.

"I'm really glad we had this chat," she said to Maribeth.

Maribeth looked at her, her eyes softening and looking as warm as they could behind the vivid ice blue of her contacts. "Me, too." She nodded. "It's not that I don't want to give you money or anything else. It's just that I don't think it would be good for you." She gave a wan smile. "The best thing I can do for you is shoot straight from the hip, just like I always have, and stop you before you make a fool of yourself."

She'd shot straight from the hip, all right. Straight into Lexi's heart. "It's good of you." Lexi gave a short nod. She couldn't believe Maribeth actually thought she was being *helpful*.

"What are friends for?"

"That's what I'm wondering." Lexi turned on her heel and walked away.

"Hey! Wait up!"

"No thanks." Lexi didn't even look back.

"Aren't we going to Ormond's?"

"Not interested." She quickened her pace, knowing that right about now Maribeth was feeling pretty embarrassed about being publicly dissed. It wasn't a quarter of what she'd made Lexi feel, but it was a start.

"Lexi!" This time Maribeth's voice was sharp. No more fake Mrs. Nice Girl.

Lexi ignored her and kept walking.

She didn't stop until she got to the customer service and returns desk at Nordstrom.

She drove home, blinded by tears of anger. There was a pretty good portion of self-pity in there, too, but she didn't give a damn. She *did* feel sorry for herself.

She had a right to feel sorry for herself.

"Fuck you, Maribeth!" she shouted at a traffic light, so loud that people looked at her from the cars to either side.

She didn't care.

The light turned and she accelerated, enumerating those who had wronged her as she blazed her way down Democracy Boulevard. "And fuck you, Leo." He'd been at the dinner that night. "Go to hell, Lauris." So had she. "And a big *fuck you* to Michelle, too!"

She went on, screaming until her voice hurt and her chest ached and there were tears streaming down her face. She needed the release. Without it, something inside her might have imploded.

"And by the way," she added, gripping her hands on the steering wheel until her knuckles went white. "Thanks to you, Mommy and Dad, for bringing me into this stupid world and then leaving me"—her voice shook, and the tears really began to flow—"to figure out the hard parts by myself."

She realized then that this was about twenty years of pent-up anguish and frustration. A lot of people would have said she "had it easy" until her father died, and financially, that was true. But she would have given up all the money and creature comforts she had just for a feeling of family and security. Even though she'd tried for years to have a close relationship with her father, he was always a little distant. She figured it was because he worked so much. And maybe a little bit because she looked so much like her mother.

But whatever had caused the detachment, he'd always taken care of her. Michelle never acted badly toward Lexi when her father had been around, so obviously there was some sort of understanding that he loved her.

There just wasn't much of a *feeling* of it.

She'd felt it once, though, so she knew what it was. Maybe that was the difference between Lexi and Maribeth and all those other jerks—maybe they were like they were because they didn't have any clue what genuine human warmth was.

Lexi wasn't sure whether she was better off for knowing or not. It sure seemed like Maribeth was happier than she was.

When she pulled into the driveway of her house—"her" house, that was, at least for a little while longer—she was spent. Every ounce of her energy had gone into walking out of the mall without crying and driving home without stopping.

So it wasn't exactly a pleasant surprise to see Greg's truck out front.

It was even worse to literally run into him as they both rounded the corner behind the pickup from different directions.

"Whoa! Where's the fire?" he asked.

She kept her head down. "Ex*cuse* me," she snapped, and brushed by him.

"Wait, are you okay?" He caught her arm just long enough to stop her but let go immediately.

Still, she whirled around and faced him. "Don't. Touch. Me."

"Sorry." He put his hands up. "Impulse. You looked upset."

"And you thought mauling me would help? Or maybe you just wanted to take a bad situation and make it worse." She felt like a boxer facing an opponent, out of breath and out of energy.

That this particular opponent had kind blue eyes and a look of deep concern should have stopped her anger, but instead it raised her ire further. She didn't want anyone feeling sorry for her.

No one.

"So you're one of those people," he said, nodding.

She shouldn't ask. She knew that. But she couldn't stop herself. "What people?"

"Those people who get nasty to the rest of the world when they're hurt. And"—he gave a low whistle—"you look like you're really hurting." There was nothing in his expression to indicate he meant this in a cruel way, but it felt like a dagger to her heart.

"Who says I've been hurt?"

"It's obvious you've been crying." He kept his eyes on her for a minute, then said, "But what do I know? I'm just the contractor. I shouldn't have said anything. It's none of my business."

"That's for sure."

"So, look, I do have a question for you. The guys are going to be working on the room next to yours tomorrow, gutting the closet and so on. Is ten A.M. too early to start?"

"Do whatever you want," she said, her voice cold, though she actually appreciated his asking. "It's not *my* house." She walked away from him.

"Okay, then. They'll be there ten, ten thirty."

She turned back to him. "And where will *you* be? Isn't this *your* job?"

"I'll be out doing estimates for the rest of the week. But here"— he took a card out of his front pocket and walked over to hand it to her—"if you have any problems or concerns, that's my cell number."

She took it. "Fine." As she walked away, she could feel his eyes on her back. She wanted to stop and thank him for his concern, but she was so filled with bitterness and toxicity that if she said anything, it was liable to be more negative than positive.

He was right about that—she always had defaulted to mean when someone else hurt her. For some reason, she was black-and-white— there were no grays in her personality. Gray was vulnerable, and she couldn't afford that.

She let herself into the empty house and went to the kitchen. Michelle kept a wine cooler there filled with champagne. Lexi took out a bottle. Charles Heidsieck 1996. Good choice. She didn't know anything about the year, but she knew she liked the label.

She popped the cork and took out a coffee mug. This was no time for a fussy glass.

The light was blinking on the phone, indicating there was a voice mail. Lexi ignored it at first, figuring anyone who wanted to call her would call her cell phone, but then it occurred to her that maybe

Maribeth had called to apologize and had just wanted to leave it on the machine because she was embarrassed.

Not that Lexi was in a very forgiving mood, but she took the handset and dialed the code into it and listened. There was one message, and it wasn't Maribeth; it was Michelle.

"*Alexis, it's Michelle Henderson.*" Like Lexi wouldn't know *which* Michelle. "*There are contractors working on the house and a great deal of that work will be on the area you're currently occupying. If there is any way for you to get your things, well, and yourself, out before the first of the month, please do so. And remember to call Mr. Larson to come over before you take anything out of the house. That's for your protection, you realize, as well as mine.*" She hung up without another word, though there was the distinct sound of festive Latin music in the background. Presumably, she'd returned immediately to the fun of widowhood after hanging up.

"Call Mr. Larson," Lexi said, pouring more wine into the cup. "Right. I'll be sure to add that personal humiliation for your entertainment." Not only did she have no intention of calling Larry Larson before leaving the house for the final time, but if she wanted anything out of here beforehand, she would damn well take it.

But what would she want? All the wonderful old mission-style furniture that occupied the place before Michelle moved in had been replaced by what looked like Donald Trump's personal collection: gilded mirrors and frames, chintz sofas, Louis XIV chairs, hand-painted china with patterns so ornate and detailed that Lexi got dizzy just sitting close to them.

Once upon a time, this had felt like home. It wasn't home anymore.

Nothing was.

And for the next hour, she poured, and repoured, the champagne and packed the pieces of her fragmented life into moving boxes to take wherever she ended up going next.

Lexi was prepared for job interviews to be nerve-racking or tedious or both.

What she was not prepared for was how difficult it would be to *get* an interview.

She began by looking in the "Help Wanted" section of *The Washington Post*. Almost none of them said in the ad what they paid, but she began by approaching any company she'd heard of. Some of the jobs were clearly outside her range of capability, though she amused herself with the idea of applying for a job as an accountant, so she narrowed her scope to administrative assistant positions.

Every one of them wanted her to e-mail a résumé.

She didn't have a résumé.

More than one of the people she spoke with asked her if she'd "posted her résumé on Monster." When she Googled the phrase, she figured they were referring to Monster.com, which appeared to be an enormous virtual job fair. She started by taking a "résumé readiness" quiz and found that, at least, she was ready to *have* a résumé. However, she wasn't quite ready to *write* a résumé, and she certainly wasn't ready to *post* a résumé.

She sat in front of that Web site for two hours, reading everything she could find on how to find a job as an administrative assistant. The more she read, the less likely she thought it was that she could get work in an office of any sort. But then she saw a small article on building experience by working for a temporary agency. She could go to one place, they would put her into the work pool, assign her jobs, and before she knew it, she'd have at least a few things to put on a résumé.

Determined that that was the best path for her right now, she looked up the number for Temps, Inc., and made an appointment for the next morning.

She didn't have the blind, foolish optimism she'd had even a few weeks ago when she imagined she was going to be a painter, but she was learning the ways of her new world fast.

If she didn't try to swim, she was going to drown.

"I'm going to have you do a computer test while I look over your application, all right?" Her name was Perry Rose, and true to her name, the tall, thin, pinched-faced woman was prickly. As soon as Lexi introduced herself, she'd looked her up and down and said simply, "Oh. I see."

But Lexi couldn't afford the luxury of turning and running away, no matter how much she wanted to, so she'd stuck it out, filling in the two-page application handed to her by a receptionist who looked about twelve, and then following Ms. Rose into one of several quiet cubicles that contained computers with privacy walls around them.

The whole place smelled like pencils and new carpet.

"When you're ready, simply click on the Start button and do the tests until the computer tells you the exercises are completed. The entire series takes about twenty to thirty minutes."

"Okay!"

"All right, then, you can return to the waiting room when you're finished."

Lexi looked at her watch. It was a couple of minutes past ten. Then she clicked the Start button.

First was a typing test. She'd never formally learned typing, but she thought she was pretty good at hunting and pecking. The timer told her she typed twenty-eight words a minute and gave her an option to try again.

Even though virtually all Lexi's office experience came from watching TV, she knew twenty-eight words a minute wasn't good, so she took the *repeat* option.

A couple of times.

Then there was a grammar and punctuation test. It was easy. She hoped she made up some of her lost time there.

Then there were other tests that she didn't feel so confident about. Spreadsheets, Microsoft Excel, PowerPoint, and others she hadn't even heard of. She muddled her way through, but by the time she finally got to the end of the series, she felt like she'd just taken a tenth-grade math test she wasn't prepared for.

She pushed Complete and looked at her watch.

It was eleven.

She went back to the waiting room, hoping against hope that Perry Rose hadn't been paying attention to the time.

"You can go to Ms. Rose's office," the receptionist told her after getting buzzed on the phone. "It's the second door on the left." She raised a limp arm to indicate a hall next to the water cooler. "Down there."

"Thanks." Lexi went down the hall to the door. It was closed. What the hell was she supposed to do? She knocked.

Nothing.

She knocked again.

The door whipped open. "I *said* we don't have a lot of time to waste here."

Lexi stiffened. "Well, I'm sorry. I didn't hear you."

"Fine, I'll send someone new."

"*What?*" This was ridiculous. There was no call for the woman to be such a bitch. They were strangers, after all, so they owed each other the common courtesy they'd give to someone on the street.

The woman held up her index finger and looked away, saying, "I'm sorry you're dissatisfied, but there's nothing else I can do."

"It's not that I'm—" Lexi stopped, realizing Perry must have a Bluetooth earpiece on under her mop of red hair.

Sure enough, she said, "All right, then, you let me know by noon if you think she's going to work." She looked at Lexi. "I am not impressed."

Lexi sat down and waited silently.

"Ms. Henderson?"

"Yes?"

"I was speaking to you."

Lexi was immediately irked. "I didn't realize it."

"You need to be absolutely on the ball when you are interviewing for a job." It was easy to imagine her punctuating her words with a rap of a ruler. "And make no mistake, you *are* interviewing for a job."

"I'm aware of that," Lexi answered crisply.

"Your testing went abysmally. I guess you know that."

It was then that Lexi first realized this was going nowhere and would continue to go nowhere until it got there. "I felt stronger in some areas than in others."

"Really?" She looked surprised. "For example, in what areas did you feel strong?"

Lexi straightened in her chair. Every muscle in her body wanted her to bolt. "I'm a good proofreader."

Perry tightened her lips and gave a half shrug. "What good is that if you cannot *apply* the corrections?"

"That would depend on the application, wouldn't it?"

"As far as I can tell, Ms. Henderson, there is not a single computer application at which you are even moderately proficient." She raked a judgmental eye over her. "I imagine you are adept at text messaging on your telephone, but you are hardly qualified to communicate with the business world, much less do so on behalf of an executive."

"What are you saying? I'm unemployable?"

"Utterly." She leaned back in her chair and spread her arms. "It's my opinion that you need to go to a technical institute and become versed in at least the most basic Windows programs so that you are at least employable as a basic office assistant."

Lexi felt like she'd been punched in the stomach. "Actually," she said, standing up, "I don't think I want to work with *you* at all." She began to walk out the door.

An incredulous Perry Rose followed her. "I'm sorry?"

"No need to apologize, it's obviously who you *are*." Lexi stopped and turned back to her, staring her in the eye. "Ms. Rose, are you aware that corporate headquarters occasionally sends *prospective employees*"—she used air quotes—"to branch offices to see how they are treated and to look for areas where there may be a need for"—she brought out the air quotes again—"*personnel adjustments* or education?"

It was satisfying to see her face drain of all color. "I . . . have heard of such things before."

Bingo! Lucky guess. Lexi was enjoying this, even though as soon as she left, they'd be able to check her application and find out she was lying. Meanwhile, a few minutes of squirming would do this bitch some good. "How do you think corporate would feel, knowing you'd spoken to me with such disrespect?"

"I . . ." Her shoulders collapsed. "I apologize deeply, Ms. Henderson.

It's been a very rough couple of weeks around here. We've had a lot of no-shows, and have lost quite a few employees to Telesec. Naturally, it was disappointing that someone as outwardly poised as you appeared to have no skills at all. I mean"—she laughed—"it was ludicrous, in retrospect."

"But not impossible for someone to come in with that level of experience."

"Unlikely. You took it pretty far. I should have realized that, in and of itself, was a test, of course, but sometimes pressure makes good people do bad things."

"And sometimes, Ms. Rose, pressure makes good people do *better* things." She shook her head and turned for the door. "Think about it." She opened the door, but it was lighter than she expected, resulting in a dramatic swoosh and then a bang as it hit the back wall.

Good.

It was the most fun she'd had in weeks.

She stopped at Wagshal's Delicatessen on Mass Avenue on her way home to pick up a celebratory knish for lunch. She would have liked one of the shepherd's pies, but they were too much for her pitiful budget.

While she waited for them to heat the knish, she heard a familiar voice behind her. "Hey, Blondie."

Oh, God. It was *him*. The guy from her house. The contractor. Greg. She turned and put on a bright smile. "I'm sorry, have we met?" This was a ridiculous act; they both knew exactly what she was doing.

He had a bottle-shaped bag in his hand. "Yes, ma'am," he answered with a straight face. He took a moment to order a turkey sandwich with what seemed to be every single thing in the fixin's bar on top of it, gave his name, then turned back to her.

"Oh, yes." She narrowed her eyes. "Aren't you supposed to be at my house in Potomac, taking a sledgehammer to all my childhood memories?"

"Nah, I've got the crew working on that. I came to Spring Valley to do an estimate."

She stared at the guys behind the counter, willing them to hurry up and give her the knish and let her go. "I'm glad to hear there is room in the future for you to do more than destroy my home."

"Hell, we've got time to destroy *hundreds* of homes in the area."

She shot him a look and noted he had a dimple denting his cheek. Someone else might find that cute, but Lexi just rolled her eyes. "Charming."

"So, is your name Anna?"

Lexi was startled. "Why do you ask?"

"Mrs. Henderson didn't say much about you, apart from making the point that you're not her offspring, but we found some things with the name Anna on them behind the wall of the closet upstairs, and I thought they might be yours. Nothing big. I think there were some old birthday cards and papers. Things like that."

"*Behind* the wall? Like, *hidden?*" For just a moment, she hoped her mother might have hidden some sort of fortune in the house that would now save Lexi from her predicament.

But he shook his head. "Some of these old places are built funny that way. If something on the shelf gets pushed back, it can fall behind the back wall. I think that's what happened. It looks like a shoe box of stuff fell and the stuff came out. The house is tight, which is good, so no mice or humidity got to it. When I saw the name, I thought that might be you."

"Anna was my mother," Lexi heard herself say. She didn't owe him an explanation, of course, but suddenly she felt very alone.

"Lexi!" One of the deli guys held up a bag for her.

Lexi's face warmed, and she stepped over to get it, saying, "I'm Lexi. As you might have guessed."

"Nice to meet you." Greg gave a quick pirate smile. "I know you can't say the same."

She shrugged. "Well." Well, what? There was nothing to add.

"So if we put the stuff on the bed in the pink room—?"

"That's fine." She nodded and tried to swallow over the lump in her throat. "Thanks. And, by the way, about the other day . . . you were really nice. Thanks."

He met her eye. "No idea what you're talking about."

She gave a laugh. "Right. Good."

They called his name, and he reached for the bag with his lunch in it. "So are you eating here?" he asked, gesturing toward the tables in the back corner.

She thought about it for a moment, and when she saw him pull a bottle of water out of the bag that she had been sure contained a bottle of Mad Dog 20/20, she was tempted to say yes.

But she shook her head. "I've got to find a new place to live," she said. "Since my current place will be . . . unavailable."

He nodded in a way that made her wonder, just for a second, if Michelle had told him anything more than what she wanted done. "She said to start on your room at the end of the month. I figured you were going somewhere."

"Yup. I'm going somewhere." Where? *Where?* "Thanks for telling me about the papers. I'll look for them later."

"You got it." He raised his bottle to her.

She left, feeling more displaced than ever.

12

Camp Catoctin, Pennsylvania
Twenty Years Ago

Lexi didn't want to wake up when the stupid horn started blowing reveille at seven o'clock in the morning. Every day it was the same thing: Wake up practically at dawn; spend the whole day doing stupid, pointless things; then *finally* be allowed to go back to the cabin to sleep, only to have to listen to those two goons, Nicola and Holly, whisper about her from their bunk until finally all the squinching of her eyes and plugging of her ears worked and she fell asleep.

Then, before one dream was finished, it seemed like it was time to get up and do it all over again.

"Oh my God," Tami complained. "It's, like, *so loud*. I *hate* the tuba."

"It's a trumpet," someone said. One of the know-it-alls. Probably Holly.

"Whatever it is, it's horrible." That was Sylvia. Lexi felt her sit up on the top bunk and reach for the ladder.

Just like every morning.

"Come on!" Brittany barked, and opened the shutters. Light slammed into the room like a missile.

Everyone groaned in protest.

Lexi rubbed her eyes and slowly tried to adjust to the light. The air smelled like fish, which meant it must have rained last night. The lake always seemed to overflow and send a bunch of dead fish onto the shore when there was a lot of rain. Honestly, Lexi couldn't understand it. You'd think fish would love a whole bunch of new water, rather than just going belly-up.

When her vision finally cleared, Lexi looked for the chain hanging on her bedpost. It was part of her routine, making eye contact with that diamond first thing in the morning. In a strange way—something she'd never admit to anyone—she felt like she was waking up and seeing her mother.

It wasn't the best connection she could imagine, but it was the only one she had.

And who was to say that something as magical looking as a diamond didn't actually have some sort of magical properties like that? Maybe some portion of her mom's soul resided there, just for her.

The thought made her smile and she reached out for the chain.

It wasn't there.

She looked. And looked again.

It wasn't there.

Without any other thought but to get it back into her hand, she scrambled off the bed and to the floor, looking for broken pieces of the ring or the chain or something that would explain this.

"What are you doing?" Sylvia asked.

"It's gone!"

"What is?" Sylvia followed her gaze to the bedpost. "The ring?"

"Your ring is right on your hand." Tami pointed to the stupid silver maple leaf ring Lexi had gotten at the mall with her friend Jillian right before leaving for camp.

"Not that ring!" Lexi snapped. "The diamond one. *On the chain!*"

"It's hanging on the bed." Sylvia yawned. "Like every night. For whatever stupid reason you do that."

"It's not there!"

"Then you moved it," Sylvia said matter-of-factly. As if Lexi had simply forgotten she'd moved it.

"I did not!"

"Jeez, calm down." Sylvia rolled her eyes.

"It's got to be here somewhere," Tami said, looking at the bedpost first, as if Lexi had missed it. "Hm. It's gone."

"No shit. That's what I've been saying."

Tami gasped at Lexi's language.

Sylvia laughed.

The other two, Tweedledee and Tweedledum on their bunk across the room, didn't move.

Lexi thought that was suspicious.

"What do you two know about this?" she demanded, stomping over to the bunk. She reached up and threw the covers back off Nicola. "Huh?"

"What?" Nicola asked, blinking.

"My ring." Lexi pointed to her bed. "It was next to me last night when I went to sleep, and now it's gone."

"I don't know what happened to it," Nicola said.

"What about you?" Lexi rattled the bottom bunk, and Holly sat up. "Stop it!"

"Where's my ring?" Lexi could tell, just from looking at Holly, that she had something to do with this. "I know you took it."

Holly's face went red. "I didn't take your stupid ring! Why would I want a big fake diamond anyway?"

"Found it!" Tami shouted, and Lexi's heart leapt.

She started back to Tami, who was pulling a ball of dust out from under the bunk.

"I guess it's not it after all," she said, shrugging.

Lexi felt close to tears. "Someone took it, and no one has been in here all night except for the people in this room right now. And no one is leaving here until they admit it and give it back."

"We're not the only ones in here at night," Nicola pointed out calmly. "There's Brittany."

Brittany! Lexi was almost sure that Holly had something to do with the ring, but the little part of her that had doubt could easily imagine Brittany taking it. Brittany would do anything to be prettier, and since it didn't look like it was going to happen for her face, maybe she'd decided wearing fancy things would do the trick.

"The senior counselors sometimes come in at night, too," Holly added, standing up, having gotten fully dressed under her sheets. Freak. "To make sure everyone's where they're supposed to be."

"I bet it was Brittany," Sylvia said, pulling on a tank top. "She's probably hoping that will make Danny Parish screw her."

Tami gasped.

"You're not supposed to say things like that!" Holly barked, but Nicola shot her a look.

"One of you is in so much trouble," Lexi threatened, but she knew the threat was empty. Her anger was being eclipsed by complete anguish, and she could feel the power leaving her like air from a balloon. She couldn't keep anyone here. She couldn't make anyone confess.

She was beginning to feel like all she could do was cry.

But she was not going to give any of them the satisfaction of that.

"I'm going to tell Mr. Frank that one of you is a thief!"

"Um, excuse me?" Sylvia asked archly.

"Not you."

"What's going on in here?" Brittany pushed open the door with a splintering crack and came in looking, as usual, pissed off.

"Someone stole Lexi's ring," Tami said.

"That gaudy thing you hang on your bed?"

Lexi wanted to throw something at her. "My mother's ring."

"I thought you said it was your stepmother's," Holly interjected.

Lexi turned on her. "You sure paid a lot of attention for someone who has no interest."

Once again, Holly's face turned red. "I just heard you say it—that's all."

"It doesn't matter whose ring it was," Lexi blustered, but did it? Was she out of luck in getting help from Mr. Frank since she'd stolen it herself from her stepmother? But the *chain* was hers. Was that okay? If not, should she just not say anything at all?

That wasn't an option. She'd do anything to get it back.

"I'm going to tell Mr. Frank," she said firmly. "Unless someone wants to fess up right now."

"You're not going anywhere except to breakfast," Brittany said, putting her birdlike arms on her bony hips. "Now get ready."

"I'm going to see Mr. Frank, and you can't stop me." Lexi straightened her back. "Why would you even try to stop me if you didn't have anything to do with stealing my jewelry?"

"I didn't take your stupid Cracker Jack ring." Brittany rolled her eyes. Again. For her, it was punctuation. "So fine, go talk to Mr. Frank. But you better tell him that I said you had to go to breakfast, because I don't want to get in trouble for you breaking the rules."

Mr. Frank was just about the only really nice thing about Camp Catoctin, Lexi thought.

He was tall and lanky, with sad eyes and a humble smile. If he grew a beard and wore a sheet and sandals, he'd look just like Jesus. She could picture him holding a little white lamb, like the Jesus on the cover of the Bible she'd gotten from Sunday school at her church five years ago.

"I understand you have something urgent to discuss," he said, gesturing at the bent-wood chair in front of his desk. "Please sit down and tell me what's on your mind. You're not feeling ill, are you?" Concern etched lines in his brow.

"No." She shook her head and suddenly found that she had no voice. It had been a long time since she felt like anyone was listening to her, or really cared, so Mr. Frank's kind manner choked her up.

"What is it, then, Alexis? How can I help?"

A sob escaped her lips. "Someone . . . stole something from me."

Mr. Frank frowned. "Here? At camp?"

She nodded. "In my cabin. Last night."

"What was it?"

This was the tricky part. She had to communicate it was of real importance without admitting that she'd gotten it under less-than-honest circumstances. "It was a necklace with a ring on it. It . . . belonged to my mother." There. That was true. The rest came spilling out of her in choked sobs. "It's . . . the . . . only thing . . . I . . . have . . . of . . . hers." She took a deep, ragged breath. "I . . . know . . . maybe I shouldn't . . . have brought it. . . ." She sniffled. "But it gets so . . . so lonely." She covered her face with her hands and cried into them.

"There now," Mr. Frank said gently. "There."

She didn't know how long she cried, but he waited patiently, watching her with care yet letting her get it all out.

She needed that.

Finally she was able to collect herself enough to speak again, though it sounded funny because her nose was as clogged as if she had a clothespin on it. "I know," she started, but it sounded like *I doe,* "I should have given it to you for safekeeping, but I wanted it with me. I thought it was safe because I kept it in my pocket all day and hung it on my bedpost every night."

"Is there any way it might have fallen or gotten tangled in the bed-sheets?"

She was grateful he wasn't dismissing this as something that didn't matter. Maybe he didn't know just how valuable it really was—even Lexi didn't know the ring's worth, although she'd heard her father talking about insuring it for tens of thousands of dollars—but he had respect for the fact that it mattered to her.

"No," she answered him. "I looked everywhere. Everywhere. I even checked outside the door and under the porch, in case it had some-how fallen and gotten kicked outside. It's nowhere. Someone took it."

"You're sure of that?"

She nodded. "The only way it could have fallen would have been if it had broken, and if that had happened, the pieces would be around somewhere. They're not."

Mr. Frank frowned. "Who is your counselor?"

"Brittany."

Something crossed Mr. Frank's expression. Did he not trust Brittany? Did that look mean he thought she had something to do with this?

"What did Brittany do when you told her the ring was missing?"

"She said she didn't take it."

He nodded. "Beyond that. Did she organize any sort of search with the other girls in the cabin?"

"No, she told me I was freaking out over a worthless piece of crap and that I should just shut up and go to breakfast." There, she'd done what Brittany wanted—she told Mr. Frank that Brittany told her to go to breakfast.

He did not look pleased. "She spoke to you that way?"

"She always speaks to us that way." Lexi didn't care if Brittany got in trouble; it was the truth. In fact, she hoped the counselor did get in trouble. "Anyway, I made everyone pull their sheets off their beds and let me look through their suitcases. It wasn't there."

Mr. Frank gave a quick smile. "You certainly do take charge when you need to."

"Brittany wasn't going to."

"Hm. So you are absolutely certain that it wasn't anywhere in your cabin?"

She nodded. "Absolutely." That was true. The ring wasn't in the cabin. So whoever took it must have had a friend in another cabin who was willing to hide it or something.

That ruled out Holly and Nicola. They didn't seem to have any friends in the world besides each other.

Sylvia, on the other hand, had tons of friends.

And she was just nasty enough to have done this and then lied to Lexi with a completely straight face.

"Maybe more than one person was involved," Lexi suggested. She had to tread lightly. If she made this sound too complicated, Mr. Frank might blow it off completely, and she needed him on her side.

"Have any other counselors been in your cabin while you've been here? Any at all?"

Lexi thought about it a moment, but she'd never seen anyone else anywhere near there. Brittany didn't seem too popular with the other counselors, though sometimes Lexi suspected she disappeared with a boy for an hour or so at night when she thought they were asleep, but she certainly didn't have any visitors coming to see her where they could be seen.

"No," Lexi said. "Except for Mrs. Marsh. She comes through at night sometimes."

Mr. Frank nodded. "I've asked her to do that some lately."

"Not that she would have taken it," Lexi hastened to add. "Of course. She doesn't even wear jewelry."

"No, no." Mr. Frank tapped his fingertips against the desk. "Well, Alexis, I'm not sure what to do beyond having a meeting with my staff to make sure everyone keeps an eye out for this ring. I'd like you to write down a description. Would you do that?"

Lexi nodded. "Do you think we'll find out who took it? Do you think I'll get it back?"

"I hope so." He stood up and walked around the desk. "But almost as important is the fact that we have to be sure everyone stays where they're supposed to at night and that our cabins are one hundred percent secure. If someone went into your cabin last night, and I'm not saying they did, but if someone did, we need to be very sure that doesn't ever happen again."

That night, after Tami and Sylvia had fallen asleep, and Brittany had slipped out to whatever rendezvous she slipped out to every night,

Lexi lay in her bed and listened as Nicola and Holly spoke quietly on their bunk.

"So how big is it?" Nicola asked.

"Not as big as other houses in Potomac," Holly said. "But I think it's perfect. Four bedrooms upstairs, and a rec room with a pool table."

Holly lived in *Potomac?*

Great.

Now Lexi would probably start running into her everywhere. That kind of thing always happened when you didn't want it to.

"I *love* pool! I totally have to go visit you."

"Oh my God, you do. That would be so much fun! Maybe you can come during fall break. Or between Christmas and New Year's! How awesome would that be?"

"Awesome."

"How far is Frederick from Potomac?"

"I don't know."

"Well, I don't care how far it is—you have to come."

"Then I can meet your little brother."

Holly sighed audibly. "He's such a pain. But yeah, you'll meet him, all right. Because he's *always* hanging around."

Lexi wished she had a little brother or sister, even if he or she was a pain. Then, at least, she'd have someone to share the misery of Michelle with.

"Oooh, your dog is so cute!" This time it was Holly. "What's his name?"

"*Her* name is Zuzu. She's a golden retriever and Lab mix."

"Awwww. And I love your yard. I always wanted a tire swing, but my dad said none of our trees are strong enough, so I have a plain old swing set that's way too small and rusty to use now."

So Holly had a brother and Nicola had a dog. Holly had a nice little house in Potomac with a swing set and a dad who was involved in her care and safety, and Nicola lived in Frederick, which Lexi knew was only like thirty minutes' drive from Potomac, though she wasn't going to tell *them* that.

All she needed was to run into them at the mall after school or something.

She resented them so much she could almost taste it.

Lexi's thoughts were interrupted by a crackling sound. "Do you want some Zotz?" Holly whispered.

"Yum!"

There was more crackling as they opened the candy. Lexi thought she could hear the fizzy centers bubbling in their mouths.

Lexi loved Zotz.

She loved them so much, she was tempted to ask if she could have one. But she knew how that would go. They'd say no and go back to their little private meeting, feeling all the more superior for having shot her down. So she just lay in bed, wishing she'd fall asleep so she wouldn't have to listen to them sucking on candy and talking about how they'd be friends forever.

"Is everyone asleep?" one of them whispered.

The bunk bed creaked as they looked around. Lexi closed her eyes.

"I think so."

"Let's go, then."

The bed creaked again, and Lexi could hear them walking across the wooden floor and opening the door as slowly and quietly as they could. The wood planks squeaked quietly as they passed Lexi's bed.

Where were they going?

Lexi waited, holding her breath, until she heard their footsteps go down the steps and out onto the dirt. Then she sneaked out of bed and peered out the window. The two of them were walking through the dark in the direction of the bridle trails.

That was really odd.

"What are you doing?" Sylvia's voice startled Lexi.

"Holly and Nicola just went out somewhere," she said.

"Where?"

"I have no idea."

"They are going to be in so much trouble!"

Lexi shrugged. "If they get caught."

Sylvia threw her legs over the side of her bunk and jumped down onto the floor. "They're going to get caught. Because *I'm* going to tell on them. Which way did they go?"

"Toward the trails." Lexi was secretly glad Sylvia was going to take the initiative. She wanted those two to get in trouble as much as anyone, but she didn't want to be the one to make it happen. Just in case that kind of karma came back to get her.

Jill had told her all about karma when she didn't want Lexi to tell anyone she'd tried a cigarette down the path by the school and she was *sure* Lexi didn't want anyone to know she'd taken that bottle of Love's Lemon Scent from Sears.

"Not for long," Sylvia singsonged, and marched out the door, letting it slam behind her.

"Wha' was that?" Tami sat up, rubbing her eyes and trying to make sense of the sight of Lexi standing in the middle of the room in the middle of the night.

"Sylvia went to find Brittany," she guessed.

"Oh." Tami dropped back against her pillows. "She's in the shed by the pond. That's where the counselors go to make out."

"I know." Lexi nodded. "That's probably where she's going." And she was probably motivated, at least in part, by wanting to catch them in the act of something.

Something really good so she could tell everyone about it in the morning.

Tami closed her eyes and was out again, like one of those baby dolls whose eyes close when you tip her backwards.

With no one to talk to and nothing to do but wait, she went out onto the front porch and sat down to watch the moon shimmer on the lake in front of her.

"We've got to hurry," Nicola said urgently. This had seemed like such an adventure last night. Tonight she just had the bad feeling that they weren't going to make it to get the ring.

A couple of times she'd almost stopped Holly, but that was silly and superstitious. It wasn't like that movie where the Scarecrow Man killed people who ventured out into the night—they were at camp.

It was *safe*.

Wasn't it?

"We shouldn't have done this," Holly panted. She was flagging, Nicola could tell. "It was a dumb idea."

"We *have* to get the ring back!"

"I *know*! The stupid thing was hiding it in the first place!"

"Well, it was *your* idea."

"I know!" Holly gulped and stopped. "Wait up a second. I need to catch my breath."

"You wait here. I'll go get it myself."

"No way. You'll get killed, and I'll be haunted by it for the rest of my life."

"I wouldn't be too thrilled by that, either."

"We shouldn't do this."

"We have to. You know we have to."

"I know."

"Let's go, before anyone notices we're gone."

"Okay."

They took off again and were almost at the tree line when a bright spotlight hit them like an open hand. It was huge, lighting a wide circle around them, throwing their shadows—huge and grotesque—against the leafy curtain in front of them. "Stop right there!" someone called.

Nicola and Holly froze, and looked at each other sideways. Holly was crying. Nicola was doing her best not to. "Just stay still," she said quietly. "We'll be fine."

"This is all my fault," Holly whimpered. "I'm so scared."

"Shh! It's not your fault." But it was, sort of. It *had* been dumb to steal the ring. What if it *was* real?

But it couldn't be!

Footsteps came up behind them, and the light moved with them, growing closer with every step. Holly was shaking so badly that Nicola thought she'd fall down.

"Names, please." It was Mr. Frank.

Nicola didn't realize how badly she herself was shaking until the moment when she realized it was him. "Nicola Kestle and Holly Kazanov," she supplied, since Holly didn't seem able to speak for the moment.

"What are you kids doing out here?"

"We . . . were . . . going f-for a . . . walk," Holly stammered.

Another person spoke then. "Number one, you know that's against camp rules." It was Danny Parish. "And number two, with someone potentially breaking into the cabins at night, it's not safe for you to be outside without supervision."

"Parish!" Mr. Frank hushed. "No need to scare them more than they are."

"Yes, sir." But Danny still flashed them a warning look.

"Is anyone else out here with you?" Mr. Frank asked them.

"No," Nicola said, and Holly stammered the same.

"All right, then. We're taking you back to the cabin. But understand that we're setting up electrical fences out here to protect the borders."

"We are?" Danny asked.

Mr. Frank growled at him to be quiet, then said to Holly and Nicola, "You might have gotten quite a shock if you'd kept going."

Nicola put a hand to her chest, imagining the horror of running blindly into an electric fence. Imagining it was probably even more terrible than experiencing it would have been.

"What's your cabin number?" Danny asked.

"Seven."

"Brittany," Danny said to Mr. Frank. "She's not careful enough."

Mr. Frank nodded. "We'll keep a special eye on cabin Seven until the campers leave."

It was only then that Nicola realized Mr. Frank was in a tattered robe, cinched over what looked like flannel pajamas. Someone had roused him from his sleep to tell them they were out here.

"I'm sorry to have woken you," Nicola said to him.

"It's all right, Ms. Kestle. But let this be a lesson to you: No leaving the cabins after dark. Period."

"Yes, sir," she and Holly both said, and followed the bouncing flashlight beam back to the cabin.

The crickets were so loud, it would have been hard to have a conversation out there, but Lexi liked it. It allowed her not to think about the things that really bothered her.

She was really starting to enjoy the solitude when she saw a group of people—three of them tall, three of them shorter—come out from a dark corner of the lake and move toward cabin 7.

Before long, she could tell it was Mr. Frank, his wife, Brittany, Holly, Nicola, and Sylvia.

As soon as they got close, Lexi could see that Sylvia looked very pleased with herself.

"Alexis, what are you doing out here?" Mr. Frank asked, his usually calm voice edged with tension.

She thought for a moment, then said, "I heard some noise and got up and almost everyone was gone from the cabin. It scared me"—she felt a little bad about lying—"after what happened last night, with the robbery and all."

"I don't blame you one bit," Sylvia said. "In fact, I was so worried that the same guy might get Nicola and Holly that I ran down to the boathouse to find Brittany, but then *she* and Brian were *asleep* there, that is, I *think* they were asleep because they were lying down—"

Mr. Frank and his wife exchanged a look.

Brittany looked miserable.

"—so then I had to run to Mr. Frank's to tell them what was going on." She crossed her arms in front of her. "I might have saved your lives," she added to Nicola and Holly.

They just sneered at her.

"Everyone get into your bunks," Mr. Frank said, then looked at Brittany and added, "*Everyone*. We'll deal with whatever discipline we have to tomorrow. For now, I want you all to go to sleep. And if even one of you steps foot outside the cabin before reveille in the morning, you will go home immediately, do you understand?"

Everyone mumbled their agreement.

"And that goes for the remaining week you're here," he added. "Sylvia is quite right: There's been some nefarious action going on around here, and we don't need anyone to get wound up in it."

As far as Lexi could tell—and she was up very late for the rest of the week—no one left the cabin between taps and reveille again.

13

The Present

Within a month and a half of Randy's conditional proposal and Holly's starving-for-matrimony act, she lost 16.8 pounds and, apparently, all Randy's interest.

The secret to the former was easy: She didn't eat. All told, she probably clocked in at about five hundred calories a day, and those were just things she thought she needed to stay alive: a little protein, a little vegetable juice, no carbs. It was miserable, but she was so determined to "win" (though she never determined exactly what she felt like she was competing for—Randy? A wedding ring? Just plain beating the weight?) that she persevered. Eventually even the hunger felt like a triumph.

She knew it wasn't a lifestyle choice. She was going to return to normal eating habits just as soon as she reached her goal.

The secret to the latter—losing Randy's interest—was not so easily determined. When they were together and she ate light, he looked pleased, so it wasn't that she was a drag to be around. Also, she made an extra effort to be cheerful with him and considerate of his needs.

So why did he seem to be losing interest?

At first Holly thought it was just her imagination that Randy was distancing himself from her. But after her disastrous attempt at seduction, she grew certain of it. He didn't return calls for hours, and sometimes not even until the next day. He broke dates or ended them early.

They had sex only once, and it ended . . . with a whimper, rather than with a bang.

The more he pulled away, the less she ate. It was a terrible cycle of longing, aching, feeling sick, feeling sad, being emotionally exhausted, being physically exhausted. . . . Finally Holly decided she just had to face Randy with it. She needed to know what was going on, one way or the other.

And the worst thing about it all was that she was the thinnest she'd ever been in her entire adult life. This was the Holy Grail of Happiness, or so she'd always thought.

But it just wasn't all it was chalked up to be.

In fact, she was less happy than she'd been in recent memory.

Eager to get things back on track with Randy, and hoping that would make everything feel better, she arranged to meet him at the gallery at closing after they hadn't seen each other for a couple of days.

"So what are you doing tonight?" Lacey asked as she turned the sign on the door from OPEN to CLOSED. The sign was an original piece by Erik Heller.

"Randy and I are going out for drinks."

"That's weird, right? Going out for drinks when you're, like, engaged? It sounds so formal."

Holly shrugged, but of course it was weird. Everything that happened with Randy lately was weird. "We need to talk."

Lacey nodded and, for once, didn't add a snarky comment. She didn't seem to like Randy. Even before the pre-engagement, which she thought was the height of stupidity, she'd always been standoffish with him. "So afterwards, if you're up for it, me and some friends are going to the Zebra Room. You should come."

"Thanks. I'll see if I can make it." Holly had no intention of going out with Lacey and her wild friends. She would feel like a boring old woman alongside them. Hopelessly uncool.

She'd felt like that since she was eight.

"You can bring him if you want."

And *that* was an even more pitiful mental picture than just Holly going. She laughed. "I can't see Randy shakin' it at the Zebra Room."

Lacey nodded. "But I think I'd pay money to." She went to the cash register and booted it down. "By the way, they're cutting back my hours at the Smithsonian, so I can pick up more here, if you want. Maybe you should go on vacation."

"Yeah, right."

"Why not? The place will keep on making money without you. And you've been really tense lately. I think you could use some relaxation."

She sure could. But it also felt like she couldn't even remember how to relax. Actually, she wasn't sure she'd *ever* known how to relax. She wasn't high-maintenance, and most people probably wouldn't think she was high-strung, but she had been so awkward and self-conscious all her life that it felt like her motor was always running on high.

"I'm fine," she said simply.

And it felt exactly like a lie.

"Right. There's Whatshisname." Lacey gestured at the front window.

Randy was peering in, his hands cupped by his eyes to block the glare of the setting sun.

Holly gave a wave and went to the door. "I'm here." She looked over her shoulder at Lacey. "You'll lock up?"

"Obviously."

"Thanks. I'll see you tomorrow."

"Or tonight!" Lacey added, knowing full well it might draw Randy's attention, but it was lost in the whoosh of the closing door.

"What did she say?" Randy asked.

"Nothing. So where should we go? Maggie's?" Maggie's was an old pizza joint a few blocks away. Holly loved the brick walls and the soft lighting and the smell of garlic that hung in the air.

"Sure."

They walked the blocks in a thick silence. Holly tried to think of something to say, but fell short over and over again. How could they have a casual conversation now, then sit down at the table and backpedal to the topic of how to fix their relationship?

He asked me to marry him, Holly reminded herself as they walked. *There's no way he's gone from marriage to uninterested in one month. No way. I have an overactive imagination. Always have.*

He's not even looking at you, another voice in her head said.

He's not touching you.

"I'm glad you suggested this," Randy said after what seemed like ages. "I've been wanting to talk."

What? Glad you suggested this? Been wanting to talk? Anyone overhearing them would think they were business associates or acquaintances, not engaged!

"What do you want to talk about?" Holly asked. They stopped at the Veazey Street intersection across from Maggie's and waited for the light to change.

Later, she'd wonder what she was hoping he'd say. *Wedding plans? What cut of diamond do you want? Platinum or gold?* Or even, *How about we get onions on the pizza this time?*

What he said instead was, "Us. I don't think it's working."

Holly shot him a look. She had to have heard him wrong. Or he was joking. Or someone else had said it. "I'm sorry?"

His mouth was a thin, tight line. He glanced at her, then back at the light and said, "Our relationship doesn't fulfill me anymore."

She looked around at the six or seven people standing at the intersection with them, wondering if they were hearing this—how could they not?—and if they found it as unbelievably cold as she did.

The walk sign flashed, and Randy began to cross, but Holly grabbed his arm. "Wait a minute! Let your audience go without us."

"Audience?"

She gestured. "Them! I can't believe you just *dumped* me in a crowd of people like that!"

He looked at the retreating backs, then at Holly. "I didn't *dump* you, Holly. Don't make it sound like that."

Hope surged in her chest. Hope that she hated herself for later. "You didn't?"

"It's mutual, isn't it? Don't you feel it, too?"

Tears burned at her eyes, but she *refused* to cry. "I'm not even sure what the hell you're saying. What's mutual? Are you breaking up with me or not?"

He expelled a long, even breath, then gave a single nod. "I guess, when you put it that way, I am."

"When I put it that way? As opposed to what way?" Her voice rose.

"You're not *dumping* me but you're *breaking up* with me? Is there a distinction there?" *Don't cry, don't cry, don't cry.* "Because if there's a difference, I sure don't know what the hell it is."

He put up a hand and *shhh*ed her. "You're making a scene, Holly."

"*I'm* making a scene? You're the one who decided to—" She stopped. She wasn't going to do this. She wasn't going to have this conversation. What was the point? There was no changing his mind. She didn't even want to. "Forget it. Nice knowing you."

It would have been a nice dramatic touch to pull off an engagement ring and throw it into the street so he could go scrambling for it in traffic, but she didn't have a ring. There was no such thing as a pre-engagement ring. Instead, she just walked away.

He said nothing. He didn't follow her. For all she knew, he went on to Maggie's and ate pizza, perfectly content with the disintegration of their relationship.

God, she had been such a fool. She had settled for so much less than she deserved.

The fact that Thin was equaling Miserable in her personal lexicon made it all that much worse. Where was the confidence she was supposed to have miraculously gained?

The relaxed attitude?

The *fun*?

She walked the two blocks back to the gallery, but the idea of going in and being alone with her heartache and humiliation was just too much. So she kept walking. She couldn't think; she could only move.

So she kept moving.

Lacey and her friends were at the Zebra Room. It was only about half a mile from where Holly was now. And she did like Lacey, though she'd always found her friends to be a bit odd. Randy had referred to them as "bull dykes" once, though Holly wasn't really sure that was the case. She'd never actually asked Lacey if she was a lesbian, but it seemed possible.

Not that it mattered.

In fact, in the state Holly was in, a night out with a bunch of people who were so different from anyone she ever hung out with might do her some good.

It beat the hell out of the alternative, which would be a night alone with wine, ice cream, TV, and a predictable meltdown around 11 P.M.

So she went to the Zebra Room.

It was crowded when she walked in, and she *heard* Lacey before she actually *saw* her. She was at a table with a bunch of women who looked like grown versions of Tuesday Addams.

"Yo! Holly!" Lacey had spotted her before she had the chance to think better of this. "Over here!"

Holly put on a fake smile and went to the table. There were two pitchers of beer and several plates of appetizers between them.

"Sit!" Lacey commanded, then introduced everyone so quickly that Holly didn't even catch their names, much less remember them.

"Hi." Holly gave a weak wave, then tried to compensate with a smile that was so strained, it probably looked demonic. "Nice to meet you all."

"What's wrong with you?" one of them asked.

"Wendy!" another said. "That's rude."

"She looks like someone just ran over her dog," Wendy said, then said to Holly, "Sorry, but you do. Are you okay, honey?"

"I've had a bad night." Holly felt Lacey's eyes on her and deliberately avoided meeting them. "I'd love a beer." Or two. Or three.

"Of course!" The girl who had chastised Wendy poured from the pitcher into a glass and handed it to Holly. "Maybe we should get some Jäger to chase that with. It's a little backwards, but it should do the trick."

"That might be a huge mistake." Holly downed about half the mug, hoping it would work quickly to numb her. "Or a good idea. I'm not sure which."

"Probably a mistake," Lacey said. There was still a question in her eyes. She'd probably already guessed what had happened and only wanted to know the details now. "Because you're opening in the morning, remember?"

She hadn't remembered, but it was a good thing, she thought. Because she might take her relationship woes out on her diet, her pillow, the person who cut her off in traffic, or a telemarketer, but one thing she'd never do was let the business she'd worked so hard to build falter because of her emotional life.

That was probably the thing that kept her from being an actual artist—the ability to separate her left and right brains and let the left rule—but it kept her financially afloat. "You're right, no Jäger." It wouldn't have tasted good anyway, though it would have *felt* good . . . for a while.

She needn't have worried. The conversation at the table took off right away and meandered from local bands to Wendy's upcoming trip to the Dominican Republic, to Lacey's new kitten (something Holly hadn't known about and, frankly, couldn't picture) and back to the parking in Eileen's neighborhood.

"I mean, it's ridiculous! I *have* the permit on my car, but they booted it anyway, so I have to take time off work to go to *court* to point out that *they* made a mistake." She took a slug of her beer. "It's not like they're going to compensate me for my time, or for the gas it takes to go down there. But if I didn't show, they'd totally have my ass in a sling."

"You should countersue," Holly said.

"Can I *do* that?" Eileen asked.

Holly had been kidding. "I don't know. But there are all sorts of legal loopholes. Citizen's arrests and things like that are legal sometimes, so why not counter an egregious parking violation with legal action? Get the paper to cover it! You'd become a local hero!"

"Penny, didn't your sister sue her ex for breach of promise after he broke their engagement?"

"Yes!" The woman next to Lacey nodded and reached for the pitcher of beer. "But that was civil court. And she caught him cheating on her. I don't think the D.C. government has been cheating on Eileen."

"Like hell! They've been distributing tickets and booting cars all over the place."

Everyone laughed.

"But your sister won her suit, right?" Lacey said, looking pointedly at Holly.

Holly hated that it was so obvious what had happened.

"Yup. Not that she got anything for it. Except his embarrassment."

The conversation was mercifully interrupted by the club DJ coming on over the microphone and announcing his first set.

It was a perfect time to escape.

Holly finished her beer and took a ten out of her purse. "I hate to drink and run, but I have to go."

There were objections at the table.

"I've got to work in the morning, like Lacey pointed out. But I—"
She was interrupted by something pulling at her hips and turning her around to face him.

She had no idea who he was.

But he was cute, in a blond-blue-eyed-twenty-one-year-old-drunk sort of way. "Dance with me," he said. "C'mon."

The music was pounding. She didn't recognize the song but thought she would have if she were his age.

"Go!" Lacey said. Then Eileen, Penny, and Wendy joined in, "Go! Go!"

Holly had had just enough beer to go out on the floor and dance, so she gave a nod and started to move.

And soon, to her utter amazement, she started to have *fun*.

"Where are you from?" the kid asked her, trying to yell over the music.

"Here!" She shrugged. She was tipsy but not foolish. "Near here. How about you?"

"There." He laughed. "But I go to school here. At GW."

He didn't ask any more questions or try to make more conversation, and Holly was glad. It was enough that he'd asked her to dance. Completely unwittingly, he had broken a long cycle in her life of being the big fat wallflower.

The song ended, and he squeezed her hand. "I'll catch you again."

"Sure!" She was sure she'd never see the guy again, and she didn't mind either way.

"Here." Lacey was at her side, thrusting a mug of beer into her hand. "Have another one. Stay. Have some fun. Obviously your *date* with Randy wasn't so hot."

"No." Holly drank, in part because it gave her a minute not to *talk*.

"What happened?" Lacey pressed.

"He dumped me at a crosswalk on the way to Maggie's."

Lacey's face registered surprise, but her voice was as blasé as ever. "In public."

Holly nodded.

"Were there people around?"

"Oh, yeah."

Lacey narrowed her eyes and shook her head. She looked disgusted. "Creep."

"I guess."

"You *guess?*"

"No, you're right."

"And you're too sober." Lacey grabbed Holly's upper arms and looked into her eyes. "Holly, you need to *feel* this and realize what a jackass that guy is. And he's not even the first one. He's hardly any different from that jerk who wanted you to be blond."

Derek. Yes, he'd been a jerk. And she'd been a fool because she *had* bleached her hair until it was brittle and so broken she had to have most of it cut off.

"You could do so much better."

Holly was loosening up, but she still couldn't let go of the angst of being dumped. "I haven't had a lot of offers, Lace," she said honestly.

Then, for a brief moment, she was afraid Lacey might make her one.

It must have shown on her face because Lacey burst out laughing. "Um, don't look at me. I'm into boys, too."

"You are?" Holly couldn't hide her surprise.

Lacey looked at her for a moment, then said simply, "Oh my God. You need to get out more."

"What does that mean?"

"It means . . ." Lacey sputtered for a moment, then threw her hands up. "Well, basically it means I'm not a lesbo, and you're not a beached whale. And losing weight isn't going to change your life in the way you want it to, because what needs to change is the fact that you're sheltered."

"I am not!" *Was* she?

"Yes, you are! Jesus, Holly, you need to get out of that box you're existing in and *live* a little! You're so stuck in a rut, it's not even funny. But the worst part is, it's not a *routine* rut—it's a mental one. You need to let go"—she tapped her temple—"up here!"

"That's not true," Holly objected, but it was such a weak objection that she would have been better off remaining silent.

Lacey rolled her eyes some more.

"Okay, if you're right—and I'm definitely not saying you are—what the hell are you proposing I do?"

Lacey was quick with an answer: "There's a guy at the bar who's been eyeing you for the past fifteen minutes, and another guy on his way over here now, and I'm pretty sure he's going to hit on you."

"Who?"

"Right on the end. Red shirt. So, if you'll excuse me—" She started to back away.

Holly grabbed her arm. "No! Wait!"

"Oops! There goes my phone." Lacey gave a devilish smile and left Holly to deal with the extremely tall, less-attractive-than-the-last-guy man who was now trying to get her out onto the dance floor.

It was great.

By the end of the night, Holly's ego wasn't exactly *fixed*, but it sure had a lot of Band-Aids on it.

And when she left the bar at 2:15 A.M., she didn't care that she was going to get about four and a half hours of sleep that night, because she'd gotten something way more important.

Confidence.

Not a lot of it, of course. This was still Holly. But she was beginning to realize she'd rather be lonely than live with someone who made her feel uncomfortable and self-conscious every minute of every day.

Lonely was far, *far* easier.

14

The world seemed to be of two opinions of Patrick Naylor Jr.: Half thought he was a brilliant though troubled actor with charisma and talent in spades; the other half thought he was a self-indulgent drug addict with no common sense and even less respect for himself than for the casts and crews of his movies.

Nicola fell into the former group, and she figured most other people did, too, given the fact that his movies did, and had, done pretty well for two decades now.

He'd had the lead in her first movie a thousand years ago. She'd gazed at him from a distance of several yards for two months during filming, but apart from a moment in which he'd asked her for a light for his cigarette and she'd actually gone looking for one (by the time she got back with it, he was, of course, long gone), they'd had little contact.

Still, she had pined for him like a teenager with a crush. Granted, she didn't have teen magazine pinups of him on her walls—with his reputation, teen magazines probably didn't feature him much—but she thought about the brief moments she'd spent with him fifteen years ago a *lot*.

So when she went to Mike's office and saw him leaving, it was like a ninth-grade girl's dream.

Especially when he'd looked at her, and his face had broken into a smile.

"Hi," she said, hating how hot her face felt.

"Hey, there." He nodded and continued to look at her as if trying to figure out how he knew her. "How're you doing?"

"Great." She splayed her arms. "Can't complain." Yes, she could. She could complain that she was being such a geek.

He smiled—and, oh, she'd sighed over that smile so many times. In real life, it was even better than on screen. More personal. For a moment, he was silent, just looking at her; then he extended his hand. "I'm Trick," he said, though it was obvious he needed no introduction.

"Nicola." She took his hand and he gave it a squeeze.

She'd heard his friends called him Trick instead of Pat or, God forbid, Patty or anything like that.

Trick. She liked it.

"Are you with Varnet?" he asked, jerking a thumb back toward the door he'd just left.

"Yes, for ages."

"Yeah? What have you done?"

She didn't want to confess that her first movie role had been as a bit player in one of his movies. That was just too . . . uncool. Particularly since he had no idea who she was.

"*Duet*," she said airily.

"No kidding. What role?"

That knocked her ego down a peg or two. "I had the lead."

"Really." He turned the corners of his mouth down and nodded approvingly. "Impressive. I hate to say it, but I think I'm the only person on the planet who hasn't seen it yet."

"Available on DVD," she rang, then could have kicked herself. He had ten DVDs out for every one of hers.

She couldn't impress him with *that*.

It was like bragging, *I breathe air!*

"I'll have to check that out now." He gave her another brief smile and started to leave, while she stood there, frozen by feeling like a complete fool, but then he stopped and turned back to her. "What are you doing after this?"

"After what?" Ugh! She was not playing this cool *at all*. She might *look* different, but she was still every bit as awkward as she'd ever been.

She had to remember—maybe she had to remind herself every ten minutes or so—that she looked different now. People weren't seeing the face that had shown all her fears and vulnerabilities.

When he looked at her, he saw something closer to Angelina Jolie than to Phyllis Diller, even though she felt she was indoctrinated into the Phyllis club regardless.

"Oh, you mean my meeting with Mike?" she asked, taking *weird* and turning it into *really weird*.

He gave that laugh she'd heard so many times in surround sound. "You're cute."

"Ditto." It was another idiotic thing to say, but she knew enough to work her new face into a sexy look. She could still turn this exchange around to her advantage. "So what did you have in mind?"

He raised an eyebrow. "Dinner?"

"Hm."

"Maybe come back to my place after?"

"I don't know, Trick. We barely know each other."

"True. But I've got a fucking amazing view." He raked his gaze over her. "You'll love it." He met her eyes. "I promise."

She couldn't pass this up. How many girls got a chance like this?

Granted, Trick's own personal record of *how many girls got a chance like this* was probably disproportionately high, but in the population at large, how many people got the opportunity to go out with someone they'd had a crush on for years?

That number was disproportionately low.

Nicola had to seize this opportunity.

"Okay." She gave what she hoped to hell looked like a casual shrug. "When and what time?"

"Little Door, on West Third." He shrugged one shoulder. "Eight thirty?"

She'd been to Little Door. She tried to imagine kissing someone after eating the tuna, and decided—if she couldn't get to a tooth-brush first—the mint in the dish would make it okay. "Perfect," she said. "See you there." She walked past him.

"Hey."

She stopped and glanced back.

"Don't you want me to pick you up?"

And see the modest place where she was living? No way. Not yet. She made an effort to give a casual shake of the head. "Nope. I'll meet you there. Eight thirty. Don't be late, because I'm not waiting around."

Lie. She would have waited all night. They both knew it.

The amount of preparation that went into getting ready for this date was not even worth documenting. It was way, *way* over the top.

And for the first time since she'd had her nose done, Nicola kind of enjoyed making up a new face. When she was in high school, she'd had fun reading fashion magazines and following their beauty blue-prints, with detailed instructions for "smoldering eyes," "the perfect French pout," "cheeks with a healthy bloom," and so on.

Tonight she pulled out all the stops.

And when she was finished, she looked pretty damn good, if she did say so herself.

She arrived at Little Door ten minutes early and drove around the block for fifteen minutes so, assuming Trick was there on time, she would be fashionably late, at least by a tiny margin.

Unfortunately, he wasn't there yet when she arrived, so instead of waiting for her and thinking, even for a moment, that she might have gotten a better offer, he came in, saw her, and perhaps concluded that she'd been there since eight, kneading her hands and waiting and hoping for his arrival.

Another fifteen minutes of circling, and she would have arrived *after* him.

"Hey, Nicky." He opened his arms as he approached her, then kissed both cheeks. "Good to see you again."

People at college who hadn't known her very well called her Nicky. For some reason, the people closest to her had never gotten that in-formal.

She decided to like that he was being informal.

"You, too."

He gestured at the maître d', who immediately ushered them to a quiet table for four in the back.

Nicola was puzzled by that for a moment, until Trick explained, "I like having some elbow room. Hate it when they squeeze me into a little table that has no room."

"Me, too," she agreed sincerely. What she didn't add was that she, like most of the population, didn't usually have any choice about such things.

The waitress filled their water glasses and lingered over drink orders, showing extra attention to Trick, even after he'd ordered and looked away from her. Her lingering drew his attention back long enough for him to say, "That's all, sweetheart." It was distinctly dismissive, and even the waitress seemed a little embarrassed as she slunk away.

"I guess you get that a lot," Nicola commented, privately feeling horrible for the poor girl.

"Lazy waitresses? You have no idea."

"Oh, I don't think she was lazy. I think she just recognized you."

He sneered. "I ordered a drink, not a blow job. She doesn't need to stick around for a drink, know what I'm sayin'?"

Nicola nodded, though she didn't love the implication that the waitress might have been equally useful giving him the drink or the blow job. But she didn't let herself get too hung up on the de-tails—he probably just had different turns of phrase.

This didn't mean anything really. Not necessarily.

Their drinks came, and they ordered dinner without anything re-markable happening while the waitress was there or after she left.

"So . . . that was you in *Karaoke Nights*, huh?" Trick asked.

"No, *Duet*." *Karaoke Nights* was a terrible teen comedy, like a bad imitation of *A Night at the Roxbury*, if such a thing were possible.

"That's right." He shot a finger gun at her and winked. "That's what I meant. Good flick."

Except that he hadn't seen it. "Thanks." What could she say now? He didn't mean what he was saying, so she couldn't mean what she was saying. This was going to get really old, really fast. "What about you? What are you working on now?"

"*Gamehunter Three*. The first two were such huge successes that they begged me to come back for another." He rubbed his fingers together, indicating a big payout. "So I agreed to help 'em out."

She laughed—he had to be kidding, right?—and said, "It's good to have work in this day and age, isn't it?"

He shrugged. "I've always got work. Not worried. So tell me something." He nodded toward her. "You're an actress. Been around a while. You've got your chops."

She flushed under his praise, however faint. "I guess so."

He picked up his Scotch on the rocks, wiggled it for a moment, then took a sip before asking, "What do you think my best picture is?"

"I'm sorry?"

"My best work. Everyone's got a different favorite. I'm just wondering what yours is."

"Oh." For a moment, she thought he had to be joking. But he wasn't. He was including her in the conversation by asking her what she thought of him. "Well. *Gamehunter* is a good one, for sure." She figured he was angling for that one since he'd mentioned it. "And, of course, *Harvest Moon*." She was careful with that one, in case he suddenly remembered the lovesick girl who was little more than an extra.

She needn't have worried.

"What did you think of me in *Dance Fever*? Too ripped?" He flexed his bicep, in case there was any doubt as to what he meant. "I don't want to get a reputation as nothing more than a pretty boy."

"Well, no." Though she gathered *he* thought of himself that way. "I think people think of you as a really good actor."

He swirled his Scotch again and gave a dry laugh. "Brinkman didn't." He was referring to Norman Brinkman, a genius director who had started working in the late seventies, with the likes of Martin Scorsese after he'd done *Taxi Driver*.

Brinkman was a genius.

Nicola would have given anything to work with him.

"You were just great in *Choirboy*," she objected. And she meant it. He'd played the angry street kid as if he meant every word. "It was an inspired performance."

"Inspired by that guy being a dick." Trick snorted. "I hated that guy. He had me pissed off the whole time."

"Oh. Hm." She didn't want to admit it, but if Brinkman had found himself with a talentless egomaniac for a lead, the smartest thing he could have done—and undoubtedly *would* have done—was just piss him off and keep him pissed off until the cameras stopped rolling.

The waitress and another server came and put their food down in front of them. Trick had ordered the rib eye steak with mushroom confit in a size so large it would have embarrassed Fred Flintstone, and Nicola had ordered the mint-crusted tuna.

At least one thing tonight was going to leave a good taste in her mouth.

"But you like my performance, huh?" Trick was saying. He didn't acknowledge the servers at all.

"Yes." Then more than now. "I did." She gave the waitress a small smile and nod of thanks as she set the plate down.

"Tell me more."

"More?" Dare she hope he wanted to know more about her? Maybe she'd read him wrong and he wasn't only thinking about himself and his own achievements. "What do you want to know?"

"Well . . ." He sawed off a big piece of steak and popped it into his mouth, asking, without chewing first, "What else have you seen of mine?"

Everything. But she wasn't about to admit that now. "I'm not sure. What else were you in?" She cut off a small piece of tuna and chewed it with her mouth closed.

For a moment, his jaw went slack; then he scrutinized her and started to laugh. "You had me going for a minute," he said, waggling a finger at her. "Pretty good."

He had her number. He just didn't know she wasn't trying to be funny. "So. I heard you were up for the lead in *Duet* at first," she said, trying to rein the conversation into something they might actually have in common, however tenuously. "That's interesting."

"Was I?" He shook his head and put another enormous piece of steak in his mouth. "I get so much shit thrown my way, you know?"

"I can . . . only imagine." Said the woman who felt like she'd been turned down for more parts than she'd even auditioned for in the past few years. She poked at her baby spinach salad. "That was the role of my life. It certainly would have been interesting if you'd been in it instead of Robert. I wonder how it would have impacted the success of the film."

"Robert?" He looked blank.

"Robert Dean Zunick." Even if her name didn't impress Trick, Bob's should. "He got the role."

"Right." He nodded, reaching for the steak sauce the waitress had left with their entrées. "Right. Good guy." He drowned the top-quality Kobe rib eye in steak sauce, hacked off another piece of steak, then nodded appreciatively. "That's more like it."

Given the quality of her tuna entrée, she was pretty sure he'd just basically smothered the best steak he'd ever eaten in what was essentially ketchup, mustard, and Worcestershire sauce.

The rest of the meal proceeded in pretty much the same way:

Trick talked about himself in between mortifyingly huge shovelfuls of food, and every time Nicola tried to inject anything that she thought might be a common interest—or something that took the focus off Trick exclusively for even a moment—he grew noticeably bored.

At one point, between the end of his steak and the arrival of his fourth Scotch, he even concentrated on cleaning his watch crystal while she told him something about her grandmother.

That was when Nicola decided she'd had enough.

There was no question of who got the check. When they were finished eating, Trick just made a *we're outta here* gesture at the waitress and got up. Obviously he had a tab running here, and they didn't need to be so gauche as to bring a paper for him to sign.

It worked fine for Nicola. By the end of dinner, she was so sick of him, she didn't think she'd ever be able to sit through another one of his movies.

Unless she was in it.

And at the rate things were going, *that* seemed about as likely as running into a *T. rex* on the PCH.

So no check meant no waiting for a check, which meant no more of this interminable conversation she was having with Trick.

He held the front door for her to exit. When she turned to say good night, he spoke first.

"So what do you say we go back to my place and"—he gave a cocky smile and let his implication dangle for a moment before saying—"you know . . ."

She sighed, not because his proposition was offensive. It wasn't. If he had been the dream-come-true she'd thought he was, before these past few hours, she would gladly have gone home with him and *you know*'d until they were exhausted.

Now she didn't want to do anything with him. She didn't want to talk to him anymore, God knew she didn't want to *listen* to him any-more, and she definitely didn't want to go home with him for the honor of, as he'd so eloquently put it earlier tonight, blowing him.

Or more.

"Actually, Trick, I've got to get back home. I've got an early call." She didn't. She didn't have any calls at all at the moment.

"Aw, come on." He hooked his hands over her shoulders and drew her close to him. "Just for a little while?"

Heaven help her, it was tempting. Looking into his eyes from this proximity, the vacancy shaded by the night, she could see the same thing every woman who loved him saw on the silver screen. His face was beautiful; his mouth a sensual curve. If he'd shut the hell up, she might have a chance at falling for the fantasy long enough to enjoy herself.

But he couldn't. "Come on, no one says no to the Trickster."

"Oh, gross," she said involuntarily. But at this point, she didn't care. "I'm sorry," she lied, "but you can't say that kind of crap to any girl with an iota of self-respect and expect her to fall into your arms. You're like a walking, talking *when you sleep with someone, you sleep with everyone that person has ever slept with* public service announce-ment." She crinkled her nose and shook her head. "No thanks."

He hesitated for a moment before saying, "Now you've really got me goin'." That smile again. "Come on, just for a little while. I can guarantee you won't want to go."

She shook her head. "Sorry. But thanks." She took her valet ticket out of the outside pocket of her purse and handed it to the guy at the valet podium. She was glad to see he gave it to a runner right away.

The sooner she got out of here, the better.

"You are so beautiful," Trick said, his mouth cocked into a half smile. "If you weren't, I wouldn't be wasting my time."

If this was what this so-called beauty had bought her, she didn't want it. Even as recently as a few hours ago, it felt like her new looks had gotten her a ticket to heaven, but now she saw that they had only unlocked a door that should have stayed locked.

It had been a lot more fun thinking Trick was the hottest guy who'd ever lived than knowing he was a self-referencing egomaniacal dud.

"You're wasting your time now," she said with a wan smile.

He narrowed his eyes and smiled back. "Ooooh, baby, you're good at this game."

"Thanks." She was profoundly relieved to see her car rounding the corner and pulling up in front of the restaurant. "And thanks for dinner. I . . . really enjoyed it."

"I'll be in touch."

She said nothing but gave him a brief smile of thanks before going to the driver's side of her car.

"Is that Patrick Naylor Jr.?" the valet asked as she slipped him a five.

"That's what I've been asking myself all night," she answered. "And now I don't even know for sure who *I* am anymore."

15

Lexi carefully lifted the torn lid of the Kinney Shoes box and set it aside. There were some birthday cards, signed by people whose names Lexi didn't recognize; a few handwritten recipes; about ten playbills; and a "nothing book," which was a blank book that Anna had used as a journal with messages for Lexi.

Finding it was like finding the Holy Grail.

Her mother had written it directly to her, so reading it was as close as she'd ever get to having a conversation with her. But, in some strange way, it *did* kind of feel like a conversation. As she read, sometimes she smiled, sometimes she cried, she had a million questions, but her frustration that they'd never be answered was overshadowed by the sheer joy of having the journal.

Anna had evidently begun it when she was pregnant, and it was filled with breezy, meandering entries about the baby clothes she'd just purchased at a yard sale and how an old friend of her mother had given her a windup baby swing and a Johnny Jump Up, and she was trying to imagine the baby who would eventually use them.

I wonder who you'll be, she wrote at eight months' pregnant. *A boy? A girl? John (for my father)? Alexis (for yours)? I went to the big consignment sale at the community center today and bought all yellow things because I don't know. Your dad thinks you're a boy, but maybe I shouldn't put this in writing, but I have a hunch you're a girl. No matter who you are, we just can't wait to meet you!*

Three days after Lexi was born, the entry said: *Well, hello, Lexi! Welcome to the bigger world! Do you have any idea how incredibly much I love you? You are better than I ever imagined, and my heart is more full than I could have dreamed was possible!*

About a year later, an entry began, *Hello, sweetheart! You're asleep in your crib, so I thought I'd take a moment to say hello to the you in the future. We had a long morning of playing Where's Lexi? with the blanket over your head. You never seem to get tired of that! And your new love is dancing. . . .*

Lexi smiled to herself. It was funny for her to imagine herself ever loving dancing, as she was so laughably bad at it now. She longed for the days when she had been uninhibited and unself-conscious, safe in the world no matter where she went because she was so cushioned by her mother's love.

It hadn't mattered a bit that they were so poor, they had to buy secondhand clothes at a consignment sale and borrow an old crib from a neighbor. To read Anna's joyful prose, it was hard to believe they'd ever struggled.

But they had. Later journal entries alluded to the fact that they'd had to move suddenly when they were evicted from an apartment in Gaithersburg and the brief time they'd spent sharing a studio in an old neighborhood in Bethesda.

Anna hadn't known then that the hardware her husband and his buddies were working on in the garage would eventually lead to the founding of one of the biggest digital communications corporations in the United States, and that, at least for eleven years or so, she would live on Easy Street.

Hers was a Cinderella story.

For a while anyway.

Then—*poof!* She was gone. Leaving a beloved daughter without nurturing and a workaholic husband who had no idea how to be a father, much less a single father.

So what did that make Lexi's story? What was the opposite of Cinderella?

Or *was* she the opposite? To go backwards would imply that she'd experienced hardship before privilege, and that simply wasn't the case. Lexi had had it easy her whole life.

Except she hadn't been like the girls she went to school with, which was difficult sometimes. As a child, she couldn't have put her finger on the difference exactly; she knew now that she'd been raised with a humility and gratitude that the old Potomac money simply didn't have.

Reading the journal now filled in pieces of her life that she might never have understood. Sure, she'd known that Daddy had "made it big" at some point in her early childhood, and there was a house somewhere in Northwest D.C. that had been the first she'd lived in, as a baby, with her late grandparents. Beyond that, she'd known no details.

Now she did. Now she knew that her parents had really loved each other. And loved *her*. Once they'd been a happy family.

Anna hadn't actually written that directly, but there was a lightness in her tone, an optimism about the future and about life in general that seemed greater than anything Lexi recalled while her mother was living.

Then again, the woman had been ill for some time, and most of Lexi's memories were based on those last couple of years, so the conclusion that poor equals happier probably wasn't a fair one.

But emotion wasn't based on *fair*. Emotion was based on very faulty intuition much of the time. Lexi knew that. Logically, she knew that.

Nevertheless, something deep inside her told her that the wealth was the cause of everything bad that had happened in her life. And, though she'd never been determined to throw away her bank account balances and credit cards while her father was alive, she did always suspect that "the other half" wasn't living so badly.

According to the journal, Lexi's mother had worked one summer as a clerk at Tiffany & Co. in New York, living in a tiny studio apartment in Midtown. Though Lexi would have loved to read more details about it, it was interesting that Anna had found the work so satisfying. She loved to go to work every day, she said, loved feeling productive and having that routine.

It was as if she were speaking to Lexi from the grave.

So maybe, in some way, it was good that Michelle had kept the money. Morally corrupt, of course, but maybe it was better for Lexi.

Maybe it was her only shot at finding out what happiness *really* felt like.

In the past, whenever Lexi had needed a little pick-me-up, she'd gone to the mall and done some shopping. It almost always helped, at least temporarily. Clothes, shoes, accessories, all those things provided the needed lift, in varying degrees.

But the cosmetic counters were the best. Intricately shaped and painted bottles, glistening lids, fancy fonts and poetic descriptions of the miracles contained within. She loved the feel of those packages in her hand, the smell of the creams and perfumes, the taste of lip glosses. In many ways, it was better than sex, though she was aware that might speak more to the quality of her former boyfriends than to sex on the whole.

Regardless, no matter what her mood, it was made better by a trip to Sephora. Worries dissolved when she crossed the threshold. Anxiety went down; creativity went up. She could think more clearly in the scented air and fluorescent lights.

If she were ever elected president, she'd have all her meetings with foreign dignitaries in Sephora.

The black-and-white office.

Things were different now. She'd gone to a career planner online and found some tips for finding the perfect career. The key seemed to be to find what you know and love and find a way to make money at that.

She knew and loved Sephora.

It was, to her, what Tiffany had been to her mother.

So she went to Montgomery Mall, that beacon of shopping delight that had warmed her soul ever since she was a teenager shopping at Casual Corner and Merry-Go-Round for leggings, scrunchy socks, and oversized tunic sweaters.

She pulled up to the garage in front of Nordstrom (no matter where she was going in the mall, she liked to enter through Nordstrom) and parked. Then she took a moment to psych herself into the confidence that was necessary when asking for a job. She needed to look like she didn't need it.

She got out of the car and walked through the familiar double doors of Nordstrom. The smell of fabric and leather greeted her. It was comforting in its familiarity, despite the fact that she was no longer able to stop and pick things she wanted to buy.

That wasn't to say she'd never be able to again. Once she had a job, she'd probably be able to get *most* of the stuff she wanted. Or at least the stuff she *needed*.

Walking through the store and out into the mall, Lexi felt a little better with every step. Because the mall, she realized, was always in the same mood, no matter what *her* mood was. There was something very reassuring about the beautiful clothes hanging there, one identical item after another, and the plastic mannequins, with their facial expressions frozen somewhere between nothing and mirth. The lights were flattering, the floors were gleaming, the music was soothing, and for just a few moments, all seemed right with the world.

Even more so when she entered Sephora. The glass case in front contained a new collection from Lorac and a set of new colors from Bare Escentuals.

This was the right thing. It would be the perfect job for her, and they would be fools not to hire her. She knew the product lines probably better than 99 percent of the customers. (There was always the chance that someone out there was an even bigger product freak than she was.)

"Hi, can I help you find something today?"

Lexi looked up to see a sales associate dressed in black and wearing a headset looking at her expectantly.

"Yes." Lexi took a steadying breath. "I was wondering . . . are you hiring?"

Getting the job was easy, as it turned out.

Finding a place to live, which she'd thought would be the easy part, turned out to be a lot more challenging than she'd anticipated, despite the fact that she found ten places on Craigslist that looked worth visiting.

Time was running out, but she decided to move into an extended-stay place she'd found in Bethesda for a week or two if she absolutely had to in order to get out of Michelle's house on time.

It bought her more time to see the prospective places.

First, there was the town house share in Bethesda. She would get a room and full bath on the ground level, and share the laundry room on the same level and the kitchen upstairs. It was $850 a month, and the circumstances were, of course, horrible. However, it hadn't taken her long to realize that her budgeted eight hundred a month wasn't going to take her very far.

"So what do you do?" one of the girls who lived there asked Lexi. Her name was Rachel, and she looked like she was about twenty-three. From what Lexi gathered, she owned the house.

So even though she was blond and vapid and wore the blue eye-shadow that some magazines were trying to contend was in right now (though as far as Lexi was concerned, it would *never* be back in), she was still more successful than Lexi.

Smarter, one might argue. She owned property.

"I work at Sephora," Lexi answered. The words sounded strange to her own ears. *Let's go to Sephora*—sure. *I need to pick something up at Sephora*, she'd said a thousand times.

I work at Sephora sounded like she was trying on a Halloween costume that didn't quite fit.

Rachel nodded. "So are you, like, a manager?"

"No." The temptation to embellish was great, but Lexi had found that the truth was working pretty well for her lately. It was certainly easier to keep track of. "I just started."

"What did you do before that?" the other girl, Debbie, asked. She was about the same age as Rachel, with deep auburn hair and the kind of tall, willowy figure that would have made her a great model in the sixties.

Nothing. The answer to the question Debbie was asking was *nothing*. But that was one truth that was just a little too hard to cop to with these two. So, rather than lie, Lexi hedged. After all, it was none of their business. "Before that, I *shopped* at Sephora." She gave a laugh.

But Debbie and Rachel just exchanged a puzzled look.

"I'm looking for someone with a really solid work history," Rachel said. "Because I need to be sure the rent's coming in."

Lexi was taken aback. Was this kid looking at her and accusing her of being a bad risk? "Of course." She waited a beat. "Obviously that's not going to be a problem with me."

"Good."

There was a short, uncomfortable silence.

"So can you tell me about the space?" She'd had only a minute or two to look at what she'd be renting. What Rachel called "ground floor" was, to Lexi, the basement. There was no door, although Rachel called the large square window with a window well an "evacuation window," which apparently made it legal for her to rent the space as a bedroom. The bathroom was not attached; she'd have to walk out her bedroom door and into the bathroom, potentially running into someone who was down there doing laundry, though it was unlikely that anyone would be doing laundry late at night, and that would have been the most awkward time to see anyone.

"You just saw it," Debbie chirped.

Lexi was beginning to hope this didn't work out. She *needed* it to, of course. There was barely any time for her to move: just three days.

So it wouldn't be reasonable for her to turn it down, but the whole prospect of moving in here was depressing.

"What I mean is, how is the climate control down there? It can be hard to heat a basement in cold weather."

"There are vents down there," Rachel said, pointing out the obvious while obviously not answering the question.

Which might have been an answer right there.

Lexi eyed her. "Are you at all flexible about the rent?"

"What do you mean?"

"I mean is eight fifty firm, or would you be willing to go to"—she was winging it; she had to think fast while not pricing herself out of the game—"seven seventy-five?"

Rachel gave a short, hard spike of laughter. "No."

Lexi recoiled inwardly at the harshness of her response. Surely it was normal to try to negotiate the rent.

"So," Rachel went on, exchanging another look with Debbie, "we're going to take a minute to talk about this. We have other applicants, too, so could you excuse us for a minute?"

"Sure." The air was stifling. "I'll step outside." She didn't wait for an answer. If she was this desperate to get out now, when she'd been there for only half an hour, how on earth was she going to *live* there?

Rachel and Debbie were just the kind of girls and women that had been a thorn in Lexi's side all her life. The way they'd met her at the door, a wall of two people, had put her off immediately. Then there were the looks they'd kept sharing. Conspiratorial. *What did you think of that answer?* and *Sephora?* and *Ummm . . . we'll talk about whether or not we think we can tolerate you.*

Well, Lexi wasn't going to do it.

She had nine more places to look at, and odds were good that they'd be better than this. She made a deal with herself: If she let herself off the hook with this one, just got in the car and drove away, she'd try that much harder to make one of them work, even if she had to compromise her ideals.

She went to her car and got in. The digital clock showed she had fifteen minutes until her next appointment five minutes away. It seemed like a good omen.

As she was reversing out of the parking space, the front door opened, and—surprise!—Rachel and Debbie both poked their confused faces out.

Lexi lowered the window. "I don't think it's going to work out!" she called, then made a broad shrug.

Of course, the two looked at each other.

And smiled.

They hadn't been about to accept her application anyway.

Two blocks from the next appointment, Lexi's phone rang and the landlord told her the room had been rented. Daunted but not discouraged, Lexi went to her next appointment.

Fifteen minutes later, she left in a fit of sneezing and with burning, watery eyes. She wasn't sure if she was allergic to cats, or if this was the kind of reaction anyone would have upon being faced with so many of them in one small space, but she crossed that apartment off her list.

Likewise, she ended up eliminating the group house on Georgia Avenue, which smelled like pot and looked like a bus terminal; the apartment on University Boulevard that was full of mouse droppings; and the converted motel in Rockville that looked like a halfway home.

That left all Lexi's eggs in the basket of Pamela, who lived in the Waterford condos on Connecticut Avenue in Kensington. She didn't know the neighborhood very well, but it was close enough to her job, and as she drove through, she could see that it appeared to have all the amenities she could want close by.

The lobby was nice, although Lexi wasn't crazy about taking an elevator to and from the ninth floor every day. She'd gotten stuck on an elevator alone at a hotel in New York once, and it took a lot longer for help to come than it should have. She wasn't sure if she'd *become* claustrophobic at that moment, or simply realized she already *was*, but she never got on an elevator these days without wondering what would happen if it stopped.

But maybe this would cure her of that, she thought optimistically.

When the doors didn't open immediately upon the elevator stopping on the ninth floor, her optimism wavered a little, but they opened a second later, and Lexi breathed a sigh of relief and made her way down the hall, looking for 915.

Pamela Bersoff was a small fretful-looking woman in her mid-thirties. When Lexi knocked, she answered the door so fast that Lexi wondered if she'd been peering out the peephole, waiting for her.

"Are you Alexis?" she asked in the tone of one trying to "catch" someone in a lie.

"Yes." Lexi put out her hand, and Pamela flinched, then shook it. "So I guess I should show you around."

"Okay."

Pamela closed the door, turned the dead bolt, and ran a chain across it.

"Is this . . . an unsafe neighborhood?" Lexi asked.

"Why do you ask?"

"Because that's a lot of locking you're doing." The thought that she might be locking Lexi *in* rather than locking the rest of the world *out* crossed Lexi's mind.

"Single women can never be too careful," Pamela said. "If you're going to live here, that's one thing we absolutely have to agree on."

"Right." Lexi supposed she could live with that. She wasn't usually paranoid about her safety, but she wasn't an advocate for danger, either. "I agree."

"This is my room." Pamela gestured toward a meticulously clean bedroom with simple mission-style furniture and a long balcony overlooking Connecticut Avenue. The sliding glass doors had multiple locks.

Would it even be *possible* for a bad guy to get up to the ninth floor to break in if he didn't have superpowers?

"And this is my bathroom." Not surprisingly, the bathroom she pointed to was gleaming and sparse. If *Dateline* came in with their black lights and bacteria cultures, they'd probably find nothing.

"It's very nice," Lexi commented, and it was. The bathroom wasn't very modern; the bathtub and shower were one unit, the sink had a built-in cabinet below it but no extras. The mirror was the door to a medicine cabinet. Convenient but old-fashioned.

Lexi was irked with herself for feeling like it wasn't good enough, but it was quite different from the house she'd grown up in. The lifestyle she'd gotten used to.

"This would be your room." Pamela opened the door on a room that was considerably smaller than the master. It would have been a nice den, with its sliding glass door to the balcony, but Lexi had never even been in a hotel room that was this small.

"Hm." Lexi stepped in. She had to consider it. She couldn't be a chooser. She opened the accordion doors to the closet. It was small, too. She'd have to keep her off-season wardrobes in storage.

"And the bathroom is here, right across the hall." Pamela gestured toward a bathroom that was identical to the one she used, only empty, except for a bamboo-print shower curtain.

Lexi stepped out of the room and tried to assess the space between the two bedrooms. There wasn't much. This would have been a perfect space for one person who had an occasional guest, but it was going to be a bit of a squeeze for two.

But, again, Lexi couldn't be a chooser.

She was a beggar.

"Can I see the kitchen?"

"Sure. It's right here next to your room, actually." She led Lexi to a narrow galley kitchen. It had a tiny table, better sized for two children than for two adults, a telephone on the wall, and . . . a cat box.

"You have a cat?"

"Yes, I do. Pooka. I hope that's not a problem."

"I'm a little bit allergic."

Pamela looked concerned. "He doesn't like sneezing."

Lexi laughed. "I don't either, but I can put up with a little bit."

"No, I mean really, he gets very agitated from sneezes." Pamela was looking agitated herself. "They give him seizures."

"You're kidding, right?"

Pamela shook her head. "I'm sorry, but if there's a chance that you will have chronic sinus problems while living here, I just can't approve you."

Lexi's nose began to feel runny. Oh, for God's sake. "I'm fine. Really. It's not a problem."

Pamela frowned. "Well . . . if you're sure . . ."

"Absolutely."

"All right. Then if you want to fill out the reference sheet, that would be good. It's right over here. You can sit at the table."

Lexi sat, feeling like a student about to take the SATs.

Pamela handed her a printout and a pen. "Three landlord references, three *verifiable* job references, past or present, and two personal references, please."

"I don't have all of those."

"What?"

"I've never had a landlord before." Or a job. "And I've just started my new job, though I'm sure they would let you know I've been showing up. And obviously I can do the personal references."

"What do you mean you've never had a landlord before?"

"I've lived in the same house for years," Lexi explained, but she didn't want to confess the circumstances. "You know, it was mine, but now I don't want to buy again until the market stabilizes a little and starts to go up." She was parroting what she'd heard on TV; she actually had no idea if the market was stabilizing or going up or down at the moment. It seemed to change by the minute.

"Oh." Pamela looked dubious. "I guess I can take your Realtor's name."

Ordinarily, Lexi would have written down names with absolute confidence that no one ever really checked references.

But she was 100 percent sure that Pamela would.

Before she could formulate an adequate response, a big beige long-haired cat propelled himself from the floor to her lap to the table, throwing up tons of hair and dander into her face.

"This is Pooka."

The thing weighed almost as much as Pamela, Lexi guessed. And was even more skittish.

"He's cute," Lexi said, and the cat leapt away, turning his face to her with an unmistakable warning in his eye.

"He's my widdle baby," Pamela cooed. "Yes, he is."

Words failed Lexi.

Which was convenient, since she had to sneeze.

Perhaps no one is ever completely ready for an animal attack, but Lexi, in the midst of a sneezing fit, was utterly unprepared to have her hands and face attacked by what felt like fifty paws with claws extended.

"Get him off me!" she cried as she felt a nail snag its way down her cheek.

"He's frightened!" Pamela's voice came from somewhere. "Stop sneezing."

"I—" She sneezed. "*Can't.* He's right"—she sneezed again and was blessed by another paw full of claws dragging its way down her temple, perilously close to her eye—"on top of me!"

Finally she grabbed the large, hot mound of living fur and hurled it away from her. She heard it make contact with the wall several feet away, a thump and a simultaneous squall.

"You can't do that to Pooka!" Pamela shrieked from somewhere in the watery blur Lexi couldn't see through.

"He *attacked* me." Lexi reached around on the table for a napkin to blot her eyes and the wounds she was certain were bleeding down her face.

"You *sneezed,*" Pamela returned, in a voice twice as accusatory as anything Lexi could have mustered. "I *told* you not to *sneeze.*"

"You didn't tell me I'd be attacked if I sneezed one time."

"I told you not to sneeze." Pamela was resolute. "You need to go now."

Lexi's first impulse was to wad up the stupid references sheet and throw it at Pamela, but her second was to apologize and try to make up for this. After all, she *needed* a place to live, and the price was right, here.

Financially, that was.

Emotionally, the price was far too high.

"You're right." Lexi stood up. "There's no way this could work." She started toward the door and reached for a paper towel from the roll over the sink, but Pamela swatted her hand away.

"No!" Pamela shouted, as she might have to a dog. As she, in fact, probably *had* to a dog. More than once.

Lexi could have argued that the least Pam could do was give her something to wipe away the blood from the wound her stupid cat had inflicted on her, but it was really obvious that an argument like that would go nowhere.

So she left, stopping to pick up the wadded references page so she at least had *something* to stop the flow of blood. Clutching her purse close to her, she hurried into the neutral territory of the hallway as quickly as she possibly could. As soon as Lexi's toes touched the carpet, Pamela had slammed the door behind her and spent a good minute turning locks and dragging the chain across the door.

"God help anyone who comes to get you," Lexi muttered, patting her temple and then checking her fingers for blood. There was only a faint stain. Maybe she could get away with it long enough to get to her car and use the antibiotic wipes she kept in the console.

She went to the elevator and pushed the button, silently chanting, *Please don't let anyone be on the elevator, please don't let anyone be on the elevator.*

There was, of course, someone on the elevator.

It was Greg. He had a baseball hat on backwards and, in the great tradition of "workman" clichés, a ratty T-shirt and a toolbelt strapped around his waist.

She stepped onto the elevator with him, humiliated. "Oh, good Lord. Am I going to run into you *everywhere?*"

"Yes." That dent showed up in his cheek again. It was probably a sign that he was trying not to smile. "So"—he gestured at her—"who won?"

She didn't meet his eyes. "The cat."

She could see him nodding in her peripheral vision.

"I'm a dog person myself," he said.

"So am I. Now." She wished she'd had one with her at Pamela's. A big-toothed pit bull.

The elevator moved incredibly slowly. It would have been an awful place for her to live, really, having to take a slow, creaky elevator to and from the apartment every day.

Yeah, a snarky little voice in her said, *a cardboard box on the street is a lot better than that.*

"Look, you should probably wipe that off." He held his bandanna out to her.

It was filthy. "No, thanks. I'll be fine."

"I'm more worried about the kids that are bound to be in the lobby. School just let out, and you'll scare the shit out of them if you don't clean that gaping wound up."

"Oh." She squinted and looked closer into the reflective doors. She *was* a mess. "I see what you mean." She took a bottle of Purell out of her purse and put it on the corner of his bandanna, then wiped it on the side of her face. Fortunately it was easy to clean.

"So," the guy went on. "Do you always fight with the cat?"

"Nope, we just met." She squeezed more Purell onto a clean part of the fabric and cleaned the other side of her face.

"A friend of yours?"

"The cat or the owner?"

"Either?"

"Neither." She finished cleaning herself up as the doors opened.

They both stepped into the lobby and she folded the bandanna and held it out to him.

His pale eyes were clearly laughing at her when he declined the return of his bandanna. "No thanks. Consider it a party favor." He smiled, and she had to admit, it was kind of nice to see him, especially after the insanity she'd just been through. She was getting used to his face, she guessed, and that familiarity was somewhat comforting.

She looked at it and shrugged. She couldn't really expect him to want the bloody thing back. "I'll clean it and leave it for you at the house."

He laughed outright. "Blondie, it looks to me like you've got more important things to worry about."

"Thanks." But she had to smile. "How blunt of you."

He splayed his arms. "Just being honest." He cocked his head. "So what were you doing up there, besides fighting with a cat and not being friends with the owner?"

"I was looking at an apartment."

"Ah." He nodded slowly. "I had a feeling you might be looking for a place. Not that it's any of my business—"

"No, it's really not."

"—but what are you looking for? You want a condo or were you looking to share or what?"

"It's none of your business." She raised an eyebrow. "Like you just said."

"True. Are you buying or renting?"

She gave him a withering glance. "Renting. Your employer has thrown me out."

"Well, actually, she's not my employer—she's my client. And I'm not surprised. When I first met her, she told me she didn't like certain minorities and hoped I would try to limit their presence on my team."

Lexi rolled her eyes. She knew exactly which minorities he was referring to—for some reason, Michelle and her friends didn't have any problem with being bigoted at all. "What did you say?"

"I told her she'd have to hire someone else." He shrugged. "I guess she didn't want to do that."

Lexi just bet she didn't want to do that. In fact, Michelle probably had plans for Greg himself when she got back.

It felt good to know he wouldn't comply.

"Look," he went on. "I know this probably isn't what you're looking for, but I've got a room to rent in a house a couple of miles from your place. The rent's cheap." He named a price. "But there's a catch."

She frowned. It was *too* cheap. "Must be a hell of a catch—what is it?"

"The catch is that I need help fixing the place up to sell. Little cosmetic things, like painting and cleaning. I had one of the guys on my crew lined up to do it, but he got engaged and moved in with his girlfriend."

Lexi was skeptical. "Surely you've got ten other guys who could step in and take his place."

He looked at her for a moment, then said, "Yeah, you're right, it's a dumb idea."

"No, wait, I didn't mean it was a dumb idea, only that you'd need . . . references . . . and—" She stopped. What *did* she mean? It wasn't like he was some freak, trying to get her into his clutches. If he were dangerous in any way, he'd already had ample opportunity at her father's abandoned estate to do her harm (something Michelle should have thought of before sending workmen to a house where she knew Lexi would be alone—or maybe Michelle *had* considered that, she thought cynically).

Anyway, Greg was offering her the chance to save a bundle on rent in exchange for the kind of grunt work anyone—even Lexi—could do in their off time.

"Where is the house?"

He told her an address. She knew the area well, as it was close to the locks on the C&O canal. She and her friends used to hang out there a lot during high school, drinking beer, as it was remote. More so then than now, she was sure.

"And how long will the rental term be?"

"That I don't know. It could sell at any time, theoretically, though in this market . . ." He flattened his hand and tipped it side to side.

Even if it were for a couple of months, that would buy her time and save her the money she thought she'd have to spend on the extended-stay hotel. "I'll take it!"

He smiled. "Cool. So, if you'll just jot down a few references . . ."

16

Holly gave a lot of thought to what she'd said in her pep talk to Nicola because, although she believed every single word she'd said to Nicola, she wasn't living that way herself at all.

Where she'd told Nicola to *own* who she was now, and wear it proudly, without regard to how she'd ever looked in the past or how she might look in the future, Holly was walking around almost twenty pounds lighter but with an apologetic posture.

It was tempting to blame Randy.

After all, she'd lost all this weight because of him, really, and he barely seemed to notice her at the end. If anything, he seemed to be paying *less* attention in the weeks right before he broke up with her.

Surely that was her imagination.

Nevertheless, Holly had been schlumping around as if her very existence were an imposition to him, while she was yelling at

Nicola—actually *yelling* at one point during that conversation—that she should be proud of who she was, regardless of anything else.

Well, why wasn't Holly following her own advice?

If she were her own best friend, she'd have some prime words for the way she was acting.

Lacey had.

And Lacey had been right to a certain extent.

So, with that in mind, Holly decided that she had to do the very thing she would have advised any of her friends to do in the same situation: She had to make *herself* feel great.

Of course, that was easier said than done. She'd left Randy a message earlier to find out if they could talk about the breakup and maybe try again to work things out. But he hadn't called back yet. So Holly was telling herself that, in contrast to how she'd usually be, she was going to just roll with it and let whatever happened happen.

Que sera sera.

Meanwhile she was going to go to the mall to get some new clothes and makeup and whatever else it took to make her feel good about herself, damn it.

Things didn't go great at Nordstrom. More than sixteen pounds was significant weight loss, but she still wasn't Brass Plum material. She tried on a couple of things that looked drapey and Chico's-y on the hanger, only to be alarmed at the way her body and underwear battled for prominence just beneath the fabric.

So it was with some resignation that she left Nordstrom and went to Sephora.

Sephora always made things seem right.

"Hi! Can I help you find anything tonight?" This question was the same every time she came into the store, always asked by some gorgeous girl with perfect makeup and the kind of willowy figure that looked great in the tailored black Sephora uniform.

"I'm just browsing"—she looked for the name tag—"Lexi. But thanks, I'll let you know if I need anything."

"Oh." Lexi looked a little disappointed. "Well, I'll be around if you need anything. I'd be glad to do a demo or a makeover if you wanted to try something new."

"Thanks." Holly went to the mascara center and was immediately lost. There was a display tree with at least twenty different mascaras on it, each one with a description that made it sound like the greatest product ever invented. "Um . . . Lexi?"

She didn't hear her.

"Lexi!"

The girl turned, looked at her, smiled, and for just a moment, Holly felt like she was experiencing déjà vu. Something about Lexi was really familiar, but she couldn't quite place her.

"What can I do for you?"

"I was looking for a good mascara and"—Holly gestured at them—"apparently they're all good, according to their descriptions."

"They want you to *think* they're all good." Lexi raised an eyebrow. "But it really depends on what your mascara needs are."

"My mascara needs?"

"Sure. Do you need lengthening? Curling? Thickening?" Holly scrutinized her. "Or, maybe, would you say . . . all three?" She pulled a Dior tube off the display.

"Actually, what I want more than anything else is a mascara that won't come off under my eyes and make me look like a panda at the end of the day." Holly reached for one that said it WON'T SMUDGE. EVER.

"Then you don't want that one. It's total crap. Twenty-six dollars, and you look like a panda within two hours." Lexi slipped the Dior and the other back in its slot and pulled out another one. "What you need is tube technology."

"*Tube* technology?"

"Yup. This stuff wraps a little tube around each lash and then dries like"—she snapped her fingers—"like rubber cement or something. Well, not rubber cement, but like that glue you use when you're a kid that dries and it will kind of hold things together, but if you touch it, it rolls off?"

"How's everything going over here?" interrupted an officious-looking little woman with way too much blue eye shadow. She appeared to be the manager, or someone who thought herself to be an authority, because she gave Lexi a quick once-over, but when she turned her attention to Holly, her brows relaxed and she pasted a false smile on. "Do you have any questions?"

Behind her, Lexi's face reddened, but she didn't say anything.

So Holly did. "I'm sorry, maybe you didn't see, but I'm already working with someone." She gestured toward Lexi.

The woman, whose name tag identified her as GARDA, whispered to Lexi, "You just called one of our products 'total crap.' I *heard* you."

"Well, it *is*. And it's overpriced."

Garda gave Lexi a dismissive glance and said to Holly, "She's new. . . ." She let that dangle, as if it explained why she felt like she just had to jump in the middle of things and humiliate her employee.

"Hm. I'd never know it. She's really well versed in the products and honest, which I *appreciate*." Holly gave a tight smile. "Thanks, anyway, though." She looked to Lexi, and said, "Sorry, where were you?"

Garda turned on her heel and left, practically *harrumph*ing as she went.

"Thanks," Lexi whispered. "She's been doing that all night. Most of the time, people start talking to her instead of me because she's so"—she shrugged—"forceful, I guess."

"Is she your boss?"

Lexi shook her head. "But I think she thinks she is." She gave a quick, dazzling smile, and again Holly had a strange sense that she knew her. "There's always at least one girl like that in every room, hating anyone who might steal her thunder, even if it's just because she knows more about shampoo."

"It's pretty obvious who knows more about makeup between the two of you."

Lexi laughed. "Well, thanks. I think."

Holly felt sorry for Lexi. Now that Holly got a better look, she could see that Lexi was a little older than the other girls working there. She might be late twenties or early thirties versus the average twenty-one that everyone else seemed to be. But she looked fantastic—better than the rest of them.

Without interference from the likes of Garda, customers would probably gravitate toward Lexi, given the chance.

"Anyway, about the mascara," Lexi went on, unwrapping a disposable mascara brush and dipping it into the tube, "it coats your lashes and then dries, so when you wash it off, it comes off in chunks instead of liquefying." She grimaced. "I'm not describing this very well, but honestly, it's awesome stuff. Because it dries that way, it will never, ever rub off under your eyes or on your clothes, or *his* clothes, or anywhere else. It's weird but cool." She handed the brush to Holly.

"It does sound weird." Holly brushed it over her lashes.

"New Japanese technology." Lexi laughed. "That's what they say, anyway."

Holly blinked and looked in the mirror. It was nice. "And it really won't come off under my eyes and make me look like a panda?"

Lexi held up her hand. "Girl Scout's honor."

"Hm. Can I do the other eye?"

"I'm already on it." Lexi handed her another brush. "I always had to do both, too. When I was just a customer, I mean. I hate it when they're stingy and let you do only half your face so you have to either buy the stuff and get symmetrical or look like an idiot all the way home."

"Me, too." Holly leaned in to do her other eye. "So is that why you work here? Because you shopped here all the time and needed the discount?"

"Actually, I work here because my father died and my stepmother kept all his money and I had no other skills beyond shopping for makeup and wearing clothes I can no longer afford." She gave a laugh. "That's my new thing. Telling the truth."

"Bold."

"I know, right?" Lexi laughed and handed Holly a shadow brush. "Try this on your eyelids. I think it will really bring out the green in your eyes."

"I barely have any."

"That's why you need to bring it out." She waited while Holly smoothed on a golden brown shadow that was so obviously her perfect color that she decided she would trust anything else Lexi said. "Did I mention that my father's wife gave me a week to move out of the house I grew up in, so now I'm living with a guy who drinks beer for breakfast and wears wifebeaters with a straight face?"

"Beer for breakfast?"

"Practically." Lexi made a face and handed Holly a round sponge. "He drinks beer, anyway. I think he even makes it in the garage."

Holly looked at the sponge. "What do I do with this?"

"It's Lorac's cheek stamp. The coral looks good on almost everyone. Here." She dabbed it on the apples of Holly's cheeks, and Holly mentally added it to her shopping bag. "But I'll give him this," Lexi went on. "He gave me a rent I can afford in exchange for me helping him fix up his house, even though I am clearly not cut out for it."

Holly looked at her. "So you like him?"

"He's okay." Lexi shrugged. "A whole lot better than Stepmother Dearest." She handed Holly a Q-tip with red goo on it. "Try this. Dolce Vita lip gloss. It's my favorite."

Stepmother Dearest. Holly had heard that one before. Who was it that used to say it?

Wait a minute—

Holly straightened and looked at her, Q-tip still in hand.

Really looked at her.

"It's not so dark when you put it on," Lexi said, misunderstanding Holly's expression. "Seriously. It's pretty neutral."

God, it even *sounded* like her. Sort of. As far as Holly could remember.

How had she not seen this before?

Lexi was . . . *Lexi. Shit, what's her last name?*

"Whose?" Lexi asked.

Holly hadn't realized she'd asked the question out loud. "Yours," she said. Then she smiled, trying to make the question less creepy. "You look familiar."

Lexi gave her a blank look. "Henderson."

Oh, of course. Of *course.* It was Lexi Henderson.

The girl who had been the source of so *much* of Holly's preteen angst. A girl she had confronted over and over again in her imagination, for years.

Now, here she was, right in front of her.

As pretty as ever.

Holly felt ill. "I've got . . . to go. . . ." She couldn't think. Couldn't come up with a coherent excuse.

Part of her felt compelled to be polite, but part wanted to slap Lexi across the face and leave.

Neither part won.

She just left.

"Ma'am?" Lexi called behind her, like some crazy echo of her former self. Not real. "What about your stuff?"

"I don't need it," Holly tossed over her shoulder, quickening her pace. This couldn't be real.

She went out into the mall, feeling like she could breathe only when she was lost in the anonymity of the crowd in the food court.

Lexi Henderson waiting on Holly at Sephora? It just didn't compute. It was just too weird. And on top of that, she'd been nice. Or she'd *seemed* nice. She probably had to—it was her job.

But since when did someone as rich as Lexi Henderson need a job at all, much less one in sales?

Holly bought a lemonade from Pretzel Time and paced back and forth, trying to decide what to do. She wanted to leave, but if she did, she'd lose this chance—such as it was—to make some sense of that old chapter in her life where one girl had bullied her into feeling insignificant.

Drawn by an instinct she couldn't quite name, Holly went back to Sephora and peered in the window from the side, out of sight. It took a couple of minutes, but she saw Lexi in the back corner, with her manager and the smug salesgirl who had tried to interrupt the sale earlier. Garda.

Lexi looked upset.

Holly made her way into the crowded store and casually got as close as she could to the scene without being noticed.

"She's trying to say you're driving customers away," Garda snapped at Lexi. "Two in one night! First there was that one you told not to buy the new Desia moisturizer because it was overpriced—"

"Garda," the manager cautioned. "Alexis, I'm just not sure this is a good fit for you. Why don't you go home for the night and come for a meeting with me before opening tomorrow? We'll talk about it then."

"But I need the hours tonight," Lexi began, then stopped. "Fine. What time should I be here?"

"Nine."

Lexi nodded and headed into the back room.

"She told that woman to go to Target," Garda said. "I *heard* her. She said this stuff cost too much and that she wasn't getting a commission anyway so she didn't mind telling the truth."

The manager frowned. "You heard that?"

Garda nodded.

Holly felt like she should step in and set the record straight, but she didn't know if Garda was talking about Lexi or not. This didn't seem like a situation Holly could fix.

Lexi swept out of the back room before Holly even had a chance to think everything through. She stepped back, looking down at the Urban Decay products intently until she knew, from surreptitious glances, that Lexi had left.

So she followed her.

Holly had never been stealth in her life—as Lexi herself could attest—so she couldn't say exactly why it seemed like a good idea to try it now. All she knew was that she couldn't stop.

Lexi went to the McDonald's counter at the food court. Luckily, Holly blended easily into the crowd. Lexi wasn't looking for her, had no idea who she was, so there was little danger of being spotted.

As she got closer, she heard Lexi ordering a couple of items off of the dollar menu. A double cheeseburger. Fries. A Coke.

It was far from extravagant.

But a few seconds after she handed her credit card over to pay, the kid at the cash register said, "Your card was declined."

"What?" She honestly looked like she couldn't comprehend this. "Can you try it again?"

"I ran it through twice."

"But I just put money in after the last—" She shook her head, defeated, and took the card back. The useless card.

Holly watched her go through the automatic door and out onto the sidewalk. There were fewer people out there. Holly couldn't go out without being spotted, and what could she say?

So she stood, frozen, next to the Panda Express counter and watched as Lexi lowered her head into her hands, and her shoulders started to shake.

She was crying.

Holly swallowed a lump in her throat. What had happened to Lexi? How had she gone from being the spoiled rich girl to someone who couldn't pay three dollars for food?

It was sad. No matter what she'd ever done, it was sad.

And if any part of this was because of her, she had to do something. She moved tentatively outside.

"Excuse me," she said, moving closer to Lexi's back as if approaching a potentially hostile dog.

Lexi looked up, wiping at her eyes. They were red and puffy. "Yes? Oh. It's you."

"Yeah, look, I'm sorry I had to go earlier. I had . . . something."
This was graceless. She didn't know what to say.

"Don't worry about it," Lexi said. "You weren't obliged to buy anything."

"Well, no, but I left because I was a little . . . disconcerted. I think
we might know each other. That is, I used to know a Lexi at camp."
This was tricky. "Well, I didn't really *know* her, but we were in the
same cabin."

"Maybe. I went to camp," Lexi said, then looked at Holly more
closely. "For years. Until I was, I don't know, thirteen."

"Camp Catoctin?"

Lexi sniffed and stood up, wiping her hands on her pants. "Yes."

There it was. If there had been any lingering doubt, it was gone now.
"I think we were in cabin Seven together when we were thirteen,"
Holly said. "With my friend Nicola, and Tami . . ." She tried to remem-
ber Tami's last name. "Something. And another friend of yours."

"Sylvia," Lexi said immediately, then gave a halfhearted laugh.
"Ugh. She was no friend of mine, believe me. She was such a bitch."
She frowned, still blotchy from crying. "Can I say that now about a
thirteen-year-old without sounding like a bitch myself?"

Holly certainly hoped so, for all the times she'd thought of Lexi
that way. "I thought you guys were pals."

Lexi gave another short laugh. "I had to act like that or risk being
on the wrong side of her wrath."

This was a point of view Holly would never have anticipated.
"Really?"

Lexi nodded. "Oh, God, yes. You should have seen some of the
things she did to the other girls there."

"I can only imagine." Except she didn't have to imagine; she knew
exactly the kinds of things Sylvia and Lexi and Tami had inflicted.

"My mom had just died, my father married that witch"—Lexi made a face—"my life was a mess enough without having Sylvia torment me in front of everyone at that stupid dance or something."

Holly looked at Lexi, really studied her, to try to find some sign of the person she'd spent twenty years believing her to be. But all she saw was a girl who was as screwed over by the Mean Girls as she and Nicola were. Maybe worse. At least she and Nicola had each other.

"So what's your name?" Lexi asked. "Because, I'm really sorry, you just don't look familiar."

It was hard to believe someone Holly had given so much thought to in the years after camp had completely forgotten her. In a way, it was a relief. "I'm Holly. Holly Kazanov. We were thirteen. It was the last year before we were too old to go there."

"But . . ." Lexi hesitated. "That summer it was me, Tami Ryland, Sylvia Farelle, and I do remember there were those other two girls. The tall skinny one and the—" She stopped.

Holly raised her hand. "Short fat one. I know."

"Oh, I didn't mean . . ." Lexi grimaced, then sighed. "Well, you know I did. I'm not going to lie. But, wow, you look fantastic!"

"Thanks to your makeup."

Lexi waved the idea away. "You look good. Not like the awkward thirteen-year-olds we all were at the time. So what ever happened to your friend? The tall skinny one? I was so jealous of you two."

Holly couldn't believe her ears. "*You* were jealous of *us*?"

"Of course. I think we all were. You two were the only ones who had a real friend at camp. Everyone knew it. Even Sylvia."

"Ironic, since the only reason we *needed* each other was because you guys were so awful to us."

Lexi looked ashamed. "Are you two still in touch?"

"Yes."

Lexi smiled. "That's really cool. You two did everything together, as I recall. I never had a friend like that. Ever."

It was amazing to Holly how Lexi could say the saddest things about her life without a trace of self-pity, even after what Holly had just witnessed. It was like she was just reporting on the misfortunes of someone else.

"So where is she now?" Lexi asked. "What did you say her name was? Nicki or something?"

"Nicola. Nicola Kestle."

"No kidding. Like the girl in that movie."

"*Duet.* That was her." Holly felt pride in saying it. She always had—*my friend Nicola, you know, the star of* Duet—but never more than right now when she could reveal the connection to someone who had known Nicola Back When.

Lexi's jaw dropped. "Are you kidding? I loved that movie!"

"I know! Me, too!"

"Wow." Lexi shook her head. "That's really something. You'll have to tell her I said hi."

"She'll be astonished," Holly said, but the words sounded flat. "So . . . listen . . . are you okay?" She floundered for a better way to say it but came up short. "I mean, you seemed kind of upset."

Lexi looked at her dead-on and gave a small but distinctly gracious smile. "Yes," she said. "I'm fine." She left no doubt at all that the topic wasn't up for discussion.

"Well. Cool." This was so awkward. "I guess I'll be on my way, then. Do you need a ride anywhere?"

She gave a laugh. She knew what Holly was thinking. "Thanks, but I have my car."

"Well." Holly shrugged. "It was good to see you again."

"You, too, Holly. Really."

Holly walked away, half wishing she hadn't witnessed any of this. Wishing she didn't have to feel this way now. Because it wasn't her responsibility. It wasn't her problem. And there wasn't anything she could do to help if Lexi was broke and out a job—

That's when she remembered the one most important thing about her history with Lexi.

It wasn't how Lexi had laughed at her when her boat went down in the little lake at Camp Catoctin, or the way she'd flounced in and out of the cabin as if she were better than anyone else.

Holly didn't care about any of that stuff anymore. It wasn't the details that had affected her afterwards; it was the way it had all made her feel.

And even that didn't matter now.

What mattered was that twenty years ago, she and Nicola had stolen from Lexi the one thing that might help get her out of the situation she was in now.

That ring.

That huge diamond ring.

It was still out there in the woods somewhere.

17

Nicola pressed the accelerator of her BMW Roadster and whipped around a curve on the PCH, narrowly missing a car that was doing the same in the opposite direction.

Evidently Friday evening was a popular time for the depressed to become reckless.

What was she doing? At thirty-three, she was a washed-up has-been. Or maybe just a sorta-was. And that should have been fine with her; she had invested pretty well, spent cautiously, hell, even the Roadster had been her agent's hand-me-down after his 007 phase had passed.

She should have been content to have had a hit and been set up so well financially.

That was what really got to her right now. She'd gotten further than 99 percent of actors did, and she should have been satisfied with that. Instead, she kept subjecting herself to one bad fit of an audition after another until eventually she had made the *critical* mistake of trying to make *herself* fit into those bad-fit roles.

Then today she'd heard that Ed Macziulkas's casting director—after asking for her *specifically,* to work on that script that had been written *with her in mind*—had passed on her, saying that she had "fucked her face up" and was "no longer interesting."

Oh, she'd fucked up all right. She'd *finally* given in to the pressures of society's demands for female attractiveness, and she'd lost what might have been her Comeback Role.

On top of that, the only seeming benefit of her nose job—getting a date with good ol' Trick—had backfired so enormously that she wondered why she'd ever wanted to run with the pretty people.

"Shit!" She pounded her hands against the steering wheel. "Shit shit *shit!*"

Hindsight was 20/20, of course, but it did suddenly seem painfully obvious that she'd never heard any great success stories about actresses who changed their look via irreversible cosmetic surgery.

Sure, there was speculation that Angelina Jolie might have had her nose done at some point. Or maybe she'd just matured—frankly, Nicola didn't think it was that obvious. The more applicable example was Carolina Madden, who'd Botoxed herself into a waxen statue and gotten a job . . . advertising Botox. The "Express Yourself" with Botox might have been a success, but it was pitiful watching Carolina trying to demonstrate facial expressions, and worse still knowing that was as far as she'd go now.

What could Nicola do now?

Unlike Carolina Madden, she didn't look anything like herself. She realized that now, even though it was painful and surreal. It was as if she would wear a Halloween costume for the rest of her life; the crazy person dressed up as Marilyn Monroe or Jason from *Friday the*

13th at odd times, who had to explain, "No, no, it's really *me*, Nicola Kestle, under here. I just can't take the costume off."

Apart from finding out if Kiss had room for a nonmusical member, or joining Blue Man Group, she couldn't imagine what job she could get in show business at this point.

And that was the most depressing thing of all. She wasn't in it for the money; she never had been. She wanted to *act*. She loved the process. She'd loved being on stage in seventh grade, she'd loved singing in front of a crowd in twelfth grade, and then she'd gotten the opportunity to work in film, and she'd loved that most of all.

Now she'd blown it.

She rounded another corner, this time perilously close to the outside edge, the cliff.

Not that she was actually suicidal. She felt like shit, for sure, but she didn't want to die.

She just wanted the adrenaline to take over and push the self-pity and hopelessness out of her veins.

By the time she got to the exit at Redondo Beach, she was a little less fiery and a little more resigned. She'd changed her face, and that had changed her life. Her career. Things would never be the same again.

Maybe no one would say she was *so ugly* at a four-way stop for a while, but it was equally clear that she wasn't going to get a good job again, either.

This one she'd just lost, though—the one tailor-made for her—that was going to hurt for a long time.

Her phone rang, and the tone made her jump. She scrambled to find it in her purse, hoping against hope that Ed Macziulkas and the producers of the *Nicola Kestle-esque Project* had overridden the casting director's initial veto and wanted her for the role.

"Hello?" she answered breathlessly.

"Oh. My God. You will not believe who I just ran into." It was Holly.

"Hey, Holly." Nicola's disappointment was so great that she wasn't sure she could be trusted to have this conversation and drive at the same time. She pulled into a shopping center parking lot. "What's up?" She knew her voice sounded weary. She couldn't help it.

They were probably smart not to hire her if she couldn't even fake that she was glad to hear from her best friend.

"Don't get too excited," Holly said with a laugh.

Nicola wasn't feeling jovial. "Sorry." She didn't mean it. She was bitter. It took this call from her friend, and her unfair anger about it, to make her realize she was really, really bitter. "I'm not having the greatest day."

"Did something happen?" Holly was immediately soft and sympathetic. "Are you okay?"

"Fine." Nicola felt guilty for wasting Holly's sympathy on her own piss-poor mood, thanks to something that was entirely of her own making. "Really. It's just one of those days." She forced joviality into her voice. "So distract me. Who did you just run into?"

"Lexi. Henderson." There was a tense silence on the other end of the line, like Holly was waiting, and holding her breath, for some great response.

Who the hell was Lexi Henderson?

If Nicola had been at home, she might have fumbled for a minute, quietly Googling the name, but she was in the parking lot shared by a Target and a PetSmart, with no Google capability whatsoever.

"Really?" she asked noncommittally.

"Yes! Oh my God, I couldn't believe it! She was working at Sephora in Montgomery Mall, can you believe it?"

That ruled out Lexi Henderson as a famous actress, politician, or model.

Well, maybe not model. Maybe some semifamous model had made a brief splash on *America's Next Top Model,* then sank, and was now working at Sephora.

"Wow." That didn't sound enthusiastic enough. Nicola ratcheted up the perk. "How did she look?"

"Fan-flippin'-tastic. Of course. What would you expect?"

"Fan-flippin'-tastic."

"I know! It was disgusting in a way. I mean, at first she was just some salesgirl helping me and doing a really great job of it, so I was beholden to her, right? Then she said something that made me realize, oh my God, this is *Lexi Henderson,* so I looked at her differently. Of course. It was quite an emotional roller coaster."

Nicola was still clueless and trying to play it cool. "What do you mean?"

"Well, obviously, you run into Lexi Henderson twenty years later and she's waiting on you in Sephora, you get a totally different perspective on her. And yourself."

Twenty years later. Nicola racked her brain. Twenty years ago. She'd just met Holly. At camp. Camp camp camp . . .

"Oh my God, *Lexi Henderson?*"

There was a puzzled moment before Holly responded, "Um . . . yes. Hello? Were you not here for this entire conversation I just— Oh my God, you forgot who she was!"

"No, I didn't."

"You totally did. I'm saying *Lexi Henderson* and you're thinking, *Is that some Minneapolis news anchor?*"

"I did not think that!"

"Then you thought something exactly like that and tried to fake your way through the conversation."

"Maybe."

"So are you up to speed now?" Holly asked with a good-natured laugh. "You know who I'm talking about?"

"Totally." Nicola gave a firm nod, even though Holly couldn't see her. "Now, repeat all the other stuff you said, because I forgot it once I remembered who the hell you were talking about."

"Oh, for God's sake."

"I'm sorry! I'm not always a mind reader!"

"Okay, Lexi Henderson. Blond. Pretty. Mean. You know who I'm talking about?"

"Affirmative."

"If you're going to be sarcastic—"

"Okay, fine, *yes*. I remember her. She was a bitch."

"Right. Or *was* she?"

"I seriously think she was. What makes you think she wasn't?"

"First of all, she was really nice before I realized who she was. But, granted, she was trying to sell me stuff. But then we got talking, and it came out that *Sylvia* was the real one in charge. The Queen Bee, so to speak. And I really think she was telling the truth, or at least that she believed what she was saying."

"Sylvia?"

"Are you kidding?" Silence plunked down between them. "Suddenly you didn't live before you graduated from college?"

"Oh, *Sylvia*!"

"Really?" Holly challenged. "Or is that *oh, Sylvia* like it was *oh, Lexi* a few minutes ago?"

"No, no, this one I remember." Who could forget weird Sylvia, with her frosted blond hair (at age thirteen!), pig nose, and bad skin?

How did she end up ruling the roost for every girl at camp? Holly had been prettier than Sylvia. Lexi certainly had. How was it that Sylvia had dominated them all when she might have been the most vulnerable of any?

Sheer will, Nicola concluded immediately. She'd seen it a hundred times before, and she was sure she'd see it a hundred more times before she hit forty.

"Good. So it turns out that *Sylvia* was the force behind all Lexi's evil. And I'm not giving Lexi a pass on everything—believe me, I'm skeptical—but from what Lexi said, she was scared to go against Sylvia because she didn't want to be the target. I can understand that."

"I don't know. That Lexi was pretty mean."

"Yeah. She definitely was. I'm only saying that you never know what's going on behind people's actions, you know?"

"That's for sure." Nicola sighed. It was hard to feel sorry for gorgeous, rich, confident Lexi. If she'd had all those gifts at thirteen, surely she had the strength to stand up to Sylvia if she'd wanted to. "So that *is* pretty interesting that you ran into her."

"I haven't even gotten to the interesting part yet," Holly went on, and, after a dramatic pause, said, "She's flat broke."

"Broke? How is that possible? She was so rich! Wasn't her dad some sort of industry chief?"

"I can't remember what he did, but he's dead now."

Nicola felt a pang. Her own father had died ten years ago, and she didn't wish that kind of sadness on anyone. "Recently?"

"I think it must have been. Because this broke thing seemed pretty new to her. As was the job. This is her first week."

"But not her first job, I'm sure."

"I don't know. It sure sounded like it. And given how rich she was, she might have been one of those spoiled rich girls who walks around with a little white dog in her purse and shops for recreation, with all the bills going to Daddy." Holly groaned. "I wish I were one of those girls."

"You do not. You'd be bored out of your skull the first day."

"Maybe. Anyway, Lexi was saying her dad left everything to her stepmother. *Everything.* And she did seem like she was still in some shock about it."

"Oh, the stepmother I remember. Lexi complained about her constantly."

"Well, I guess she had good reason to, because not only did she keep all the money, but she kicked Lexi out of the house. Lexi's living with some guy in exchange for working on his house."

"No way. There is no way I believe that. She's playing you." Nicola shook her head to herself. "That's what amateurs do, they always add that one detail that takes everything too far. I believed it all the way up to that point."

"I don't think she's lying." Holly's tone was serious. "Look, you were nominated for a Golden Globe, and I didn't buy your *I remember Lexi* act. There's no way this girl was outacting you."

"Come on, you've known me for twenty years. Of course you know when I'm lying. You can be a good actor but a bad liar." She remembered a guy she'd slept with last year. He seemed so perfect until she found out he was married. "Or a bad actor and a *great* liar."

"I'm telling you—she wasn't lying. In a way, it was the absurdity of that detail that made it ring true. Whatever. I believe her—and when you see her, you'll see what I mean."

That brought Nicola up short. "What do you mean when I see her?"

"You and I need to fix this for her."

"Fix *what* for her?"

"We've got to get the ring back."

The ring. Shit. Nicola had forgotten all about that. "Are you out of your mind? I'm not coming back and digging around in the woods for some old cubic zirconia."

"You said you were *sure* it was fake!"

"Yeah, well, I was also sure we'd be going right back out the next day to get it back once Lexi had freaked out."

Nicola remembered what it had felt like that night, walking through the inky darkness and being startled by the camp counselors appearing out of nowhere and marching her and Holly back to their cabin.

"Come on, Hol, do you really think that was a real diamond? I don't even see how that's possible. Do you know how much it would have been worth? Good Lord, there's no way her stepmother would have let her get away with that!"

"Her stepmother might have had no idea she was the one who took it. You know how rich people are—they have maids, gardeners, drivers, all kinds of people working in and around the house. If they noticed a big, ostentatious ring was missing, they probably wouldn't have leapt to the conclusion that an adolescent kid had taken it."

"I guess you could be right."

"What if I am? I don't even know if I should hope I'm right or wrong, but if there's any possibility that the ring was real and *we stole it,* that's a *felony!*"

A sick feeling balled up in Nicola's stomach. "And you're thinking that if she's broke now and *if* that ring was real, it could really help her out."

"Exactly."

"Assuming it's still there and they haven't razed the entire Camp Catoctin area to make a housing development or something."

"I already looked it up online. It's still there, same as ever. You can see the whole area on Google Earth."

"Can you see the ring?"

"Very funny."

"Did you tell Lexi any of this?"

There was a long hesitation. "No. Truthfully, I didn't think of it until I was leaving the store but . . ." She sighed. "I don't know, would there be any point in telling her? What if she got her hopes up and it was all for nothing?"

Nicola could see that point, but there was more. "And what if you tell someone you did something terrible to them and then you have no way to rectify it? If we told her the truth then couldn't find the ring, all we'd be doing is reminding her of something painful."

"And potentially setting ourselves up for liability."

Nicola doubted that. "We were underage."

"But we haven't been for fifteen years. There could be some legal loophole where you're responsible for *not* returning something if you know about it once you're of age."

"Holly."

"What?"

"That's ridiculous. And you know it's not the point."

"Okay, the point is that we did something really, really wrong. And, I'll admit it, I'm ashamed to go to that poor woman now and confess it. But at the same time, does it serve any purpose *at all* to tell her about it if we can't get the ring back? I mean this sincerely—I think all we'd be doing is stirring up a bunch of angst."

"Or answering a question she's been asking for a long, long time."

"Or stirring up angst."

"Okay, or both." But Nicola knew that if something that meant a lot to her had been stolen twenty years ago, she'd probably still be wondering what the hell happened to it and if there was any way to find it.

Admittedly, she hadn't remembered Lexi's name when Holly first said it, but now that she was thinking about her, Nicola could clearly picture that blond-haired girl lying four feet away on her bottom bunk, staring at that ring every night as she went to sleep, as if she were wishing on a star.

Whether or not the ring had had any great monetary value, it was clear it had a *lot* of sentimental value.

"You've been saying you wanted to come for a visit anyway," Holly was saying. "Maybe you weren't exactly planning on traipsing around in the woods of the Catoctins, but, hey, it will be good quality time for us to spend together."

Nicola laughed. "It's definitely not what I had in mind. But I miss those East Coast twilights, and it's been a long time since I really dug in the dirt. It might do me some good."

"And if things go as they should, it will do Lexi some good," Holly said, then added, "which, okay, I'll admit, will do our guilty hearts some good, too. It's a win–win–win situation."

"Hopefully."

"Yeah, hopefully. So can you come?"

"I don't know." Nicola thought about the alternative. She could stay here and continue to drag her sorry, pessimistic butt to auditions when she was in a foul mood; she could hang out in her house, watching less-talented actors make more money on sitcoms than she had made for a hit movie; or she could go to Maryland and try to shake off the weirdness she was feeling, possibly coming to some sort of new peace.

"Randy broke up with me," Holly said suddenly.

"*What? When?*"

"A little more than a week ago. I would have said something sooner, but . . . I was hoping it wouldn't stick. I didn't want to tell you and have you hate him and then . . ." Over the phone line, it sounded like Holly took a shaky breath. "Whatever. I could really use a visit, regardless of the ring, though I think that would be a fun adventure, if nothing else. What do you say? Could you take even a couple of days away?"

Now it didn't seem like that hard a decision.

"I'll let you know my flight information in a few hours," Nicola said. "Meanwhile, get a map and some Deep Woods Off! We're going on an adventure."

18

The decision to move to Greg's had been easy. Not only did it seem like fate, running into him that way, but it wasn't a huge commitment. She could still take her time finding a more permanent solution to her housing problems, so she wouldn't end up stuck in a terrible place or living with an awful roommate.

Which was more to the point: Given the potential roommates she'd encountered, his "known evil" seemed far less risky than the "unknown evil" she might have ended up with instead.

"This will be your room," he said, opening the door on a room that was about half the size of the one she'd had at the house in Potomac. There was no attached bathroom, so needless to say, no Jacuzzi tub or bidet.

It was a simple room with hardwood floors and a view of a wildly overgrown garden out back.

She could get used to it.

"Think you can deal with it?" Greg asked. "I mean, I know where you're coming from, and this isn't quite so lavish."

"Not quite." She smiled. "But it's perfect. Really."

"The bathroom across the hall is yours. You can put all that girlie stuff of yours in there."

"How do you know what I—?" She stopped. He knew everything about the way she kept her room and bathroom. He'd traipsed through them countless times over the past few weeks. "Never mind."

"You gonna miss it?" he asked, and something about the sincerity in his eyes made her feel a little like sinking into him and just crying away the weeks of hurt and confusion she'd experienced.

"I don't know," she said honestly. "I left in such a hurry. . . ."

"You kind of had to. You ran out of time."

She nodded. "It was hard to say good-bye. To think about it. I grew up there, you know. My whole life, I didn't realize it was such a palace."

"No, it was home."

Lexi remembered an entry in her mother's journal. She'd written it to a four-year-old Lexi. Her father had hit it big, and her parents were moving to the house in Potomac. *Tomorrow we're moving to the house on Carriage House Drive*, she'd written, and even her handwriting had seemed to show her excitement for the new place. *You'll just know it as "home," of course, and it will be the place where you and your siblings will grow up. Maybe you'll even get married in the backyard someday, by the pond your daddy has promised to put in back by the weeping willow tree. . . .* The pond had never materialized.

Neither had the siblings.

It seemed almost nothing had gone the way Anna Henderson hoped.

"Exactly," Lexi said, trying to shake the mood. "It was home. But it isn't anymore." Saying it didn't make the pain go away, but it reminded her of the truth. It *wasn't* home anymore. It wouldn't have done her any good to sit around in the rubble and dust, reminiscing with herself about how it used to be or could have been and how horrible Michelle was for taking Lexi's mother's home for herself. "And this is perfect. Why are you selling it?"

"It's what I do. I flip houses. Not so much as I used to a decade ago when the market was hot, but it's still a pretty nice financial supplement."

"Aren't you attached to it?" she asked. The place was adorable. *She* could get attached to it. "Won't you miss it?"

He shook his head. "All I see is the structure and what I can sell."

"Hm." It was like what everyone said about ob-gyns—they stopped looking at a woman's parts as a roller coaster and saw them clinically.

She didn't know him well enough to joke that his house was a vagina.

Instead, she said, "Even a few months here will give me time to get back on my feet and move on."

He studied her. "You'll have to tell me about that sometime."

She laughed. "Tell me when you've got all night."

"I've got all night tonight."

She didn't know what to say.

He must have sensed that because he added, "I'm serious. I've got a six of Sam Adams and all the time in the world. Let's order Chinese, and you can tell me what I've gotten myself into by letting you move in."

"It would bore you to tears."

Again he gave that smile. "You have the capability of doing a lot of things to me," he said, and even though he did not move his eyes from hers, she suddenly felt naked under his gaze. "Boring me is not one of them."

A tingle ran through her. Oh, no. No, no, no. She could *not* get the hots for this guy. That was one thing she absolutely could not afford. "Not tonight," she said, her voice a lot stiffer than the molten lava that her insides had become. "But another time, maybe. Thanks."

The spell was broken somewhat the next morning when she encountered the kitchen. Or, rather, the room that would have been the kitchen if it weren't just a receptacle for dirty dishes and beer bottles.

"How can you live like this?" she asked incredulously. "I can't even find a toaster to heat up a bagel. And I'm pretty sure I wouldn't be able to find a plate, either."

"What are you talking about?" Greg asked over a cup of coffee and the Metro section of *The Washington Post*. "There's about fifty of them in the sink."

"A *clean* one," she corrected. "This is just . . . ew. I did not sign up for this."

"Ahh . . . You should have read the fine print."

"There was no print."

"You didn't sign the contract?" He was trying not to smile.

She put a hand on her hip. "You mean the contract *you* didn't sign, either? I think you might have missed the fine print my imaginary lawyer put in, too. Like the part about you doing your dishes *as you use them*."

He laughed outright. "Touché. I'll have my imaginary lawyer contact your imaginary lawyer and hash this out."

"Ugh. This is so gross."

"I know," he said. "I had some guys over for preseason football a couple of days ago and we grilled out. I just haven't had time to deal with it yet. It'll be clean tonight."

"Yes, it will." She turned on the water. "And in the future, you should get paper plates."

"Hey, what are you doing?" He put his cup down and came up be-hind her. "Don't do that. I don't want you doing my work."

"It's the only way I can be in this house and breathe," she joked weakly. He was so close to her back, she could feel the heat coming off his body. "Leave me alone to do this."

"No way." He elbowed her out of the way and reached for the dish soap.

"Greg!"

"If you *have* to have this clean, I'm doing it myself," he said, then glanced at the clock over the stove. "Or at least whatever I can get done in the next five minutes."

She stepped back and put up her hands. She wasn't going to fight that hard for the "prize" of doing some guy's dishes. "This is why it's a good idea to clean as you go along."

"That's what my mother says."

"She's right."

He raised an eyebrow at her, then returned to rinsing the dishes and putting them in the drying rack. There really weren't so many as she'd initially thought.

"You know what you need?" she asked, leaning back against the wall.

"A new roommate?"

"No, a dishwasher."

"Maybe my new roommate could be a dishwasher."

She smirked. "Very funny. *Or* you could get an automatic dish-washer, like everyone else in the world has. It gets dishes a lot more sanitary than that stuff you're doing there does."

He stopped and looked back at her again. "I'm updating the entire kitchen while you paint the front rooms. Don't worry your pretty little head about it, Blondie—you'll have your dishwasher. At least until the place sells."

"What a relief."

He finished the last dish, wiped his hands on a bar rag that was hanging next to the sink, then turned back to her. "Tonight. Here. You and me. We're going to talk."

Dread coursed through her. That was the kind of thing Michelle used to say. "Why?" She hated that her voice sounded so small and defensive.

"Because I hardly know a thing about you," he said simply. "And I want to. I know you're not that great at talking about yourself, but I'm hoping after a couple of beers and some lo mein the stories might flow."

She smiled. Genuinely smiled, from her heart. That was so nice. "Make it merlot, and you've got a deal."

"Is that the only condition?"

"So far . . ." It had been a long time since she'd flirted.

It felt good.

He gave a single nod. "Fine. See you here at seven."

"Done. Meanwhile I'll paint the front room that awful tan shade you picked out."

"Excellent."

She walked on air for the rest of the day.

"It never occurred to me that you might need to be told how to paint a wall." Greg took his Washington Nationals baseball cap off and scratched his head.

He'd been at her father's house all day while she painted the front room. Until now, she'd thought it was the *color* that made it hideous, not the paint job.

"Didn't you notice the holes as you went along?" he asked. "Any of them, if not all nineteen thousand of them?"

She noticed them now. Tons of tiny nail holes, all the more obvious because she'd just painted the wall a pale beige. "I figured they would be less noticeable when the paint dried."

Greg looked at her with a raised eyebrow. "Yeah?"

Her face felt warm under his gaze. "In fact, I thought the paint would *fill in* the holes. Obviously I see now that it's not the case."

"Good." He started to walk away. "Then spackle and repaint tomorrow."

"Spackle?"

He stopped, looked at her, then let out a long sigh and went to the pile of painting supplies he'd left in the room for her. Most were untouched.

She was actually proud of the job she'd done, apart from the holes, because she hadn't dripped paint anywhere. There was a tarp included with his supplies, but when she'd tried to lay it down, it was so thin that walking on it made it get caught in her shoes and rustle up the wall. She figured she was better off going without it and cleaning up any spots as they occurred, because she *did* know that latex paint was water soluble.

Apparently she wasn't going to get any kudos at all for being tidy.

"This"—he held up a big tube that looked like toothpaste—"is spackle."

"Okay. What do I do with it?"

"Good you should ask." He gave a quick smile and picked up a tool. "*This* is a putty knife. Now come here, Blondie, I'll show you how to use them *together*."

She narrowed her eyes. "You're kind of enjoying this, aren't you?"

"I am. I shouldn't be, but I am."

"A couple of months ago, I could have bought and sold you."

"That's what's making this so much fun."

She nodded and headed toward him. "Don't you owe me dinner? And some sort of alcohol product?"

"I think we said seven." He took the lid off the not-toothpaste tube. "Meanwhile, here's a lesson for tomorrow." He took her hand and put the tube in it. "Squeeze a tiny bit of that into the hole you're filling." He nodded at her. "Go on."

She tried. It came out in a rush and a big blob of it hung on the wall for a moment before falling to the ground.

She looked at Greg. "Too much?"

He laughed. "Little big. Here." He came up behind her and held her hand up, squeezing the tube with her fingers so just a little came out. "See? Then you take the putty knife." He handed it to her and guided it, in her hand, to the spot, and smoothed it over, leaving a smooth, if discolored, surface. "And . . . that's it."

He was so warm behind her, and the feel of his hands on hers was so comforting that she had to fight herself not to collapse against him.

"I'm not sure I got that," she said. "Can you do it again?" She was glad she wasn't looking at him because her face would have shown too much.

"It's not rocket science, Blondie. Put the spackle on," he did, "then smooth it over. Easy."

"What do you do with the mess left on that?" She pointed to the putty knife, even though she already figured she could hang a rag from her waistband and wipe it on there.

He let go of her and walked around, probably not noticing the way her face was flushed. "For this, you just take a paper towel and wipe it off."

"Got it."

"Are you sure?"

She cocked her head and gave him a look. "Pretty sure, Greg."

"Great. So *after* all the spackle has dried, which means it will turn from that pink color to white, you can paint over it again."

"Got it."

"No questions?"

"Only one."

"What's that?"

"Why are you painting this room such a dull, blah shade? Look at all the sunlight that comes in here. If you went with a light butter yellow, it would look so pretty!"

"No." He smiled. "We're going for *neutral* here."

She liked the way the laugh lines crinkled at the corners of his eyes. They probably wouldn't be so pronounced if he used a moisturizer with sunscreen, but this was one example of a person who looked *better* with a few years carved into his face. Clearly he'd always been hot—dark hair, light eyes, that clichéd chiseled jaw—but the laugh lines took him from "pretty boy" to "handsome" in a way that most guys didn't have.

"Well, you've got neutral all right," she said, shaking her head. "But I think it would sell faster with *pretty.*"

"It will sell faster with neutral." He started to leave again.

"Why does everyone say that?" Lexi asked, bringing him to a halt. "Why would *blah* be more attractive to a prospective buyer than *zing?*"

"Because what's *zing* to one person might be *eek* to another," he explained with a small chuckle. "You know, half the time I think you're pulling my leg."

She put her hands up, spackle in one of them. "No pulling here."

He laughed again, then said, "Neutral is the rule of thumb. Let the place be someone else's canvas. If you're finished with the crazy questions, I've got to go bathe so my date doesn't run out on me tonight."

"Good thinking. I'll just keep working because I don't care what my date thinks of me." She tucked a rag into her pants and started spackling, making an effort not to look back at Greg.

But she heard him leave.

And only then did she stop for a moment and look back at where he'd gone.

She was excited about their dinner.

She'd spent too much of her life in her little sheltered area, never getting out and meeting different kinds of people. If she hadn't, she might have been able to scrape Maribeth and her ilk off long before they decided to scrape *her* off and then she might have met someone like Greg sooner.

Not that there was anything romantic there. The beauty of it was that there didn't need to be—*she* didn't need that—having a friend, and an honest friendship, was far more fulfilling than romance ever could be.

At least for now.

So it really kind of stank that they were both working their tails off to get the place sold because Lexi wasn't sure what she would do next. Her rent here was so low she'd never find anything like it again. What would she do next?

It was tempting to do a bad job so buyers would be turned off, but Greg would notice it long before anyone else did, and he'd make her fix it anyway, so there was no point.

Plus, if she didn't do this well, she'd have no job at all. That one night where she'd lost two sales—especially that one girl who'd looked like she was going to buy a ton—had done her in. Garda had wasted no time in implying to their manager that Lexi was deliberately turning customers off.

Lexi hadn't had the energy to argue about it.

It was time now—actually it was *past* time—to think about getting another job. Maybe one that would pay enough for her to put a down payment on her own place. Much as she loved Sephora, she was only there part-time. What she needed was to go full-time and get her own place.

She knew she had to do it.

She'd known that this deal was finite from the beginning.

So, whatever her silly girlish feelings for Greg, she needed to keep them in check. It would be just plain stupid to fall for the guy right before they went their separate ways.

It would be wine and lo mein but nothing more.

Period.

Holly wasn't ready to commit to "skinny clothes" yet, even though she was officially down 20.6 pounds, but she loved the little boutique Louisa Remley's at the Rio Center in Gaithersburg, so she decided to go in anyway. They carried unique clothes from size 4 to 16, and she'd spent many happy hours there, shopping for special occasions, from the time she was in high school.

In fact, when she entered the store, she realized that she wasn't as happy as she used to be.

Actually, now that the shock of Randy's leaving—and never even bothering to return her calls—had worn off, her appetite *was* coming back.

And she was glad of it.

"Holly!" Rosa was the manager, and she'd been working there as long as Holly had been shopping there, so they knew each other by name. "Girl, I almost didn't recognize you!"

"Oh!" What could she say? *Thanks* just didn't seem appropriate. "I guess I look different lately."

"Lately! You look different than you did ten minutes ago! I need to wear my glasses!"

"What do you mean?"

"When I first saw you out here with your boyfriend, I didn't think anything was so different. But now that I look at you . . ." She shook her head admiringly. "Mmm-hmmm, you look *good*! How'd you do it?"

"Complete deprivation," Holly answered. "What do you mean you saw me with my boyfriend?" The "ten minutes ago" thing was confusing her. "You mean last winter?"

"No, I mean when you first came in, whenever that was—ten, fifteen minutes ago? You were over in the lingerie section."

"You must have me confused with someone else. I just came in." Holly idly fingered a red-and-white Empire-waist dress. "I love the summer stuff."

"It's a good season this year," Rosa agreed, but she was frowning. "Are you saying you *weren't* standing right over there with your boyfriend a few minutes ago? That tall blond guy with the big nose?"

Sounded like Randy, all right. "No, we broke up. Must have been another fat girl with a tall blond boyfriend."

Rosa nodded but looked uncertain. "I feel like I'm going crazy. I was *sure* it was him, and from the back I just assumed it was you, too. Then here you were." She shrugged. "Weird stuff. But forget that—is there anything I can help you with? I know you liked our nightshirts, but, honey, I don't think they're gonna fit you anymore."

"Come on, Rosa, I'm not *that* different." And it was true. She felt exactly the same as ever. If she were in a better mood, she might even try to shop for a few things, though she was realistic enough to admit that she'd outshrunk many of the things in the store.

In a way, that kind of felt like a shame, because she loved their stuff.

"You just let me know if you want me to help you out with anything," Rosa said. "And if I'm in the back, you know Shelly can help, too." She pointed toward a girl putting shoes away.

"Thanks." Holly did spend a few minutes wandering around, looking at things, but her heart just wasn't in it today.

And the thing with Rosa thinking she'd seen Holly and Randy earlier was kind of disconcerting. Holly, always ready to be superstitious, wondered if it might somehow *mean* something. Was she supposed to get back with him? Try to make it work?

She dismissed the thought as soon as it came to her, but its sticky residue remained in her mind as she walked out into the bright sunshine and down the row of shops to do what she'd actually come for—to prepare for Nicola's visit. She stopped in Pier 1 and picked up some candlesticks, then went down the road to FineWines and picked up a red and a white, along with some cheese and crackers.

It was going to be fun to have Nicola in. It had been so long since she'd had a good old girls' night, with wine and bad TV and junk food. She couldn't wait.

She put the stuff in a cooler in her car, then locked up and went back to the shopping area with the idea of walking around the lake before heading back home.

It was a nice day, despite the heat, and her optimism about having her friend over put a bounce in her step.

But as she passed the wide windows of the Corner Bakery, something—or rather, some*one*—caught her eye. She looked in and saw Randy sitting at a back table.

Her first thought was that it was unfathomably weird that here he was right after that exchange with Rosa. For a split second, it was hard for Holly to dismiss the idea of fate.

Until she noticed the girl he was with.

How she'd missed her at first, she didn't know, but now that she looked closer, what she saw was someone who, at least from the back, looked a little like Holly—same hair color and length, same height.

Except this woman weighed more than Holly did. In fact, she looked even *bigger* than Holly had been at her biggest.

Holly's jaw dropped, and she tried to form a thought, but it was impossible.

Then he laughed at something his companion said, and he leaned across the table to kiss her.

And it was as if Holly were seeing some strange echo of her own life playing itself out now.

But it wasn't that.

It was just Randy making out with a fat girl.

After making Holly lose weight as a condition of marrying her, then dumping her once she did.

All at once, it became horribly, disconcertingly clear to Holly who Randy was and what he was all about.

He was a chubby-chaser!

Actually, he was worse than a mere chubby-chaser. He preyed on women with that vulnerability so he could manipulate and control them in a way he could actually *watch*. He hadn't missed the fact that Holly had lost a lot of weight when he told her he could "pinch an inch"—he'd have had to have been blind to miss it!

But he got some sick thrill out of pushing her to do it, to lose more and more.

Then, once she had, she was no longer of interest to him.

He'd found his new mark.

For about five minutes, Holly stood there, paralyzed, watching the two of them nuzzle and flirt. Part of her wanted to go back to her car and drive far, far away, hoping to erase this image—and this truth—from her mind.

Yet part of her wanted to go in and strangle him.

To say nothing of warning the poor girl he was with what he was all about.

A series of scenarios ran through her mind: things she could say to each of them, things she could dump on Randy's head, but when he looked up and caught her eye in the window, what she did do was leave.

And she didn't look back.

"Hey! Holly!" Randy called behind her.

She quickened her pace.

Now that she could.

"Holly!" Footsteps closed in on her, and she felt his hand on her shoulder.

She whirled to face him. "I do *not* want to talk to you."

"Why not?"

Why not? Of all the things he could have responded with, what he decided on was *why not*? How could she even *begin* to answer that one?

"You are a pig," she said, her voice simmering with hostility. She wanted to hit him. She really, really did.

"What did I do?"

"You really need me to tell you?" She glanced in the direction of the Corner Bakery, then back at him, trying to formulate one clear, succinct *fuck you* that would satisfy this moment for the rest of her life.

Unfortunately, *fuck you* was the only thing that came to mind, and she wasn't going to give him the satisfaction of going so lowbrow.

"Okay, so you think I was seeing Monica before we broke up, but I promise things didn't get serious until *after* you and I were over."

"Monica would be the plus-size girl you left in there, probably in the middle of some deal whereby you'd give her the emotional satisfaction she's craving in exchange for her, um, dropping a few pounds, is that right?" Her anger was boiling over. "Am I close, Randy?"

"I don't know where this is coming from, but I don't deserve it."

"Yeah, well, you shouldn't have chased me out here to get it, then, should you?"

"What happened to you?" he demanded. "You used to be so nice."

"What happened to me? I'll tell you what happened to me: *You* happened to me! You made me feel like I wasn't good enough for you unless I met a certain physical standard. You told me you'd marry me *if*—and *only* if—I lost weight. You watched me struggle, you watched me starve, you didn't care about my health, all you cared about was watching and seeing the magic your manipulation created. Once the trick was over, you moved on to the next one."

"That's not true." His objection was weak. It was as if he'd never thought of it in such clear terms himself and recognized the truth only when he heard it.

"It's *one hundred percent* true. I just can't believe I didn't see it sooner." She wanted to kick him. "What's her name? Monica? Maybe I should go in and warn Monica what you're all about. Maybe spare her some heartache and yo-yo dieting." But the truth was, Monica wouldn't believe her.

Holly wouldn't have believed some strange woman saying these things, either.

"This is none of your business."

"You're right. But if I thought I could help her, I wouldn't care if it was my business or not—I'd try."

"You're just jealous," Randy said. Oddly enough, he sounded like he was trying to soothe her, though his voice was having the opposite effect. "You need to move on."

"I need to move on, all right. I need to get the hell out of this box I've been stuck in."

"Box? What are you talking about?"

"I'm talking about the fact that I led a sheltered, fearful life and you *loved* that. You totally took advantage of my insecurities in order to dominate me. Did it make you feel big?"

He straightened and started to object, but the way his face colored told her he'd probably already been accused of this. "If you're in a box, it's not my fault."

"No, you're right. I should have gotten out a long time ago." She looked at his smug face and felt like she was really going to lose her mind if she stood there one more moment. "I just didn't know I could. Now I do." She didn't wait for an answer but just hurried away, desperate to get to the safety of her car.

She'd realized, in bits and pieces, that her relationship with Randy had been unhealthy, just like her relationship with Derek before him had been, but it wasn't until tonight that she fully realized just what a toll it had taken on her.

She'd let those relationships affect almost every part of her psyche and self-esteem. She'd been manipulated, but only because she'd allowed it.

Thank God Nicola was coming. Thank *God*.

It had been so long since Holly felt like herself that she didn't even know what it meant anymore.

But she did know that if there was one person she'd always been unself-conscious with, it was Nicola.

She couldn't wait to see her.

Holly waited by gate 2C at Dulles International Airport, looking for her best friend, whom she'd been warned she'd know only by the fact that she wouldn't recognize her anymore.

The passengers from Nicola's JetBlue flight filed out of the security doors, and Holly waited, half holding her breath, wondering if Nicola looked *anything* like herself, or if she should just wait for perhaps a beautiful Asian woman to come running toward her, arms outstretched, saying how long it had been since they'd seen each other.

It was funny, though—she knew Nicola the minute she came off the plane. Sure, she looked a *little* different, but to Holly it was as if Nicola had red lipstick on, not a whole new face.

"It's so good to see you!" she cried, throwing herself into Nicola's arms.

Nicola held tight. "You, too! You look different." She drew back and frowned. "What's changed?"

"Nothing." Holly laughed. "Everything but nothing. It doesn't matter. You're here and that's all that matters. Well, that and whatever's going on with *you*." She was concerned at the pale, serious look on Nicola's face. "Are you okay?"

Nicola nodded. "I've had a few long weeks with work and . . . everything. And the last part of the flight really tested my stomach, but everything's fine now. For the first time in ages, I feel like I'm home."

"Good. Because I feel like you're home, too." Holly hooked her arm through Nicola's. "Let's go. We'll have some wine and eat junk food until we're ready to burst."

"Good. You look like you need to have a snack."

"I know, I couldn't eat after the whole Randy thing—"

"Or *during* the whole Randy thing."

"Right. That, too. It's funny how being thin isn't as fun as I thought it would be."

"I feel the same way about being pretty."

Holly laughed. "Who would believe it?"

Nicola smiled. "Neither of us would have." They walked a few minutes in silence; then Nicola asked, "So we're off to Camp Catoctin tomorrow?"

"If you're up for it. I think it will be a blast."

"It's kind of cool, huh? It's almost twenty years to the day that we left that place for the last time. I never thought we'd be back."

"Me neither. Because we were too old. Imagine if we'd known we'd be back at thirty-three!"

Nicola laughed outright. "We thought we were old *then!*"

"Ugh. I know."

Nicola looked at her again. "I can't get over how . . . different you seem. Happy. I like it."

They went to the baggage carousel, where Nicola's bag was, miraculously, one of the first ones off.

"So you're sure the place is still there?" Nicola asked. "The camp, I mean?"

Holly nodded. "I did some research. From what I can tell, it's unchanged. They're not using it for kids anymore, at least not this year, but the main facility is being used as an adult education center. There's been no development, from what I can tell."

"Unless Mr. Frank is still there and decided to build himself and his wife a house out in the woods."

"If that's the case, and if they ended up exactly where we're going to look, I think we'd have to take that as a sign."

"No kidding." Nicola laughed uneasily. "But we don't believe in signs."

"Nope!"

They stepped through the automatic doors, into the night air. "Keep reminding me of that, okay?"

20

"This is so creepy," Holly said. They were standing in front of what remained of the crescent of cabins that used to be Camp Catoctin. The buildings were overgrown now, with weeds growing into—and out of—them. Some of the roofs were sagging, and most of the windows were broken.

Cabin 5 had QUINCE RULES spray-painted on it in black, whatever that meant.

"It is," Nicola agreed, heavyhearted. "It's sad seeing something that seemed so big and lively so small and broken now."

Holly nodded. "I wonder why it closed."

"It's probably like all those quaint old ghosts of restaurants you see on the side of old interstates. Maybe they used to be in vogue, but as cities got tighter and more people moved in, the service industry moved in, not out."

"Plus, no one can afford anything anymore."

"Yeah, there's that."

"Should we go look at our cabin?"

Nicola hesitated. She might regret this. "I'm thinking we have to."

Together, they walked from the gravel parking lot toward cabin 7. For a while they didn't say a word; they just walked across what was once a sweep of green grass but what was now a mangy old dog of a patch, with crabgrass and bare patches of dirt, to the cabin they'd both loved and hated for four weeks twenty years ago.

The wood was rotting, and there was a pale 7 faded into the peeling paint where once there had been a large brass number.

"How long has it been closed?" Nicola asked.

"I don't know. They still use the meeting hall for adult education and retreats, so technically, it's not closed. But when I called to make sure it was still here, the person who answered the phone said it hadn't been a kids' camp for 'years.' Who knows how many? Maybe it closed the year after we were here."

"If only it had closed the year *before* we were here." Nicola laughed.

"But then we wouldn't have met!"

"Sure we would. People who are meant to meet each other meet one way or the other. We might have ended up in line together at Dulles Airport. It didn't need to be here."

"Yes, it did," Holly contended. "Because you don't make lifelong friendships with people you stand in line with at the airport."

"I don't know—lines at the airport have gotten awfully long."

"Be that as it may, I'm glad we met here."

Nicola smiled. "Me, too."

"On the other hand, I'm not so glad we're here right now. It's way spookier than I thought it would be."

"It is." Nicola took a tentative step.

"Maybe this is the penance for going back to the scene of our crime."

"No, no, the statute of moral limitations has expired here. We're back because we're good people, not because we *have* to come back—"

"Really?"

"Okay, we *have* to come back and look for the ring, but we don't have to cop to it."

"So far we haven't."

Holly rolled her eyes. "Do you want to banter or atone?"

"Atone. This time."

"Fine. Let's go." She turned around and looked. "But do you want to go in first?"

Nicola grinned and nodded. "Of course!"

Holly took an uncertain step onto the wooden porch. She could totally picture the entire thing breaking and splintering under her weight. Not that the embarrassment would have been that huge with just Nicola, but she didn't want a serious accident, and given the looks of the entire campsite, it seemed like anything was possible.

"Remember how the horses neighing and galloping would keep us awake at night?" Nicola asked behind Holly.

For a moment, Holly closed her eyes and remembered the sound from outside the windows—the soft neighs and the hard pounding of dirt. So hard, she could picture the clouds of dust rising from beneath galloping hooves. "Yes." She smiled. "Though now you could add that sound to one of those spa-effects clock radios, and I'd probably sleep like a baby."

"Let's go in." Nicola pulled the screen door to the cabin open. The hinge was broken, so the door dropped limply onto the porch, and she had to scrape it across the planks. "Do you remember that squeaky sound?"

"Yes, but only from those nights we were trying to sneak out without anyone hearing us."

"That's the only time I was so aware of it, too. Weird how even now it's familiar."

Holly nodded but said nothing. This was proving to be a lot more melancholy than she'd anticipated. They stepped over the wooden threshold and into the sleeping space.

It was a lot smaller than she remembered it.

Seriously, the room was about twelve feet square, with two of the three bunk beds still there. Both were rusted, with some of the springs popped and sticking out. There was a mattress on one top bunk—Nicola's actually—and the rest were bare. How was it that someone had come through and cleaned up just that much—to remove one complete bed, three mattress, but to have left two frames and one mattress behind? Was there some sort of emergency that interrupted them to the extent that they never came back to finish the job?

Thanks to the state of disrepair—in addition to the mouse droppings and spiderwebs—it was obvious they weren't still using the cabins for guests, so why hadn't they completed the job of razing them?

Standing in the small space, Holly was overwhelmed by memories and a strange protective feeling for the child she'd been. This wasn't a happy place for her. This was a place where angst and misery were almost literally soaked into the wood-beam walls and the mattresses that remained. Her nights here had not been happy ones, gazing out the window and fantasizing about whatever bright future she might have, but instead of misery and self-consciousness, trying to stay awake and be the last to fall asleep so that if anyone started talking about her and laughing at her, she'd be aware of it.

What she'd imagined she'd do with that information, she didn't know.

She'd never gotten that far.

"Let's go," she said. She actually heard herself say it before she realized she was really going to say it.

"What's wrong?" Nicola asked.

But when Holly looked at her, she could see that Nicola was being haunted by very similar ghosts. "Don't you find this disconcerting?" she asked her.

"Totally," Nicola said. "But it's fascinating at the same time. Not only is this place a ghost town, but it's *my* ghost town." She pointed to the window. "I used to look out that window right there and watch the moon cross the sky. As long as it made it from one pane to another, I knew time was passing and that I'd be able to get out of here sooner or later."

"I just closed my eyes and willed myself to sleep," Holly confessed. "I knew that as soon as the sun came up, another day had passed and that was another black X across that day on the calendar."

"Do you think it's healing to be here?"

Holly thought about that for a moment, then shook her head. "I don't know. I'd like to think so, but to tell you the truth, I'm standing here now feeling almost as nervous as I did when I was a kid. Like Lexi and Tami and Sylvia are going to come prancing through that door any minute and say something mean. Something to make life miserable."

"Yet you want to help her. Lexi, I mean."

"That's right." Holly nodded, but there was a bit of the fearful girl she used to be in her expression. "Go figure. Now, can we get out of here? I'm terrified that the floor is going to crumble under our feet and we'll fall into some sort of termite hell."

"Let's go." Nicola led the way and opened the door for Holly, then followed her out.

Holly was profoundly relieved to breathe the fresh air again. She was a thirty-three-year-old woman with her own business, and her own house, and a new lease on life—she shouldn't have been afraid of ghosts in an old camp cabin, and yet she was quaking deep down in her body.

She picked her way down the steps carefully, glad with every step she took that she was getting farther away from the cabin. Mr. Frank's office and meeting hall were barely visible behind a curtain of ever-greens in the distance, but she was glad to see them nevertheless. "So where do we go?" she asked, digging her heels into the dirt. "It's left, right?"

"Eleven o'clock from the front of the cabin."

Holly looked at Nicola. "You just happen to remember that?"

"Hey, this was a big deal for me. I had mental maps to everything around here. Don't forget I was the one who had to navigate home on the water in the middle of the night. Alone."

"True. You're lucky you didn't become one of those short-lived news stories and long-lived urban legends. Can you see kids lying in these cabins talking about it? 'She left the dance and took a rowboat back to camp, but before she got there, a slimy hand reached out of the inky black water and grabbed her—'"

"Ew! Stop! I remember the horrifying details well enough—you don't need to embellish them with disembodied hands."

"It wasn't disembodied, but that's a nice touch," Holly said. "That's the kind of gross detail that makes the story stick. And, believe me, I have a bunch of stuck old horror stories in my head."

"This is the place for them." Nicola started walking across the weedy landscape, and Holly followed her.

"Maybe we should have brought a compass. Or water or a candle or some sort of safety stuff. Do our cell phones work out here?" Holly took out her cell phone and turned it on. One bar. "Oh my God, maybe we don't even have cell service."

Nicola stopped and turned around. "There's your car right there." She pointed. "We are not that far from civilization. This place isn't nearly so big as it felt when we were little. Get ahold of yourself."

"Easy to say now." Holly glanced at the comforting sight of her car, then at the thick woods ahead. "But when we're there . . ."

"How long has it been since you left the city?"

"A long time. Months. Maybe years."

"You're just being princess-y. It's fine. These are very thin woods, and we don't have to go very far."

"How long has it been since *you* left the city?"

"Fourteen years."

Holly's jaw dropped. "Are you serious?"

"Sort of. We filmed in Upstate New York about fifteen years ago, then I went back to L.A. and did two more movies in the studio, and . . ." She thought about it. "Yeah, I guess if you're talking about when was the last time I left the city or suburbs, it's been a while."

"Great."

"What difference does it make?" Nicola laughed outright. "If I'd been hiking along the Appalachian Trail last year, it wouldn't make a bit of difference to what we're doing right now! What we're doing is *time travel*, not hiking."

"True."

"And time travel is much worse. So stop wigging out about this, and start trying to remember where the hell we're supposed to go."

"I thought you had mental MapQuest going on."

"It's not infallible."

Dread simmered in Holly's veins again, but this time she didn't mention it. "I followed you. Get us to the entry point, and I might be of more use. Though I do remember it as being just about this angle when we went into the woods."

"The trees are bigger now."

"And there was a gap to the right—"

"Oh my God—I remember that!" Nicola pointed to the spot. "Where the counselors from a couple of years before us had a fire and burned out part of the woods!"

"It's grown back now."

"That's good. Environmentally speaking."

"Navigationally speaking, it sucks."

"Fortunately we're a lot bigger and a lot older now." Nicola took out her BlackBerry and looked at it. "And *some* of us have two bars, so we should be fine. Now follow me."

With more confidence in the "two bars" thing than in anything else Nicola had said, Holly followed her into the thicket and along the overgrown path. Obviously, whatever they did at the adult education and retreat center, they did not hike, because where Holly remembered a narrow clearing through the woods that had been easy enough to follow even in the dark, now the pathway was closed in and there was only the merest hint of clearing along the way.

She wasn't even sure she wasn't imagining it.

But Nicola was on a roll, walking through the woods like Helen Keller on a mission, knowing exactly which way to go and when.

"I can't believe how this is all coming back to me!" She stepped over a fallen log and held some branches aside for Holly to follow. "I feel like I did it yesterday!"

Holly glanced back uneasily in the direction of her car but said nothing about it. "Good thing, because I'm following you. I can't believe we did this in the dark. We must have been nuts!"

"We were motivated, for sure. Actually, I used that experience when I did *The Black of Night*."

Holly looked confused.

"That slasher picture I did."

"Oh! The one where you were *actually* invited to the casting couch for a bigger role?"

Nicola nodded. "Hence, my small role."

Holly cracked up. "Little did he know you'd become a big star anyway. What's next, by the way? Did you get the *Nicola Kestle Project*?"

"No."

"No?" Holly stopped. "Are you serious?"

"Dead serious. I didn't even get an offer to blow someone to get it." It was a lame joke, and it fell flat.

"I'm so sorry," Holly said. "I can't imagine what they were thinking."

"Apparently they were thinking I no longer look like Nicola Kestle." Nicola started walking again. "And they're not the only ones. I sat next to a self-proclaimed fan on the plane, and she not only didn't recognize me, but she didn't *believe* me when I told her who I was."

"Holy cow! Did you show her your license or something?"

"No! I didn't need to prove myself to her!"

"I would have."

Nicola smiled at her friend. She used to think that way about being famous, or semifamous, too. Turned out, it really wasn't so great as she'd imagined. "We're getting close, I think." Nicola stopped, almost like a hound dog sniffing the air. The contours of the woods had changed, but she was almost positive she knew where she was. "It's right over there." She pointed to a place twenty degrees off the path they were following now and tramped through the brush.

"Are you sure?" Holly was beginning to wonder if they should have been dropping bread crumbs behind them. "We're getting really far from the car. . . ."

"Oh, come off it, Holly, we're not *really far* from the car. You're thinking like a kid. We're not even a quarter of a mile into the woods."

"That's a long way!" Holly objected. "A quarter of a mile of woods is a *lot* of woods."

"In the dark. When you're thirteen, but now—" Nicola stopped and frowned.

"What?"

"Shh!"

"*What?*"

Nicola shot her a look. "Jeez, it's a good thing I wasn't trying to silence you so a grizzly bear didn't hear us!"

"You cannot just stop like an English pointer in the middle of the woods and shush me and expect me to do my nails!"

"*Shhhh!*"

This time Holly did.

"Never mind, it was only a bird."

Holly glanced around uneasily. "You heard something unusual? Do you think it might be a person?" Suddenly the things in the woods were far less of a concern than the people who might also be there.

"It was a mourning dove. Wow, you are really a scaredy-cat."

"I am not!"

"You absolutely are."

She was. It was only hitting her now, but she really was. Take her out of the coddled safety of her urban neighborhood, and every little nature sound freaked her out. "You're the one who's freaking me out," she lied.

"Oh, okay." Nicola's dimple showed, though she didn't actually smile. "So. Here we are."

"Where?" Holly looked around. "Where are we?"

"This is the clearing. Or it *was* the clearing." Nicola wrinkled her nose. "Nature is taking over everything. It's good, of course, but it's also like a science fiction novel, where nature wins no matter what."

"And it happens quickly, like we're standing here and vines begin to wrap around our legs." The air was thick with gnats and humidity, and Holly was beginning to feel like she couldn't breathe. "Where's the birdhouse? Oh my God, what if it's not here anymore?"

"It's got to be here. They took down the house but not the birdhouse. Who would come back for the birdhouse later?"

"True." Holly scanned the tangle of trees and limbs and leaves, looking for a box, or even the broken remains of one, high in them.

"It has to be close to one of the bigger trees," Nicola said, "because it was solid as a rock when I climbed up it."

"That narrows it down." Holly found a thick, gnarled trunk and looked up into the foliage. "Is that it?"

"Where?" Nicola squinted. "No, that's just bramble."

They walked around, searching in silence, apart from the crunch of dead leaves and twigs under their feet, for more than half an hour before Holly finally felt like it was time to give up.

"Maybe this was a stupid idea." She was sure it was. In fact, she really wished she'd never run into Lexi Henderson, because now she was going to wrestle with the guilt of it forever, and it was all for nothing. There was not a thing she could do to help Lexi or to make up for what she'd done to her.

Nicola looked at her. "This was *not* a stupid idea. This was a really good idea. A *noble* idea."

"I don't know how *noble* it is to remember, twenty years later, that you stole something from someone and, only then, want to make it right."

Nicola shrugged. "A lot of people might not have even bothered. We at least deserve credit for that."

Holly nodded, but she wasn't convinced. "It doesn't really matter now one way or the other, though, does it? I don't see the birdhouse, and we've been looking for it for ages here. How long are we going to tramp around in here before we finally admit we've failed?"

Nicola sighed. "We have gone over every inch of this area. It's not here."

"Maybe it came crashing down, and the ring was dislodged. You know what we should have brought? A metal detector."

"Wow. That *would* have been a good idea. I wish we'd thought of it."

"There's a Toys R Us in Frederick." She'd seen it when she went to pick up frames from an estate sale a few weeks ago. "We could go down and find one, then come back. It's only about half an hour away."

"Let's do it!"

With their optimism invigorated, they headed back in the direction they'd come from. It was a little after noon, so Holly felt confident that they had enough time to get to the store in Frederick and back before they lost all the daylight.

They'd been walking only a couple of minutes when Holly heard Nicola shout behind her and turned to see her fall heavily to the ground, breaking her fall with her right hand.

"Oh, no!" Holly rushed back to her. "Are you okay?"

Nicola was pale, and her face was tight with pain. "I *slammed* my hand. I think it bent all the way backwards."

"Ugh!"

"My wrist is killing me." She lifted her right hand, which was at an odd angle.

Holly sucked air in through her teeth. Just the sight of it made a shiver run down her spine. "We've got to get you to an ER, fast."

Nicola nodded. "Yeah, this hurts like hell."

"Should I call nine-one-one?"

"No, it's not an *emergency*."

"Are you sure?" Holly winced, looking at Nicola's wrist, which was swelling as she watched.

"Yes. Let's just go. It's not an emergency, but the sooner I get a painkiller, the better." She gave a short laugh. "I've had a lot of experience with broken bones, cartilage, and narcotics this year." She gestured at her now-perfect nose.

"You poor thing. Let's get out of here. We can come back in a few days when you're drugged."

"Sounds good to me."

But not five minutes later, Nicola said, "Stop!"

Holly started and turned to her. "Are you okay?" Her eyes fell on Nicola's wrist, which did not look okay at all.

"I think this is it."

"What?"

Nicola was looking around urgently. "I think this is the place." Her eyes fell on something, and her expression sharpened. "There it is!" She pointed into the trees.

"There's what?" Holly followed Nicola's gaze and saw it. A little birdhouse high up in the trees. "Are you kidding me? We spent all that time looking in the wrong place?"

"I'm not a human compass."

"You're pretty close." Holly shook her head. "I can't believe that's it."

"You have to go up."

"What? *I* have to go up?"

"Well, *I* can't climb with this." Nicola lifted her hand. "You're going to have to do it."

"But we have to get you to the hospital!" There was no way Holly could picture herself climbing up that tree. It had to be thirty feet up there, maybe more.

"We can't leave now that we've found this!" Nicola argued. "God knows we might never find it again. You have to go up. There's just no other way."

"I can't!"

"Why not?"

"Because I'm not a climber! I can barely hike through these woods in a straight line! If I climb up there, I'll fall and kill myself!"

"Holly Kazanov, you had me come all this way for this, you have been *obsessed* with finding this ring for Lexi, there is no way I'm going to let you give up this opportunity."

"We can make a chart of where we are, and when *you* are well again, we can come back and *you* can climb the damn tree, since *you're* the one who's good at it."

Nicola shook her head. "Get climbing."

"I'm scared."

"Then this is the most valuable thing you'll ever do in your life. Trust me. You can do this."

Holly looked dubiously at the tree. There were a lot of branches sticking out. Chances were decent that, if she fell, she'd get caught up in them at least long enough to slow her fall.

"You can do it," Nicola said again. "Now, come on." She went to the tree and pointed to a large knot. "Put your foot here and reach up for that branch there."

It looked doable. But everything in Holly was resisting. She *never* did this kind of thing. Not when she was a kid, not when she was a teenager, and definitely not now. "I'm too old. I'm too fat."

"Actually, Hol, you're not nearly so fat as you think you are, *and* you're perfectly proportioned. It's not like you're going to tip one way or the other. Whatever your boobs do to pull you forward, your ass counters."

Holly had to laugh at that. "Thanks."

"Any time. Now get moving."

Holly swallowed hard. If she didn't do this, if she walked away now, she would be disappointing Nicola, failing Lexi, and solidifying her position in this world as a fat girl who couldn't get out of her own way.

But more important, if she *did* do it, she would prove to herself— and to the rest of the world, too, but mostly to herself—that she was *not* the loser fat girl.

That maybe she never really had been.

She put her foot in the knot and hoisted herself up, reaching for the branch. She missed the first time but caught it the second time. Thoughts of her late nana came to mind. Nana who always said *Jesus will save you.*

She hoped Jesus was here now.

"Good. The rest are closer together," Nicola said. "Step here and reach for that branch now. See?"

"Yes." Holly nodded and reached. This time it was easier.

All her life she'd felt constricted by the clichés about fat girls. That they couldn't run, that they were ugly, that they were unworthy (of too many things to mention). This was her chance to shoot every one of those things down for herself. To hell with the kids who had teased her in elementary school!

She took another step, reached for another branch.

To hell with Randy!

Another step, another branch. Already her hands were getting sore, but she didn't care. She wasn't losing strength; she was gaining it.

To hell with the bitches at camp who had made her feel like an embarrassment to them all. From Brittany to Sylvia, Tami, and even Lexi. To hell with Lexi!

Holly wasn't risking her life here for Lexi. This had ceased, at least for the moment, to be about Lexi. She was doing this for *herself*.

"Keep looking up!" Nicola called.

"What?" Holly glanced down.

She nearly fell.

It was a long, long way to the ground. How had she gotten so far, so fast? She froze. How would she get down?

"Shit, I'm sorry! I shouldn't have said anything. But seriously, keep looking up. You'll be fine."

"I'm scared."

"Look at the birdhouse. It's one more step away. See it?"

Holly looked. She did see it. She could almost reach it now. And actually, there was something comforting about it being right there. Someone had put it there. She wasn't on the magic beanstalk high in the clouds; she was just in a tree, heading for that box, and she was almost there.

"One more step," Nicola repeated. "And there are, like, ten branches you can choose from. You'll be fine."

Holly took a short breath, fastened her eyes on the birdhouse, and reached for a higher branch. The step was easy—she felt around with her foot and eased herself up.

She was there.

Now what?

The holes were tiny. There was no way she could fit her hand in there. She looked for the chain Lexi had kept the ring on, hoping, perhaps foolishly, that it was still sticking out.

"Can you see anything?"

"No." The house was made out of metal, not wood, as she had thought at first. She reached out for it, and the sheets of miniature siding shifted easily under her touch. It was rusted. "Hang on, I might be able to see. . . ." She pushed at it gently, and a piece of rusty metal fell to the ground. "Look out!" she called after the fact.

"Don't worry, I'm fine!" Nicola called back.

Holly pressed her lips together in concentration and reached in again. This time she thought she saw something. It wasn't a glittery, shiny mass, the way she remembered the ring, but a lump covered in dirt and dried bits of grass and leaves.

A lump with a chain attached to it.

"Oh my God!"

"Did you find it?"

"Oh my God! Yes! I think so!" She tugged at it. It didn't move. She pulled again. A little harder. This time it did move. She was able to reach in and grab it.

It was the ring.

"Tell me what's going on!" Nicola called.

"I've got it!" She was laughing, but tears rolled down her cheeks. She'd done it. She couldn't believe it, but she'd actually climbed up the tree, reached into the mystery box that may have had the ring or may have had a dead bird in it, and she'd gotten the ring.

She had never, ever felt so accomplished in her life.

Keeping her eyes focused up, she felt her way down the tree. It seemed to take forever. She was dying to examine the ring, to see if it was real or if it was a fake that had mottled and chipped with age. At the moment, she didn't care which it was, because she had gotten all the way up there to retrieve it.

She'd *done* it!

"Careful," Nicola said. Her voice was close.

Startled, Holly jerked her head in the direction of the voice and lost her footing. Branches scraped down her leg, tearing into her flesh as she fell. It was only about three feet, but it was an unexpected three feet. She flailed her arms, trying to grab on to something—anything—to stop her from falling.

Instead, all she did was smash her arm against something soft and warm.

Nicola's face.

The blood gushed from Nicola's nose immediately—and dramatically.

"Oh, shit!" Holly shoved the ring into her pocket and reached for Nicola. "Are you okay?"

Instinctively, Nicola recoiled. "I'm okay."

"You're bleeding like a fountain!"

"I am?" She pulled her hands away from her face and looked. "Fuck. It's my fucking nose. Again."

"Here!" Without thinking, Holly pulled her shirt up over her head, turned it inside out, and handed it to Nicola. "Put this against it with a little pressure."

Nicola did, and Holly led her by the crook of her arm to the car. They'd passed a hospital sign about ten miles down Route 15. They'd be there soon. Everyone just had to stay calm.

They got to the car, and Holly opened the door for Nicola and helped her in.

"It's okay," Holly reassured her in a voice she hoped was convincing. "We'll be at the ER in just a few minutes."

Nicola said something, but it was muffled.

"What's that?"

Nicola moved the shirt aside. "Let me see the ring!"

"The wha—?" In her panic, Holly had all but forgotten it. "Oh! Here." She pulled it out of her pocket and handed it to Nicola. "It's filthy. Don't touch any open wounds now."

"I've got plenty."

Relieved that Nicola was able to joke, Holly gave a laugh and went around to the driver's seat.

Her hand was shaking, but she put the key into the ignition and started the car. She drove out of the gravel parking lot. "Are you okay at all?" she asked, afraid to steal a glance at Nicola for fear of what she'd see.

"I'm not dying." Nicola dabbed at her nose with the T-shirt. "Though you'd think someone had cleaned up a murder scene with this. Head wounds bleed so much. Yuck."

"Oh my God. Oh my God." Holly couldn't stop her trembling. "Did I break your nose? The nose you spent a lifetime wanting to change? The nose you just spent a *fortune* on?" This was a catastrophe. She'd ruined her best friend's life.

"It's my wrist that really hurts," Nicola said. "My nose will be fine." The way she said it, though, it was clear that she didn't really think so.

It was clear that Holly had ruined *everything*.

Holly swallowed and pressed a little harder on the accelerator. "Don't worry, I'm sure they can fix everything at the hospital. Just hold on a few more minutes."

"Do you still have any water left?"

Nicola reached into the cup holder on her door and handed

Nicola the Dasani bottle she'd been drinking from on the drive up. "It's warm."

"That doesn't matter." There was a sharp intake of breath. "Holy cow."

"What? *What?*" Holly glanced nervously over at Nicola and saw she was holding the ring up in the light. The chain still hung down like an old vine.

But the facets of the ring glittered in the light like Dorothy's ruby slippers.

"I can't believe it, but"—Nicola shook her head—"I think it's real."

"B elieve me, sweetie, you could look a lot worse."

Nicola was waiting for her discharge papers so she and Holly could get out of the ER, but the nurse would not stop talking. The only remotely medical thing she'd done was hand Nicola some Tylenol 3 in a little plastic cup. "Huh?"

"Your face. It could be a *lot* worse, after what you've been through."

"Oh." What else could she say? *Thanks?* No thanks. And *shut up* just seemed a little too harsh.

"You might not *feel* so hot," the nurse went on, "but someone who's been through what you've been through might have come out of this a mess."

For some reason, she had it in her head that Nicola had been in a fender bender, rather than a walk in the woods. Nicola had already corrected her once, but she was too tired to keep doing it. It didn't matter.

"Here's a sheet on what we call the RICE treatment for your sprained wrist. Rest, ice, compression, elevate. For the first forty-eight hours, ice is the most important thing you can do, and most people slack on that because they don't think it will help."

All Nicola wanted was more codeine. "I'll ice it."

"Take the splint off first." She handed Nicola another sheet. "For your nose, you're going to want to be very sure there are no dramatic changes, like an inability to breathe or a large bruised bulge on one side or the other. If you leave a septal hematoma untreated, your nose can just"—she snapped—"collapse. Right into itself. It's one of the scariest things you can ever see."

"If I can't breathe, I'll see a doctor." She was going to have to anyway, to repair the damage cosmetically. Nicola sighed. "Okay. So what do I do to get out of here now? Do I have to sign something?"

"I'll go check and see if your papers are ready." She pushed through the curtain barrier and clopped down the hall.

A few minutes later, there were more footsteps, and the curtain scraped open a little. Holly poked her head in. "How are you feeling?"

"Like leaving, how about you?"

Holly came in and sat down on the chair next to the bed. "The same. What did they say?"

"Sprained wrist, bonked nose."

"Bonked? Is that the medical term?"

"I did an episode of ER once. I'm pretty sure that's the medical terminology."

"I saw that episode! You were a med student. I guess you're practically a doctor now."

"Exactly. Though I doubt CVS would honor my prescription for Percocet."

Holly laughed. "They gave you Tylenol Three, huh?"

"It's better than nothing. A little."

The nurse came back in with a clipboard. "Okeydokey, you are all set to leave. You just have to sign here." She pointed to a line on the page. "And here. Good. Here are your prescriptions, and you'll need to follow up with your doctor in a couple of days."

"Thanks." Nicola started to stand but felt woozy and sat down again.

"Take it slowly," the nurse said. Then she looked at Holly. "Were you in the accident, too?"

"Accident?" Holly glanced at Nicola.

Nicola rolled her eyes and shook her head.

"Um, no," Holly said.

"Good, so you can drive her home."

"That's the plan."

"All right. Good luck! Hope all goes well for you!" She waved her clipboard and went into the next cubicle, where Nicola heard her say, "Oh, my! All of this happened from falling while you were on a hike?"

"Ready?" Holly asked, assisting Nicola to her feet. "I was thinking we ought to just hang out and rewatch season one of *The O.C.* tonight. You up for it?"

"Definitely."

"Think you could hook me up with Benjamin McKenzie?"

Nicola gave a laugh. "If I could, you'd have to get in line behind me."

They started to walk slowly out of the ER. Nicola ached all over—her head, her arms, her back, her butt . . . everything was sore.

"I've got it!" Someone shouted behind them.

Nicola glanced over her shoulder as the nurse came bustling toward her. "Do you know who you look like? Well, apart from the black eyes and the blood and stuff."

At the moment, she couldn't even imagine. "Who?"

"That girl—" She frowned and clicked her tongue against her teeth. "She's an actress. What *is* her name? She was in that movie— *Duet.*"

"I just can't get over it. This concealer of yours is amazing." Nicola was looking at her reflection in the visor mirror of Holly's car. It was two days since they'd gone to Camp Catoctin, and the swelling and bruising had gone down enough so she could put makeup on her face and actually look normal.

She actually looked like herself again.

Her *real* self.

Not *exactly*, of course. The break hadn't happened so neatly that she'd gone back to being an exact replica of her former self, at least not to her own eye, but as Holly had pointed out, she looked *enough* like herself to do a damn good impersonation.

"It's Benefit Erase Paste. Maybe you should get some."

"Definitely." They were on their way to Sephora to present Lexi with the ring. Nicola was both excited at the prospect of helping someone out in this pseudo–fairy godmother capacity and terrified at the idea that Lexi would instead see them as thieves.

Which was way more accurate.

"What do you think she'll say?" Nicola took the ring out and examined it for the millionth time in the light. It was gorgeous. A clear stone, with perfect facets that caught the light and scattered it all over the inside of the car like little stars. If it was a fake, it was a magnificent one.

They'd cleaned it up with jewelry cleaner Holly had gotten from

Target, and with every stroke of the cloth, the metal had bloomed with luster and the stone had grown clearer and brighter.

Holly pulled into the parking lot by Nordstrom and put the car in Park. "Are you ready?"

"I'm not sure. But I know we don't have a choice. We have to do this."

"It'll be fun!"

"Yeah. Maybe."

"Maybe."

Simultaneously they each took a bracing breath and got out of the car.

"Let's do it!" Nicola said.

"We *are* entering through my lucky door," Holly pointed out. "We could stop in the shoe department on our way out."

"Sounds like exactly what the doctor ordered." They stepped into the air-conditioned vestibule. "That and Tylenol Three."

"Which one do you think will help more?"

"No contest. The shoes."

They took the escalator to the second floor and walked into the bright artificial atmosphere of the mall. "Wow, it's changed since I was last here!"

"Which was, what, like twenty years ago?"

Nicola nodded. "Fifteen, twenty. I think Nordstrom had just come in."

"There's some good stuff here. We should make the drop and then make a day of shopping!"

"I thought you had to get to the gallery."

"Nah. I'll let Lacey cover it."

"Well, listen to *you*—I haven't heard you being so spontaneous in . . ." Nicola thought about it. "Apart from this week, I'd have to say *ever*. I haven't *ever* known you to be so spontaneous."

Holly nodded and, for just a moment, looked uncertain. "Ever since I saw Randy with that girl . . . I don't know, it was like I realized I've been so wrong about so much for so *so* long. What I thought was up turned out to be down. Black is white. Fat is thin. And thin"—she shrugged— "is fat. I've spent a lifetime trying to figure out what everyone else is thinking without ever giving any consideration to what *I* think."

"I've tried to tell you that for years."

"True. But what I didn't realize until I actually hit the bottom was that being good to yourself doesn't mean you have to be bad to everyone else. I always thought it was either-or."

"So you were good to other people at your own expense?"

"Sometimes." She paused. "A lot of times. I lost all this weight because I thought Randy would love me more if I did. How sick is that? But I realized a few days ago that I had more power over my own fate than I was admitting. So I decided to take control." She gave a laugh. "Now I'm just trying to hold on to that control."

Nicola smiled. Holly had a magnetic charisma no matter what she weighed. There was no way to convince her of that, but for the first time in the years that Nicola had known her, it sounded like Holly was finally realizing something of her worth *without* regard to how much she weighed.

It was like a miracle.

Or, better yet, it was like it *should* be.

"I think that's incredibly brave," she said to Holly. "I am so damn proud of you for figuring out that no man was worth what he put you through. And I don't mean the weight. You could lose that or gain it, depending what you wanted to do, regardless of what some guy wanted.

But the thing is, you wasted so much *thought* on him. So much energy. You gave him more of yourself than he deserved. But somewhere out there, there's a guy who *does* deserve you."

"And I'll know him if he doesn't ask me to lose weight in order to marry him."

"That'll be a start, anyway."

They laughed.

Then Holly said, "So I had a strange opportunity recently. To do something utterly unlike myself."

Uh-oh. Nicola braced herself. What was coming next? Self-acceptance was one thing. Dyeing your hair black, calling yourself Sasha, and moving to Russia—or something similar—would be quite another. "What is it?"

Holly stopped and faced Nicola. "You might think I'm crazy."

"I'm ready." Nicola raised her brows in question.

"Have you ever heard of Guy Chacon?"

She thought about it. "I don't think so. Who is he?"

"An artist. He was regionally popular at first, but now he's making it big all over the nation. The JW Marriott in San Francisco just bought a bunch of his work to display in the lobby."

"Oh! Is he the one who did all those impressionistic paintings of the cherry blossoms?"

"Bingo."

"Okay, so . . . what? He asked you out?"

"No. No, no." Holly paused. "He just asked me to take my clothes off for him."

Nicola took a moment to process that. "I'm sorry?"

Holly gave a nod. "Seriously, he asked me to model for him." She glanced right and left, then added in a stage whisper, "*Nude.*"

Nicola clapped a hand to her chest. "Are you kidding me?"

Holly crossed her heart with her index finger. "Totally serious."

"Are you going to?"

"Well . . ."

Nicola stopped again and put her hands on Holly's shoulders. "Tell me you said yes to a famous painter wanting to paint you!"

"Actually I said no. Or, more specifically, no thank you."

Nicola got her reaction in check. She was from a different place, after all, a more artistic community. Maybe, to Holly, such a suggestion was shocking or too immodest. Maybe she was just too shy. It wouldn't *hurt* her if she declined his invitation.

But what an opportunity to accept and possibly be part of history in a great artist's portfolio.

Still, she let go. "At least you were polite."

"I was." Holly hesitated. "Do you think that was stupid? To say no, I mean. It's the chance of a lifetime, in a way."

"No. I don't think it's ever stupid to do what your inner voice tells you to do—or not to do, as the case may be."

Holly frowned and nodded. "That's what I thought. I just can't help but feel that it's foolish to refuse to pose for a famous painter."

"Not if it would make you uncomfortable," Nicola assured her. "And speaking of paint, here we are." She swept her arm forward.

Holly followed the gesture and saw the storefront for Sephora. "Mecca."

"What if she's not working?"

"Then we wait for her shift. I was here again on Thursday and that was her day off, so the way I figure it, she's got to come in today."

"Unless she's part-time."

"Don't borrow trouble. I'm sure she's here."

They walked in and looked around.

Nicola wasn't sure what she was looking for, since she hadn't seen Lexi for twenty years. And the fact that Holly saw the woman *and* her name tag for as long as she did before she put two and two together made her even more skeptical of recognizing her. "Tell me if you see her," she said, and set about checking the name tags on every employee they passed.

Everyone looked twenty.

"I don't see her," Holly said after about ten minutes. "I'm going to ask. Oh! There's the cashier who checked me out the last time I was here!" She hurried over to a kid who looked about eighteen, and Nicola followed.

"Excuse me," Holly said, drawing the girl's attention. "I'm looking for Lexi Henderson. She works here."

"Lexi?" the girl repeated. "Hey, you were here before!"

Holly nodded impatiently. "I was, and Lexi helped me. She'd just started then. Do you know if she's working today?"

The girl shook her head. "She doesn't work here anymore."

Even Nicola felt the sting of that. "She doesn't work here anymore?" she asked.

The girl looked at her, then at Holly. "What, are you guys cops or something?"

"Cops?" Holly looked so incredulous that Nicola decided not to add anything to further how ridiculous the accusation was.

Holly's shock was clearly proof enough of the truth.

"No," Holly said to the girl. "We knew her years ago and have something she might want."

That was bad. Nicola decided to step in. "Actually, she was a friend in camp, and then when my friend"—she indicated Holly—"ran into her here, she was so surprised, she didn't think to get her phone number. She just thought she'd be able to come back and find her, but apparently that's not the case."

She wasn't sure, exactly, when the girl had stopped listening, but it didn't matter. She was on to Nicola.

"Ohmigod, are you Nicola Kestle?" she asked, glancing nervously around as if she hoped no one else would join them in this moment.

"I am." Nicola was so glad to be recognized again that she didn't bother with false modesty or trickery.

"I am *such* a fan of *Duet*. Can I have your autograph?"

Holly glanced at Nicola, and her meaning was clear.

"Sure," Nicola said. "But, first, do you know where Lexi is?"

"Well . . ." The girl put a finger to her chin. "She *might* have left a new address on file for her final check. Do you want me to look?"

"Would you?" Holly asked.

"Please?" Nicola added.

She shifted a glance from one to the other, then gave a single nod. "I'll take a quick look, but don't tell anyone."

As soon as she'd walked away, Holly turned to Nicola. "Who the hell does she think we're going to tell?"

"Her boss, I'm guessing," Nicola said quietly. "Now, *shhh*. Don't draw their attention."

"Fine." Holly turned away and assumed a face of overplayed nonchalance.

Nicola hoped the cashier wouldn't notice and think something weird was going on, since, to look at Holly, there was.

"This is the address we have on file," the girl said as she returned. "I have no idea if it's right, but . . . whatever."

"Thanks." Nicola took the paper and shoved it into her front pocket. "We really appreciate it," Nicola said as she gave her autograph. "There's just one more thing."

Holly shot her a death look.

Suddenly Holly was an expert on when to shut up.

"Can you show me where the Erase Paste by Benefit is? I need to pick some of that up before we leave."

"So what should we do next?" Holly asked over a BLT pizza at California Pizza Kitchen. "Should we just go straight over there? Or warn her somehow first? Maybe try a reverse lookup on her phone number?"

"We came here without warning her," Nicola pointed out, reaching over to trade a piece of her Caribbean jerk pizza for a slice of the BLT. She'd wanted to try everything on the menu. "So what's the difference?"

"This is a public place. It's not so much of an ambush when it's a public place, because there are so many people around. Going to her house . . . I don't know—it just feels like there's a different protocol."

"Hm. I see what you mean."

"On the other hand, this should be such good news for her that she won't care if we warn her first or not."

"*Should* be. Then again, it might be more of an 'I could have had this all these years if it weren't for you' than a 'thank you so much, I thought I'd never see this again!' for her."

Holly shrugged. "We don't *have* to tell her we took it. We could say we were hiking in the woods today, found it, and remembered it looked like the one she'd lost."

Nicola tried to keep from laughing, but she couldn't. "Not even Meryl Streep could pull that act off."

"No?" Holly laughed. "I guess you're right. We have to face the music."

"*After* we eat." Nicola took a bite of the BLT. It was amazing. Given the choice, she would have preferred to sit here all day and eat every different pizza on the menu.

"Excuse me," a voice interrupted.

For a second, Nicola thought it was the waitress and was about to ask if she could bring one of the pear gorgonzola pizzas over, too—after all, they could save the leftovers and eat them during their O.C. viewing tonight. But it wasn't the waitress. It was a woman who looked to be in her mid-twenties, with a stylish dark bob and red lipstick.

"Yes?"

Holly set down her pizza and dabbed her mouth with her napkin.

"I'm *really* sorry to interrupt, and I swear I'm not usually this person, but"—she rolled her eyes—"I have to say, I am *such* a fan."

Nicola swallowed. "You are?"

Meanwhile, Holly, oblivious, asked, "Of what?"

Nicola shot her a look.

Uncertainty crossed the woman's eyes. "Wait . . . you *are* Nicola Kestle, aren't you?"

Pleasure flowed through Nicola's veins. "Yes."

"Oh!" Across the table, Holly's face went red. "Sorry! I always forget!"

This was the second time in an hour Nicola had been recognized. She was thrilled.

"Can I get your autograph?" the woman asked, looking around haplessly. "I don't have paper."

"Here's a napkin." Holly handed it over. "And I have a Sharpie in my purse." She started to dig.

"You just happen to have a Sharpie in your purse?" Nicola asked.

"You'd be amazed how often this comes in handy. See? Now you can sign the napkin, a pizza box, a glass, whatever you want."

The woman's jaw dropped. "Oh! A *glass*! What a *great* idea!" She reached for Nicola's water glass and handed it to her. "Would you mind?"

Nicola looked around. Could she get in trouble for writing on a glass? Would anyone even care? Well, she didn't, she decided after a moment. This was a great moment, and she'd sign the wall if someone wanted her to. She wiped the condensation from the glass with her napkin, then asked, "What's your name?"

"Phyllis. Spelled the usual way."

Over the years, Nicola had learned there was never a *usual way*. "*P-h-y-l-l-i-s?*"

Phyllis nodded. "So will there be a sequel to *Duet?*"

"There's been talk." Yeah, talk of a new actor and actress taking on the *next generation* roles. "But nothing is sure yet. We'll see."

"I would sign a petition, anything. I just think you are the best. You're so *real*. I felt like I could relate to you."

This gorgeous woman felt like she could relate to the Nicola Kestle she saw on-screen? That was amazing. Because, frankly, if *she* had been on screen, there was probably no way Nicola would have felt she could genuinely relate to her.

Of course, everyone had different personal demons, and there were probably few people in the world who were so physically beautiful that it made up for anything and everything else they might feel.

"Thank you," she said to Phyllis, though she was growing consumed with thoughts about keeping her nose in its current broken state rather than healing or going back to a cosmetic surgeon to have it "fixed." The "fix" hadn't worked the way she'd hoped it would.

She didn't want to be "fixed" anymore.

"Thank you," Nicola said, handing the signed glass to Phyllis. It still had water in it.

"No, really, thank *you*." Phyllis looked her over. "I really almost can't believe it's really you."

Join the club, Nicola thought, but she said, "It was a real pleasure meeting you, Phyllis."

She watched, pleased, as Phyllis walked away with an obvious bounce in her step. It had been a while since Nicola saw someone react to her in any way even close to that. She had to admit, her ego liked the boost.

"Oh my God, you're, like, a movie star!" Holly said.

"Sort of. For the moment. What happens if this is all swelling and my nose goes back to being small and straight?" Never before in her life could Nicola have imagined this being a concern to her.

"I don't know. I guess you'll just have to learn to deal with being classically beautiful."

"But I don't want to be classically beautiful anymore! I want to be *me* again. No matter *what* that means!"

"You've always been you!"

"Come on, don't start that Glinda the Good Witch stuff with me. You know damn well I looked cripplingly different when you first saw me this week."

"I wouldn't have said it was *crippling.* . . ."

"My *grandmother* didn't recognize me," Nicola argued. "*That* was crippling. My agent didn't recognize me. The producers who wanted to audition me based on the fact that they'd *written the part* with me in mind didn't *recognize* me, so they hired someone else." Nicola closed her eyes for a moment and pinched the bridge of her nose. "I appreciate your support, I really do, but the time for honesty has long since arrived. I look like some dull Barbie doll. My stupid New Nicola Project was a complete failure. You could find a million mes just walking around West Hollywood with your eyes open. Now."

"Except . . ." Holly sort of winced. "I'm not sure that swelling is going down that much more. I'm afraid it looks like I sort of knocked the cartilage . . ." She couldn't finish, she just gestured. "*Out of line*, I guess."

"I hope so." Nicola sighed. "I seriously hope so."

"Seriously?"

"Seriously. If you broke my nose back into a reasonable replica of its former self, I'll be indebted to you forever." Nicola smiled. "I can't tell you what a nightmare it has been having a face that isn't my own."

"I can imagine it was disconcerting, but not to the point where you'd want it *smashed*."

Nicola laughed. "Well, no, I guess I wouldn't have specifically asked for you to *smash* it. But if people recognize me again, it's got to be better. To hell with being beautiful, I want to be *me*."

Holly looked at her and nodded. "I think I know what you mean."

Nicola suspected she did. "I used to think it would be the ultimate dream come true to get my nose fixed and to be what people might actually consider *pretty*. But to look in the mirror, or pass a store window and catch your reflection, and to see someone . . . *else* . . ." She shook her head. "It's like having someone ape your every move. It's been disturbing."

"You know, when you hinted toward this before, I thought you were being falsely modest." Holly took a sip of chardonnay. "Not that there's anything wrong with that. Modesty is good. And you are so beautiful that who could believe you were really unhappy with it?"

"Look, I don't know how 'beautiful' I actually look right now, but I do know, for a fact, that I'd give anything to feel like myself again. Anything."

"Now *that* I understand." Holly gestured toward the food in front of her. "I'm eating what I want to for the first time in weeks. And it's not to say I'm going to pig out and purposely gain all the weight back to make a statement, but it feels damn good to eat what I want. Wait, make that, to *do* what I want."

"And what you want is to have some pizza."

"That's right!"

"So it's not so weird that I want to go back to ugly from pretty."

"You were *never* ugly!"

"You know what I mean."

Holly laughed. "Yeah, I guess I do. You want to go from pretty to ugly, and I want to go from thin to fat again." She pointed a finger at Nicola. "We've learned our lessons and want to tap our heels together now and go back home."

Nicola raised her wineglass. "There's no place like it."

"So now we get there by taking the yellow brick road to Lexi's house."

As it turned out, Lexi was surprisingly good at painting.
Walls, that was, not pictures.

"It's all about the tools," she said to Greg after he marveled at the precision with which she'd painted his bedroom and then the dining room with its complicated angles and elaborate crown molding. "Once I had the spackle and I discovered that old album cover was the perfect maulstick. I mean, *look* how perfectly straight my lines are!"

"Old album cover?" Greg's eyes fell upon Bruce Springsteen's *Born in the U.S.A.*, which was now covered in less-than-patriotic beige, tan, and primer. "Are you kidding me?"

She pressed her lips together. "Remember yesterday when I went to the garage to ask you—and I specifically said this—an important question?"

"The Redskins' pregame was on!"

She shrugged and dabbed a little touch-up semigloss white onto the doorframe. "It would only have taken a few seconds to answer."

"So you decided the answer was yes?"

She gestured at the perfect paint job she'd done. "Are you saying the answer was no?"

He looked at the walls, scrutinized the corner, even *touched* the baseboard. "No," he said at last. "I guess not."

"Ha!"

"Actually, I have to say the furniture looks really good the way you moved it around in there, too. You made it look like a model home."

"Isn't that the idea?"

"Yeah, but I . . ." His voice trailed off. "It's not exactly my gift."

She laughed. "No kidding. But you had the furniture all wrong. Heavy pieces all bunched up together makes it look like the room is half the size."

Greg shrugged. "I will absolutely bow to your superiority in this area."

"Good. You should. And you shouldn't have brought that stupid La-Z-Boy back in."

"It's comfortable!"

"It's huge and ugly."

"Granted." He folded his arms in front of his chest and leaned back against the doorframe. "But it's comfortable."

"We are never going to agree on this." She smiled. She didn't mind disagreeing with him.

Which was a good thing, since she was certainly getting used to it.

"You know," he said. "I wasn't really sure this arrangement between the two of us was going to work out at first—"

"You weren't exactly my Barbie Dream House roommate either."

The dimple showed in his cheek. "And yet you hid it so well."

"Right. I should be an actress."

He gave a half smile and looked at her in a way that made a shiver tickle down her spine. He took a step toward her. "The thing is, I think we work pretty well together."

"Apart from your piggy ways, leaving dishes in the sink, and so forth," she softened, just talking about it. "I think you're right." For all his faults—and she was ready to point out scores of them—he was really pretty endearing.

Actually, when she watched him do his thing, using power tools and turning a wall into, say, a gorgeous arched entryway, he was more than endearing.

He was sexy.

"I mean really well." Greg hesitated and then, practically circling his toe on the floor before him, added, "I got an offer on the house today."

That stopped her in her tracks.

She put the paintbrush, bristles up, in her front pocket. She'd given up on keeping these jeans clean a long time ago. "Did you take it?"

"Not yet, but I will."

"Oh." She swallowed. This sucked, but it was what he wanted. It was what they'd both been working toward. "Congratulations. That was a lot faster than I expected."

"Yeah, well, when the Realtor said he wanted to bring people by, I figured we'd just get some helpful feedback, not an offer. But since we're in this to sell it, I had to be open."

"Of course. Why not?"

"Because . . . well, I know you thought you'd be here longer."

It had been only a month. Initially they'd talked about this taking eight months or so, and when he pointed out there were no guarantees, it was probably both of them who thought that meant it might be longer.

"How long until we have to be out?" she asked.

"A couple of months. The best I can hope for is a late September or October settlement date."

She nodded, mute. Obviously she'd known she couldn't do this forever. When she started, she wouldn't even have minded the idea of wrapping up quickly. What she hadn't planned on was actually feeling at home with this guy in this house that needed so much work.

"We're damn good, aren't we?"

He nodded. "That's what makes this all the more difficult."

"Makes what more difficult?" What now? Wasn't it bad enough that she had to find a new place to live? That her time with him was over before it even felt like it got started? What could possibly make this more difficult?

"This." He cupped her face in his hands and kissed her.

Lexi had been kissed before—there was no denying it, from Josh Stenberg in first grade right on through Drew Ardner three months ago—but this kiss felt like the first. She could have died satisfied if it was the last.

Then he pulled back and said, "So, there's *that*. And I've got a proposition for you."

"Wasn't *that* a proposition?"

He smiled and looked right into her eyes. "I guess it was. Maybe I should wait for an answer on that before I give you the next one."

She raised her chin. "I'll have to think about it."

He shook his head. "Then you're going to have to think about it in conjunction with this: There's another place, down River Road, close to Seneca. I've had my eye on it for years. It's gone into foreclosure, and I was thinking, if you don't have other plans right away, that maybe we could . . ." He was clearly struggling to come up with the words. "Do our thing there."

"Our thing being . . . ?" She could think of quite a few things she'd like to do with him.

"What we did here." He gestured around them. "Renovating. Staging. Selling. Or maybe not selling—I haven't gotten that far. But I know I just complicated things, and you might not want to stick around, knowing how I feel."

"That's right, you took a big chance on getting slapped, didn't you? I might have been shocked!"

"I wouldn't put it past you." His smile widened. "I wouldn't put anything past you. I think that's one of the things I like best about you. You feel what you feel, and you put it right out there."

She laughed. "Oh, sure, you say you like that *now*—"

He pulled her back into his arms so close, their breath mingled. "I will *always* like that about you."

Warmth spread through her chest and out into her limbs. This was unlike anything she'd ever felt before.

Happiness.

When he kissed her again, she sank into it, allowing herself to feel every sensation, every clichéd butterfly of it.

Until they were interrupted by the doorbell.

"Ignore it," Greg murmured against her mouth.

"We can't! What if it's the Realtor?" She smiled as she drew away. "Besides, we have *work* to do."

"Fine. There's a hole I need to patch in the back room anyway."

"Go!" Part of her wanted to run back into his arms and ignore the rest of the world, but most of her wanted to string this out as long as she could, enjoying every moment of it.

How long did it take to fall in love?

When she opened the door, she was greeted by two faces, both of them familiar but out of place. She cocked her head, hoping it would come to her before she had to admit she had no idea who they were. "Yes?"

"Lexi," one of them said. She was the shorter of the two, with glossy brown hair, warm brown eyes, and—

That was it, Lexi remembered. "Holly! How nice to see you! How . . . *weird* to see you—?"

"One of your coworkers at Sephora gave me your address," Holly said quickly. "After I swore up and down that I wasn't a stalker. And I'm not," she hastened to add.

"O-kay." This was odd, but not scary odd. Lexi wasn't sure what to do. She looked from Holly to her friend, who also looked familiar. Tall and thin, with long auburn hair and light blue eyes. Her arm was in a blue sling.

"We need to talk to you," Holly went on, speaking in urgent tones. She gestured at the woman with her. "This is Nicola."

"Nicola Kestle." The other woman held out her good hand, and Lexi knew who she was all at once. The movie star! No wonder she hadn't been able to place her—she was so *out* of place. "We were in the same cabin as you back at Camp Catoctin back in eighth grade," Nicola went on.

"Right. Of course, I've seen you since then." Lexi looked her over. She looked a little different. Maybe it was because her child face was still hovering somewhere in Lexi's memory, mingling with the woman before her now.

"Can we come in for a minute?" Holly asked.

"Oh!" Lexi stepped back, opening the door farther. This was completely weird, but she was willing to go with it. "Yes, sure, come on in."

"Thanks," Holly said, and tossed a look at Nicola, as if urging her on.

Lexi led them into the front room—they referred to it as the living room, though it had only one chair and one love seat. The walls were a plain antique white, and until the house sold, Lexi thought they were in desperate need of some paintings. She'd even brought in the ones she'd inherited from her grandmother, but they were still sitting on the floor, leaning against the chair rail because she decided they weren't actually good enough to put on the wall.

They all sat, and after about half a second of awkward silence, Nicola spoke. "This is really awkward. For all of us. In fact, you might hate us when you hear what we have to say, and we don't blame you, but we just had to come back and do the right thing—"

"What she means," Holly interrupted, "is that twenty years ago we wronged you and we're here to make it right."

It was a good thing Holly had spoken, because Nicola had really kind of freaked Lexi out. "What are you talking about?" she asked, assuming anything that happened twenty years ago had to have happened at camp, and what could these two former mice have done to warrant her hating them now? "Are you here to give me a Three Musketeers bar because you didn't share back then?" She was immediately sorry for saying it. What if that *was* what it was about in some way? Maybe they were here trying to complete some sort of twelve-step program, and she'd just made fun of them.

"What?" Holly looked stunned. "No. We're . . . no." She frowned. "Did you actually care about that stuff back then?"

"Oh, it was just—" Lexi waved it away. This was their deal, not hers. "I was jealous, that's all. Everyone seemed to get stuff from home, even horrible people, except me. I was jealous of everyone." She gave a short laugh. This *was* awkward. Why the hell were they here? And when were they going to leave?

Holly nudged Nicola and gave her an *I told you so* look.

"Okay, you guys are going to have to tell me what you're up to," Lexi said. "Because you're sort of freaking me out."

Nicola spoke in a reassuring tone. "Listen, I know this seems really out of place, and it probably is. We all know people in our past that we could have treated better, and we all know people in our past who should have treated us better. Life is just one big mess that way. But when Holly ran into you at the mall and saw that you were in trouble—"

"I didn't *see* that," Holly interjected. "You told me, straight up. It's not like you *looked* destitute or anything."

Lexi nodded and went rigid. No. No way. "Please tell me you're not here to give me some sort of charity."

"No, not at all!" Holly said, so effusively that it almost made Lexi laugh.

"We're here to give you this." Nicola took something out of her pocket and handed it to Lexi, pressing it into her hand.

"I thought we were going to lead up to that," Holly said in a stage whisper. "Tell our side first."

"We were sucking at that. She just needs to have it." Nicola returned her gaze to Lexi and gave an apologetic shrug.

Lexi almost laughed at their cartoonish exchange, until she looked at the thing Nicola had put in her hand.

She shouldn't even have had to look.

She knew instinctively what it was, just from the feel of it, the cool metal, gliding like water into her hand. She'd held it so many times in her childhood that she could never forget.

"You found it," she breathed, looking down at the gleaming piece of gold and rock in her hand.

"Yeah." Holly cleared her throat. "So, I know it's been a while—"

"Where did you *find* it?" Lexi's hand began to shake. She looked at them with tear-filled eyes. "It was my mother's." She looked down at it again and said, more to herself, "Finally." She sniffed, and Holly noticed a tear drop onto her jeans. "I can't believe it." She closed her hand around it and held it close to her heart.

It would have been easier if she'd just yelled at Holly and Nicola and kicked them out.

Now they had to watch this painfully poignant scene in silence and wait for whatever tonic chord Lexi was going to play to end it.

"Where did you find it?" Lexi asked, her voice just barely more than a whisper. "How did you know to bring it to me?" She looked back at it, then dangled it on the chain and looked at it in the light. Her laughter was sudden and startling. "My God, it looks like new!"

"It was exactly like you had it," Nicola said carefully.

Lexi looked at them and swiped tears from her cheeks. "I'm sorry. You must think I'm a total weirdo, crying over this, but it symbolizes so much. . . ." She unclasped the chain and pulled the ring off, then set it aside, still clutching the chain.

"Tell me, really," Lexi said, "how did you find it?"

There was a moment of silence.

"See, that's where the whole thing about you hating us comes in," Holly explained, eyeing the ring Lexi had set on the table. She was absolutely mortified to have to fess up to this, particularly on the heels of this scene. "We . . . took it from you."

"It was only supposed to be a prank," Nicola added quickly, but to Holly's ears, it didn't soften the blow. "For one night. But we got caught and everything got confused."

"*You* took it?" Lexi frowned, apparently uncomprehending. "When? How?"

"We took it off your bedpost while you were sleeping one night in the cabin. We only wanted to hide it for a day, but they caught us going back for it and wouldn't let us."

"But *why?*" Lexi asked, looking completely earnest. "Why would you do that?"

"Well, we were thirteen at the time," Nicola said. "So our reasons were stupid like only a thirteen-year-old's can be, but"—she shrugged, embarrassed—"you were really mean to us and we wanted to get back at you."

"We thought we'd be able to just take it for one night and put it back the next one, like Nicola was saying," Holly said quickly, not wanting that point to get lost in this. "But Mr. Frank and all the counselors got involved, and when we tried to go back and get it the next night, they stopped us. And"—tears made her eyes gleam—"we were afraid to tell you, or anyone else, the truth."

"It was and is totally wrong," Nicola said plainly. "And you're probably really mad that we took this from you and it was missing for so long, and we don't blame you one bit. But after Holly saw you and you told her about your situation, we remembered the ring and thought maybe it would help."

"And we hope it does," Holly added eagerly. "Really."

Lexi looked from one to the other of them.

They waited, bracing themselves for the worst reaction.

But Lexi was strangely calm. It was like a peace had come over her when she took the ring into her hand. "Wow," she said. "Not a lot of people would do that."

"Steal, keep it secret for years, or bring it back?" Holly asked.

Lexi laughed. This was all too weird. "Um. I guess all of the above. I wish you'd let me know somehow before now, but then . . ." She looked thoughtful and then shrugged. "I probably would have wanted to go look for it, and there's no way I could have found it."

"We couldn't get back, either," Holly said. "And Mr. Frank told us that he was putting up electrical fences along the border, which, now that I think about it, was probably a big fat lie, but it just made it sound like, no matter what we did, we couldn't make this right."

"And we were scared to death to tell you the truth," Nicola said. "We hope you'll forgive us, but neither of us blames you if you can't. More than that, we hope it helps you out, we really do."

Lexi didn't speak, but her expression spoke volumes.

"Honestly, we would have said something back then if we'd thought it was real, but it was so big and so elaborate that we had no idea it might be real," Nicola said earnestly. "Neither of us ever saw anything like it in real life before."

"The ring?" Lexi asked, then gave a dry laugh. "Oh, yeah, the ring was magnificent. The real one, I mean." She shook her head. "Not this one. It's just a copy."

They both looked at her, mute.

"What do you mean?" Holly asked at last.

"Isn't that real?" Nicola followed up.

"That?" Lexi glanced at the ring. Even from a distance of several feet, it was obvious to her now in a way that it wasn't when she was a child. Of course, she had a lot of other information now, too, about how Michelle had siphoned money out of the marriage via a veritable pipeline of jewelry replacement and sales. "It's a really good knockoff of the real thing," she said. "But it's a fake."

I t's a *fake?*" Holly asked.

Lexi nodded. "It was the *chain* I was upset about losing." She could tell from the expressions on their faces that this was surprising news. "It was my mother's. She wore it every single day." Every day it had touched her skin, separated by mere millimeters from her heart. This one small gleaming rope of metal that even Michelle couldn't be bothered with meant more to Lexi than anything. She'd been anguished at losing it.

It couldn't have mattered more if it were worth millions, for all the love she'd burned into it, all the secrets it had absorbed. She almost felt that if she looked in its shining links, she'd see her adolescence play out on them. Her thoughts and hopes and dreams, everything she'd concentrated on while wearing it or holding it, frozen in the gleam of metal.

"I thought the ring was real at the time," Lexi explained. "Obviously

I can see why you remembered it as something potentially big. But I learned a couple of years ago that my father's wife had decoys made of all her jewelry, so she could sell it if and when she pleased. She probably sold the real ring that this is copied from months before I ever took this."

Holly raised her hand to her mouth. "Are you sure?"

"Oh, I'm very sure." Lexi looked again at the ring and then held up the chain. "But *this* means the world to me. It has so much sentimental value for me. Maybe even more, now that your story is attached to it. I can't believe the two of you took so much trouble to come back all these years later."

"You have no idea," Nicola said with a laugh. "We've spent the last day trampling around in the woods looking for it, climbing trees, getting injured"—she raised her wrist—"and then trying to work up the courage to come bring it to you and admit what we'd done."

"I'm not sure I could have done that," Lexi said. Actually, she doubted she would. "And I can assure you I know people who have yet to admit what they've done." She fastened the chain around her neck. It was warm from her hand and felt like the touch of an old friend.

"But are you *sure* the ring is a fake?" Holly asked.

Lexi nodded. "Absolutely. Even the family jeweler admitted he'd done it, though he contended he made the copies 'for insurance purposes.'"

Holly looked disappointed. "I'm really sorry. Not only for making you so upset all those years ago, but mostly because we weren't able to help you now. I really thought this would be a huge help to you."

"It is!" Lexi said, and meant it. For these two girls, now women, whom she'd been so jealous of during her formative years, to come back and fess up to something that could have gotten them into a lot of trouble was really remarkable. "You've brought closure to one of the biggest mistakes I ever made, taking the necklace to camp and then losing it. It was awful."

It was clear the two before her had hoped to be giving her something that would save her financially, like one of those great big cardboard checks from Publishers Clearing House that would solve all the problems of her life.

"We're sincerely so sorry," Nicola said, standing up. "You shouldn't have had to go through that."

Holly joined her in standing. "If there's anything we could do to make it up to you. Ever. *Anything.*"

Lexi waved that off. "It's water under the bridge. I'm just so glad to have it now." She smiled. "I can't tell you"—her voice faltered—"what it means to have it back."

"Remember, if there's anything we can do," Nicola said, shrugging her slinged arm. "To help in any way. Right, Holly?"

But Holly didn't answer. She was staring at one of Lexi's grandmother's old paintings. "What is that?" she asked.

"Holly!" Nicola said in an urgent whisper.

"Ugh, I know," Lexi said. She should have put them away. They looked ghastly. "I know it's a mess. It's just something I inherited from my grandmother."

Holly moved toward it as if being drawn by some unseen force. "But it's . . . I mean, I *think* . . ." She moved closer. "Is this a Patronienne Jordan?"

"I don't think—" Lexi stopped. She had no idea *who'd* painted it, and the thing was such a grimy mess that there was no way to see a signature. But she remembered a name from long ago. "Would that be Patti Jordan?"

Holly laughed. "It would if this is an original."

It was strange how the name had come to her out of the blue like that. She hadn't thought of it for years. Decades. "All I know is the paintings were done by a friend of my grandmother's. I think the name was Patti Jordan, and about all I remember about her is that we went to her house on the James River down in Smithfield when she was sick. Dying of cancer, I think. I was really young, but it was freaky enough that I remember her name."

"She died in 1977," Holly said, looking from Lexi to the painting. "Do you have any more?"

"I have four," Lexi said. She was still holding the ring fast in her hand. It was crazy, but she felt like it gave her luck.

Holly gasped and put a hand to her chest. "Are you serious? Can I see them? Not that I'd blame you if you said no, but I'd love to check them out."

"Well . . . yes." She exchanged a quizzical look with Nicola and led them to the other three paintings.

"I don't know if you'd want to part with these," Holly said after a preliminary look over them. "After all, I realize they were your grand-mother's. But, Lexi, I have to tell you, if these are what I think they are, they're worth a fortune."

Lexi's eyes widened. This was not the kind of news she thought she'd get. Ever again. "A fortune?"

Holly nodded. "Yeah." She glanced at Nicola, then back at Lexi. "Millions."

"So let me get this straight," Greg said, popping the top off a bottle of beer. "You can buy and sell me now, but you've decided, instead, to stick around to work on houses?"

Lexi, who had just gotten an official—and very high—appraisal on her inherited paintings, laughed. "Of course! As I see it, I can retire from my glamorous career in wall painting and spackling, but I prefer to stay productive."

"Here?" He held the beer out to her. "With me?"

She took it and gave a nod. "Here with you."

He scrutinized her. "Are you sure this can make you happy?"

The question was so absurd, she almost laughed. "What are you talking about?"

He sighed. "Look, I know where you came from, the kind of life-style and environment you came from." He gave a quick self-effacing smile. "I've spent weeks dismantling it. When you moved in here, it was because you needed a place, but now you have all the choices in the world."

"*All* the choices in the world?" she asked, moving toward him.

He nodded. "Looks that way."

"So I can pick and choose whatever I want, according to you." It was an easy choice. After an unsatisfying lifetime of cruising on credit cards and enjoying whatever she wanted, she'd found her bliss in work and in the man who'd shown her how to do it. She wasn't stupid enough to give the money from the paintings away, of course, but she was smart enough to realize that she had more fun being productive than she did being coddled.

His grin was so sexy. "Just about anything."

"Any house, any car?" She blinked. "Any man?"

"Oh, Blondie, I'd bet money on that."

"In that case, Mr. McKenzie," she draped her arms around his neck and smiled as she felt his warm hands on her lower back, "I choose *you*."

They were calling it "the comeback of the year"—Nicola Kestle was going to star in a movie biopic of Ann Radcliffe, directed by none other than Wynton S. Balademas, whose film version last year of the monk's story from *The Canterbury Tales* had won him huge critical acclaim, three People's Choice Awards, and two Oscars.

No sooner had Nicola's casting been announced in *The Hollywood Reporter* than Oscar buzz began about her.

"I was so lucky to get her," Balademas was quoted in the article as saying. *"I've had this project on the back burner for a long time, and it was just sheer luck that I was flipping channels in a hotel room and came across an old movie of Nicola's. It was then that I knew I had found my Ann Radcliffe."*

The movie everyone would think he meant was *Duet*, but Wynton had told her that it was, in fact, *The Black of Night*.

It was ironic, since that was her first movie and she spent most of it in the shadows and darting behind trees and buildings to get away from a serial killer. It wasn't her face that had captivated Wynton so much—he could barely see it—but the way she carried herself, the way she moved, the very awkwardness of her height and gait.

Knowing this made the victory of getting the part that much sweeter.

"Who is Ann Radcliffe?" was Holly's first question.

"She was a writer in the 1700s. She wrote *The Mysteries of Udolpho*, which is generally acknowledged to be the first Gothic novel."

"You sound like a Wikipedia entry."

Nicola laughed. "Where do you think I looked her up?"

"It sounds like it will be really spooky and moody," Holly said. "Where are you filming?"

"Prague." Nicola was so excited about that, she could hardly stand it. She hadn't been to Europe in years, and she'd never been to Prague—but lately, with everything that had happened, she'd been feeling like she needed a change of scenery.

As opposed to *being* a change of scenery.

"That sounds wonderful," Holly said wistfully. "I hear it's really beautiful there."

"I can't wait!"

"And is there a Mr. Radcliffe?"

"They're talking Colin Firth."

Holly groaned. "Are you *kidding* me? I want your life!"

Nicola laughed. "Well, you're certainly welcome to come along! Filming begins in mid-November."

"I can't leave the gallery."

But Nicola knew Holly didn't want to leave the gallery. Despite the fact that she occasionally got caught in a rut, Holly was most content when she was just being a homebody. Even their trip an hour north to Camp Catoctin had clearly taken her out of her comfort zone.

"The offer stands," Nicola told her, and she meant it. "Anytime."

After they hung up, Nicola went to her powder room and looked at her image in the mirror. It was something she hadn't done much lately because she was always afraid of what she'd see. She'd attached so much baggage to every image this mirror had ever held that it almost didn't matter what it showed her anymore. She was going to feel weird about it.

Surprisingly that wasn't the case this time.

The face that looked back at her wasn't that of the girl she'd been when she and Holly had met, and it wasn't the eager young actress who had won the role in *Duet*. It certainly wasn't the generic Hollywood Barbie face it had been a couple of months ago, thank God.

Instead it was, as they said, the face she'd earned.

She'd come by the lines honestly, both the laugh lines *and* the frown lines. And she wasn't sure she'd do anything in her life to change them or make them go away, even the bad stuff. The crying she'd done over lousy boyfriends, lost jobs, and anything else in her past had all led her to who she was now, and all that angst had gone into the sincerity of her performances.

The laugh lines were something to be proud of. As Vivi always said, *Anyone who's smiled enough in their life to have laugh lines really has something to smile about.* It was typical Vivi sugar talk, but it was true. Nicola had never appreciated it more than she did today.

Her eyes were her father's. She'd see him every time she looked in the mirror for the rest of her life. Her cheekbones and her hair were from her mother. Even when her hair eventually grew threaded with gray, it would be the same as her mother's was today. It made her warm inside to realize how much personal history she carried with her everywhere, every day.

And how that personal history had led her to where she was

now—on the edge of an exciting new chapter in her life—and everywhere she would go in the future.

She would never take it for granted again.

Holly was glad for Nicola; she really was.

But at the same time, she envied Nicola's glamorous life, even while she didn't want it for herself full-time. It would be nice to get up and go someplace totally different, and *be* someone completely different, for a few months at a time, then land safely back in your own life.

Holly had been safely in her own life for so long now that she didn't know how to do anything else.

Granted, she'd broken her cycle with Randy. And there had been some personal reward in getting that ring—well, the *chain*—back for Lexi Henderson, particularly since she had climbed the tree herself instead of waiting below for Nicola to do it.

Actually, she thought, that was a good metaphor for their relationship. Holly had always been the grounded one, while Nicola was the one reaching for the stars. It had been cool to be the one up in the air for once.

But even that was compelled by trying to right a wrong, and it had done so, even if it wasn't in the way she'd anticipated. She'd done it for Lexi and because it was her moral obligation as well.

If it had been just for herself, would she ever have done something so risky?

In the end, it had benefited Holly financially—Lexi had agreed to sell her Jordan paintings to the Macomb Gallery—yet she was still unfulfilled.

It was one thing to realize she'd felt bad about herself almost all her life, based primarily on how guys acted toward her, but realizing it didn't simply erase years of flagging self-esteem.

She didn't really understand the idea in psychology that once you realize what's at the root of your problem, the problem goes away.

She had to do something.

Something drastic.

Something life-changing that she couldn't undo.

And she knew just what it was.

This was a secret she would keep to her grave.

She couldn't tell anyone—*anyone*—about this. Ever.

What would they think? Every person who knew her would be shocked. Most of them would probably think she'd lost her mind. Some of them might even be concerned enough to make her seek help.

But Holly was absolutely sure she wasn't making a mistake.

She wound her car through the woodsy curves of Seven Locks Road, watching the street signs as her headlights flashed onto them. Carteret Road. English Way. Dwight Drive. Cindy Lane. She swallowed hard, knowing she was getting closer to her destination and that she was about to do something she wouldn't be able to *undo*.

She didn't care. Or, rather, she *couldn't* care. She could no longer afford to care about what was *right* or *wrong* or, especially, what other people would think.

This was her emancipation.

Tonight she would become a different person.

She turned onto River Road, then almost immediately saw the remote little country lane that she was looking for.

She slowed down and put on the high beams.

I can do this, she said to herself.

Her mouth was dry. Her heart pounded. Her hands were cold and clammy, and though she couldn't see them in the dark, she knew she was clutching the wheel so tightly that they were like ghost hands.

Then she got to the house.

She put the car in Park, took the keys out of the ignition, and waited in the dark for a moment, willing herself to do this, to go through with it.

It would be so easy to start up the car again and floor it out of there. She was only a few miles from Starbucks. If she wanted to, in ten minutes she could be sitting in the homey familiarity of the coffee shop, sipping a hot chocolate and relaxing in the knowledge that no one had anything on her, that she could not be blackmailed.

Of course, worry about blackmail was pretty far-fetched.

For one thing, no one would probably ever know it was her.

Her phone rang, startling her so much, she shouted. She pawed through her purse, looking for it, and flipped open the phone. "Hello?" she asked breathlessly.

"So Willand's rep called and said the contracts are wrong," Lacey said. "He said they were offering only a twenty-percent commission now."

Holly sank back against her seat, grateful for the moment of normalcy. "I don't remember talking to him about that."

"Does that mean you don't remember or you know you *didn't?*"

"It means . . ." She put a hand to her chest. Her heart was still beating a mile a minute. "I don't remember. He could be right."

"That's less of a commission than we take on anyone else."

"I know, but he pulls in a lot of revenue, and it's going to be more now that he's a part of that garden festival thing down in Disney World next spring."

"So what do you want me to do?"

"Fix the contracts. I'll initial them tonight, and we can messenger them to him tomorrow."

"Oookay." Lacey sounded dubious. "But I hope no one else gets wind of how easy it is to talk down your commission."

"It's not easy," Holly snapped. "I've just got other things on my mind."

"Not that jerk again!"

Not *again*. *Still*.

And not just *that* jerk, but *every* jerk she'd ever dealt with. Every jerk who had ever made her feel subpar or unworthy or fat or desperate or ugly.

Randy symbolized them all, of course. But not for long.

Things were about to change.

"Look, I can't talk about it right now. I have something to do. But I'll talk to you later, okay?"

"Hang on, Holly. I don't like the way you sound. Are you okay?"

"Yes, I'm fine."

"Are you *sure*?"

Holly gave a short humorless laugh. Her nerves were taking over. "Yes, I'm sure. Go out, Lacey. Have a good time. I'll see you later."

"All right, but you know you can talk to me if you need to, right? Like, about anything."

Holly nodded, alone in the dark. "Yes, I do. And I appreciate it. Leave the contracts out, and I'll initial them later on."

"Fine, fine. Call me later if you want to meet for a drink or something."

"Will do." But she wouldn't.

She clipped the phone shut, put it in her purse, and shoved her purse under the seat. She wasn't going to need it tonight.

She got out and hit the lock button on her fob. Even though she was just a few yards off River Road, the woods were thick and silent, except for the light song of crickets. Fireflies floated deep in the thicket, on and off, and she had a vague memory of playing Ghost in the Graveyard in her parents' backyard when she was a child.

It was a comforting thought, and she decided to hold on to it.

She walked across the dirt driveway and to the door of the little house in the woods. With one final deep breath, she raised a shaking hand, hesitated, then pounded on the door.

Nothing.

He *had* to be here.

She knocked again.

This time she heard footsteps approaching on the other side of the door and a voice saying, "Come on in, then." Then the door opened and he stood there. "I thought you might not be coming."

She opened her arms. "I'm here."

"Excellent. I'm so glad. Come right this way." He led her down a hall, then stopped in front of a closet full of clothes, mannequin parts, musical instruments, and other props. "You can change in there, then come on into the back room when you're ready."

She wondered if this was what it felt like to be Jenna Jameson or one of those other porn actresses.

Barely noticing how ragged her breath was, she slipped out of the cotton dress she'd worn and into one of the robes he had hanging there. She wondered for a moment if she could get away with leaving her underpants on, but that was stupid. He'd make her take them off anyway.

It was what she was here for. She needed to get used to that fact right now or else leave.

But there was no way she was leaving.

She'd come this far; she was going to see this through.

She pushed open the door and walked back out into the hallway, taking tentative steps in the direction he'd indicated.

This was terrifying.

She'd never been so scared in her entire life.

What if he saw her shaking? Would he make her leave?

One thing she knew was that she absolutely, positively could *not* afford to blow this. Somehow, and it no longer mattered how, she'd gotten it into her head that this was her last chance.

It was her *only* chance.

"There you are! Come on now. Right over there, on the stage. That's right. I hope the lights aren't too hot for you. I have a fan if you want, but we have to use it carefully."

"It's fine," she said, her voice gravelly. She cleared her throat. "I think I prefer it warm anyway."

He nodded. "Very well. It's entirely up to you, Holly. So . . . whenever you're ready." He sat down and watched her expectantly.

She swallowed and heard the gulping sound herself.

One . . .

She untied the belt on the thin silk robe.

Two . . .

She pulled it off her shoulders, trying to breathe, trying to keep from falling down, trying to keep from screaming or crying or running away.

Three.

The robe dropped to the floor.

And . . . it wasn't so bad.

"Now, if you'll just lie back on the chaise, sort of on your right hip only leaning back slightly," Guy said, gesturing with his pastel stick like an orchestra leader.

She got on the chaise. The crushed velvet fabric was warm. It was soothing, kind of like lying on a heated massage table. She followed his instructions, moving her arm like *this*, her left leg like *that*, her chin up higher, her eyes half-closed.

It didn't take long for her to fully understand and believe that she was a prop, no more or less sexual to the artist than the bicycle tire she'd seen in the room when she was changing.

"Make sure you let me know when you need a break," Guy said, studying her ankles as he spoke.

She could feel his gaze there like it was a spotlight.

"I could just work all night and my models often complain that I forget to offer them breaks. So what I say to them, and to you, is that I'm not psychic. If you need to stand up, stretch, use the facilities, or get a cookie, just give me a few moments' notice, all right?" The entire time he spoke, he didn't look her in the eye. His gaze moved over her and his hand moved rapidly over the canvas. He was sketching her in umber first, she knew. It was a technique she'd seen before. As soon as he'd finished the first draft, so to speak, she could move, but not until then.

What was interesting was that she didn't feel the need to move. All her impulses—to run away, to go home, to make up an excuse for never coming back and doing this—disappeared like smoke the moment she'd dropped the robe.

Just as she'd hoped, so did her self-consciousness.

And, despite the fact that the only person viewing her now was clearly doing so in a piece-by-piece manner, perceiving her one shadow and one curve at a time, for the first time in her life, she felt truly beautiful.

And free.